MEGALONYX

AL ZACH

MEGALONYX

This is a work of fiction. All of the characters, names, incidents,
organizations, and dialogue in this novel are either the products
of the author's imagination or are used fictitiously.

Archway Publishing books may be ordered through booksellers or by contacting:

Archway Publishing
1663 Liberty Drive
Bloomington, IN 47403
www.archwaypublishing.com
1 (888) 242-5904

ISBN: 978-1-4808-6526-6 (sc)
ISBN: 978-1-4808-6527-3 (hc)
ISBN: 978-1-4808-6525-9 (e)

Library of Congress Control Number: 2018962526

Print information available on the last page.

Archway Publishing rev. date: 04/30/2020

This is Dedicated to Terri

CONTENTS

CHAPTER 1

Monster Chase: The I-95 Corridor

FRANK PORTER SITS UNEASY in his Ford Taurus after driving ten hours straight. His right hand presses down on the metal brace supporting his fractured leg to accelerate the car. His other hand holds a cigarette, and the steering wheel simultaneously. Ashes are everywhere on the console, and topples into his coffee mug because he misses the ashtray most of the time. The car swerves every time his cigarette hand moves off the wheel because his other hand is busy stabilizing his foot on the pedal.

Frank Porter quit smoking five years ago, but now, this is not apparent to him. He sets the cruise control, and to some relief, he relaxes a bit. Suddenly, pins and needle sensations attack his hand and arm which are numb from holding his fractured leg. He needs to find a service area to stretch his body. A strike of pain radiates from his injury. It is time for more morphine.

Frank Porter, a respected man, who writes for the *Tannersville Gazette* in Virginia, is delirious. His lips tremble as he whispers," Gotta pee. Gotta pee. I need to already have peed."

Then he shouts," I need more morphine!"

A filled, piss jar lays next to him on the passenger seat. He wants to stop and empty the smelly contents. The usually reserved man, who writes articles on bird migrations, realizes a toilet, or even a tree, would serve him better than a mason jar.

If only his dead mother could see him now. How many times did she scold him that only crazy people talk to themselves. She also preached that fools try to live out childish fantasies. On this point, his dead mother's philosophy is totally wrong. Frank Porter is chasing a monster. This by far is not childish or foolish because it is not a fantasy. The claw marks across his back sting with a painful reality. The red, gas empty light flashes on the dashboard. And of course, his dead mother appears in the back seat.

Next to the piss jar, lays an open box of morphine syringes. He needs to inject himself. The pain pulsing from his leg feels like dog fangs ravishing his flesh. His head aches like it is being squeezed by a vise grip. Frank Porter loses count of how many times he has self-administered the morphine. His pain needs are great, and addiction use overrules safety protocol.

The syringes are stolen, and he is not familiar with the dosages. He probably is close to overdosing, but the pain constantly persists. Glancing in his rear view mirror, he notices his dead mother sitting in the back seat, knitting. This morphine sure is potent stuff. Frank Porter's mom looks up from her needles and yarn, and gives him a quaint smile that he learned to live, love, and despise.

He needs a fix fast so he can grab the double barrel shotgun which strategically is placed on the back seat. The man of peace, the animal lover, Mr. Frank Porter, knows nothing of guns. He lives in a small country town, with hunting as a major sport, if one considers shooting innocent animals a sport. This man could not hurt a fly.

At a gas station in Virginia, he pleaded to a teenager working the pumps, to explain the handling and usage of the gun. Frank Porter told of an attack by a crazed raccoon, he needed to take down. The gullible kid believed his story, and yearned to come along for the kill. Is Frank Porter really going to shoot down some sort of creature? The answer is yes or at least he believes so.

On the dashboard lays a folded newspaper with an add circled in red:

Buford's Circus of the Bizarre
TALE OF THE SNOW CREATURE
May 1st, Saturday, Pennatoc, Florida

Frank Porter is somewhere in Georgia on the I-95 highway. His goal is to reach Florida, and destroy the snow creature. This seems moronic considering Florida is hot and sunny, and the word "snow creature" would relate to cold and blizzard-like. He drives non-stop from Virginia. Hoping to catch up with the beast, he indulges in this dreadful adventure with no sensible escape.

The rain flows steadily onto his windshield as the car's headlights light up a road sign that reads, "Rest Area 3 Miles." He really needs to recuperate, and tank up the car. Frank Porter's six-foot-one-inch stature, cramps him greatly on his trek. Again, a morphine shot is well overdue. He will simply park the car, inject some drugs into his leg, hobble into the men's room, pee, and wash up. His clothes also will be changed for some new ones. Hopefully, nobody will notice the bloody clothing while he is doing the hobbling.

The late afternoon reflects cloudy and rainy, which probably is a godsend. The previous forty-eight hours brought on raging fires all over Georgia, due to the spring drought. Just three hours ago, Frank Porter could barely see the highway in front of him due to the smoke. At one point, the smoky air was affecting his breathing, and he had concerns of turning around. Instead, his Ford Taurus endures ahead through the haze, only to miraculously confront the opposite- pouring buckets of rain.

He is driving with good turn around time, since the state troopers are busy battling the fires. Most of the action is north of him, and the I-95 south is clear travel without much police control. The rain feels good on his face which he sticks out the open window. The car's head-lights flash onto the road sign,"Rest Area 0.5 Miles." The red light for empty gas gleams from his dashboard.

Frank Porter can relax more with the cruise control on. He regrets he did not think of this earlier. With his head sticking out of the car win-dow, he recognizes an old truck about ten car lengths ahead. Victory is at hand! Yes, it is they. It is them. Bill Meyers, Bogey Wilson, and the snow creature are in that truck.

Driving through the night pays off for Frank Porter. Maybe he will ram them off the road, right here and now, ending his too surreal ordeal (a daring feat for a Ford Taurus). Bill Meyers is one of the few survivors of the Tannersville killings, and old Bogey Wilson, is the accused, mad murderer. The snow creature is the abomination that fits the missing pieces of the bloody puzzle.

Frank Porter, with wet strands of hair matting his balding head, cries out, " I stab at thee with vengeance! I end this cat and mouse game of demons and terror! You now are in my controlling embrace of no-mercy termination!"

A women in the lane next to him, shrugs to her driving husband, to take a look at the crazy man shouting out at the rain. The husband slows down to keep away from the madman.

Frank Porter notices their concerned eyes, and in a sneering voice he exclaims," You better move away! You better get as far as hell away! I'm the man. I'm the man to kill the snow creature!"

The couple are both stupefied and fearful.

His dead imaginary mom murmurs, " Hmm, hmm, hmm, my poor boy. Where did I go wrong?"

Frank Porter rolls his eyes with disapproval as he sees his mother's reflection in the rear view mirror. He peers side to side with contempt, and in a half /yell, half/whisper, exclaims,"Mother, shut up! Always were you a backseat driver. Now shut up!"

Frank Porter's delirium and need to stop vanishes. Vengeance helps erase the pain. His rest area was seeing that old milk truck owned by Bogey Wilson, an eccentric black man, who junks cars in Tannersville. They must of taken their time, not realizing he is still alive. The truck rolls ahead like they have no concerns. This is odd considering there exists a national manhunt for the accused killer.

Frank Porter wonders if they started those fires to draw off attention from the criminal search. He refuses to let them escape. He keeps a close yet secretive stalk. The red flashing gaslight taboos his moment. He forgets the car needs gas. Frank Porter hopes the stories about cars traveling miles and miles on a empty tank are true.

"Do I tank gas, or do I continue? Do I tank gas, or do I continue? Maybe I should flip a coin. No! I am going on. Continue I will, unleashed to kill!"

Frank Porter remembers that last line from a heavy metal song, back during his teenage years.

Lost in vengeance, unconsciously peeing on himself, he jabs his leg with a stolen, morphine syringe. A quick flush of relief stimulates him, both mentally and physically. The sensation tingles of goodness, pushing aside his anger, fears, and pain.

During his euphoria, he unknowingly drives off into the rest area. There is something wrong. He glances over where the old truck veers left, staying on the I- 95. The Ford Taurus veers right in a lane heading for the rest area building.

He yells at himself, " Damn! Frank, You idiot! What in the devil's name am I doing over here?"

Crazy Frank Porter cannot believe how stupid exiting is going to screw things up.

Every time he speaks, his imaginary mother politely scolds him from the backseat.

"Oh quit it Mom! You are dead! Yes, I am talking to myself. Yes, I should watch how I drive! No, I am not going to stop yelling at you!"

She makes a cute joke," You say I am dead to you, so why are you yelling at me?"

Well, how odd is it, a man talking with no one. Odd maybe, but not really true, because he actually is speaking with his imaginary mother, or dead mother, or maybe- a ghost? His dead mother who is present, but cannot be present. Somehow, she can speak, and hold a conversation with her son.

Now, madder than ever, he drives through the service area, while Bill Meyers and the gang are getting away on the I-95 southbound.

"Oh yeah! No gas? I am in the wrong lane? No problem. I will simply get back onto the highway. I'm going to smash, smash, and smash them right off the road! They end, and I win. Win! Win! Win! I am the man. I am the man who slays the snow creature!"

Crash! Crash! Crash! The Ford Taurus clips the back bumper of a red sedan. Frank fails to realize the cruise control is still on, while he plows through the rest area. He loses temporarily control of the steering wheel. His car scrapes up against a guard railing, and speeds out of control.

The loud screeching catches the attention of a state trooper,standing at the entrance of the refreshment building. Of course, the only cop not fighting forest fires, is enjoying a donut and coffee. What luck, with a Georgia state trooper lounging at this particular rest area, where Frank Porter performs a doped up, loony car exhibition.

The police officer stares in shock at the speeding car. Ram! Bam! The Ford Taurus smacks straight into the rear of a large camper. The back of the camper is all crushed with vehicle stuff flying all around. Frank Porter's car bounces off to the side of the camper upon impact, still traveling at fifty-five miles-per-hour. The front of the car is all dented and smashed but still running. His previous plan to push the old truck off the road is obviously not going to happen.

The state trooper drops his coffee, spilling some on his pants. He jumps into his squad car, and peels out in seconds flat. The officer probably would have been better off assisting the forest fires. A "gun ho" cop, like himself, craves this kind of action once in awhile, but should have been more modest for what he wished for.

Frank Porter realizes that he is all discombobulated. Only a professional writer could imagine such a word as discombobulate at a time like this. Frank Porter regroups his morphine soaked thoughts, and manages to turn off the cruise control with success. Small relief satisfies his agitated state of mind.

Suddenly, he swerves, avoiding an old lady with a walker, crossing on the safety walk. Taking a quick glance, the old lady appears to be his mother.

He yells a few words." Okay Mom, I know that is you! Giving me a wake up check, uh Mom?Testing me so I don't screw up? Get out of my life damn it!"

The old lady tilts over onto the concrete, scared out of her wits. She listens to Frank hollering like a lunatic as he drives away.

Lying down and cannot get up, she yells," Fuck You! Fuck you! And fuck your mother too!"

Her dear husband is driving them to their Florida, vacation home. The husband annoyingly sings non-stop. The old lady's tolerance is going to break if she hears another verse of Frank Sinatra, vocalized by her spouse. The "F" word dooms to appear sooner or later. She feels better, though, cursing at a stranger than her dear old hub.

Frank Porter heads back on the highway while regaining the control of his car. He moves directly behind the old milk truck which made little distance on the I-95 southbound. He hears a siren, and notices the state trooper car in the rear view mirror. Some gibberish vocals resonates from a loudspeaker of the police vehicle. Frank Porter cannot understand the official request, and he cares even less.

He thinks how fantastical this event is playing out. Like in a movie, he races in a car with a loaded gun, being chased by the police. This all is happening to mild manner, Mr. Frank Porter. He is losing precious time to end this chase. Who cares about the cops? His dead mother would care, but is she really here anyway?

The shotgun briskly lifts from the backseat in Frank Porter's hand. This action is ignored by his busy, knitting mother. He points the gun out the window, and fires. Frank Porter, holding it cowboy style with one hand, blasts a slug into the left rear tail light of the truck. The guys in the truck realize what is happening, and increase their speed. They know it is Frank.

A large metal door is closed and loosely hinged at the back of the truck. There exists an open space between the side and back door. A large shadow shifts in this space. A nasty animal odor, like an unclean cage smell, engulfs Frank's nose. The stink revitalizes his memory of the last months' horror. His vengeance focuses on his target- "The Beast".

Like ducks in a row, the old milk truck, the Ford Taurus, and the state trooper vehicle, head off the next exit in the pouring rain. They all end up turning onto a dirt road. Bill Meyers obviously is attempting to escape the pursuit. The police vehicle frantically swerves, attempting to pass and cut off Frank Porter's car.

Frank Porter once again raises the shotgun out the window, and hits the back metal door, dead center of the old milk truck. A loud, disturbing howl is heard, and sword-like incisor protrudes in and out of the back door space.

Again, verbal noise fills the air from the state trooper's loud speaker. His dead mother says, "The nice policeman is asking you to please pull over." She then appears to him with a devilish face and says, "Or the cop is gonna blow your bald head off!"

The rain continues, but with less force. The dark skies begin to take on a lighter gray. The speeding vehicles move at a good clip on the muddy, old road, surrounded by woods and meadows. The officer constantly transmits back to base for assistance. However, due to the fire crisis, this "gun ho"cop is on his own.

Bill Meyers makes his move. Suddenly, the old milk truck brakes to a full, short stop, with pin point accuracy. Frank Porter, caught off guard, slams down hard on the brakes, and skids toward the right. The driver's side door smashes into the corner of the truck where he shot out the red tail light. Frank Porter is pinned in his seat by the inflated safety bag.

The state trooper's vehicle swerves haphazardly, and ends up in the road ditch. The front of the trooper's vehicle sags due to a busted ball joint on a front tire. Because of all the excitement, he forgot to strap on his safety belt, back at the rest area (shame- a violation of highway law). The officer cracks his head into the windshield, and sits stunned. A spiderweb crack fills his view in front of him.

Wrecking the police vehicle is not wanted in a criminal arrest. An anxious attitude exclaiming, "I am above the law", will always be their downfall. The blood trickling in his face is a unfortunate bonus. This whole incident annoys the tough, young cop. He reports back to the office base. Unfortunately, due to the emergency of the forest fires, there is a delay for the confirmation of more police assistance.

Frank Porter is smothered in his seat by the air bag. He cannot breathe, and finds it difficult to move his position because of the lack of physical strength. The situation makes him gasp for air, air which he seems he cannot find with this rubber material in his face. Miraculously, the safety bag pops, and Frank Porter sucks in a large gulp of oxygen. Any longer, he surely would have perished.

He looks through the open window. Directly in front of his face, is the slit between the truck's side and the loose fitting back door. A sword-like incisor comes slashing down at him, missing the side of his head by inches. Again, the putrid odor overwhelms him bringing those feelings of disgust. The sword-like blade continues slicing at him. Frank Porter avoids getting cut by keeping his head off to the side. Every now and then, it brazes his shoulder. The huge claws must have pierced the safety bag, which temporarily saves his life.

Frank Porter is thinking where is a cop when you need one. The state trooper's door is jammed, and he attempts to crawl out the window. His small gut is not complimenting his escape. The officer tumbles to the roadside, and awkwardly stands up. The blood is wiped out of his eyes with a white towel, already soaked red. Slow moving, the state trooper orients himself back into a professional mode.

Back at Frank Porter's car, are thrusts of the huge incisor, loud animal growls, and putrid air. He still reaches behind for the shotgun, but cannot snatch it. His mother, who really is not there, is useless. The huge blade begins scraping deeper into his shoulder, spattering blood. It is a failure to move in a safer position, due mostly to his tall length. He fears a mighty blow will kill him.

Suddenly, the old truck quickly moves and stops ahead around five car lengths. Bill Meyers waves his hand from the driver's seat, and honks the horn several times. The old truck then quickly peels out ahead. It zips through a brushy field, and disappears into the trees. Bogey Wilson, although a drunken eccentric, is an excellent mechanic. He must have optimized the truck for road performance. Back in Tannersville, most of Bogey's cars took top winnings in demolition shows.

The rain sprinkles lightly as Bill, Bogey, and "The Beast", are gone. Frank Porter's mission ends in failure. For what ever reason, they spare his life. This is unexpected.

Out of nowhere, Frank Porter finds himself flying through the window, and next, face down in the mud. The Georgia state trooper lifts and drags him to his police vehicle. He strides hurriedly back to Frank Porter's car, grabs the shotgun, and flings it into the tall grass next to the road. The trooper's shirt tail is sticking out of his pants, with his gut protruding through the bottom of his undershirt. The officer heavily huffs with a bloody forehead. His police work grades impeccable, and never such injuries occur on the job. His demeanor is definitely off balance.

"I am Officer Bongo. What the hell was that! You both loaded on cocaine or some shit. You violated all the laws in the book! Nobody, I mean nobody, messes with my highway! Welcome to Georgian jail time my friend. We do things differently around here, when it comes to disrespect. This is not just about traffic violations, mister. You violated me! You injured me! And don't bet that your friends are going to get away. I will nail their ass too!"

Frank Porter settles down. He is returning back to his old self, like mild mannered Bruce Wayne in the "Batman Movies". Instead of changing into a superhero though, he played the psychotic joker, or the two-faced villain. He is oblivious to all the pain, and can barely stand against the police car. His body slumps against the police car door, which he uses like a crutch. He feels nothing from his fractured leg as if it was cut off and gone.

His feelings are calmer with a numb rationale, though he is still under the influence of the morphine. He will be put in jail, and serve time. Nobody is going to believe his "Tale of the Snow Creature".

Officer Bongo's voice becomes incoherent as Frank Porter's mind begins to slip away. He visions his dead mom standing up the road a bit. She has her hands bent on her hips, and looks toward him with disapproval. She slowly turns away and flaps her arms down with disgust. He visions his mother walking away, and disappears into the horizon.

He always did his best for her, but feels she never approved much of his choices. The fact that he married in his small, religious town, but later divorced, always disagreed with her. She probably appeared to embarrass him on this crazy, car ride. She always ridiculed his immaturity as a grown man. Frank Porter becomes unconscious, but past events become alive in his drug ridden state.

Some Background

Frank Porter reports on the Tannersville Killings for the local gazette, back in Virginia. He interviews with Bill Meyers, a survivor of the horrid events. In the beginning, the deranged man makes no sense at the psychiatric ward. When the month of March rolls in, with the promise of springtime, he begins to show signs of mental recovery. The uncontrollable yelling lessens to small outbursts per week. The self-slapping episodes seize, so the ward's assistants remove him from the straight-jacket therapy. Sometimes, Bill Meyers would clasp his hands together, like in prayer, and rattle them against the padded walls like a jack hammer. He actually would bore a hole in the wall with the stuffing coming lose.

Bill Meyers on occasion, speaks in thought-provoking statements. One of his favorite ones goes something like this.

"Suzy! Sex-death Suzy! Don't need your sex and death? Girl, can I meet you half the way? Oh sorry, so sorry Slutty Suzy."

Tannersville, Virginia, simply lies between the Yew and Allegheny Mountains. Nothing happens here. The killings place Tannersville as a bloody red dot on our nation's map. The *World Inquiry* and *National*

Exposed Magazines, exaggerates a tale of a savage beast, a beast of unknown origin, ripping apart and eating people. Bogey Wilson is marked as the lunatic who killed and dismembered his victims. The stories of beast, or man, or both, circulates with craziness. The religious town of Tannersville loses part of its normalcy from the trash gossip.

Frank Porter sheds some light on this local tragedy with his article in the Tannersville Gazette. He finally writes a story with intrigue, and revelations. Sheriff Gibbs, who pompously called himself -Thee Sheriff Gibbs, denounces the insane material, and literally shoves him out of his hometown. The sheriff is well-known in keeping the town's fine, pseudo-reputation. He hates all the bad press, and horror-fiction gossip about his quaint community.

One of Sheriff Gibbs favorite thought-provoking comments is something like this," If the people knew everything, I would not be doing this job. And so they don't know everything. It's my duty not to tell them everything."

The day of Bill Meyer's release approaches near the end of March. Frank Porter knows that this young man held back information. He sits very relaxed and quiet. A mound of ash from his cigarette smoking becomes part of the concrete floor next to where he simply sits everyday. The routine smoking acts as a time filler for him to complete a greater task.

Back To Officer Bongo

Officer Bongo yells into his radio transmitter," I got a 2-20, a 10-20, and a mess of everything! I need back up off the I-95 at the Broad Street exit. A rusty white truck needs comprehending, last scene heading through a brushy meadow, probably heading to Pittstown."

He waits for a response. The officer gazes into the horizon gathering his thoughts. The sun breaks through the clouds after all the rain, and it looks like they are going to have a nice sunset.

Frank Porter watches the officer, and notices that he seems to be quite shaken up. Everybody assumes that the police are well experienced in these matters, but this seems to be Officer Bongo's first real action drama. Vocals resonate from the receiver which sends the officer in a frenzy.

Officer Bongo speaks with temper, "What do you mean I have no back up! I am not letting these assholes get away. That old truck cannot drive to far in the next thirty minutes."

Obviously the Georgia state troopers are all caught up assisting the fire outbreaks. Officer Bongo stares with anger at Frank Porter, while arguing into his police mike. This officer is about to take matters in his own hands. His police vehicle is broken down from a maniacal chase, and his blood pressure rose to a point of no return.

Also, that gut of Officer Bongo hangs there for a reason. He drank his share of beer last night and felt withdrawn. He feels especially withdrawn, since Frank Porter denied him his afternoon snack and coffee.

Officer Bongo remarks, "How the hell did your buddies drive across that brushy field with that old truck?"

"First of all, they are not my buddies, and one of them is a mechanic." Frank Porter simply replies.

Officer Bongo continues, "What in heaven's name was all that ruckus about back there? I pulled your I.D. up, and the files show you have no criminal record or anything. You could have killed someone. You and I are going to have a private conversation. And by the way, when I was talking to command, you were mumbling, like you were talking to someone."

"I was arguing with my dead mother." Frank Porter truthfully answers.

"Oh boy, You are a real nut job! So, you are going to claim your mother instigated all this, right? I heard it all before psycho man. Sure, blame it on Mom." Officer Bongo sarcastically chuckles.

Frank Porter is exhausted, and has no energy to deal with the officer. Again, he feels like he is going to pass out any second. As he slumps against the police vehicle, Officer Bongo forcefully straightens him up, and stares straight into his eyes. He is trying to intimidate him so Frank Porter reveals information. The officer pushes him hard against the police car, and walks over to the side of the road. He contemplates that this has to be big, like a drug deal gone wrong, or a murderous love triangle.

Surprisingly, a nice sunset develops after all the rain. Frank Porter falls over, and sits against the squad car on the muddy road. Officer Bongo slips on his police gloves with a determined look, like you know what is going to happen next. Frank Porter, as a news reporter, has a feel for people. This young, brash cop is going to be trouble.

Roaring sounds are suddenly heard from the north side of the muddy road. Large trailer trucks are seen hauling tons of cedar wood. The officer awaits for the trucks to pass, and then he will interrogate his prisoner. There is no back-up police coming, and he is taking matters in his own hand.

The first trailer truck nears the police car, and Frank Porter figures a lumber company is saving its pricier cedar wood from the fires. One of the truck driver wonders what crime this guy might of committed. It looks serious, and he keeps the eighteen wheeler moving. Officer Bongo waves his hands, leading the lumber trucks pass the wrecked vehicles. Four huge trucks pass with mud flinging at Frank Porter from the huge tires. How much more humiliation is the broken news reporter going to endure?

Although Frank Porter is still dosed on morphine, he is feeling more himself. He regrets the crazy behavior that he allowed to overtake him. His strength is low, and it is difficult to stand up.

The hallucinations of his dead mother disappear. Did some psychological friction between his mother and him surface in connection with his unstable behavior? Their past relationship remained good, but something triggered her appearance. Frank Porter could not explain. Her death brought sorrow, but he never blamed himself. Oh well, blame it on drugs.

The last trailer of lumber begins to pass them. A smaller truck appears behind the lumber one. Frank Porter meets eye to eye with Bill Meyers behind the wheel. It is the old milk truck. Bill Meyers grins at Frank Porter, and turns directly at Officer Bongo straight on. The police officer's instincts respond immediately to the sudden surprise. Frank Porter is stunned to see Officer Bongo draw his pistol, and simultaneously jump off to the side.

The officer's split second reaction is not enough. Bill Meyers drives over the officer's legs. Shockingly, Frank Porter admits to himself that the officer's attempt was commendable. However, his actions are not enough to avoid his legs becoming smashed. His pistol goes flying in the air, somewhere, into a muddy puddle at the road side.

The old milk truck stops about thirty yards ahead. Officer Bongo frantically scrambles for cover. He props himself against the front bumper of his squad car. His legs do not respond, and feel like dead weight. He wildly thinks about his next move as his eyes lock onto the idling truck. The pistol whereabouts are unknown to him, but he remembers where the shotgun lies in the tall grass, which he threw from the backseat of the Ford Taurus.

The truck turns off the engine, and all is quiet. The officer pulls himself with his arms across the road, dragging his body through the mud. Officer Bongo lost his "gun ho" attitude. He becomes frightful. Only a few more yards to the spot where the shotgun should be. Pain now resonates from his legs below. In the wet, tall grass. he clumsily searches, but nothing found. He nervously looks this way and that way, and then sees a flash of metal. The shotgun reflects a small shine from the disappearing sun.

Clouds suddenly cover over the sky, and blot out the sunset completely. A menacing feeling invades Officer Bongo in the twilight. He is scared. He rushes towards the shotgun. This is one chess move too late.

A huge roar echoes out from the truck. The back door slams down to the ground with a metallic bang. Officer Bongo cannot see clearly in the tall grass as he looks over his shoulder. He tries to focus on a huge mass rumbling towards him with blades rotating in all directions. For the first time as a cop, he is really scared. He moves hysterically forward to grab the shotgun. A painful, burning sensation strikes across his back.

He is roughly handled, and flips over, only to witness a large, stinking mass towering over him. A throated growl vibrates his ears, and warm breath of stench engulfs his face. A quick painful sting to his stomach, a crunching squeeze to his head, and a sight from his eyes inside the creature's mouth, are the last human events of Officer Bongo. There is blackness, and then nothing.

Bill Meyers nonchalantly steps out of the truck, and walks over to Frank Porter, still sitting against the police car. He stands against the twilight of the new evening, and looks down at Frank Porter's helpless predicament.

Bill Meyers boldly speaks,"You could not leave things alone back home. You, and I, are lucky that we not dead like the rest. You should of said nothing. That wacko sheriff warned you. I would not have returned for you. No one does or ever will believe -"The Tale of the Snow Creature. I would have enjoyed the mockery that people would comment about you. Writing of monster stories? Really. Only fossil remains can prove this creature ever existed, and to capture a live one, well, we both know who has the only one."

Frank Porter replies," Why do you despise me now. I was the only person truly sympathetic towards your plight. What is the whole point of this. I am willing to work with you, and have a proper investigation with the right authorities. All those lives."

"Oh shut up! Of course you do not get it. Hey Bogey! Get over here with Big Meg!" He yells.

He calls the snow creature- Big Meg? He named it? He trained it? Frank Porter cannot tilt his head in the direction the beast is heard lumbering over. Quickly, Frank Porter is airborne, and slumps over on the back of this stinking, woolly mass of a carnivore. He bops up and down, moving in darkness as this evening of the car chase finally ends.

★★

Officer Bongo awakes in excruciating fits of bodily pain. He stares at a amazing starlit night. It is extremely hot, hot to the point he can not breathe. His body is partially propped against a tree, and flames engulf around him. Officer Bongo stares at his bloody insides protruding from his stomach. His legs are all smashed up with one foot pointing in an impossible, physical direction. He glances at fire dancing around him, and creepy shadows forming with the black night. He suddenly has a sensation to vomit, and a bloody mess pours out of him.

This is it. Officer Bongo can hardly speak, and in his last thoughts, realizes- This is it.

He never listened to his mother. Like Frank Porter talking to his dead mother, he should of talked more with his living mother. She scolded him to be an accountant- a safe, stable job. A job supporting a wife, a family, where he could be home to enjoy them.

His mother called him an idiot that he joined the police force. It will be the death of him, she always promised. If he dies on the job, she is not going to his funeral.

In his dying state, Officer Bongo attempts to speak, "Well, Mom, your wish came true. There are little human remains, so a funeral casket is out of the question. Mom, you won! Yes, I should of a been a boring, shitty accountant! You taunted me till my true end."

How he wished these last words were not wasted about his aggravating mother. What a way to go. Thanks Frank Porter for reminding him of her.

A flaming tree collapses on the pitiful, dead, Officer Bongo.

CHAPTER 2

Good Ol' Tannersville U.S.A.

IT WAS WEDNESDAY, DECEMBER 3, 1986. Bill Meyers closed Charlie's Place early, because business was slow on a week night. The snow storm forced customers out of the diner as well. Standing by the front door with burgers in a bag, Bill Meyers turned off the lights, and locked up the place. All he could hear was the pitter-patter of snowflakes falling onto his parka, and people noise coming from the Tannersville Bar and Grille. The snow accumulated to about a foot high, with snow piles blocking parked cars.

Bill Meyers turned the key in the ignition, and listened to the rat-a-tat-tat, rat-a-tat-tat of the cold engine attempting to start. On a third try, the engine turned over, and the old station wagon shook while the car warmed up. A snow plow earlier, pushed mounds of snow against his father's station wagon. It was fresh powdered snow, and the car would simply drive over it. Wet or icy snow would of produced a slippery situation.

His father always spent the money for good snow tires. Bill Meyers remembered as a child, when he sat with his father at K-mart's tire dept. His mother always bought him a pair of new shoes in the fall. That year he got no shoes. He thought this was strange.

"Sorry son. Those old shoes still have some wear and tear in them. They will have to do for winter. New tires for the family wagon may save our lives this season. These harsh winters, here in the hills, can snow bound us for weeks. Skidding off a cliff, is no way to die."

The dramatics his father vocalized almost made you believe, that living in this small town could be life or death. Bill Meyers realized as he grew older, that his father needed to validate his family decisions. They were financially burdened that year, and the snow tires outweighed his boy's feet.

Bill Meyers remembered as a youngster his reply," And new snow shoes would stop me from falling, cracking my head on the icy walkway at school."

His father stared at his boy with surprise. A small frown developed on his face from his son's snappy reply. His father somehow was taken back by his child inquisitiveness.

Bill Meyers waited for the car to warm up.

He muttered to himself, " Another year past away, and nothing important I have to say."

He needed money to do the things he wished to do. The snowfall this year was plenty, and maybe skiers will visit the local resort at Ridgewood. This would increase the business at Charlie's Place, and stick more bucks in his pants pocket. However, the skiing around here was mostly local with few tourists. The job at the diner will never strike like gold. Nothing really happened in good ol' Tannersville, U.S.A.

Bill Meyers was medium height with a buzz haircut. He was physically fit, and played first year football at Ridgewood University. Like most people who lived in Tannersville, his family was low income. He needed that football scholarship to afford college. The diner assisted in paying small bills, and daily expenses. He could not save much money, and still lived at home. His twenty-first birthday in August, brought little to his table, and felt he was missing out on this profound year of manhood.

Bill Meyers was not necessarily depressed, but lacked fulfillment of personal satisfaction. His mother prayed at the church religiously, like a lot of the people here in this town. Her churchly influence on him, added to his unaccomplished achievements for other interests. Bill Meyers always sacrificed for his family, and loved his parents. But now, at twenty-one, the pay off from supporting family values, interfered with the pay off of his desires.

The stale air inside the station wagon always reminded him of his father. It smelled like this as far back as he could remember. He turned up the vent to let in some fresh air in from outside. That stale odor remained, only making the inside colder than it already was.

Nothing could rid the car's aged smells. This car had to go. It reminded him of his past as a child. How could he afford new wheels to attract girls? He cannot. It was embarrassing when he pulled into the university parking lot with a family station wagon, a station wagon from the 70's. Something needed to change, and that something had to be now.

Like all young men, Bill Meyers desired sex. Yes, he desired to experience real, physical sex. The girls in high school were attracted to him, but in a safe way, like a relationship one has with a big brother. Bill Meyers was a good man, but not the "stud" man. This year of manhood of twenty-one years, was to brand him his sex-hood. Hell, other fellows on the football team lost their virginity years ago.

His friends, who were girls, always complained about the difficulty in meeting a nice guy to settle down with. Was he not a nice guy, sitting right next to them in the cafeteria? Then at a town festival, he would witness these girls, who were just friends, drinking beer, or tongue tied with some loser.

They would probably be grabbing at his pants in the woods some-where, back of a stinking, pick-up truck. These were guys with low grades, skipped classes, and probably could give daddy's little girl a sexual disease. Girls wished for nice guys. Uh.

Bill Meyers saw people meandering outside the Tannersville Bar and Grille in his rear view mirror. Loud voices were heard from this small crowd behind him. It seemed curious, and he thought about checking it out. It was late, he wanted to go to sleep. His car pointed in the direction of his home.

He pulled out into the street, heading to a red light at the inter-section on main street. He really did want to get home, but wondered who those "bar stoolers" were. Who would be hanging out at the Tannersville Bar and Grille during this wicked snow storm.

He decided to do a u-turn at the intersection, and shoot the red light. There was nobody in sight, and those dull thoughts about his life, brought out some mischief in him. What the hell, he thought, and drove through the red light.

This action had its merit. Main street was one of the few roads plowed. Bill Meyers grinned a little as he circled in the intersection disobeying the traffic law. A television show popped in his mind. He began singing. " Bad boy, bad boy. What you gonna do when they come for you. Bad boy, bad boy."

Bill Meyers headed down main street, passed Charlie's Place, and noticed people standing around the corner of Tannersvile Bar and Grille. He noticed a girl being pushed onto the sidewalk. A stocky man circled her, and was hollering with anger. He recognized Mr. Ratchet, a co-worker of his father, tugging at the girl's coat, as she crawled to get away.

Hmm, this did not look good. An unusual jolt broke in his nerve, changing his curiosity. The nervous jolt broke into waves among his bodily parts. This kind of stuff was not his expertise. No time to start gutsy decisions like saving a damsel in distress. Bill Meyers was second string football player, and there was a reason for that.

The station wagon had no choice but to go straight passed the crowd. He recognized the girl, spitting at the older men. It was Susan Conti, a classmate from his high school. His heart picked up in beats, accompanied by a slight sweat on his forehead. Bill Meyers was never a take charge kind of guy, and wished he could turn around and avoid this altercation.

What could he do for her anyway? His mind kept flashing an alert - abort, mind your own business, you will get yourself in big trouble. The road consisted of a one way due to the amount of snow, and turning the car away was not an option. Susan Conti scrambled to her feet, and punched Mr. Ratchet smack center on his nose.

Yes, Bill Meyers recognized "Slutty Suzy", Susan Conti's reputable nick-name. She dated some of the football team, and a whole list of guys around town, who unfortunately for her, bragged about their sexual exploits. Of course, Bill Meyers was not one of them. All the boys back in high school turned their heads, when Susan Conti strutted down the hallway. The rumor was she put out.

Bill Meyers fantasized many of times of being with "Slutty Suzy", but never actually asked her out on a date. He tutored her awhile in algebra, and barely spoke a word to her. She could not grasp the math, and he ended up completing her reports, so she could get a passing grade. One year, a story circulated that she was flunking out of school.

In order to graduate to the next school level, she had a thing with Mr. Appleton, the biology teacher. Whether the stories were true about "Slutty Suzy" or not, Bill Meyers desired her, like all the boys who heard the stories.

Bill Meyers planned to keep going straight pass the commotion at the corner bar. He noticed the stop sign, but that was not going to cause a problem. He already drove threw a red light, and committed an illegal u-turn. He visioned Suzy Conti's jacket being tugged at, and then, it ripped open with the insulation fabric busting out. Bill Meyers saw all this out of the corner of his eye while looking at the road ahead. He possessed this uncanny sense of peripheral vision.

He was going to drive through the intersection and not look at "Slutty Suzy" biting Mr. Ratchet on the hand. He also did not see the guys pushing and tossing "Slutty Suzy" back and forth in their bully circle. Nope, Bill Meyers kept away from this stuff with a ten foot pole. In football, he was second string, and never started in the game. This put him at second string in life. He lacked to take charge, and do the right thing.

The station wagon was near the corner. He kept driving nonstop passed Mr. Ratchet grabbing Susan Conti's pants. Damn that peripheral vision!

Crash! Bill Meyers unknowingly veered left into a parked car across Tannersville Bar and Grille. He was so busy not looking over at Susan Conti, that he smacked into a car, because he really was not paying attention to the road. [Damn that peripheral vision]. Everyone stopped due to the crash, and Mr. Ratchet yelled, "Hey, you hit my car!" Susan Conti quickly pushed Mr. Ratchet off her, and ran in the snow as fast as she could.

Bill Meyers attempted to reverse the car, but the tires kept spinning in the slushy snow. What happened to dad's super snow tires?

He panicked, and downed the pedal to fast. Again, spin, spin, spin. He eased up, and finally, the station wagon reversed.

"Open the door! Open the Door", Susan Conti yelled.

He definitely was not opening the door. Again, the super tires spun in the snow because he downed the pedal too fast. The high grade tires were useless against the wet, icy snow.

"Open the Door! Open the Door!" Again she yelled.

Bill Meyers was not opening the car door.

"Open the door! Open the Door," Susan Conti pleaded as she skidded in the slush, now nearer the passenger side.

Bill Meyers was not opening the door.

Susan Conti opened the door, and jumped into the station wagon. The door was never locked. A typical action for no reaction from the infamous Bill Meyers.

Her wet long hair flew in his face as she fell over to his side. It smelled good. The men rushed into the street towards them with fists in the air.

Bill Meyers downed the pedal. This time, he had some traction. The station wagon swerved left to right in a forward motion through the intersection. His attention was lured to her invigorating fragrance even in this traumatic situation. Then he sped, right through the stop sign. This was no big deal since he already drove through a red light.

Bill Meyers' anxiety, and feelings of fright, were now added with an aromatic smell of "Slutty Suzy". The station wagon changed. The air changed in Dad's car. It was a miracle! New jolts, and twitches rippled inside him. He was reacting to fear and delight simultaneously. The sensation reflected a person who enjoyed eating sweet and sour together.

Bam! A delivery truck swiped the station wagon on the passenger side. Susan Conti screamed from the impact, and jumped over to Bill Meyers. The weight of her body pushed his foot on the accelerator, which sent the station wagon into a half spin after the crash. The station wagon in full speed, misdirected, headed straight to the corner bar.

Mr. Ratchet, who led the pack of drunks, barely saved himself, as he flung sideways into the slushy snow. Immediately, Bill Meyers slammed on the brakes. The front of the car smacked into the doorway of the Tannersville Bar and Grille with Susan Conti screaming. The damage was lessened because of the last minute braking, but the bumper was dislodged, and a headlight was broken. The front door of Tannersville Bar and Grille had a huge crack in it.

Bill Meyers was light headed with panic. He heard mumbling outside, his fingers tingled uncontrollably, and his nose smelled satisfying fragrance, a lovely nuance engulfing his dad's stenched station wagon. He just sat there.

"Go,! Go!", Susan Conti yelled as she pushed Bill Meyers with both hands. He pulled out of a two second trance, reversed the car, and drove once again through the intersection They passed the stalled delivery truck with the driver shaking his fist.

Susan Conti exclaimed, "Why did you drive through the stop sign? Are you stupid?"

"No, I'm a bad boy," Bill Meyers blurted in his mindless state.

"What? What did you say? Are you nuts?" She remarked.

Bill Meyers, with Susan Conti, continued on main street with no talking . He reached the outside of the town, and had to pull over.

Mr. Ratchet stood in a half-way position as he panted severely in the snowy intersection. Suddenly, he became dizzy, and tilted over in the street like a falling bowling pin. His buddies tried to help him as Mr. Ratchet laid unconscious. An ambulance came 15 minutes later, and took him to the Tannersville Medical Center. Later, Mr. Ratchet was treated for a mild heart attack in the intensive care unit.

"Are you okay, Suzy?" Bill Meyers, the boy scout, responsibly asked.

She replied, "Are you okay Billy boy? That was insane back there."

When she said that it was insane, does she mean the assault on her by grown family men,or his miraculous escape, which could of ended up in a deadly accident. They both still were unsettled. In the mix of all this trouble, his mind could not help returning to her alluring smell. If she knew what he was thinking right now, after all this commotion, she definitely would think he was insane.

He politely asked,"Should I drive you home?"

She nervously replied, "No, not yet. Take me somewhere."

Bill Meyers obviously was not driving her to his house, with his religious mom, and his strict father. In front of him, read a sign- Meade Lake Next Right. He decided to take her to Meade Lake, alias "Make Out Lake", which everyone called it back in high school.

He drove along River Street next to the water, but the entrance to the parking lot was snowbound. They stopped along the plowed road.

The lights were on at the parking lot, and shone quite serene reflecting on the frozen lake. Snow clumped up on the pine branches, and with a break in the clouds, stars were seen scattered in the sky.

The whole view was a copy of a Christmas card, and helped both of them calm down. Susan Conti peered out the window, with a relaxed mood, unlike the panic-stricken girl he just witnessed twenty minutes ago.

Bill Meyers sat with Susan Conti at "Make Out Lake" in his father's station wagon. His life was changing with a positive- Wow!

"You did good back there, Billy boy. Thanks for saving me from those creeps." She replied.

Susan Conti settled down, and became more comfortable sitting in the station wagon. She unzipped her ski jacket, and took it off. She tugged at her damp white sweater, tightly snug around her breasts. Bill Meyers leered at them, although they were not huge. She definitely aroused him. He desired her with her stringy long hair, her damp sweater, and her squirming in the seat with her wet, tight blue jeans. It could not get better than this for a young man.

In any other crisis, Bill Meyers would be crapping in his pants about the car damage, and the future confrontation with his dad. What repercussions would develop with Mr. Ratchet, who knew his father from childhood. Right now, he did not care. Bill Meyers cared for the lovely body which suddenly moved over to his side, giving him a kiss on the cheek, and followed with a warm two minute hug. Actually, the snuggling lasted for one minute and 32 seconds. He counted.

"What happened back there?" Bill Meyers finally asked.

She positioned herself back on the passenger side, and stared at him quietly. She gathered her thoughts, and every now and then, looked out at the wintry scene. Bill Meyers whiffed the smell of alcohol every now and then. Her being wasted did not outweigh the importance of sitting with a hot looking girl at the lake.

Bill Meyers knew she drank in high school, but the gossip was drawn from her living with her alcoholic father. The loss of her mom to lung cancer added to her situation. Susan Conti was pegged as a party girl. Her personal grief might of brought on a lifestyle, which became misconstrued by others.

"I could not find my Pop in the afternoon, and with the coming snow storm, I began to worry. My Pop usually is home watching the television on a weekday. He might go out to the market, but he comes straight home. Sometimes he hangs out at the Tannersville Bar and Grille. He usually shows up home around five to have dinner. I always have a little something for my Pop, even though I am not a great cook. It was strange that he was missing, considering he dislikes driving in the snow."

For him, so far, logic dictated Susan Conti's story.

She continued speaking," Anyway, at four in the afternoon, I decided to go look for him as the snow started to fall. My pop hangs out at the Tanny Bar a lot, so that was my first stop. I met Mr. Ratchet and the other guys, who said they did not see my father all day. This is when the trouble started. They began to buy me drinks, and at first, we were having a fun time, laughing and telling jokes. Mr. Ratchet kept trying to put his arm around my shoulder, and I politely gestured to him to stop. The time went fast and it was getting late. The conversation began to get creepy, saying offensive stuff to me. How could those men believe a nice girl like me would put up with such trash talk. They disrespected my womanhood."

"Well, what things did they say to you? Mr. Ratchet's wife belongs to the "Ladies of Jesus" group. I would think he would be a perfect gentleman." Bill Meyers added.

Susan Conti exclaimed, "That 's right Billy Boy! You would think. I was trying to be polite for awhile, and then threw a whiskey shot in Mr. Ratchet's face. They said things like- what position do I prefer when doing the deed. Do I take it up the ass? Really, the ass? Everyone knows the dimensions are not for that. Did I ever do more than one guy at a time. That story is only partly true, I started with two guys down in Ridgewood on a Friday night, but I stopped. It did not feel right, and it was hurting me. I knew God did not approve of this."

"Well that is good. You followed the right choice if God does not approve." Bill Meyers spoke with support.

He really did not believe her, and heard the story about the threesome. She kept gabbing about the drunken men, and his mind contemplated about this scenario of three. In a way she disgusted him, and in another way, he lusted for her. He found her totally desirable.

She continued her babble, "Anyway, Mr. Ratchet tugged at my arms, and requested for a little sugar from me. He will buy me the pretty necklace, I admired in K-mart jewelry department. I mentioned it to them earlier in our conversation over drinks. I had no desire for that fat, stinking man, not even for jewelry. Well, maybe if it was the handsome Matt Johnson, the general manager at K-mart."

"Yeah, Matt Johnson looks like a hot guy." Bill Meyers felt idiotic for that statement.

He thought," Stupid! Gay. What a stupid, gay thing to say,"

Bill Meyers knew in what direction her story was heading. She was a known tease, and enjoyed the free drinks. When events began to get out of hand, Susan Conti panicked. Her reputation as "Slutty Suzy" did not help her situation. These guys were not thinking straight. The implications were steered in a direction which would bring disaster and public embarrassment.

Bill Meyers quickly thought that those "bar stoolers" were not going to say a peep about the car incident. Their own reputations would be blemished. Old Mr. McCory, who owned the Tannersville Bar and Grille, will probably write off the damage to the insurance company, claiming an unknown car smashed up his door after closing hours.

Susan Conti's babble continued, " I scolded them to stop it, and to keep their hands off me. Mr.Ratchet claimed that this is what I wanted. Yeah, right. It was not my problem their wives are not putting out for their hubbies. So one of them blocked the door, and I realized trouble was brewing. I softened up my attitude, and ordered another round of whiskey shots. I swayed by the juke box, and selected some tunes. I seductively massaged the chest of Mr. Ratchet. I wrapped my arms around him, starting to lick his ear lobe. Then, I quickly shocked him with a knee bolt in the groin! He heaved over immediately. The other guys became distracted, and I escaped out the front door."

Bill Meyers exclaimed," That is really unbelievable." He actually meant those words.

Susan Conti with a change in tone, replied,"Well, I guess you know the rest. I could not believe what was happening. Those old men, and me? You are like my knight in shining armor. Yes, Billy Boy, my knight to protect me."

Susan Conti seemed more relieved after telling her story. She was less upset. Bill Meyers loved the bit about the knight in shining armor, and him saving the day. If she only knew that his real attention was to flee. He wished to retreat from her bar brawl, and would deny he ever witnessed it. Instead, by accident, Bill Meyers now was idolized as a hero. She continued to compliment him, and she began to check him out with her seductive eyes.

During her non stop chatter, she took out a pill, and popped it in her mouth like she was taking a candy.

Bill Meyers looked on confused and said, "Is that so wise after all that drinking? You really should sober up. Drugs are not going to help your situation."

"On the contrary, this "Oxy" is just what I need to straighten out. The pill levels me off from the liquor. I guess I should head home. I hope I find my Pop passed out on the couch. This is very unusual, especially with the snow storm and all."

Bill Meyers confidently replied,"I'm pretty sure your father is back at your house. Like you said, he probably went out on a errand (like buying alcohol).

Susan Conti agreed, and gave a last glance at the serene, wintry scene. She kissed him romantically, and repeatedly thanked him. She will never forget this moment, here at Meade lake. He had a way of comforting her. He radiated a sensible calmness, probably from his big brother attraction. Bill Meyers started the car, and took the scenic route to her house because some streets were just not plowed yet.

When he reached the Conti's house, it was dark, and quiet. Her father's pick-up truck was not there. Susan Conti became nervous again. Bill Meyers parked the station wagon in the street. He helped her over the mounds of snow blocking the sidewalk. They got to the front door, which was unlocked. Susan Conti claimed that she never locked the front door. There justified no reason because they did not own anything worth stealing. The house was chilly, and Bill Meyers first turned on the thermostat for some heat.

Susan Conti said, "I hope there is enough oil in the tank. Lately, due to cost, we are only burning wood in the fireplace."

Bill Meyers assuredly said, "Well Suzy, the fireplace will take awhile to heat up your house. Obviously, your father was not here during the afternoon, because I assume he would of started up a fire. I hear the oil burner turning on."

She then noticed the blinking light on the answering machine. She quickly jumped over to the phone, and pressed the play button.

"Hi honey, it's dad. I assisted a man who broke down on Rte. 3, and drove him up to Helix Point. He is a scientist who works at the observation center. Due to the storm, I am staying here with him. Wow, it is a really nice set up. I did not know they had such comforts and supplies. I will be home tomorrow as long as the snow is passable. I love you, and will see tomorrow."

Bill Meyers exclaimed, "See. Your father is okay. He actually is doing someone a honorable deed."

Susan Conti, in a comforting voice, said,"Oh, that is my Pop. He always helps the less fortunate. You know he drinks a lot, especially after the death of my mom. He never was able to fill the emptiness of my mom's presence in the house. We almost moved a few times, because everything reminded him of her. But Pop always is there for the helpless to lend a hand."

Suzy Conti became even more relaxed, and hugged him. Again, she expressed her thankfulness as the alcohol vaporized into his nose. Her eyes looked glazed and droopy. He told her to lay down and get some sleep. Everything will seem better in the morning. He told her to forget about those guys, that it was the liquor doing the talking. They will be to afraid to speak about this night's altercation.

"I am going to jump into a hot shower", She commented

"Everything is better now that you are here, Billy Boy. You wanna join me in the shower?" Suzy replied with a sly voice.

Bill Meyers immediately became embarrassed, and was at a loss of words.

She replied," Take it easy, Billy Boy. I am only joking with you. Do you honestly think I jump into the shower with every guy I just meet?"

Yes! Yes! Bill Meyers answered her in his mind. She stared at him with surprise, as if she heard him telepathically.

While walking out of the room, she remarked, "You know, You can be a bit of a dope. Sit down in the living room, and grab a beer."

He answered," It is too late for that, and I do not drink. I will wait for you, and help you to go to bed."

"Oh, that sounds good. I will see you in my bed then?" Susan Conti replied as she left the room.

Suzy Conti again was joking. Or was she? At this point, Bill Meyers did not know. He lacked experience for intimate situations. He heard the shower go on, and sat down on her couch as the heating vents rattled.

Was he going to have sex tonight? No. If the sex resulted as uneventful, or lousy, she will not see him again. Bill Meyers needed strategy.

The best thing was to ask her out on a date. She looked so drugged and drowsy. It would not be fair to take advantage of her. The sex will be more meaningful, if he was patient. First, build up a personal relationship, and then, the deed.

Bill Meyers heard her in the bedroom, and he yelled in from the living room, "I think I will go home. You get some sleep now."

Susan Conti rushed out to him, wearing a long sweater and bare shapely legs.

"What do you mean?" You are going to leave me in this lonely, chilly house with my Pop gone?"

He stuck to his strategy and said,"Get some sleep. Listen, how about you accompany me on Friday night to Ridgewood. Would you like to go to the "Science Fiction Fest" at my university?"

Susan Conti delighted replied, "You mean like Star Trek stuff and geeks dressed up in costumes?"

"Yep." He said simply.

She embrace him with a big kiss.

Susan Conti said, " Shut up! Yes, yes, I definitely will go! It sounds like a real blast, and a real date with my knight in shining armor, who saved me from those creeps. Let us take on the world together Billy Boy, and start a new adventure."

Susan Conti again kissed Bill Meyers all over, but this time much more seductive. She touched him here, and caressed him there. At one point, Bill Meyers felt like she was going to devour his whole face. The kissing was good, really good. He wanted more as he grabbed one naked ass cheek under her long sweater. However. he restrained and stuck to his gentlemen strategy.

She happily commented, "I love you Billy Boy. Where were you all these years? Why did you not ask me out once? I always noticed you, and would say to myself, what a great guy. If only he could be mine, all mine."

Bill Meyers spoke, now ending the evening, "Suzy, we will have loads of fun on Friday. We will continue this after the festival. You do need some sleep. You look as if you are about to pass out in my arms."

In a slurred, sly voice, she said, "I only wish, Billy Boy."

Even with her brushing of the teeth, the presence of alcohol was lingering. He brought her to her room, and she pulled off her sweater, Totally naked in front of him, she crawled in her bed. He threw the covers over her, and kissed her on the forehead. In seconds, her eyes were closed, and quiet.

He left the room, and just outside he door, she whispered, "I love you, I really love you."

Bill Meyers left the house, and out of habit, locked her front door.

Outside, he looked up at her bedroom window and he exclaimed, "See you on Friday."

Bill Meyers went into his car, turned the ignition key, and heard the rat-tat-tat from the engine. His nose sniffed the lingering aroma of Susan Conti. His thoughts respectfully acknowledged - "My Suzy".

Eight Hours Earlier

Harold Olgleby piled supplies along the shoulder of the road. His temperament increased as the snow would not let up. The tools and spare for fixing the flat of his old van, had to be buried somewhere underneath the trunk floor. The van was packed to the max with equipment. The unloading of stuff in the ceaseless snow storm, was unbearable. He found a latch, pulled it, and "eureka"- he located the spare. As a scientist, with a P.H.D. in meteorology, you would think figuring out how to elevate the van, and change the tire to be simple. Harold Olgleby cursed as he cut his finger on the contraption that lifts the car.

His finger would not stop bleeding. He searched for the first aid box, and dug around his stuff, making more of a mess. He had everything well organized, but could not locate what he needed. This incidence increased his temper. The blood dried on his hand and became sticky as it froze from the cold. He wrapped it in gauze, and returned the glove onto his damaged hand. Harold Olgleby sat in his van, and recuperated while he cursed at the continuing snowfall.

The scientist complained,"Damn that weather channel! This is more than five inches of snow."

He wiped the moisture off his eye glasses as he sat with the heat on full force. Stranded along Rte. 3, was going to be the day when everything goes wrong. To add to his misery, his van conked out. He turned the ignition, and nothing. Again, he attempted to start his van, and nothing. He accepted the bad luck. Harold Olgeby dialed for Roadside Assistance on his CB radio. His radio received no transmission in the Virginia hills.

The cold began to penetrate the warmth inside the van. He zipped up his parka. He pounded onto the steering wheel which brought no results to his predicament. Just as he blurted another curse word, a muffled voice was heard outside from the snow. A man knocked on his window, and asked him if everything was all right.

Harold Olgeby stepped out of his van, introduced himself, and explained he got a flat. After that, his engine died. Mr. Phil Conti introduced himself, and told him not to worry. He will fix the flat, and then check the engine. Relief overcame Harold Olgeby. Helplessness was a trait he dreaded and responded poorly to.

He thanked Mr. Conti, and showed him the flat tire tools. Before, Mr. Conti started, he walked over to his truck, and grabbed a beer from the backseat.

While Mr. Conti was fixing the tire, Harold Olgeby made some small talk. "I am heading up to Helix Point to the research center. Two weeks ago there was significant readings on my seismology instruments. Maybe you remember the small earthquake last summer in the papers. I am following up on the data. I believe this area will be affected real soon with a larger quake any day now."

Mr. Conti glanced over to this gentleman every now and then. He listened to the scientist, and his research. Mr. Conti noticed that Harold Olgeby had a nervous personality. He was a skinny, pale man making a lot of hand gestures, and kept pushing his glasses back up his nose bridge like a brainiac in some college movie.

Mr. Conti on the other hand, had tan, rough skin from working outdoors with a muscular body. He worked slowly, reflecting a man becoming older in age. who just cannot move with the same energy as he use to. His alcohol problem was not apparent at first, until Harold Olgeby saw the empty bottles in his back seat of the truck.

Mr. Conti explained, "Your engine is kaput. You need a new distributor cap. It is getting late, and with all this snow, I recommend that you leave your van for the night, and pick up the broken pieces in the morning."

Harold Olgeby exclaimed, "I cannot do that. It is out of the question. Listen, I will pay you 100 dollars plus gas to take me up to Helix Point with your pick up truck. It is essential I arrive at the research center."

Mr. Conti was surprised at the young man's determination, and quick reply. His frail character contradicted that of an adventurer. There was only eight inches of snow, and he really could use the money. This scientist looked like one of these rich city types, so he requested 100 dollars, and a fast pit stop to purchase complimentary beer. Harold Olgeby leered at him for a few seconds, and agreed to the money.

The scientist felt slightly annoyed, that Mr. Conti was taking advantage of him. On the other hand, this local man assisted him with his broken down van. The price seemed a little steep, considering they were only thirty minutes away. It was, however, a treacherous drive into the snow bound hills. The snowfall looked thicker, and conditions were worsening.

They loaded the equipment into the truck, and headed down Rte. 3 to Cliff Drop Road. They stopped at a Quick Mart with 100 dollars to buy beer and snacks, Harold Olgeby sat contemplating his lousy financial situation. You think the University would have loaned him a van for the expedition. But no. He was spending his money, with his own crappy van.

Harold Olgeby excelled in his field, with college honors and two degrees. Yet the most money offered from a company did not amount to even thirty thousand dollars a year. The young scientist was the best in meteorology, and he knew it. He lacked the showmanship to equal his intelligence. Things were going to change. Harold Olgeby held a secret about Helix Point, which could bring him the prestige he longed for.

His earlier career in the sciences, founded itself in the value of knowledge and new discoveries. Like many, desiring to better help the productiveness of society, the naive student learned quickly about the competitive, capitalistic world. The wishes to promote quality of life, instead, kindled a flame for vengeance, to win what was lost from life's harassments.

His meek frail display, branded him as unimportant, useless, and strange in school. He was mocked to extent, and so he lost himself in his studies. In the earlier school years, the kids who roughed him up, and called him names, he learned to despise. A loneliness developed existing in a society which alienated him, but yet one still belonged.

Wise guys, cutting up the class, always bragging like they were important, attracted and drew the attention of the student body- the sheep people. Their false demeanor gained them the respect, which was not generated from a discipline life. Bull crap could earn respect and prestige. That was, if you had the talent for it. Over the years, Harold Olgeby learned to enjoy the smell of his own crap.

Harold Olgeby wondered what those kids amounted to. He grinned to himself, imagining the "D" and "F" students stocking shelves for minimum wage, driving truck routes, and cleaning bathrooms. But, he also remembered the "C" students who succeeded in business, earning six figures. He received a "B" average, and the "Van Huesen Gem Trophy" for his work in diamond synthesis. He wrote papers on the stability of synthetic diamonds. Quite an accomplishment, he thought. Unfortunately, one summer morning, his dog buried his trophy somewhere in the backyard.

The snowfall increased with intensity, but Mr. Conti drove without a care in the world.

Harold Olgeby mentioned, "Are you sure you should be driving so fast, and drinking a beer in this blizzard?" .

Mr. Conti chuckled as he turned and skidded onto Cliff Drop Road. "Oh, this is only my fourth beer. Maybe two hours ago, when I had a nasty headache, we would have had a problem."

This answer did not alleviate the uncertain probability of flying off a cliff because of a "drinking redneck". The view was spectacular in these hills, and the snow thickened over the dirt road. Harold Olgleby took a pill out of his shirt pocket, and swallowed it. He suffered from anxiety, and wished they arrived at the research center.

They reached a side road with a metal gate. Harold Olgeby had the key, and he walked to the entrance to unlock it. Now it was a matter of driving straight upwards to Helix Point. His medicine kicked in, and the last part of this trip was enjoyable. Excitement filled inside of him. The research was very important to him. Harold Olgeby visioned this project to open his door of success. His colleagues would applaud him for his discovery.

What Mr. Conti did not know, was the skinny, nervous man, was more cunning than his appearance lead off for him to believe. Harold Olgleby stumbled on some fossils from last summer's earthquake, which he did not share with the rest of the team. They consisted of remains of an animal living in the primeval forest, thousands of years ago. The fossils of a missing link, a snow creature, during the Pleistocene Era.

They pulled into a parking lot next to the concrete building. The lot was large, and designed to park many cars. The county used Helix Point as a recreation park also. They held festivals, and all sorts of outdoor affairs here. Many of these gatherings were charity oriented, and helped support the research center for nature conservation. For a remote site, it was very modern, and clean. People picnicked up here in the summertime as well, enjoying the outdoors and view.

Mr. Conti was impressed with the conveniences the building offered. From all the years coming here, he never stepped inside, and was surprised. For him, this was like taking a vacation at a nice hotel. While Harold Olgleby brought in his equipment, he simultaneously began setting the instruments for operation. Mr. Conti grabbed his beer, and a bag of potato chips, and plopped down on a comfortable couch.

Mr. Conti said, "This place is awesome. That observation window, with the whole view of hills and valley, is incredible! Oh wow, look at that screen and video console."

He was enjoying his stay as he flipped through a bunch of video cassettes, hoping to find one to watch.

Mr. Conti concerned said, "Oh gosh darn, my daughter! I forgot to call my Suzy where I am."

He quickly looked for a phone, and found a satellite phone. He dialed via the self-explanatory instructions on the wall, and left her a confident message not to worry. He explained that he will most likely be home tomorrow. Helix Point had exceptional accommodations, better than his dilapidated house.

Around 9:00 P.M., the snow slowed down. Harold Olgeby was working with his technical toys, and Mr. Conti watched a video. The quiet, non interactive scientist suddenly changed his stoic behavior. He grabbed a beer and sat next to Mr. Conti.

Harold Olgeby began to loosen up, and be talkative." You know, these woods have their origin to a primeval forest from a prehistoric, mammalian time. Some of these trees are ancient, and have a vast history of the past. It was called the Pleistocene Period. The time was 10,000 to millions of years ago. Some animal species existed, like the saber tooth tiger, and the woolly mammoth. The species which interests me, was called the giant ground sloth. The fossil showed huge claws, and it was dubbed Megalonyx, meaning Great Claw."

"Meg-a-loo-nix? Well it does sound like a dinosaur name." Mr. Conti replied.

"On the contrary. It was nothing like a dinosaur, but similar to a present day bear with unique features. It was a huge ground sloth." Harold Olgeby corrected.

The scientist continued speaking, "Megalonyx, is kind of a misnomer. At first discovery, the fossil claws were thought to be of a big cat, like a prehistoric lion."

Mr. Conti spoke drunkenly to verify the point of approval their conversation had reached. "Okay, Boss, Megalonyx it is. The fossils of, you supposedly found in these hills."

Harold Olgeby continued his speech, " Last summer, you probably witnessed all those government agencies. I was part of the team. Working on the earthquake, I discovered a hidden crevasse, a cave like crack in a remote cliff. I was following a personal theory concerning the quake, which lead me to a area away from the other technicians."

The sudden, chatty Harold Olgeby stood up, went to the fridge, grabbed two beers, and sat back down with Mr. Conti. Sleepy eyed, from almost drinking a case of beer by himself, Mr. Conti showed lack of interest in the story. Harold Olgeby gave one of the beers to his assistant, and toasted, both clanking the two beer bottles together.

The scientist's lecture continued, and said, "While spending the late afternoon, down in that cracked hole, I dug up unusual bones, fossils, which at first I could only partially identify. I decided to leave them there, and return another time. Suddenly around twilight, I heard calling from the others, and quickly left my secret cavern, and diverted my team mates. The fossils, I examined were unique, and I planned to get sole credit for the discovery. I covered my tracks well, and nobody found out."

Harold Olgeby took his last swig of beer, and belched. Mr. Conti was intrigued with the story, though he was drunk and tired.

"Please, finish your tale, I think I am about to fall asleep." Mr. Conti added.

Harold Olgeby stood up, and walked into a back storage room. He spoke as he pushed into the room, a package wrapped up in a old tarp on a dolly.

"I returned in the fall of this year for a week. I dug out the fossil remains. It was a tedious task climbing into the steep crevasse with equipment, and carrying everything out, including the fossils. At one point, I really did not think I could pull it off. That is alone." Harold Olgeby remarked.

"Patiently I worked, and methodically I worked. No rushing, so I did not bring physical harm to myself, or my discovered load. What I am about to show you, is priceless. I hope Mr. Conti, you can assist me. I will share the rewards with you. It will take the utmost secrecy of you, for us to accomplish this goal." Harold Olgeby slyly explained.

Harold Olgeby untied the crumpled tarp from the huge package, which he hauled into the main area on a dolly. Mr. Conti's sleepiness was still there, but subsided from the intrigue. The uncovering of the item revealed a long, thick fossilized bone, having features of a sword made of stone. Mr.Conti saw a line split the 4 ft. bone down the middle of it's length. It reflected that of a curved scissor.

Harold Olgeby exclaimed, " I see you notice the center indentation of this fossil. I believe this mammal used this huge incisor as a clipper to grasp its prey, like a crab does. The point of the massive clipper/ claw was helpful to pin down its predecessor, and to offensively attack. Closed, the claw acted as a shovel to dig, or push away snow and dirt. This creature existed during the pleistocene period of prehistoric mammals."

The scientist spoke with enjoyment and fascination, while the intoxicated local began to lose interest. He had no interest in bones, research, and test tubes. Mr. Conti acknowledge the man's discovery, and longed for bed. He plopped down onto a cot, and fell asleep immediately.

Harold Olgeby realized the stupor of his new assistant, and decided to continue his scheme over some coffee in the morning. Mr. Conti will be useful to his project. He needed a simpleton to help protect his new found treasure. There existed more bones in these hills, which would bring him handsome prices. Harold Olgeby knew he could easily manipulate this alcoholic for his personal means.

Beer made him bloated, so he took out a small whiskey flask from his luggage. He sat down in front of the massive observation window. Harold Olgeby enjoyed the view, which was lit up from the patio lights. His mind raced with ideas about Megalonyx. This animal was definitely a carnivore. The teeth were like fangs which supported his theory.

It was odd, however. The snow creature appeared to be similar to the plant-eating ground sloths which lived during this period of prehistoric mammals. These sloths were herbivores, and grew very large, becoming trapped in caves and underground passages. They could have been easy targets for the meat eating Megalonyx to hunt.

Maybe, these carnivorous sloths fed off the plant eating sloths. The unknown extinction of these herbivore sloths has been well documented. Maybe packs of these snow creatures slowly wiped them out, and then these carnivorous sloths lacked a food source with oncoming variables and also became extinct. Megalonyx could of aided in the extinction of the woolly mammoths as well.

No previous fossils were ever found because this species was short lived and possibly regional, only in the Appalachian territory. Darwin's theory of evolution documented extensively about hundreds of animal species which did not survive, and we presently know nothing of their limited existence. Harold Olgeby possessed the first found fossils of the Megalonyx carnivore.

The fame swept scientist slowly nodded off, and entered his fantasy. In his dream, he spoke to a large audience concerning his discovery of the snow creature, fossils of a different Megalonyx. It followed by a five minute standing ovation.

Billy Boy & Slutty Suzy

The smell of new leather smothered Bill Meyer's bedroom, which he shared with his younger brother, Kyle. It was Friday morning, the day of the historic date with Susan Conti. Tonight, he was taking her to the Sci-Fi festival at his college in Ridgewood. He purchased a brand new leather jacket, which set him back 300 dollars. It was worth every dime he earned.

This purchase depleted half his savings, but he considered this buy a momentous addition for his first, real date. Past dates with girls, were not really date dates. In those days, he was lucky to get a hand shake, or a respectful hug, and always took care of the girl's expenses, gentleman-like. This time, Bill Meyers desired payback. The girls used to take advantage of his nice guy routine.

Kyle kept carrying on all over the house about the disgusting smell. His brother Billy was poisoning him. It did not take long for his mother to find out that something was out of the ordinary. The smell of coffee at breakfast could not drown out the new leather odor in the house. She walked into her son's bedroom, and saw the jacket lying neatly on his bed.

Mom politely asked, "What is going on Billy? You bought a dressy coat ? It looks expensive. Bill Meyers kept buttoning his shirt, and did not acknowledge his mother.

"I mean really. You spend all this money, now, before Christmas. It seems foolish. Especially, with all your comments about wanting a new car." His mother pleaded.

Defensively, he said," I need new stuff. I gotta look sharp, not cruddy with that one beat up parka you gave me three years ago."

Bill Meyer's mother peered at her son with natural instinct concerning the ill sensible purchase.

His mother explained,"This is about a girl, right? Oh Billy, you do not just spend your hard earn money on someone you just met. Girls can be deceiving. First, you need to get to know them better. A Christian girl loves a boy who respects them for their self worth. That Suzy Conti is not worth a dime of your time, or for that matter, the rest of your money."

Bill Meyers asked,"How do you know it is Suzy Conti?"

"You have repeated her name all over the house yesterday, and in your sleep. A mother knows these things. In the past, I heard about her less desirable ways. I always felt you were smarter than the other boys around here. I mean, really, 300 dollars on clothes? How much more is she going to pilfer off you." His mom spoke in a scolding tone.

He exclaimed, "I like her. She is misunderstood. She wants to go to the Sci-Fi festival with me."

His mother still speaking with a stern tone, "I thought you promised Kyle, your brother, to see the festival?

Bill Meyers defensively said, "He will be in our way. I am a man now, mom. I have no time for Kyle, the child. Anyway, he is annoying, always sneering at me, and cracking irritating jokes. He needs a good sock in the face!"

"Bill Meyers, how dare you! Your brother will be devastated. He bought that action doll for that "what's his name actor" to sign. That famous actor is making a special guest appearance at the festival." His mother scolded him.

At this point, Bill Meyers delved into other family issues which bugged him over the years. His mother intensely listened, though she argued back defensively. The heated discussion developed into an insane argument. The lack of reason surfaced in the verbal lashing, and personal viewpoints were shot at each other with literal honesty.

The nasty tone in the house only stopped, after Bill Meyer's father yelled for everyone to shut up.

Bill Meyers put on his old parka, and stormed out of the house. He was working all day at the diner to earn some extra money for his date.

He was doing well with his college studies, and so skipped classes (Bad Boy, bad boy).

At the diner, Charlie quickly noticed Bill Meyers' sour mood. A few customers at lunch were becoming irritated at the lack of service. Bill Meyers made unhelpful replies, and food dishes were clumsily placed in front of the patrons. He spilled beverages as he impolitely placed them on the tables.

Charlie pulled his usual, trustworthy assistant aside, and asked him what was the problem. Bill Meyers explained he had a fight with his mother.

Charlie expressed his understanding, and said," We all have personal problems. Just remember that here- the customer is always right. Your other issues leave at the door."

Bill Meyers calmed down, and thought about his Susan Conti. They were going to have a great time. The thought of them, together, helped him withdraw back to an accommodating waiter. He was going to break soon, and call her about tonight's engagement. He cannot wait, for his first, sex date!

He apologized to a tall, quiet man sitting, writing in a booth alone. It was Frank Porter, the newsman, a man who soon will play a key part in Bill Meyer's future.

"Do not worry. We all have our bad days," Frank Porter mildly stated.

The two stared at each other for a dejavu second, feeling some connection, an unknowing karma. Soon these two will be joined in a bizarre connection.

A boisterous bunch entered the diner. Todd Bloomfield and crew from the football team, barreled into the diner acting like they owned the place. Suddenly, the room tilted and wavered as Bill Meyers focused his sight on Suzy Conti. The massive quarterback's arm was wrapped tightly around her waist. The crew passed him without a notice. He stared at her hand rubbing his back, then heading down to his jeans.

In his mind, Bill Meyers exclaimed," Holy crap! What in heaven's name is going on here?"

He could not believe his own eyes.

The gang took a booth, laughing and having a grand time. Bill Meyers state could best be described as irritably perplexed. He instinctively walked over to take their orders.

Polite, and casual, he replied,"Hi guys, what are you gonna order?

Todd Bloomfield confidently said, "Well, I will have a deluxe cheese burger, fries, and a coke. For dessert, I will have a piece of Suzy Pie."

Susan Conti picked up some sugar packets from the table, and jokingly threw them at him. He pulled her over and smacked a big mouth kiss on her.

Susan Conti giggled and simply replied," Well, comparing me to sweetness is better than calling me a hunk of meat."

Everyone laughed, that is except confused Billy Boy.

Bill Meyers felt like he was shuffling a deck of cards. His meek attempt to solve this confusion, was about to have the shuffled cards scatter onto the table. His poor decisiveness needed to maneuver a solid offensive to keep up in this game.

Bill Meyers awkwardly blurted out." You will be ready tonight, to go with me to the Sci-Fi Festival?"

For a few seconds, Susan Conti appeared stunned from the question. Then, she realized what was going on.

She burst out laughing, and slyly remarked," Sci-Fi, on a Friday night? Me, and you? Oh, I remember, yeah well, I just meant if I had nothing to do. Maybe I would go to see the geeks and freaks. Todd and I are going to the basketball game tonight."

Things became more blurred for Bill Meyers. He became disorientated as the room swerved to the left, and then to the right. Did he dream all that stuff the night of the snow storm? Did he imagine saving Susan Conti from the creepy old men? Did he fantasize the kissing, hugging, and snuggling with her? Did he smell her alluring, attractive perfume, which aroused all his manly desires?

What the hell was going on! His temperament was rekindled from earlier. First his mother, now this bitch.

"What is the matter, Bill. Did you see a ghost? I do not remember approving this?" Todd Bloomfield mocked him.

The sarcastic comments and laughing, pulled Bill Meyers into a murky area, which developed right behind his normal demeanor.

"You did not really believe I would go out with you. I was glad you took me home, but that was it. What were you hoping for? A blow job?" She replied as everyone laughed.

Everyone laughed continuously, and more. The jokes echoed throughout the room. Bill Meyers remained wordless and his face red. It was a like "Slutty Suzy" was a witch, and threw a curse on him.

He could not speak or defend himself. He was zapped, stung, and paralyzed.

He turned away, and headed behind the counter. He threw his apron, unknowingly landing on the stove top. Charlie noticed all the commotion, and asked again to Bill Meyers to cut the crap. Harsh words were spoken between boss and employee.

Bill Meyers exclaimed, "I quit".

In the main area, the others poked fun at Bill Meyers as he stammered towards the door.

Todd Bloomfield replied,"Oh, poor Billy Boy will not get laid tonight. The guys on the team always knew you were a virgin. I noticed you leering at Susan Conti and I after school all the time. Like some weirdo!"

"How about fifty dollars, and I will do you Billy Boy", She sarcastically remarked.

The repetitive embarrassment percolated this murky, obscure side of Bill Meyers. He felt urged to beat Todd Bloomfield to a pulp. Because of the diner patrons, he kept his menacing thoughts controlled. No anger, no temper, and always a gentleman, that was his calling card. Though the card's words read – stupid moran!

"No, two hundred dollars baby!", Todd Bloomfield jokingly supported her.

"That is enough! All of you, get the hell out of here!", Charlie yelled at the bunch.

Todd stood up, and defensively replied, "Yeah let us go. The food always sucks here anyway. I am in the mood for pizza. Susan Conti embraced Todd closely, and they stormed out the door with the other guys. Bill Meyers grabbed his stuff from the back room, and headed out as well.

Before Charlie could stop Bill Meyers, he smelled smoke in the dining area. The apron caught fire from the stove top, and smoke filled the room. Patrons quickly got up and left without paying. Charlie was really pissed off, and took care of the smoking grille. He now had to service everyone by himself the rest of the evening. He relied on Bill Meyers with such dedication that there was no back up.

The newsman, Frank Porter, briskly walked outside, and wondered if there was a story here with the small fire at the diner. He realized how lame his reporting has become. No interesting intrigue ever sprouted in his little ol' Tannersville, hometown U.S.A. What the heck, he thought. A small mention in the weekend paper will probably be the talk of the town. He longed for an absorbing investigation, a story he could be proud to write.

Bill Meyers drove furiously in the station wagon, and stopped as he unknowingly parked by Meade Lake.

He shouted out the car window," That slut! No good "Slutty Suzy"! What is wrong with me. Why, why, why!"

He figured she was more wasted than she appeared to him that night. Abusers of drugs and alcohol distort their views. This was his answer to his night with Susan Conti.

How stupid could he be? He was not going to allow them to ridicule him anymore. Revenge was all he could think about. "Slutty Suzy" was going to be taught a harsh reality, a lesson never to be forgotten.

This week reflected that of a roller coaster ride. In the end, the ride ended with no thrills or cheers. He was alone and miserable. Respecting others? What ever did that get him? Justice was to spite his enemies who wronged him. Hell with all the goodness, and hell with his endless accusing mother. Everyone took advantage of his better self for their own devious goals.

He started the car, and left Meade lake, alias "No Makeout Lake for Billy Boy". He plotted a revenge on "Slutty Suzy", and the dumb ass, Todd Bloomfield.

CHAPTER 3

Cliff Drop Road

MR. CONTI PULLED A sleigh full of equipment to the fossil site. The time was around 1:00 P.M. Friday. On his third haul, the work developed into a hassle. He drank a few beers already to help lessen his hangover. Generally speaking, Mr. Conti was in no mood to do laborious work today, no matter how much the financial payment. He popped two aspirin because the beer only partially aided to rid him of his headache.

The sun shone brightly, the temperature held just right under freezing, and the winds were down. If you were planning to be in the wilderness around winter time, this was a beautiful day to enjoy it. However, he still lost interest, and wanted to go home and sit on his own couch. Even with the 31 degrees F', his shirt was soaked in sweat.

When he reached the spot, he yelled down the small chasm to Harold Olgeby. "Listen up, I want another hundred for this job. It is too much. I think I am going to leave."

Harold Olgeby listened to his assistant's complaint. From where he stood inside the crevasse, he could not visually see Mr. Conti.

Harold Olgeby yelled back up to him. "Just hang in there. I will be done before evening, and you can go. I will do what I can to pay you. Remember my trustworthy friend, we are working in a gold mine here."

Gold was something that Mr. Conti heard all before. In the end, he would be standing with no gold, but only the shovel. Drinking alcohol was his trustworthy reward over the years. He could feel good any time. His fantasies became real. Hard work for dreams amounted to little cash, even off the books.

He exclaimed, "I am not lugging no more stuff. My clothes are all sweaty from the sun. I am exhausted. I did not really want to stay the extra day. It is Friday, and I wish to go home."

While Mr. Conti was speaking, Harold Olgeby was already climbing up. When he reached the top, panting heavily, he showed a partial skull with large fangs.

The scientist spoke assuredly, "You see this my friend. This piece of our snow mammal could bring easily ten thousand dollars".

Mr. Conti flipped it carelessly back and forth in his hands. One of the sharp fangs pierced his finger.

"Ouch! That hurt. This bone is worth that much?" Mr. Conti asked.

Harold Olgeby said, "Work with me, partner, and I will share my findings. There are dozens of bones down there. Your name will be read in the published work. How would you like to show your buddies at the bar, a *Time Magazine* with your picture in it?"

The pitch appealed to Mr. Conti. But every now and then, in the last twenty-four hours, this pale looking guy seemed more untrustworthy by the minute. It almost brought out a defense mechanism inside of him. Harold Olgeby appeared to be a straight up guy, but he could not put his finger on it. However, his little speech convinced Mr. Conti to trudge down with him and dig up fossils.

The cave-like fissure was fascinating as they climbed down the steep rock formations. The sunlight glistened on jutting ledges spattered with snow. Different shadows brought intrigue with them, carefully stepping deeper into the hidden crevasse. Inside the cave, there were tight and spacious areas. Battery operated lights lit up the excavation site. Two large bones, like the one he showed him at the observation center were lying on a tarp. They resembled blades, and one fossil took the shape of an open scissor.

Mr. Conti figured it would be only a few more hours. He brought a few beers in his coat to help past the time. He shoveled where he was ordered to shovel. He hauled rocks from one side to the other to make space around the fossils.

The scientist used a smaller shovel and brushes. These tools were for finesse work around the structure of the bones. Mr. Conti did all the hard labor, and not used to this kind of work for years. He really lost interest. His lower back began to spasm, and his arm muscles were sore.

Harold Olgleby waved him to head back. The scientist could not stand the disgust that Mr. Conti made while digging. The disgruntled assistant headed back to the research center. The scientist told him he was going to continue his excavation into the evening. He politely asked Mr. Conti to please spend one more night. He could leave next morning. Harold Olgeby still requested his help to fix his broken down van.

Mr. Conti agreed to stay one more night, but only on the basis he was going to be a rich man. He hauled one last sleigh of fossils into the disappearing sunlit afternoon, and that was it. The pushy scientist will need to gather the rest on his own. Mr. Conti agreed to help him with his van, but actually was plotting to call a tow truck when they got back to town.

Harold Olgeby was annoyed. He needed help because his physique was definitely lacking the labor part of this project. He sat underneath the floodlights, loathing over his discovery with great apprehension. How did he ever imagine to accomplish this task alone. His selfish motive directed him into a disorganized state. His mission would not be completed, and would have to come back another time with others.

How will he deal with Mr. Conti's word of secrecy? Hopefully, the local will be on his team. Harold Olgeby lied about the funds, the funds which lacked to buy him off. He started to gather his things, and left buried fossils for another time. The conniving scientist realized that he was sinking deeper in false misnomers.

Suddenly a portable seismograph, began to show readings of earth tremors. Harold Olgeby marked the time at 6:00 P.M. Within seconds, the needle bounced into the orange range. This was his worst nightmare. The orange zone was right before the red zone. The red zone meant- get the hell out of here! The big one was approaching, and with unanticipated fury. The instrument printed out patterns which he analyzed before. It was coming soon like in hours or less.

His technical skill ranked exceptional. The tremor readings were demonstrating serious recordings. He needed to lug all his stuff out of this cave quickly. He was not prepared for this split second change as anxiety overcame him. Even if he called on the walkie talkie, he knew Mr. Conti was incapacitated. His helper would be of zero assistance. Within minutes, everything changed for the worst.

He started to gather things to head for the surface. Even if he successfully brought all the unearthed fossils and equipment, he would not reach Rte. 3. The consequences of the oncoming quake was going to be damaging. Will he get out alive? Harold Olgeby moved quickly to transport the prehistoric bones.

He estimated two, maybe three hours before the earthquake. Holding up at the observation deck was the only solution. Trudging with the sleigh full of fossils and pertinent equipment, presented a difficulty with the night approaching. He estimated a thirty minute trek.

He popped all sorts of pills. Pills for his allergies, anxiety, and the pain from all the digging and climbing. This cocktail of medicine sparked confidence and energy for him to keep moving. Should he leave all the stuff, and get the hell out of here as fast as possible? His greedy instinct ordered him to push forward with his fossils, and dump equipment to lighten the load.

Helix Point—Research Center

Mr. Conti settled in at the warm observation complex. He plopped onto the couch with a few beers and relaxed. He did not bother to shower up, and sat dirty, while slamming down some more beer. He turned on the video player, which already had a nature program in it. He calmed down to the nature sounds- birds singing, a stream flowing, and a soothing voice of the narrator. Sitting around drinking beer while watching television brought him relaxing enjoyment.

He slowly dozed off with all the day's events circling in his mind. The quality of the sofa was not bad. Mr. Conti laid comfortable, and the fabric construction helped sooth his aching back. It appeared new, like no one used it yet. He was just able to kick off his wet, and muddy boots with his feet, until deep slumber overpowered him.

Mr. Conti fell asleep as he usually did from drinking all day. His dreams entered a world, a wilderness world which time forgot. He stood amongst the pines in the snow. He did not feel cold like he was physically there, but more as a spectator watching a television show. He glanced upon massive elk, three doe and a bull with a magnificent set of horns. The elk's rack must of protruded 10 feet in all around its head. A true trophy for a hunter.

The whole scene looked different than his normal hunting treks in the woods. These animals had longer tufts of fur, and the massive size would easily break today's record. The bull elk towered over Mr. Conti. Somehow, he knew this was a past time, a prehistoric time. Again, he physically stood there, but was not there, as the majestic elk did not sense his presence.

Mr. Conti was not fearful at all. Again, he felt like an outside viewer looking into some sort of crystal ball of the wilderness past. The elk were jumpy. The bull snorted once, then twice in a row, as the air vaporized from the cold in front of it's face. They were on alert, an emergency alert of a threatening situation. Mr. Conti felt the fear as well, and knew the elk were a fraid of something else which had nothing to do with him. The bull stamped and hoofed at the ground, but could not sense where the danger existed.

This male deer needed to protect his harem. The females made short trots, and pranced in circles, confused where to go. A terrible thing was approaching, or watching, right there, but where. The bull elk bugled and wheezed. Its evolutionary instincts demanded aggression against his predators, to defend his females, and to defend to death. But, this bull elk was sparked with new unknown feelings of fear.

Snow exploded around the elk. The old stag buckled where it stood, as it collapsed to the ground. A large incisor snapped one of the back legs, and another one hooked onto a front leg. The woolly white head with beady red eyes, popped out from below the shocked bull elk. It sunk it's fangs into the meaty body. One loud bugle escaped the captured elk, and next a bloody gasp.

Mr. Conti could here sucking noises and heavy breathing as the blood gurgled out of the side of its mouth. The snow creature had two large fangs, like that of a saber-toothed tiger. These teeth aided in tearing and holding onto the prey. Its snout was similar in size like a bear.

The bull elk struggled, but a struggle in vain. This predator perfected its skills for attack in a wintry setting. The beast readjusted its massive claws with its death grasp. The backbone snapped, and the defeated bull elk was dragged under the snow.

Mr. Conti awoke suddenly. It was not really a nightmare, but still shocking enough that his body tingled with goose pimples. The dream seemed so real, like someone or something was educating him about the snow creature. He sat on the couch in thoughts, realizing he did drink too much. But it was so real. It seemed as if he took a leap back in time to the aged forests where this snow creature lived. The wilderness looked similar to where the excavation site existed.

He remembered well the stories about his Grandma's dream visions. The family would joke about her, that Grandma was crazy. They say she possessed the second sight. The townspeople called her "Conti the Witch". He wondered how unoriginal a nickname.

Many things she claimed, while she spoke and pointed her finger. Her cursive words became destiny's truth. She frightened many folks with her gypsy foretelling sessions for five bucks. She predicted deaths of husbands, illnesses of family members, bad weather, and could pinpoint tragedies.

His grandma would make outlandish statements like," On Saturday, when the moon is half full, a walk with a loved one will reward the pain of a your forgotten ones below."

Then, that person, walking with another on a pleasant eve, would stub their foot, or fracture their ankle.

People visited her to get tragic visions, instead of wishful fortunes. She had a reputation for ruining your week for five bucks. It was all fun and games for her tragic fortunes, but the customers never returned for a second time.

Did he have this second sight? Many times, Mr. Conti felt he could foresee the future. He could solve problems, as if someone whispered answers in his ear. The more he drank, the more vivid the truth. He told nobody because living with old granny's reputation was enough ridicule.

Something dreadful overcame him about these bones. That was why he felt uneasy working in the cave. A bad sensation badgered him since he met Harold Olgeby and his discovery. Old granny's presence seemed close by.

He swore he heard the words, " Blundering Fool," over and over in his mind throughout the day.

This made little sense. Who was the fool? Was it him or about Harold Olgeby? Maybe his Granny sent a foreboding warning? It could be him. Sometimes Mr. Conti felt like a blundering fool. The more he thought about it, others have actually called him a blundering fool.

The outside flood lights shone onto a figure rushing up the trail out of the snowy woods. He noticed Harold Olgeby pulling a sled outside the observatory windows. The scientist was waving furiously as if to get Mr. Conti's attention. Mr. Conti headed to the main door to see what the excitement was about. Harold Olgeby sped into the hallway bringing with him the evening chill.

The scientist loudly exclaimed, " A terrible quake is coming! Our lives are at stake!"

T.G.I.F

Kyle Meyers danced and strutted about the house with a teenager glee. His older brother was treating him to the Sci-Fi festival down in Ridgewood. He was thirteen years old, and chubby. His parents called his physique- baby fat. Kyle Meyers enjoyed reading fantasy/super hero novels, watched way too much television, and showed little interest in sports.

His parents wished that he followed his older brother in football. Kyle Meyers needed exercise to take off that baby fat. His father noticed that his younger son needed to man up, and move away from his childish behavior. The thirteen years old youngster entered the transitional period from boy to man, and needed to discipline his behavior.

Bill Meyers sat at the end of his bed upstairs. In disgust, he listened to his brother carry on at the dinner table downstairs. Kyle Meyers ate with a healthy appetite this night, and swallowed his food quickly. He also babbled about his science fiction knowledge, and how he was going to get an autograph from the movie star "Dash Hogan", who starred in the blockbuster hit, "Planet Abomination". Tonight, Bill Meyers was going to be tortured by his brother's nagging.

Bill Meyers could hear his father mumbling, " Hm, hm, Hm hm. Okay. Hm, Hm".

His father was not listening to son's crap about his fantasy heroes. His parents planned a trip to Aunt Mary in Richmond, and were heading out this evening. His dad worked a night shift, and drove his best off hours.

Susan Conti was suppose to be his date on this Friday night, and not his kid brother. She traumatized him with her total blow off. Was she so whacked on Wednesday night, that she forgot all those intimate moments they shared? What happened to his reference as a knight in a shining armor? It burned deeply. Bill Meyers felt like a sucker, and this ridicule happened too much in his life. He demanded revenge on Todd Bloomfield and "Slutty Suzy" tonight.

Bill Meyers put on his spanking new leather jacket while his mother was giving him last minute instructions. He did not comprehend any of it except,"...and be home before midnight boys."

He headed out to the station wagon, and his younger brother followed behind. They sat in the car while it warmed up.

Kyle Meyers began to complain," What is that disgusting smell! I think I will throw up. I ate too much of mom's meatloaf. You bought a new coat that stinks Billy Boop!"

Bill Meyers explained," New leather gives off an odor. After awhile, it fades away. I already told you about a hundred times."

"Oh, I forgot. Oh yeah, you and Suzy were suppose to be on a date. All that wasted money for new leather, and for the town tramp. Well, I knew that was not gonna happen. Hey Billy Boop, did you buy condoms? I want to see them." The younger brother chatted continuous.

Bill Meyers annoyed, and said," Be quiet. Stop calling me Billy Boop!"

He ignored his younger brother, and pulled out onto the street. He planned to take Route 3 down to Ridgewood. The Science Fiction festival was being held at the University. The drive should take about forty minutes. Kyle Meyers sat next to him holding his Dash Hogan action figure.

Bill Meyers reflected upon the last hour before he left the house.

His mom entered his room, and said," Why don't you eat some dinner? Look, I apologize for the argument at lunch. Your are a grown up, and can make your own decisions. It is just that girls and sex, can lead to events. Events that can change you life forever. One day, you will meet someone special, and have your own family to love under God's care. I am sorry for yelling at you."

Bill Meyers answered," That's okay mom. You were right. Susan Conti is a slut."

His mom ignored the foul word, and said, "Anyway, I am glad to see you acting your usual self. Now, your dad and I are leaving for Richmond in a hour to visit sick Aunt Mary. As our discussion last weekend, we went over the list how to take care of yourselves, and the house. The roads seem to be okay from the snow storm two days ago, so we still plan to leave tonight. You know how your father hates traffic, and likes the freedom with night driving."

"Give her my best, and good luck," Bill Meyers answered his mom.

His mom hugged him gentle, and said," This is a really nice thing your doing for your brother. God appreciates your sacrifices for others, and shining forth happiness. Try to buy something to eat at the festival. Here is a twenty. You two enjoy yourselves, and no fighting."

He replied, " Thanks Mom. We will see you both in a week."

It was a good thing God appreciated him taking his brother to the festival, because he was definitely hating it.

Bill Meyers still fantasized about having sex with Susan Conti down at "Make Out Lake ". He would forgive her, even now, after all the ridicule. A tingle stirred within, and the tingle was struck from"Slutty Suzy's" aromatic smell. It still lingered inside the station wagon. The perfume smell coaxed him to believe that he was in love.

During the drive, Kyle blabbered about movies, his friends, and a mixture of things he wanted to accomplish tomorrow. Bill Meyers understood how his father trudged through time, when his mother nagged in the car. Kyle Meyers was excited tonight, and glad his brother had to cancel his other plans. At one point, his chubby brother spoke so quickly, he burped and almost brought up his dinner. His childish joy overwhelmed him, and he refused to relax, and control himself.

Bill Meyers did not pay attention to his younger brother at all. Instead, he contemplated how to placate his rage about Susan Conti and Todd Bloomfield. Maybe, she would change her feelings after some healthy, spiteful revenge. He wished to evoke pure embarrassment on them both.

Within seconds, his insatiable lust for revenge was activated. A red pick-up truck zipped by and cut him off. It was Todd Bloomfield with Susan Conti sitting next to him. He had an ax to grind, and his evil duo were right in front of him for the chopping.

Bill Meyers drove to keep up with them, but stayed behind enough, so it was not obvious that he was tailing them. From the light of the oncoming cars, he saw her silhouette kissing Todd Bloomfield. Kisses meant for him.

Vengeance charged his neurotic mind. Spiteful poison bubbled in his veins. A dark side awaited for its moment to control Bill Meyers. He would find out where they were heading, and initiate their punishment. A christen was not to be found in this station wagon tonight.

He would start with simple pranks. Maybe they were going to the movies, and he could throw popcorn at them. Oh no, that was too lame. His dark side, his new consult, smacked his head from the inside. Visions of driving them off the road was more like it. Those two deserved something sinister. Hell's fire would be ignited for Todd Bloomfield and "Slutty Suzy".

The red pick-up truck turned left on Cliff Drop Road. Hmm, this action was interesting. Bill Meyers wondered why Cliff Drop Road? The route traveled through forest, and headed into the hills. Very few people lived on that road, and those who did were loners, real country folk, who usually did not take kindly to outsiders. Maybe Todd Bloomfield was buying moonshine, or was going to score some illegal drugs. He remembered seeing their quarterback and crew parked down an alley-way, behind the football field, smoking weed.

Then his dark energy maneuvered in his convoluted thoughts. Todd was planning to have sex at Helix Point! Who said that Bill Meyers was not a genius. Well, his mother always said this, but it was beside the point. He deductively deduced their plan to have sex on this Friday night, the night which was suppose to be Bill Meyer's night of manhood.

Bill Meyers took a left onto Cliff Drop Road. His younger brother immediately realized the wrong turn.

Kyle Meyers immediately exclaimed, "What are you doing? This is the wrong way!"

Bill Meyers replied, "We are taking a short detour. I need to find out something."

"Why are you following that truck? Billy Boop you lied. You are not taking me to the festival to see Dash Hogan!" His younger brother persisted.

Bill Meyers irritated said,"Be quiet! We will go soon, and stop with the Billy Boop."

"You lied, you lied, you lied! Billy Boop, Billy Boop, Billy Boop is a rotten liar!" Kyle Meyers carried on.

At this point, Bill Meyer's temperament had it. His anger at everything stressed his sensible limits. The strength of his dark obscurity oozed thick and black, pressuring behind his eyeballs. He slowly, strangely, confidently stopped. He idled the station wagon. Big brother glared at little brother with an evil eye.

In a deep, almost satanic tone, Bill yelled at Kyle, "I told you a million times. DO NOT CALL ME- BILLY BOOP!"

Kyle Meyers froze in silence as he watched his brother's physical demeanor morph. Out of nowhere, Bill Meyers pulled his arm back and high, with a clownish smile ear to ear. He swatted his younger brother with full force across his face. The sting was piercing. The intent was to hurt. Kyle Meyers sat crumpled in shock.

His brother never hit him. Tears swelled up inside Kyle Meyers. A few seconds passed in horrid silence. Then, a loud, baby cry resonated followed by a river of tears on Kyle Meyers face. The thirteen year old boy felt terribly violated as his tears continued uncontrollable. The tears flooded down the face of Kyle Meyers, who did not truly understand. He felt betrayed, lost, helpless, and scared.

His older brother simply sat with the same evil eye. Bill Meyers spoke very even toned, and appeared deviously confident.

Big brother exclaimed, "Grow up! It was just a small hit. Life is full of smacks. I told you to stop it, and you refused."

Bill Meyers sat with his head lower, like a hunchback, not helping the spooky situation. His head, containing the black ooze of disturbing infiltration, jutted side to side with unnatural motion.

Kyle Meyers clutched the door handle for a quick escape. He figured that his brother lost it. He would kill him next. Kyle Meyers noticed the multi-expressions appearing and then disappearing on his brother's face. His brother looked possessed.

Bill Meyers did not enjoy what he did, but did not hate it. It was urged to be done. So simple did the ripened vulgarity present the gratified facts. The smack was simple, so devilishly basic. Next, the two ahead in the pick up truck needed a good smack.

He started the car, and continued his hunt on Cliff Drop Road. Kyle Meyers stopped crying, and in silence kept touching his stinging cheek. The tissue turned red, and swollen. He dared not move quickly, that his insane brother would pounce on him again.

His older brother glanced over, and said, "Everything will be fine. The bruise is hardly noticeable. Relax while I finish what I have to do."

Kyle Meyers confused, replied to attempt normal communication," You promised me my autograph with Dash Hogan. You are not going to take me."

Kyle Meyers noticed the other vehicle up a ways, and how his older brother was keenly watching them. "Are you spying on that car? Did they wrong you?"

Bill Meyers became pleased with his brother's interest, "It is a pick-up truck with Todd Bloomfield and Susan Conti. I am watching where they are going."

The elevation picked up, and the cliff ahead turned to the right. The trees, empty of leaves, made it easier to see long distance in the dark. The truck's headlights were still. Todd Bloomfield and Susan Conti stopped for some reason. Bill Meyers moved up his station wagon a bit, but kept his distance from his unknowing prey. He decided to sneak up to them on foot, and spy.

Bill Meyers whispered," They stopped. Stay here and do not move. I will be back. Do not follow me. If you screw this up for me - I will, I will kill you!"

He was going all out. A smack here, and a threat there. If he had a gun, well, what the hell, stick a bullet hole in someone's head.

Kyle Meyers sat frightened.

He continued,"Yes, I know what you are thinking, my brother Kyle. I should throw them over the cliff. Not bad kid, you are learning fast."

His speech was spoken with such routine, monotone, flavor, as if he spoke sensible objectivity. Kyle Meyers was only thinking of escape.

The older brother left the station wagon, and said," Stay here while I creep, yes creep up to see what is happening. Now sit tight, or else!"

Kyle Meyers nodded his head up and down, meaning yes.

Bill Meyers stalked along the wooded edge of the road as he positioned himself to spy on the two. The red pick-up truck idled with its headlights on. Bill Meyers watched under the moonlit night, as "Slutty Suzy's" shadow disappeared.

While Kyle Meyers sat in the station wagon, he was frantically plotting. He felt overwhelming frightened and hatred towards his brother.

The fear though, slowly disappeared. He was glad to see him walk away. What did he do wrong? Nothing. Kyle Meyers did not recognize any wrongdoing.

He suddenly felt childish sitting with a doll, (though really an action figure). A man hit him, and he took it like a stupid kid. Kyle Meyers threw the Dash Hogan action figure on the car floor, and stomped on it with his feet. Maybe his older brother was right about one thing- he needed to grow up.

Kyle had the urge to runaway, and that was what he did. He flew open the door, and ran into the snowy woods. He was thinking, but could not think. His upset emotions jumbled the thirteen year old thoughts. Kyle stopped running. Standing and panting in the darkened forest, it became all clear to him. He will be an action superhero. Joy tingled up and down his spine.

This Friday night definitely sparked a series of nervous breakdowns, and the worse was yet to come.

He looked around at sticks and rocks, and decided to be "The Mighty Caveman". This super hero will gain his strength from the wild, and live in a secret cave. The fight with his brother welcomed his true calling. "The Mighty Caveman" will help down-trodden children, who became abused by their family. He will teach them the simple things of nature, in order to cope in an intricate people's society. Sharp sticks and stones will be his mastered weapons. The first order of business - find a secret cave.

Everyone, Meet Megalonyx

"Why did you stop here?" Susan Conti asked puzzled.

"Why not. This is as good as any place for that blow job you promised me." Todd Bloomfield stated the obvious.

He won the bet- a blow job if he won, or to buy her some stupid necklace if he lost. The bet was to see if he could eat 6 hot dogs with buns in one minute. One hot dog to swallow every ten seconds.

She replied,"It looks kinda gloomy out here. You could not find a more romantic spot?"

Todd explained,"I need some prime stuff, you know, what you asked for. Old Bogey Wilson lives at the end of this road. He sells the good weed."

An expression of sheer glee overcame her, and quickly tugged at his pants.

Happily Susan Conti remarked,"I will do almost anything to smoke pot."

She shuffled her body below as she positioned herself comfortably.

Todd glanced down during her preparation, and mentioned," By the way, what was all that gruff about you and Bill, and a date."

Susan Conti replied,"I have no idea. He gave me a lift after those "bar stoolers" were bothering me. All guys adore me. You know that. Billy Boy took my goodness for something more. Billy Boy is a geek, you know that. All those years in high school, he stared at me with his disgusting pimples. Oh, such a boring guy. Anyway, I am here, and only yours. Todd, you are truly my knight in shining armor. Oh my, look, you pulled out your sword."

Bill Meyers stood in the trees peeping towards the red pick up truck. The built up aggravation with his mother, the misconstrued date with "Slutty Suzy", and the years of irritable pranks from his brother, boiled a concocted mix of delusional madness.

The moonlit night helped his spying, but it was not clear enough. Stalking closer with a flashlight would expose his position. He noticed Susan Conti's silhouette disappear. She was going down on Todd Bloomfield. His revenge strategy was lame, and his anger converted into more miserable madness. This really lacked a sound plan at all.

He desired that action. How could he kill Todd Bloomfield? Any attempt against him, would probably backfire. He would be receiving his own revenge, and be beaten up into oatmeal. He stood watching like a peeping tom, and that was as about how good his revenge hashed out. His devious feelings became disrupted with embarrassment, as he received punishment, viewing someone else having his sex (how pitiful).

The quarterback enjoyed her expertise as his dissipating ecstasy parelleled the emotions of a scored touchdown.

The truck shook slowly, and a faint rumbling was heard. Todd Bloomfield realized her actions can be wild, but shaking the truck so vigorously? The truck continued to rattle while she took a two second break wiping her mouth with her hand.

He exclaimed, "Wait a minute. This shaking is not you, Suzy!"

He noticed snow clumps falling out of the trees, while the truck rocked harder back and forth. Todd witnessed a small tree collapsing, and then louder rumbles. A jolt sent the truck into the air, and Susan Conti's head smacked into the steering wheel. The impact from the wheel knocked her out as she laid at his feet unconscious. Another tree fell with continued rumbling. Todd realized that an earthquake was occurring, like the one last year.

The truck slowly slid to the cliff side, tilting in that direction. The road split aggressively into a fissure, pushing them towards the cliff edge. The jolt which knocked out Susan Conti, occurred from the road buckling beneath them. A crack formed through the rocks, and widened across the road. The truck teeter-tottered on the edge of Cliff Drop Road. The drop was steep enough to do real damage to themselves. A small avalanche of snow poured down the hill onto the driver's side, blocking Todd Bloomfiled's view out the window.

Bill Meyers realized what was happening as he heard the earthquake rumbles. His legs wobbled and had difficulty with balance. He headed back to his station wagon with a falling tree just missing him. He stumbled most of the way. His football finesse, or lack of as a second stringer, did no good against the unpredictable shaky ground. He took a few nasty falls, and thought about Kyle, and the safety of his brother.

Bill Meyers' madness crumbled along with the crumbling of the forest. Suddenly, he worried about his brother. Worrying for others than himself, that was his normal behavior.

By the time he reached his station wagon, the earthquake had stopped. He first searched for his brother, who was not in the backseat. He only cared to find his brother. The earthquake literally shook him back to his senses. It was wrong to hit him. He realized his eccentric emotions over Susan Conti was petty. He really needed to find him soon.

Kyle stumbled through the snow, while heading back to the station wagon as well. As soon as Bill Meyers caught sight of him, he ran to his one and only brother. He grabbed him in an embrace, and both of them fell into the snow.

Bill Meyers whispered, half cried in his brother's ear, "I am so sorry. That was so wrong. Please forgive me for hitting you. I am not a man, but you are, to have taken that smack. My spitefulness was that of a boy."

For Kyle Meyers, when the earthquake started, flakiness replaced his heroism. He fled back to the station wagon with childish fear. This bothered him greatly. How can he be respected as "The Mighty Caveman", when he just chickened out with the ground shaken. This really bothered Kyle Meyers immensely. He wanted to be a brave super hero. His thoughts were kept to himself, and figured his brother would not understand. This calling of his to be a protector of the down-trodden, needed fine tuning, and Kyle Meyers decided to keep "The Mighty Caveman" a secret for the time being.

Both were glad to see each other. How immense was his feelings for his older brother to recognize him as a real man. The eratic changes of his brother still kept Kyle cautious, but was glad to see him after the earthquake.

"Let us get the heck out of here!" Bill Meyers stated, and turned the car on.

"I am with you Billy Bo..., I mean Billy," Kyle Meyers politely answered, and corrected himself.

The two brothers made eye contact with a new understanding.

He cared less now about Todd Bloomfield and Susan Conti. Disgusting feelings about this whole charade, disgusted him. Bill Meyers did not even care about how those two fared.

They felt good about heading back home to safety. In no more than a minute of driving, a large oak tree blocked the road ahead. Bill Meyers stepped out of his station wagon, and walked all around, searching for a detour to drive around the blockage. There was no escape. To the sides of Cliff Drop Road, the terrain was filled with natural obstacles and high snow. The old station wagon could not handle the rough terrain.

It seemed bleak to walk to Route 3. Bill Meyers decided to head back down the road to Bogey Wilson's house. There, they could recuperate, have access to a vehicle, and possibly escape on a back road which circumvented the hills down to Millens Road.

Bill Meyers said,"Too much snow and debris blocks the road from the quake. Kyle,we will head to Bogey's place for help. Heading back to Route 3 looks messed up. The other side of the hill may not be affected."

Kyle Meyers agreed. As they walked, Bill Meyers realized that they were going to pass Todd Bloomfield and Susan Conti. Maybe together, joining with them, a plan for escape could be worked out. Kyle Meyers looked up at his brother, and felt more like his equal. During the walk, he was silent. He did not blabber about every little thing like a five year old. He matured quickly from his squabble with his brother.

"You okay? Suzy, wake up!" Todd Bloomfield exclaimed.

Todd Bloomfield shook Susan Conti, and sat her upright in her seat. All she did was moan with her head hanging limp. Todd rubbed her back, and kept yelling for her to awake. She slowly lifted her eyelids, and then they drooped. Suzy did not realize she suffered from a concussion.

She murmured,"I am okay, okay already. Leave me alone."

He knew this was not good. She must stay awake. He decided to crawl out of his pick-up truck, and then lift her out next. The snow crammed his door, so he opened the small window behind him which lead to open cargo area. His lean body easily snaked through, but with the truck teetering and squeaking.

It hung on the edge of Cliff Drop Road. Todd Bloomfield stood at the cliff edge. He observed the situation, and contemplated how to lift her out of the hanging truck. Every time he put weight on the truck it moved, moved in the direction down the cliff. All his ideas lacked any safety. Susan Conti could be heard whimpering, not really sure what was happening.

Todd Bloomfield, needed to calm down, and restore his composure-similar to a nail biting football game. Suddenly, as he contemplated his ideas, the ground shook again. It must be an aftershock. He turned his head toward crackling branches up on the hill. Bushes were pushed to the side as a large mound of snow actually moved down the slope.

It headed towards the road directly at him. Todd Bloomfield looked stunned at the mobile snow mound rumbling towards him in the moonlight. The slushing sound reminded him of a truck plow pushing snow off the street. This was no earthquake.

Concerned anxiety overcame him as he ran on the road. He figured a large rock was broken loose from the quake. Todd Bloomfield moved quickly in knee deep snow to deviate from its path. This rolling snow-ball changed in direction with him. Struck with fear, Todd Bloomfield could not fathom why or how this object followed behind him. He dashed away as fast as possible in the foot deep snow. He dared not to look back.

His thoughts conveyed to him that this was not an earthquake. This was not a fallen rock. What the hell was chasing him? Rumbling and the breaking of branches became louder, and moved closer. He caught a whiff of a terrible stench.

With a swooshing sound, he was airborne and felt a tight clamp around his waist. His body lifted above the snow covered floor. All was quiet, and now nothing moved. He gasped for air, and frantically grabbed at his painful stomach. His body locked onto something. This something began to move again, as he stared all around, shocked and confused.

Susan Conti stuck her head out the truck's back window. She screamed when she saw Todd hanging above the snow. The truck shook with her movements. Todd swooshed towards her, and it appeared like he was snow surfing. Todd watched with difficult breathing as he moved in the air helplessly. Helplessly, he stared as he sped towards his red, pick-up truck.

In seconds, he smashed into his truck, locking eye to eye with Susan Conti. He tumbled down the cliff after the collision. The contact tilted the truck enough, to also fall down along the side with him. The vehicle took a flip before it crashed to the ground below. He laid among some rocks and snow, but freed from what ever clapped on to him.

She felt her body ache as she still was hanging out the back window. She watched her boyfriend stop tumbling in the snow. Suzy could barely lift her head as she stared straight towards him for help.

"What the Fuck!" Todd Bloomfield yelled, feeling spellbound and frightened in this surreal disaster. His mid-section hurt to the touch.

He could not decide on what actually happened. He knew something had grabbed him, and that something smelled worse than his uncle's pig farm.

"Help, help me", Susan Conti spoke in a hoarse voice.

She found it difficult to free herself from the window. All she could do was look at Todd Bloomfield a little ways in front of her. She watched as he stood unsure of himself.

Both were not aware that the beast crouched below Todd Bloomfield in the snow.

Well, it was not hibernating any more, and had not a bite to eat in thousands of years.

Susan Conti watched as a woolly head popped out from spattering snow. It had two beady red eyes sunken in two gray pools. Eye to eye with Todd Bloomfield, the snow creature roared a body rattling, ear vibrating, menacing call. In shock, his body took a stiff composure. He showed no signs of fright, pain, or anything. He was like a clock where the ticker just stopped.

Two large fangs, sunk into Todd's mid-section. He was dragged away across the snowy woods. He was stiff like frozen, and could not scream. He could not scream his last giving right to life. Branches scraped onto his face as he traveled helplessly through the trees.

His head suddenly smacked into a tree trunk snapping his neck. He died instantly. Todd Bloomfield never had to witness the beast salivating over him like a steak dinner. He escaped the pain of the beast crunching on his bones, and devouring him quite disgustingly.

Susan Conti screamed and cried. An animal, extinct for thousands of years, awoke in her small town. A 10 foot long, 2 ton carnivore, somehow survived its hibernation. The snow creature, a type of Megalonyx, surfaced, full bodied, over its kill. She visioned the beast about 30 yards away, visible in the strong moonlight from the clear night sky.

Susan Conti laid limp in the truck window, helplessly fearing the creature would attack her next. She stayed quiet, noiseless as possible. This deemed impossible as she could not stop making pouting noises, and hysterical outbursts.

The snow creature scraped and flung snow, as it roared victory over its kill. Maybe, it was just glad to be awakened- back on the prowl.

Megalonyx resembled somewhat of a crossbreed of a sloth and a bear. The fur, white, perfectly blended in the snow environment as it hunted. The huge mammal was a carnivore, and a voracious one at that. The prehistoric creature burrowed underneath the snow packs, and used its long, blade-like claws to shovel its path through the snow. The forearm muscles were thick and strong. Few obstacles could halt this plowing machine as heavy boulders could be moved out of its way. The long fangs added a sinister character to the face of an already nasty looking animal which could tear you limb from limb.

The beast disliked the clothes as it teared them away to the bloody flesh. Todd Bloomfield's muscular body presented a good meal, but only an appetizer for this mammoth. Again it roared, as if to claim its right to the forest. The true "Master of the Winter World" has returned.

The snow creature clasped the rest of the uneaten torso, and swiftly submerged in the snow to find a cozy place to eat.

Bill Meyers heard the screams, and the metallic clunking noises from the falling truck. He quickened his pace, and felt something wrong. They witnessed the giant open fissure across the road, and the truck imprints leading over the cliff. He peered down at the wreckage.

Bill Meyers spoke in charge, "Kyle, stay here. I am going to head down, and see if they are alright."

He called, "Suzy, Todd, are you okay?"

He repeated his call several times with no return answer. The truck hung on a rocky outcrop. This was lucky for them, Bill Meyers thought. The smaller fall increased their survival chances.

As Bill Meyers headed down to the wrecked truck, Kyle Meyers noticed the trail of shoveled snow through the woods. It appeared similar to snowmobile tracks. The thirteen year old assumed it was caused by the earthquake. What or it, could make such tracks?

As soon as Bill Meyers arrived at the wreckage, he immediately found Susan Conti, half drooping out of the back window. He climbed into the loading area, and she was unconscious. The responsible boy scout, Mr. Bill Meyers, automatically took over.

He politely spoke, "Wake up, Suzy. Are you okay? C'mon, wake up. Are you alright?"

She lifted her head and screamed. Bill Meyers attempted to comfort her, realizing her traumatic state. A calming hug was given from him. This was not his first time, and now easier to touch his, well, in his mind, true girlfriend.

Bill Meyers said, "It is okay. It is okay. Calm down, my Suzy."

Somehow she knew it was Billy Boy, although it made no sense how he was here in the woods.

His mental weirdness surfaced upon seeing her. Saving her once again, was attributed has a sign- a sign they were meant to be. Todd Bloomfield disappeared, and for a justified reason. Bill Meyers dark energy started bubbling inside. It assisted in closing the love triangle. His vengeful spirit some how aided in Todd's Bloomfield's disappearance. Now the true date, the coupling meant to be, would be kindled.

Bill Meyers took volunteer medical courses in high school. He checked her out in the window position before trying to move her. She could move parts of her body, but risky, if her back was damaged. He could not leave her here. He remembered the physical check list, and administered his training. He thought what a great man he was, and he got to play doctor with "Slutty Suzy".

Then, carefully and cautiously as he could be, he patiently lifted her body through the window. She called out a few times in pain, but seemed to be mobile. By the side of the truck, she actually stood, which was a good sign her back was not critical. In his mind, he wondered where Todd Bloomfield disappeared to.

Bill Meyers yelled up to the road, "Kyle come down, and help me aid Suzy to the top."

They slowly brought her up to Cliff Drop Road. The whole time, Susan Conti spoke bizarrely- Todd was flying above the snow, she heard roars of a monster, and saw Todd bit in half by a monster. She kept repeating words about bloody fangs, and Todd's helpless expressions.

Bill Meyers did not know what to make of her stories. Todd Bloomfield must be lying somewhere, and she witnessed his deadly fall. He, like his younger brother, also saw the snowmobile like tracks in the snow. Nothing made sense, except that they just experienced an earthquake.

Bill Meyers examined his choices. Heading for Bogey's place still seemed the best solution for immediate help. How helpful an old, crazy man would be, could be only answered in a hour hike on Cliff Drop Road. Susan Conti was by far not coherent, both physically and mentally. Tears and pouting were all she added to an already frantic situation. Her arms clutched tightly to Bill Meyers as Kyle Meyers held his arm across her back.

Around the bend, they came to the entrance to Helix Point. All of them immediately noticed the tire tracks in the snow, and the opened gate.

Bill Meyers immediately stated, "Someone is here!"

The trek up hill to the Point would be treacherous on foot. With the consideration of her condition, Bill Meyers decided to continue for Bogey Wilson's place. There was no way to communicate with the person or people at Helix Point, and yelling for help, was a definite waste of time.

Susan Conti began to shiver uncontrollably. They were not not going to make it. Bill Meyers carried the emergency kit he took from the station wagon. He decided to make a fire from the matches. There also was a butane canister, used to fill his father's cigar lighter. He gathered the least damp branches he could find, poured the butane on them, and to his surprise, the fire started quickly. The warmth from the fire, installed a confidence after the disaster.

Susan Conti passed out against the body of Kyle Meyers.

The younger brother found the touch of her body, the infamous "Slutty Suzy's" body, to be pleasing. It bothered him to feel this way during a disaster, but it felt pleasing to the touch. Her perfume still strong, possessed an attractive scent for the thirteen year old. He never touched a girl, and this stirred his insides. He only experienced girl fantasies lying in his bed. He felt now, very manly.

However, he contemplated that these feelings were unacceptable for a super hero. "The Mighty Caveman" must possess manners, and not primitive desires like his ancestors. His first training for super heroism,was to suppress personal emotions. The lives of the ill trodden ranked first, and then pleasure with girls.

Bill Meyers stated, "I will continue to Bogey's place while you stay here with her. She cannot do the walk in the cold snow. Maybe he has a truck with a plow, and I can come back for you. Maybe the people up at the Helix Point will pass, and assist you. Get Suzy to a hospital immediately."

Then it began, again. They all heard the rumbling coming from the direction they already walked. Another earthquake? Susan Conti's face struck with fear. She knew it was coming back. It was coming back to eat. She clutched tighter onto young Kyle Meyers. He too became startled from her change in mood.

Bill Meyers lacked answers, but he witnessed a large mound of moving snow knocking everything out of its path. Something registered in his brain that it was not an earthquake. The moving snow approached with beastly growls.

His first instinct was to run, but instead, in a strong whisper, Bill Meyers said," Do not move! Nobody moves!"

He clamped his gloved hand over Susan Conti's mouth.

His father taught wilderness tactics when they used to hunt. If you see a bear, the best thing to do was to stay still. Suddenly the snow mound stopped. They heard heavy breathing, and more grunts. He never saw a bear do anything like this, but you would be surprised what odd things the wild outdoors could present.

The snow creature lost its focus on the vibrations and noise of its prey. This carnivore evolved a keen sense of smell. It knew food was near by. Food like Todd, though deer tasted better, smelled near by. The alluring scent was her perfume. The snow creature still needed the motion. Prey would be overwhelmed while fleeing. The fleeing signaled the snow creature to capture its next meal.

Bill Meyers observed the snow mound to be about 20 yards. A huge woolly head popped out of the snow like a prairie dog. Kyle Meyers and Susan Conti surprisingly stood still as Bill Meyers ordered. The beast huffed with vapor inhaling and exhaling quickly from its mouth. Two large fangs hung below a small black nose at the end of its snout. The eyes were beady red, ever searching. The head turned this way and that making gulping mouth noises. The snow creature was investigating the situation.

The heated fire disturbed the creature, and refused to creep closer. Bill Meyers was a good observer, being a peeping tom and all. He noticed the the beast disliked the flickering flames. True, bear and coyotes would shy away from fire like most living things. Their camp fire probably saved them temporarily. The creature popped backed down into its domain, and simultaneously took off into the woods. The snow mound laid still about a distance where the night made it dark from the firelight.

Bill Meyers never saw an animal such as this. At least, he never witnessed a creature with those physical characteristics in these woods. Was it a deformed bear? It had a bear-like quality. Both those huge bony blades resembled something like a crab's pincers. Was it a mutated bear like in a science fiction movie? Those monsters only happened on the Hollywood screen, and not real life. Something inside of him connected this snow creature with the earthquake.

"It is a sloth. It looks like a sloth from those animal kingdom shows I watch," Kyle Meyers whispered to the group.

Bill Meyers agreed quietly to himself. Those fangs reminded Bill Meyers of a saber toothed tiger from the prehistoric times. Was this a prehistoric creature which surfaced from the earthquake, like in a science fiction movie? This thought made sense, and no sense to him.

Kyle Meyers again in a whisper said," There used to be ground sloths hundreds of years ago which are now gone here in America. They were huge, but plant eating. This big guy definitely is meat eating, and seems similar."

Bill Meyers interjected, "It was more like thousands of years ago, which is impossible. Right now anything goes, but we need to get to Bogey's place. I doubt our little fire is going to stop that thing."

They could walk with torches, and use them as weapons. But again, their supplies were limited to construct sound defensive tools here in the woods. There were missing items in his emergency bag from the station wagon. He never needed it, and did not check it properly. Once he took the flashlight during a black out, and never replaced it. Torches will have to do.

Susan Conti refused to walk away from the fire pit. Bill Meyers changed the plan. She was going to toughen up, and trudge with them. He prepared the torches, and gave his younger brother the bigger one to lead the way, Kyle Meyers was proud as "The Mighty Caveman", who would lead the way with the torch.

They started slowly, still watching the motionless mound off in the woods. Maybe it fell asleep? Maybe it left. They all took quiet steps as possible. The boots on the crunching snow did not make it quiet at all. They left their protective fire camp.

Bill Meyers spoke motivating words, "Suzy, we are leaving for Bogey Wilson's house. Walk along my side, hold this torch and very shortly we will have shelter, Soon, we will be sitting alongside a nice fireplace."

Reluctantly she agreed. Her helplessness forced her to follow orders blindly. Bill Meyers knew she was in a state of shock. As a good boyfriend, he was obligated to protect her. As for himself, he was well past a state of shock.

They slowly walked through the snow, feeling the cold nip in the air. The fire offered a security which the dark gloom around them did not. The night sky lost the moonlight as clouds crept in. Their make-shift torches shone weakly, bringing them uncomfortable feelings. Bill Meyers could see the outline of the Cliff Drop Road ahead, but only about ten yards at a time.

No sound of the creature was heard. They covered over fifteen minutes of walking in shadows, surrounded by darken silence. Maybe, the snow creature was digesting Todd Bloomfield, and decided on a snooze. Maybe it disliked night hunting? No appearance of the beast was a good thing.

Small confidence built up in all of them. They were going to make it. The road began to slope downwards where Bogey's house lied. The threesome continued in a silent walk. Their destination was close, and becoming closer.

Kyle Meyers whispered,"Look a light! A light! Down there I see a light!"

He was right. The blurred lighting seen through the trees, were strings of lights Bogey hung over his junkyard of cars. The house remained a distance off, but in their sight.

Suzy understood immediately what the whispering was about, and also witnessed the lights. She started cheering, "We are here! We made it! Tell Todd. Yeah! Hooray! Hooray!"

Quickly Bill Meyers looked behind. The large snow mound plowed through the trees alongside the road. Her loud gibberish alerted the stalking beast. Bill Meyers hated himself for not forewarning everyone to remain quiet. Instinctively they ran forward. It shot past them knocking them all over like bowling pins.

The snow creature did more of a bump and run tactic. Maybe the light from the torches helped, but Bill Meyers was not positive. He noticed the large rock formation along the roadside, and told his younger brother to jump up onto the ledge. Susan Conti was knocked separately away from the impact of the beast. This might have been the offensive tactic of the predator in order to scatter its prey.

Bill Meyers leaped over to her as fast as he could. In this motion, he knocked her over just as she was standing up. Her pocket book hit a rock, and its contents spilled out, He grabbed her, and as best as he could, pulled, dragged her to the rocky outcrops on the high side of the road. He knew it was too late. The moving snow ball with its pincer claws flying as high as 10 feet above them, roared at their heels.

Strangely, the beast passed them. It attacked Susan Conti's bag. Bill Meyers knew immediately why this action occurred. The perfume attracted it! Todd Bloomfield probably had lingering smell of her perfume on him. The snow creature connected food with the fragrance.

Bill Meyers pushed, and shoved Susan Conti with sloppy precision. She scrapped her thigh against the jagged rocks. Bill Meyers and Susan Conti joined his young brother on the ledge. The snow creature lost interest in the perfume, and smacked into the rocky ledge with all its force. It yelped from pain or defeat. It scurried this way and that against the rock wall.

Bill Meyers realized this outcrop traveled almost all the way to Bogey's homestead. The distance looked a little more than a football field. Every now and then, the aggravated beast charged the rocks with its huge claws. The collision sent flying stones into the night air.

They walked cautiously on the ledge towards Bogey's house. Bill Meyers could not stop thinking that the snow creature could simply plop up and climb onto the rocks. The height was not really high.

Maybe this reasoning power was not in its nature. They drew closer and closer. It kept zipping back and forth, idling near them, but not pin pointing them.

The rocks soon were going to end, and their would have to be a last dash through the junkyard, and into Bogey's house. The snow creature stopped. Bill Meyers hoped it was exhausted, and was resting. Turning up all those rocks, and stones had to exhort a lot of strength.

Before they could think of a strategy, an engine noise was heard. Bill Meyers saw a moving vehicle with lights heading in their direction. Old Bogey Wilson was riding his tractor, hitched to a large hay wagon. The snow creature was not in site. The tractor drove closer and closer. Kyle Meyers waved his torch which they assumed was how Bogey noticed them. Bill Meyers waved as Bogey stopped about 30 yards away.

The headlights shone onto Cliff Drop Road, and suddenly the snow creature rumbled straight at the tractor. Instinctively, Old Bogey grabbed his shotgun at the moving target, and unloaded two rounds into this unknown thing. An unexpected yelp, a sound expressing pain, rang into the night. The beast's momentum still headed forward, and brushed the tractor. It quickly retreated back the other way it came.

Bogey Wilson said,"Is that you Billy Boy. Is that young Kyle, and the young lady, yeah I know you." He refused to say out loud her name.

He spoke calmly. His expressions reflected like this was an every day event, with him shooting at some unknown monstrosity.

Before Bogey could say another word, Bill yelled," Quickly everybody, into the wagon. Mr. Wilson there is something attacking us!"

The two boys assisted Susan Conti into the large wagon, and all three felt relief from their predicament. The rocky outcrop diminished, and so the tractor had enough clear area to turn around and head back to the house.

Was the snow creature hurt? Maybe Bogey Wilson shot it dead? Somehow Bill Meyers new their troubles were still brewing. He hoped the snow creature lost its appetite. Could it have reasoning for revenge?

Sitting in the tractor wagon brought feelings of safety and relief for them all. This vehicle was sound and stable, built for real farming. Bill Meyers still looked over his shoulder into the gloom, awaiting another attack. Something "pinged" inside of him to stay alert. This definitely was not over.

A large, pincer claws clamped onto the back of the wagon as everything shook. The wagon rocked back and forth. This beast had strength to halt the tractor. Those two shotgun slugs obviously were useless. The tractor wheels began to slip in the snow, as their strong foe stopped them dead in their tracks.

Susan Conti screamed with hysteria. Bill Meyers fell into the side of the metal wagon, bumping his head. Bogey Wilson cursed as he in vain tried to unleash the tractor from the beast's powerful grip.

Kyle Meyers was fed up. Although first not found, energy of heroism engulfed him. The distress of his group unleashed the power of "The Mighty Caveman".

He roared. "Aargh! Aargh, Botta bing ! Botta Boo! Aargh!"

The changes in his manhood this day, and all the hype of comic book heroes, dynamically morphed him into a action hero. Kyle Meyers molded in body and soul as "The Mighty Caveman".

Making gestures like a half ape, and half human, this action hero searched for a weapon. He discovered a pitchfork.

"Ooh, Ooh, Ooh," Kyle gestured positively in caveman language.

He then bellowed a Tarzan yell. In a split decision thought process, where superheroes possess a marveled genius, he realized the Tarzan yell belonged to a different franchise. His superhero will need a signature call, as well as fresh background to be respected seriously.

"The Mighty Caveman" grabbed the pitchfork, held it high over his head, and leaped without a fear onto the woolly back of the snow creature. His aim was exceptionally good as the pitchfork embedded deeply. The chubby, 13 year old slipped one of his arms between the creature's body and the well planted pitchfork.

The beast caught totally by surprise, unleashed the wagon. It shook violently with its claws flaring violently over its body. Kyle was able to be close enough into its furry back while the claw motioned over his head by inches. The wooden handle of the pitchfork rattled back and forth every time the huge claw smacked into it. So far, it could not dislodge it.

Bogey felt the tractor jolt forward, and did not look back. Bill Meyers, grabbing his throbbing head, was spellbound by his brother's actions. Susan Conti just screamed and cried. They headed into the junkyard underneath the white holiday lights which brightly shone in the dark night. The super hero desperately held on without knowing his next move. The offensive attack assisted his companions escape, and that was heroic enough. But how does he save himself to fight another day?

The frantic bunch on the tractor looked back, while inching slowly through about thirty rusted automobiles. They could see Kyle Meyers still riding on top of the snow creature.

Still irritated by the itch on its back, the beast's demeanor became out of whack. Its huge claws slammed into cars like punching cardboard boxes. The fanged mouth opened and closed with vicious growls, as it tried to bite over its shoulder at the intruder. "The Mighty Caveman's" arm started to hurt with his elbow locked around one of the pitchfork's pointed bars.

Bill Meyers stared at the full body of the beast. The two ton carnivore possessed a huge, hanging gut, which could process a lot of meat. It stood at an impressive eight feet high, with a dimension length at about ten feet. A nightmarish entity did the snow creature represent as it gawked with its beady red eyes, and its flaring claws of fury.

Kyle Meyers weak point now surfaced. All action men needed training. His physical stature was flax. His grip was loosening. The angry snow creature rammed into a junked car pushing it about ten feet. Kyle flew off and landed over another car. He rolled tight against an old junker.

The annoying itch stopped. The snow creature turned its appetite at the distance noisy tractor. It moved, staying above ground with huge, slow stomps. The angry roars continued as it banged the cars in its way. The huge claws would get tangled into the lights shredding them down, as bulbs were heard popping against the car metal.

Bogey saw that the beast gained ground on his tractor.

Bill Meyers also noticed this as well, and exclaimed, "Quickly, let us make a run for the house!"

Bogey Wilson shut off his tractor as Bill Meyers assisted Susan Conti from the wagon. This slowed them down more as the snow creature hustled close behind them.

Then, Bill Meyers famous peripheral vision detected a small dark form moving towards his left. Two car rows down, the shadow yelled to distract the snow creature. It was his brother Kyle. The ruse worked, and the snow creature chased the super hero, who it recognized as the annoying pest on his back.

This helped the others escape into Bogey Wilson's house. They hustled into the front door where two other people were looking on with fearful surprise. The stuffy warmth of the house felt good after all the cold, dampness spent in the woods. Bill Meyers attentively stayed at the door awaiting to see his younger brother sprinting behind them. Nothing entered- no younger brother.

Outside, a loud, childish scream was heard, like someone in severe distress. Bogey Wilson shut the door, and pushed Bill Meyers inside towards the living area. The young man crumpled down against a wall, and cried. Bill Meyers thought the worst about his brother.

Half-dazed Suzy Conti giggled, and spoke," Oh Todd, no, I mean Billy. Uh, my knight in shining armor."

Bogey Wilson peered out the front door window perplexed, and said," I thought I seen it all. Granny always spoke of the evil monsters of the woods. Damn, that beast sure seems evil."

Bill Meyers pitifully cried. For the first time tonight, the tears flowed. Now his younger brother was dead. His tears dropped from his cheeks forming a pool at his feet. All his tension, and built up pressure, was released in a tantrum. Bill Meyers was uncontrollable. Old Bogey Wilson left the young man to calm down naturally. If that was even possible.

CHAPTER 4

Battle at Bogey's

OLD BOGEY WILSON STOOD with outstretched hands over his fireplace. A tall, black man whose skinny appearance, reflected someone who rarely ate. However, Bogey did drink, and he drank his homemade moonshine. His lean, muscular body walked with a limp. Tonight's shocking events called for liquoring up, as Bogey Wilson would comment. He challenged his common sense about the going on with drinking. However, the liquoring up part started two hours ago with an argument with his son, Gilroy, and girlfriend, Jesse.

A moonshine operation in these hills was not unusual. Law enforcement tolerated such matters, as long as local disruption was kept at a minimum.

Frank Porter, the local newsman, published articles concerning illegal moonshine.

He discussed about this government blindness in a special report, "People who chronically intoxicate themselves, veer away from the community structure, and develop into less responsible citizens. The ignorance of the people, is manipulated by our politicians for control of the people. Politicians are commonly referred to as puppets. Financial developers and investors are the puppeteers, who control the politicians for self gain, as the drunken population remains blind to their true, society needs."

The newsman Frank Porter always attempted to shake up the awareness of Tannersville. Many times this mild man, wrote boldly and heaved up the adage- "Nothing ever changes around here".

Old Bogey Wilson was well-known for his moonshine, and his mechanical skills on cars. The demolition derby were legendary around here with his touch of magic on the junked autos. The car shows acted as a cover for the illegal alcohol, and other illicit drug trafficking.

He stayed here in Virginia most of the time, but traveled down to Tennessee every now and then. He transported mason jars of illegal alcohol to sell in the south. The Tennessee law cracked down on moonshine operations. His contacts discovered it was more cost effective to publicly transport the stuff into the state and sell it. Bogey Wilson stacked up thousands of dollars a year. He got caught a few times, but received minor police charges.

A young couple lived in the house also. Bogey's son, Gilroy, and a white girl he shacked up with, Jesse, looked on with awe at the whole situation. Gilroy Wilson was more medium built, and shorter than his father. He looked nothing like old Bogey. He had a stocky stance, and unlike his father, he liked to eat when he drank. His Mom left them both years ago because of the alcoholism.

Jesse, Jessebelle Quentin, was extremely attractive. Probably, could of done a lot better with her relationships. Even though she was born of poor stock, she definitely shined as the white swan in a duck pond. Her curly, brown hair and perfectly shaped buttocks, easily could of attracted a middle class, stable man from the city. Jesse was too stupid to realize what goods she possessed.

She pranced around barefooted in a night shirt, exposing her legs right up to her thighs. She plopped down on a couch, and propped her legs onto a coffee table. Her feet bottoms were black with filth as this girl obviously wore no shoes or socks.

Jesse spoke with concern," Gil, what's happening? Where did these people come from. Is there a bear outside? And now in winter?"

She nervously twisted her brunette hair with her fingers. Gilroy Wilson just shrugged his shoulders, and took a swig of liquor from a mug. Bill Meyers still whimpered, squatting against the wall. Bogey Wilson helped him up, and sat him on the couch with Jesse. Susan Conti sat in a lounge chair with her head slung forward. She looked half dazed. The mixed company represented a confused group with fearful apprehension.

Bill Meyers realized his wits needed to remain intact. Half of his wits were already gone. He explained their happenings in an orderly fashion to Bogey Wilson, attempting to sound rational about these unseemingly events. Somehow, the old man accepted the story as truthful, and peered out the window.

His Granny spoke of monster tales and witchcraft when he was a toddler. Bogey Wilson knew such unexplainable stuff existed in the world. He did not get a good look at the snow creature, and so he could not make sound judgement based on these kids stories.

Bogey Wilson stated,"Well everybody, welcome to Bogey's home. This here is my son, Gilroy, and his white women, Jessebelle Quentin. She's from Georgia. I think we all need a drink."

He brought some glasses and a jug of pure grain alcohol. Bill Meyers and Susan Conti passed. She had no idea what she was saying no to. To Bill Meyers, it seemed like this bunch was drinking already. They just needed an excuse to drink another drink again.

Susan Conti looked around with lazy eyes, and realized she sat with people she did not know. She suffered from a concussion, and needed medical help. Blood clotting in her brain was now a real potential. The old, black man brought a ice bag for her to put on her head.

Bill Meyers stood up, and attempted to take charge. "We need a plan. This thing is preying on us. It's aggressive, strong, and relentless. I believe it awoke from thousands of year hibernation. How did this happen? I have no idea. We need the police or probably, the army corp. from Ridgewood. Cliff Drop Road is knocked up from the earthquake. However, there were signs that someone is staying at Helix Point. Going back, I believe, will not help. I suggest we take the back roads around Helix Mountain to Millens Road."

Gilroy Wilson's eyes bulged and squinted at this stranger. This intruder spoke like he owned this place, his father's house. Gilroy Wilson questioned- who is this guy? Coming here ordering everybody around. Coming in their living room taking charge of them. Does this fool think we are stupid because we are black? Well, Jesse was white, but white men are all alike. Gilroy Wilson refused to take any of this crap.

He broke in on Bill Meyers speech. He sounded slurred in speech, and quickly Bill Meyers realized this guy was trouble, and he was stinking drunk.

Gilroy Wilson said," Who you, come in here. Who you order in Bogey's house, my fadder's home. I drive the tractor with you all in da hay bin . My Pop will guard shotgun as I in charge."

Bogey Wilson's son stood proud. He spoke up against this, this nobody. He decided to taken control. He would drive their tractor. But why would he drive the tractor in the middle of the night? He was drunk, and did not understand what actually was happening. Gilroy

Wilson, with a defensive reflex, told off this stranger without realizing their was a beast attacking them.

"You are not driving at all," Bill Meyers spoke with authority.

Gilroy Wilson pissed off said, "Who are you, white boy, tilling me what to do. You learn respect, like Jesse here, who serves me and my Pop. Her white ass belongs to me, and your white ass now belongs to me."

Gilroy Wilson glanced at him with rolling eyes. He literally checked out Bill Meyers backside.

Bogey Wilson broke into the conversation, and said, "Oh shut up boy! There is no need for such chatter here, in my house, old Bogey's house. And no homo talk out of you Gil! Leave these nice people alone."

Bogey Wilson spoke about himself in the third person alot.

"I will fuck him if I want! I do what I want." Gilroy Wilson yelled, and stood swaying in his stance.

Bill Meyers entered into a bizarre situation, here in the backwoods. Who the hell was fucking who? This guy was a nut. A hillman who would screw anything his private thing could fit into. Bill Meyers needed to eat, but decided to consume nothing out of their toaster oven.

"Again, you are not driving the tractor. You, Gilroy, will jeopardize our lives. You have been drinking too much." Bill Meyers again, stated the obvious.

Astounded and insulted, the young black man exclaimed," Drunk? Who, what, uh? Your white ass is mine, here in dis' place. I in charge. You see?"

He turned to Bill Meyers back, and joked," Kinda flat butt, but I will do you. If you not give in, I rape you! I jump you! I know dis very well, the rape."

Gilroy Wilson reflected back to his time in the state prison.

The conversation veered off into a place, a place worse than the horrific encounter of the snow creature.

Bill Meyers replied," You will not come near me, but if it makes you feel better, I will shove this fire poker up your ass!"

Gilroy Wilson attacked Bill Meyers in a drunken fashion. A poorly aimed punch whizzed past Bill Meyer's face. This instigated to release built up stress. He grabbed the fire poker, and whacked it across the man's behind to humiliate him in his drunken stupor.

"You are enjoying this, right homo!" Bill Meyers shouted,

Bogey Wilson cocked the shotgun, and yelled to everybody to shut up.

Bogey Wilson yelled,"I shoot to kill! My son ain't no homo. That was just a year at the state pen, many years ago! No homos in old Bogey's home. Enough of this guff. No jail time, homo stuff, or fighting in Bogey's home! I is in charge."

A long, sinister bellow echoed outside. The sound was close, so close like the snow creature was outside next to the cabin wall. The bellows continued with the floor vibrating from the creepy vocals. Thumping, and scratching resonated from the wall of the living room. The young ladies screamed, adding to the noise coming from the wall.

Everyone moved to the opposite side of the living room. The eerie sounds stopped. They all listened for more bumps around the house. Bill Meyers quickly scanned the dwelling, and realized the place was falling apart. A sudden, high volume howl overpowered their senses, and they all screamed at high volume as well.

"Ssh, ssh! We need to calm down. More noise will attract this beast," Bill Meyers demanded.

Gilroy Wilson responded," Ssh you. I hear you scream like a girl. A girl who wants it in the..."

"Stop this ass trash talk!" Bogey yelled.

A loud bash came from the far wall. They all quieted down immediately.

The snow creature was busy scoping out the structure. The beast from the past did not necessarily mean it was stupid. Prehistoric meant older in history,but not a reflection of intelligence. The perfect killing machine existed, even though fossils or evidence never had been found. No one knew of its productive evolutionary skills.

The beast wondered as it eyed Bogey's house. Its vision was poor, but could make out structure. It never seen this shape before, but it looked similar from its past memory. It smashed something like this wooded form many times, back in its territory thousands of years ago.

Bill Meyers said," How soon will it bust in, and attack us?"

Everyone else wondered the same, except dazed Susan Conti.

Another plan for escape was needed, and needed within minutes. The drunken homo was useless, and would slow them down. Since Bill

Meyers lost his younger brother who he loved, he gave little worth to this Gilroy loser. He decided to use this guy as bait. When they were to escape, maybe onto the tractor again, he would feed Gil to the beast.

Bill Meyers had no idea how ruthless, and uncaring his convoluted mind swung in and out of his routine thinking process. His brother was gone, and he cared less about this fool. Kyle Meyers was only 13 years old, and did not deserve to die in his innocence. He would not die, and he would protect his girlfriend, Susan Conti.

He spoke in his thoughts," Hell with the drunken hick!"

Never in a million years, would Bill Meyers have contemplated about killing a fellow human being.

Bogey Wilson and Bill Meyers hashed out the specifics for their getaway. Both agreed this house was useless for defense. They gathered firearms. Bogey Wilson owned enough hunting equipment, and their existed a good chance of killing the beast. If not, the shooting, hopefully, would keep it at distance. They then could escape on the tractor wagon.

Bogey Wilson whispered,"All that snow and damage from the quake, might be suicide as we take the lumber roads through the woods. We should go back on Cliff Drop Road, and where you got stuck with the falling tree, we could chain saw it out of the way. I own plenty of stuff to cut wood."

Bill Meyers actually respected Bogey's incite. Stopping and cutting the trees out of the way, made sound judgment. He was right. Taking a different path after experiencing all this unpredictable danger could be worse. They at least knew what to expect on Cliff Drop Road. Bogey Wilson had a reputation as a fool, but an experienced wise, old fool.

Bill Meyers stated, "Okay, we make a diversion for the snow creature, hop onto the tractor wagon, travel back on Cliff Drop Road,
escape to Rte. 3. We have a plan. Let us put together all the supplies."

All were basically satisfied, but not totally confident. Gilroy Wilson
murmured unhappily to himself. Jesse Quentin just shrugged her shoulders. Droopy eyed Susan Conti nodded her head up and down without
understanding the plan, or even where she was sitting. Bogey Wilson's
left eye twitched uncontrollable every now and then.

Crash! A large claw swung through the window, missing Bogey's
back by inches. His loose shirt stuck onto the point of the claw, which
bodily flung him into the adjacent wall. Bogey Wilson hit the floor, and
quickly crawled back to the others, who all huddled near the fireplace.

The snow creature easily tore apart the wall connected to the
broken window. They all witnessed its body massiveness, and ugly,
fanged face. It approached with positive dominance in this dilapidated
house. They awaited to be rushed, and killed. Instead, another ear
piercing roar trembled their bodies, and vibrated Bogey's junky stuff
in the room.

Bill Meyers grabbed the fire poker from earlier, and attempted flip-
ping burning logs towards the snow creature. The logs rolled all over,
and started a fire on some curtains, and one fell onto the couch. Bogey
Wilson snatched a shovel just in time as a huge claw swung towards his
head. A large clang could be heard from the collision. Bogey got pushed
back from the strength of the blow, but being hyped up, he cursed and
swung the shovel, blocking all following incoming claws. The old man
was fighting for his life, and expelled all his energy.

This distracted the snow creature enough that allowed Bill Meyers
to land some burning logs right in it's face. The fire definitely irritated
the beast as it head shook from the heated sting. Singed, black marks

dotted its head. It backed off, and quickly dug into the snow outside. The two young ladies, and drunken Gilroy Wilson, yelled nonstop through the whole ordeal.

Bogey Wilson took a wild swing with the shovel just when the beast retreated. He lost his balance, and plopped to the floor. For a second, all was silent.

Bill Meyers helped Bogey up, and they shook hands. They acknowledge each other and did a high five. Both acted like players winning in a game, but in a deranged game.

A fire grew in the living quarters which grabbed their attention. The two girls went back into the kitchen as the men hauled water buckets from the sink to douse the fire. The coal stove was warming the kitchen well, and seemed to be a good hide out for the time.

Bill Meyers shouted, " It shies away from fire. We need to plug that hole by the window! If we control the couch fire, and with the fireplace, this hot zone might keep the beast away. I believe it prefers the snow and cold. The adaptation for its survival. Maybe it developed anti-freeze blood to aid it in harsh freezing climates." Bill Meyers blubbed out facts which no one was really listening to.

"I do not know! I do not hell know! Old Bogey's house is ruined by that demon monster. I am gonna kill it, and hang those claws over my fireplace." Bogey Wilson stammered.

He quickly added and said," Gil, go with Billy Boy to the back hall. We have those 6 by 4 ft. plywoods we were going to use in the liquor cellar. Go quickly as I load my shotgun. No wait, I need my high powered rifle!"

Bogey gave some orders, and Gilroy Wilson reluctantly brought Bill Meyers to the plywoods. As they carried each piece to the broken wall from the back, obscenities filled the room by the two.

Bogey Wilson anxiously stared towards the dark woods. hoping to shoot his best scoped firearm, with high density, piercing bullets. This beast's day would be the last.

Gilroy Wilson hammered nails into the wooded panels with surprising accuracy, considering his condition. As the plywoods became partially nailed, Bill Meyers let go, and stomped out fires spreading onto the floor. He noticed flames licking the wall and catching onto the old, dusty wallpaper from the fiery couch. Once again, he grabbed the trusty poker, and with one good push, the flaming couch rolled to the center of the room.

The plan seemed to be working well until the next booming crash! The couch exploded into firelights with floor fragments flying. The creature erupted from underneath the room, and raged in full stance with its huge, clawed arms above its head. The claws jammed into the ceiling as plaster crumbled down. A deafening roar exploded across the chaotic living room once again. The fire did not seem to be an effective deterrent as before.

Time slowed down in motion for Bill Meyers. Bright lights of orange and yellow, flickered all around with pieces of the house sprinkling his view. In the center, the hugeness of the beast deflated any heroism he filled up on. So big, so intimidating, portrayed the snow creature.

Unfortunately, Bill Meyers meek personality resurfaced.

Bogey Wilson turned at the house invader, but could not take a shot. The high powered scope blurred his sight being so close up. He fired his weapon improperly, and the back kick from the rifle, flew out of his hands. It smacked hard down into his knee leaving a painful bruise. Bogey Wilson did not know if the bullet hit the beast at all.

A pincer claw swung at Gilroy Wilson. As he stood in drunken shock, similar to the same defeated stupor of Bill Meyers, his forearm sliced off his body from the claw swishing past his face. Gilroy Wilson stared at his stump. His screaming cries mixed in with the bellowing roars of the beast. Bogey Wilson pulled his son fast into the kitchen.

Bill Meyers saw the rifle on the floor, but still moved in slow motion. He instinctively jumped down, to grab it. He lost his aggressive nature. It seemed forever to grab the firearm. He awaited the death blow from the beast.

He clumsily laid on the floor, aimed the rifle at the woolly body which filled most of the fire lit room. The scope was useless, so he just pointed the gun at the bulking mass. He pulled the trigger. The kickback of the rifle, sent it flying, spinning to the other side of the room, into the fire. The bullet hit its target and pierced the hide of the mid section. It was a solid meat shot, although not lethal, definitely tissue tearing.

The raging beast reacted to the pain in its side. It twisted and turned in all directions, smashing everything it touched.

Somehow, Bill Meyers dark energy oozed back into his psyche. The roar from pain, and not from victory, showed weakness from the beast. That rifle shot installed in him the strength needed to survive.

Fire, uncontrollable, danced all around the room. For a split second, Bill Meyers contemplated kicking Gilroy Wilson over towards the snow creature. Bogey Wilson would have had broad view of the sinister act. The human sacrifice might be only temporary, and the creature threat would still have existed.

A few rifles or other types of guns were propped against a wall. Bill Meyers snatched one of Bogey's guns, aimed and fired. The shot seemed to land between the beast's shoulder, and huge bicep. Nothing changed in the demeanor of the snow creature. If anything, it became more pissed off. Bill Meyers pulled the trigger again, but to an empty clinking sound.

The rifle was thrown at the the beast, who now focused on him. He laid on his back as the creature smashed his pincers claws into the wooden floor like anchors, and hovered above him.

During the shots made by Bill Meyers, Bogey assisted his son in the kitchen. There existed a large, deep freezer in a corner. Bogey Wilson lifted a half carcass of a deer, and dragged it into the living room. With all his might, he flung the meat into the air.

Horrible breathe overpowered Bill Meyers below. Up close he witnessed the stained fangs, and victim's tissue enlarged around its teeth. The beady red eyes met his popping blue eyes, as its woolly, monstrous head slowly pulled back to spring forward an attack. The kill bite was headed for Bill Meyer's face. Defeat pulsed like electric shocks through his body awaiting the piercing fangs.

A heavy weight thumped onto his face, and pain resonated from his nose. The snow creature sunk its fangs into the frozen carcass of the deer, pulled back, and dropped it down confused. It expected the warm rush of tasty blood, but instead, savored on the cold metallic flavor of frozen meat.

It peered this way, it stared that way, and somehow, gave a look like - I had enough of this. It snatched the carcass with its large claws, and burrowed back into the floor's hole.

The last sounds heard were the snow creature's rumbles from digging away underneath. Crackling from fires resonated amongst the silence. Bogey Wilson, with his hurt knee, doused out fire flames in vain. The living room was destroyed, and became engulfed with uncontrollable fire. Bill Meyers stood up holding his painful nose. Hopefully, it was not broken, but at this point, it seemed to be the lesser of the life threatening situations. These two joined the others in the kitchen, the safest place right now.

Bogey Wilson helped his son bandaged his arm stump. While they were fighting the snow creature, Gilroy Wilson rammed his bleeding elbow onto the hot top of the coal stove. It burned shut the wound. He was too inebriated to recognize his own shock, and sat surprisingly calm. It seemed he would live. Bill Meyers, though, really could of cared less.

Bill Meyers wondering, asked,"Where's my Suzy?"

"She muttered repeatedly that she was hungry. I gave her something to eat, and brought her into the bedroom." Jesse Quentin spoke nervously while twisting her brunette curls.

"What? You gave her something to eat? You gave her something to eat while we could have been eating? Why did you not help us you idiot!" He yelled at her.

The young lady replied,"She is in the back bedroom."

"You mean you left her alone?" Bill Meyers claimed.

"I had to help Gilroy, you know, his arm! I, I do not know what I am doing! God help me!" Jesse spoke crying, and fell onto Gilroy Wilson's lap.

Bill Meyers left the kitchen with disgust, and searched for Susan Conti. Upon entering a bedroom, a stench of rancid meat, like a smelly salami, overwhelmed his senses. Bill Meyers saw Susan Conti on the floor with her back propped up against the old wooden wall. In one hand she held a piece of white bread, and the other some sort of sausage. A box of meat sausages were ripped open on top of the bed.

That Jesse girl was a stupid idiot. Susan Conti could not stomach that seasoned meat in her frail condition, even if she really was hungry.

Susan Conti raised the smelly sausage in her mouth with erotic motion. She was half-dazed, and lost in her mind. He guessed she mimicked what she knew best. "Slutty Suzy" definitely knew how to handle sausage. Bill Meyers quickly took away the meat, and broke up the bread for her to eat.

Then, he noticed it. He noticed a hole, like a large mouse hole in the wooden frame. He imagined the snow creature's claw poking through that small opening, searching to snatch his girlfriend. His imagination relayed this horror possibility to reality. He started to take a step in her direction to lift her away from the hole back to the safe kitchen.

She heard him touch her, and opened her eyes.

Susan Conti softly said, "My hero, my knight in shining armor. Come take me away. I want to start over."

Billy Meyers felt remorse for her. She did not deserve all this unwanted, traumatic experience. How, in a weird way, he still longed to be with her. His bubbling ooze inside lusted for her, and branded jealous ownership to her body. Her very essence was to be absorbed by him, like swallowing a drug. His sex fantasy existed real in his erotic imagination. Yet, it never happened.

Susan Conti choked a bit on the pieces of bread. Bill Meyer left the room for some water back in the kitchen. At the sink, Bogey Wilson was bandaging his son's arm stump. Jesse Quentin stood looking on useless. Bill Meyers pushed around them, ignored them, and filled a glass of water from the sink. Quickly, he headed back to Susan Conti laying against the old, bedroom wall. No one was on guard, and a snow creature attack could be the end of them.

He stopped to glance at her, and her condition.

Susan Conti spoke before he brought her the water."I am sorry."

"What do you mean, Suzy?" Bill Meyers replied.

She exclaimed,"What do you mean what do I mean? I am sorry for everything. For making fun of you. For always teasing you, even when we were young. You always were polite and nice. I am no good."

Bill Meyers stated," Do not be so cruel on yourself, Suzy. Sometimes we do things unknowingly, and do not really mean what we do."

Susan Conti readjusted herself from her sitting position. It helped little as she was all sore.

"You see, you are always nice. You say nice things, and there is a monster killing us." She considerately said.

Bill Meyers replied," Here, have a sip of water. We are going to be alright. That beast took off with Bogey's deer meat."

She replied,"I wish to start over. All of it, my whole life. I truly am sorry, and wish I could take it all back. You are the right man for me. I am going to be different."

A kind a joy, pleasurable energy rocked his body. Bill Meyers accepted her forgiveness, and wanted to start anew. "Slutty Suzy" was to be his real girlfriend, and no one but he was to call her by this nickname ever again.

Susan Conti asked," So the monster is gone. I am glad. You said it took Bogey's deer meat, and left for good? I feel safe now."

Bill Meyers confidently said," Yes, the monster is enjoying his meal miles away from us. Nothing to worry about."

He bent over to hand her the water glass. Calming down, Bill Meyers convoluted thoughts became categorically filed: the sausage box on the bed was processed from deer kill, it filled the room of deer meat scent, and the snow creature currently chomped on a deer meat carcass.

She drank and looked refreshed. Before he could hug his new or fake girlfriend, and drag her out of this butcher room, the beast's signature claw exploded through the mouse hole just like he imagined. The frail wood behind her splattered in pieces. The snow creature hugged the half awake girl with its powerful pincer claws.

Those beady, red eyes stared intently at Bill Meyers, as if expressing," I got your girl! She is all mine you sucker!"

It sunk it's fangs into her shoulder.

She pleaded," Billy Boy!".

It took off with her into the snowy night. The meaty aroma of Bogey's homemade sausage attracted the carnivore. The smell lured it to Susan Conti. Bill Meyers chased quickly and frantically through the opening of the bedroom wall.

His attempt was useless. He yelled a curse of revenge.

He screamed with hatred," I swear I will kill you, you bastard! I will set forth misery for the rest of your shit filled life!"

Now, all energy was all directed against the beast.

Bill Meyers took her death personal. His uncontrolled thoughts imagined them as a loving couple. By far, reality did not dictate this romance. His breakdown mashed his fantasies with realities, and truly believed Susan Conti was his steady girlfriend, his only love, till death do them part.

He unconsciously, concocted memories sharing their love. Special nights of romantic sex in bed. A picnic on a warm summer afternoon, which never existed. Bill Meyers remembered the naked, crazy sex in the forest, which never happened. But how he remembered and so enjoyed that forest day.

Bill Meyers believed that the snow creature spited him. This, his dark, or new personality knew. The devious beast destroyed the happiness this young man wished on his twenty first year of manhood. Deranged Bill Meyers spoke solemnly to himself to avenge the death of his beloved, "Slutty Suzy". The knight in shining armor, would slay the snow creature.

Susan Conti disappeared into the night without a whimper. Bill Meyers prayed she felt nothing. Todd Bloomfield, his brother Kyle Meyers, and now her, were all dead. But not dead like how people normally die. They were freakishly eaten dead, like we eat chicken for dinner.

Bill Meyers cried, squealed, yelled, and raised his fists at the moonlight. He demanded his slutty girlfriend back! He cursed the Almighty God.

Bill Meyers exclaimed with authority, shouting at the night sky," God, you are the slut of life. You take, take, and give back nothing. A God of no rewards!. My true, new God is the almighty Susan! My only true love, my only true God, is named- "Slutty Suzy"!

Bogey Wilson grabbed his shaking body, and said. " She's gone! Gone! We gotta go. We need to leave now. We must go before it returns!"

Bogey was right, and Bill Meyers knew it, even in his psychosis. Swiftly Bogey worked, loading the tractor wagon as Bill Meyers stood helpless. He assisted the limp, young man in a side seat of the tractor. Bill Meyer's moved slowly with his mental overload.

"Damn! Now where are the other two." Bogey Wilson replied, searching for his son and the white girl.

He had no time for this. Out of a garage, a four wheeler sounding a loud muffler moved in front of the tractor. This vehicle sat high off the ground with high performance, thick tires. Fancy "do da" lights shone all over, presenting the truck off as a celebrity item. This four by four crushed over junked cars in one of the derby shows.

"Oh no, oh no! Mr. Maverick payed me lots for that truck. He will pick it up next Saturday, and owes me a big two thousand for the mechanical work. No one is touching that machine." Bogey Wilson spoke with anger.

"I want to be alive. Me and Jesse heading through the deep woods. Da monster can not follow. Not in, through the thick forest. I need a a doctor." Gilroy Wilson exclaimed.

His father yelled,"Get out of the truck, Gil! I need to check your bloody stump!"

"Uh, no. I been soaking my stump in hooch. No more blood, no hurting." His son replied.

Before Bogey Wilson could grab his shotgun, the two took off on the snow filled trail. The high performance vehicle confidently rolled through the forest with Gilroy Wilson laughing, "Yahoo!" They could hear in the distance, an empty alcohol bottle smashing against a rock. The car engine became less and less.

Bogey looked disgusted, and said," Well, screw them. That boy was a real homo anyway. I hooked him up with that Jesse girl. I thought he'd change. Okay, I got no son Billy Boy, I guess it is just me and you."

In reality, Bogey Wilson always felt his son was a fool. The homosexuality did not truly bother him, but was raised by his religious mom, who followed the bible teachings. She believed the bible read against such ways, and were evil. Even though Bogey Wilson never believed much in church, some teachings stayed with him, like his mother blasting man and man relationships.

Did he show signs of being homo as a youngster? He wondered, being she mentioned such sins many a times.

Deep down, he also felt that his boy would not survive this night. It was a wrong move for them to take off and separate. They would most likely smack up into a tree. The snow creature would finish them. Bogey Wilson accepted the facts right there and then.

The old, black man returned to the business at hand, and said, "Maybe we should sit tight together on the tractor, and disconnect the hay wagon. The extra weight will slow us down, and risk getting stuck."

Bill Meyers never replied, and Bogey Wilson continued without expecting a real answer. The young man's hatred built stronger against the snow creature. He watched Bogey Wilson grab some guns, ammo, and two chainsaws. Some of the supplies were left.

Together, they set out on the tractor. It moved a little quicker without the hay wagon. It was a still night, about 2:00 A.M. in the early morning. Both were silent as they anticipated an attack at any time. Were they going to survive this ordeal? Half the people who were involved were already dead.

Bogey cursed his son. Together, they would have had a better chance to fight off the beast. He kept mumbling, over and over, that his son probably smacked into a tree and then the snow creature ate them.

"You are not crazy at all," Bill Meyers suddenly spoke.

Bogey Wilson laughed and said," Oh, I am crazy alright. Put a crazy man in a crazy situation, you get a normal man doing normal things."

Bill Meyers held tightly onto the shotgun, as Bogey Wilson drove the tractor back onto Cliff Drop Road. They rolled at a good clip, putting Bogey's burnt house behind them. Time past quicker, as Bill Meyers realized they were already near Todd Bloomfield's truck along the cliff side. Without the snow creature on their heels, the drive on Cliff Drop Road seemed shorter.

Soon, they passed the entrance to Helix Point. Bill Meyers mentioned that the gate was unchained, and tire marks lead up the hill. Should they check for people? The tractor kept moving. They could care less about anybody up that snow-clad hill. They were escaping out of the woods with their lives.

The tractor reached the large falling pine tree. The station wagon was still there, undamaged. First, Bogey Wilson searched for a way to drive around the huge fallen pine. No escape route was accessible. They had their work cut out for them. The tractor was shut off as they sat in dark silence. The flashlight shone upon the wrecked landscape, lighting a gloomy effect. There actually was more than one fallen tree.

Will the chainsaw buzzing and whirling attract the beast to them? The removal of the blocked trees remained to be their only choice. Bogey Wilson was in his upper fifties, and all the crazy, physical stuff brought a soreness on, and his his homemade hooch only partially numbed him. He climbed off his tractor, and lit a cigarette.

His aching back called out for a nice, smooth rub from a local lady, Miss Divine Feel. Thinking of her floppys, and sucking long drags from his cigarette, helped Bogey Wilson calm down and forget all the mayhem. Mrs. Divine Feel, now Miss, lost her husband to a lumberjack accident five years ago. Bogey Wilson provided services for her lonliness, and recieved some back, like her special massages. He also needed to include a few bottles of his hooch.

"I really have to quit," Bogey Wilson iterated while blowing out smoke.

Bill Meyers watched the old man, but did not reply. He glanced at him smoking, and then scanned the eerie night.

Bogey Wilson said,,"My cousin, Bingy Wilson, is bed ridden, full of cancer, down in Miami."

"Excuse me," Bill Meyers questioned, not comprehending the switch of small talk from their crisis.

"Bingy, my cousin, he is dying of cancer." He repeated saying.

"His name is Bingy?" Bill Meyers spoke now joining in on the casual banter.

What strange names the Wilson family used- Bingy, and Bogey. Then Bill Meyers thought of a strange, unfortunate name that Gilroy Wilson could get branded with. Imagined being nicknamed "But hole".

It seemed to relax the old man by discussing about cousin Bingy.

A flask was handed up to Bill Meyers, who refused the alcohol. Then, the old timer swigged a hit of his own hooch.

"This drink will help take off the edge of a winter night. Well, Bingy's real name was Bart. Every time he coughed, sneezed, or for that matter laughed, one heard a metallic bing sound connected to his vocals. Kids branded him the name- Bingy."

Bill Meyers replied," Well, that was not very nice. One should not make ill of someone's idiosyncrasy.

The old timer took another swig of his hooch, and continued to survey the damage to be chainsawed.

He then replied," That's right, idiosyncra... sycrat, well, what you said. People have no right. You appreciate your life and others, when crap like tonight stinks towards your way. Bingy always had that embarrassed look from all the jokes. My cousin got no respect. Now he is dying. People have no respect."

"Speaking of nicknames, what is the deal with the name Bogey?" Bill Meyers questioned.

Bogey Wilson rolled his eyes up to Bill Meyers on the tractor, and then rolled them out to the darkened forest.

He explained, "You see the white color at the ends of my frizzy hair. This color combo came with my childhood. This only cursed me for the other kids to ridicule, and call me a spook. I was Bogey, like a ghost. When I speak of kids, I mean the white kids in town. Like Bingy, I was embarrassed when my Mom sent me to Tannersville on errands."

Bill Meyers stated, "'And I guess Bingy earned his nickname from the white children as well."

Bogey Wilson peered up at his new acquaintance, with a matter of fact expression,

"To a black man, spook can mean other things. You know? So Bogey stuck to me instead." He commented.

Bill Meyers suddenly became irritated. He was being attacked by a savage beast, and he was stuck in a racial discussion. The snow creature only discriminated against their lives right now, and that was all he could handle.

Bill Meyers annoyed said, " Cut the crap! I was ridiculed just the same, and bullies are bullies, no matter what race you are. Kids will be kids. Are you claiming the other black children did not mock your bleached ends of your hair?"

Now Bogey Wilson became irritated a bit. After a few seconds, stared nasty at Bill Meyers,

He blurted," Spook."

"What"

With a little growl in his voice, Bogey Wilson exclaimed, "The black kids called me spook too, okay!"

"Okay, I will to respect your black heritage, I will call you Spooky Wilson." Bill Meyers commented.

The old black man exclaimed, "You cut the crap! I am not a spook! I is Ol' Bogey Wilson. Bogey is my name."

Bill Meyers realized the conversation was over, and accepted the ending- not Spook, but Bogey. It was time to return back to reality. They needed to cut away the falling tree, and get the hell out of here. The darkness was letting up as the sunrise was due in about an hour.

Bogey Wilson walked away with a chainsaw, and felt a little disgruntled. He was glad the talk was over. He refused to convey to Bill Meyers, that he was the kid who nicknamed Bart Wilson- Bingy. He was the wise guy kid, who branded Bart originally with the joking Bingy name. It caught on with the others.

He now felt ashamed, because Bart was dying from cancer and all. Meeting of the beast, did put life in certain perspectives.

"Stop putting pressure on me. Let's get to work," Bogey Wilson exclaimed.

He turned with disgust, and pulled on the chainsaw. The branches became stripped from the falling trunk. He needed to make space, so the larger chainsaw could have access at the trunk.

He claimed, "This will take awhile. I have to cut chunks of the trunk in sizes, so we can physically move it out of the way. Then, maybe we can take your station wagon, and finally get the hell out of here. Why don't you make use and see if your ol' wagon starts."

Bill Meyers sat in his car to start it. The engine started, and began to rattle the station wagon. Within seconds, everything was shaking.

But also another tremor started and rumbled. He shut off the engine, and felt the car still shaking. He guessed it was another quake. The trees all around dropped snow from the vibrations.

Before he could move from the driver's seat- bam! A pine tree took a tumble, smashing on the hood of the station wagon. A tree collapsed swiftly, destroying the entire front of the station wagon. The front windshield shattered in all glass sizes. Luckily, he only suffered some small facial cuts. If the pine tree fell a few feet differently, Bill Meyers would have been crushed to death for sure.

As fast and terrible these tremors hit, they also subsided, and all was again quiet. The car was useless. Their bad luck continued as if they were not destined to leave the woods. Bill Meyers made the sign of the cross, and prayed he was alive. After all the escapes from the snow creature, his life almost was erased by a falling tree.

Bogey Wilson simply gestured," I guess our escape stays with the tractor."

"I do not believe so." Bill Meyers remarked as he stared at a flat from one of the huge tires. The insane traveling was probably one bump too much. Maybe earlier, the beast punctured it during an attack. Both were loss of words. The flat tire ruined an already ruined night.

The flashlights lighted the gloom, only to create shadows to enforce their helplessness. What else could go wrong. They wanted to be back at Tannersville.

"I am tired," Bogey moaned, " and I am achy. I need to grab a few winks."

Bill Meyers shook his head in agreement.

Both jumped into the back seat of the station wagon, found a blanket, and layed close for warmth. It was before sunrise, and both fell asleep quickly. In any other situation, these two opposites characters would never had shared a blanket together.

Then, sounds of a moving vehicle were heard a few hours later. After the encounters with the snow creature, both became light sleepers. It came from the direction of Helix Point. Someone, that is someone else was coming.

Other Part of Forest

Gilroy Wilson was lost. "Damn shit! This ain't no road. What the hell! Jesse, I told ya to watch out for the road."

He glanced over at her with his glazed eyes, and he poked her with his stump. She retaliated with a punch in his shoulder. Gilroy Wilson yelled in double pain from her punch, and his hitting her with his wounded stump.

They darted through small, broken clearings between the trees. Mr. Maverick's demolition truck handled well. It had good traction in the snow, and climbed over rock easy. However, they still were lost. Because the fancy truck handled so well, he drove like a maniac, not paying attention to where he headed. Putting distance from the monster, seemed to give them a feeling of safety.

Gilroy Wilson and Jesse Quentin took the old lumber roads to circumvent Helix Point to reach Route 3. This was opposite the guys on the tractor route which headed back onto Cliff Drop Road. He felt faint, but still determined to escape the forest in his state of intoxication, and his shock of losing his forearm.

"I have to be here. I know where is am. I am up front, by our fields". He stated confused.

Gilroy Wilson knew these forest trails like putting his personal buddy into another man's ass without hands. But where is the potato field? He pushed the truck hard over some brush, and plopped out onto a large open field. He reached the potato field. He then bragged how he knew he was never really lost.

"I knew we ain't lost. See, I knew it, you dumb Jesse!" He hollered.

The young lady just looked relieved when they drove out of the thick woods. He put the petal to the metal as they sailed over the snowy field with speed. The nippy air felt good, blowing on their faces. At the other end was a tractor trail to Rte. 3.

They both glanced over their shoulders, expecting this monster to suddenly appear. They were apprehensive out in the open field, now that they were finally escaping the forest. The snow creature could not attack them on the concrete road, at least this was in Gilroy Wilson's convoluted thoughts. He sped quickly, wishing to be on the highway immediately.

He took a last swig of alcohol, and chucked the bottle out the window. The two were totally wasted. A problem existed though. This clearing was not the potato field, but the corn field. The corn field which laid high above on a cliff over Rte. 3. Again, no potato field, but the corn field, as they sped on the high cliff. Upon reaching the end, speeding close to seventy miles-per-hour, Maverick's "stud" truck shot off the cliff to a 30 yard drop. Stupid Gilroy Wilson did not know his corn from his potatoes.

The high performance truck was not designed for flying, It hit hood first into the forest floor as the truck smashed in on itself. Both of them flew into the windshield, and the truck turned onto its back. Gil laid all twisted, and could not free himself. He felt warm liquid, which was his blood oozing all over him. Jesse Quentin was either dead or unconscious because she did not answer when he called out her name.

He could hear cars nearby. Rte 3 was only a short distance, but he could not speak or move. He heard footsteps, and clanking, like someone was investigating the wreck. Someone must of heard the crash. He noticed distant lights, lights similar to roadside, utility vehicles. The electric lines were down, and repair crews were out around the clock to fix them after the storm.

Gilroy Wilson felt immediate joy as he stared at the flashing utility lights. They would call for medical help, and this nightmare would be over. He heard metallic rips, like someone tearing off the truck door. Jessebelle Quentin was pulled out as Gil felt her body relieve pressure from his back. He could not hear well because his head was smashed into the seat cushion.

A loud rumble, and violent shaking overcame the wrecked truck, which brought unbearable pain all over his body. As the truck took a different position, he flopped in agony over to the passenger side. Then, Gilroy Wilson saw his beloved woman. Jesse's half face looked back at him with one eye smashed. Very delicately, the snow creature's claw picked pieces of brain from her open skull. The large pincer had remarkable precision as it moved back and forth from the bloody head to its mouth.

Gilroy Wilson's ability to move was non existent. He was forced to stare directly at his girlfriend, being ripped limb from limb. The snow creature made little sound, and looked quite comfortable chewing, slurping, cracking bone, and belching. Gilroy Wilson watched in horror as the monster ate every part of Jesse, except her clothes. It sat relaxed, licking it's pincer claws, without a care in the world. Time passed slowly, maybe an hour.

The beast seemed to be ripping apart Jesse, piece by piece, deliberately, and slowly. It fearfully distressed Gilroy Wilson. To him, or maybe because he was so drunk, he swore that the creature ate her mockingly on purpose. It boasted its victory by tormenting its subdued opponent.

Slowly, the snow creature got on all fours. One of the claws reached into the wreck, grabbed him in the mid-section, and pulled him out. His body was forced out from its stuck position. Bones and limbs snapped as he was hauled out. His pain soared to a ten plus, as white lightening appeared in his eye's vision. Gilroy Wilson prayed to pass out. He wished the alcohol worked better in numbing the pain. He simply watched the snow creature eat him until he bled to death as the second course.

The two utility workers kept sleeping soundly in their van. It was an exhausting work night. Not even a car crash could wake these boys up.

CHAPTER 5

Caves of Sorts

HAROLD OLGEBY AND Mr. Conti survived the earthquake. The shaking and vibrations decreased slowly, and then all ceased. The quake was not bad at all. Harold Olgeby scanned his equipment, and satisfactory results were displayed- all back to normal. He needed to rethink his situation. Should he grab what he collected and take off? Maybe he should go back to the excavation site and continue for a few more days. Mr. Conti's face expressed a vote for an immediate getaway.

"That could have been a lot worse", exclaimed the scientist.

Mr. Conti answered, "I want to get the hell out of here. Let us go now Mr. Olgeby."

The scientist lacked a decisive choice. Suddenly, Mr. Conti was searching frantically through his stuff.

"Crap, I am missing my backpack! Oh no, my stuff, the keys to the truck, there not here." Mr. Conti realized he left his supply bag at the excavation site, or thought he did. All of his whining, and lazy attitude made him leave the most important thing in the woods- the truck keys.

"Well, the way you were carrying on about the work, and the amount of beer you consumed, I am not surprised," Harold Olgeby stated sarcastically.

Mr.Conti replied," Complaining, explaining my weaknesses will not make the truck keys appear."

Annoyed at Mr. Conti, the scientist stated the obvious." Well, I guess we have to go back to the cavern, and find them. Now listen, since you screwed up, we are going to haul more stuff back, which I left due to that earthquake."

Reluctantly, Mr. Conti agreed. They dressed up for the winter elements and prepared the sleds. There existed a chance they will not find the truck keys. Harold Olgeby simply suggested only then, he would call for emergency assistance.

Trudging in the snow, the scientist took the lead. While staying watchful for damage, a rhyme repeated in Mr. Conti's mind. Instead of a catchy song to pass the time, like "On the Road Again," by Willie Nelson, it was down beat, with a dismal tone-.

"Fall... Desperate... Unknown. Unknown... Helpless...Violent on Stone. Fall...Gravely...Shatter to Earth. Earthquake...Savage....Sudden Alert."

Totally stoned on weed, Willie Nelson could not concoct lyrics ominous like these. Mr. Conti remained confused, and did not understand how to interpret the words. To himself, he repeated the words of unusual obscurity.

Along the forest trail, little damage was noticed. Harold Olgeby was confident, and they were back to business as before. When they reached the excavation site, things changed. The crevasse, in which they were digging at, had split larger. They walked along the edge, and noticed a separate opening, much deeper- a new cave.

Harold Olgeby shone his flashlight into the darkness. Falling rock from the surface laid at the bottom, of a subterranean cavern. The earthquake unearthed a hidden cave. All Harold Olgeby could think about was discovering more prehistoric items. Pure glee filled up inside him.

The scientist remarked,"Quickly, get the ropes and pulleys! I am going down."

Mr. Conti responded," Oh no, This is steeper than the first site we worked at. The only way down and up is with a rope. We cannot climb out of there. We need better equipment."

"We will be fine. C'mon, where is your adventurous side." Harold Olgeby replied.

Mr. Conti said," I already told you. I left it by the roadside before I met you, when I was doing a beer run. Anyway, I need to find my backpack."

Harold Olgeby said," Secure me a harness, and gently lower me down. You look for the truck keys, and I will peek around the new cavern."

Mr. Conti reluctantly fixed a rope harness. He tied and knotted the universal chest sling for Harold Olgeby. He lowered his newly found partner, ascending 20 ft. down. The brand of rope was high quality, and much better than plain nylon. The more expensive rope had little elongation or stretch, resisted abrasion, and twisted less when hanging. These walls were jagged and sharp, and sparing no expense was smart on Harold Olgeby's part.

The fresh breaks of rocks were noticed by him while being lowered. He realized this cave was not created by the quake, but ancient. The quake just opened up the access to its secrecy. At the bottom, he quickly scanned its hugeness, and it continued deep at one end. The back of the cavern tapered off into a narrower cavern, and then, like a tunnel.

The previous digging site was a crevasse, and open to the outside mostly. He did not supply himself with hard hats. He could of used one to prevent from banging his head, falling debris, and ducking under hanging formations.

Mr. Conti yelled down," It looks like a hard hat would have been a plus."

"You read my mind, business partner."

The partner crap did not work on Mr. Conti. He wondered for a moment if he really did read his mind. Was Granny's ghost present, watching over him?

Harold Olgeby led himself with a flashlight. He quickly recognized well formed stalactites and stalagmites. There existed an indent, an opening to smaller cavern space. He found pieces of fecal matter on the floor. The droppings seemed fairly fresh. Could there be an opening down the cave tunnel, and here slept a hibernating bear? The scat was that of a large animal. It seemed as if the small cave was sealed, and now opened into the larger cavern. This explained the broken rock, and loose dirt. Did something break out of this smaller locked section from the earthquake? How did it stay alive?

Scuffling echoed down the narrow tunnel. Harold Olgeby's anxiety unleashed again. He stood motionless, and shone his light down the rocky corridor. He realized he possessed no weapon. With all the excitement, he forgot to bring protection. Such matters did not come to him naturally, like packing a six shooter. Maybe he needed a rifle to blow off the head of a grumpy bear awakened by the earthquake.

He stood motionless, and again, heard a sound. Again, a shuffling echoed from the tunnel. He held a crowbar, which would have to do as his defense. What kind of defense was this, against a hungry bear. His body began to tremble. Harold Olgeby held the weapon above his head, ready to ram it down upon his attacker. He slowly turned to head back to the opening above because his attempt to fight was in vain.

A shriek broke the cave silence, and a moving body attacked the scientist. The flashlight fell from his hand, and shone onto the cave walls, giving off shadows. Harold Olgeby saw a boy. The boy struck with a pointed stick as the scientist crashed down onto it with the crowbar. He grabbed him and both wrestled. Harold Olgleby sat on top of him, pinning the teenager.

"What the hell are you doing down here?"

"Ugh! Ba, Ba, Bash! I am The Mighty Caveman. " Kyle Meyers proudly yelled out.

Was it possible this boy was trapped in the cave for a long time, and could not speak English? This idea was truly an impossibility.

Harold Olgeby asked,"What is your real name?"

"The Mighty Caveman" replied," My human name is Kyle Meyers, when I am not in super hero status."

Kyle Meyers kept struggling, refusing to be defeated by his foe. Harold Olgeby lessened his grip, which gave the teenager enough time to loosen one of his hands. He grabbed a small rock, and sent it against the scientist's head. Kyle Meyers," The Mighty Caveman", scrambled to his feet, and meandered ape-like down the dark tunnel. Kyle sent off another caveman yell. Oops, it sounded like another Tarzan call. He needed to start originating his superhero franchise.

Harold Olgeby stumbled back to where Mr. Conti awaited above.

"What happened? What was all that yelling," Mr. Conti stated complexed.

"I do not rightly know. There is a wild boy down here. I cannot figure how he got down here, or what. I think he is deranged." Harold Olgeby stated perplexed.

Then, a groan, followed with a deep throated gurgle, sounded from the dark tunnel. Harold Olgeby did not realize he stood in the lair of the snow creature, and it returned home. His thoughts returned a to bear again. Maybe, the kid devised some prank. He felt confused. He was attentively scared. He did not know one of the fossils lived, breathed and now stalked him.

"Get me the hell out of here!" Harold Olgeby yelled.

Was it the wild boy. a bear, or what the hell. Harold Olgeby demanded out of the hole.

Mr. Conti heard the groans as well. As he fumbled with the pulley system, a large deafening roar exploded out from the cave. The sounding blast disoriented him as he slipped in the snow. He carelessly dropped the pulleys, which fell down at Harold Olgeby's feet.

"You idiot! Quickly another rope!" The scared scientist again yelled.

Mr. Conti said, "I'm sorry! That confounded sound, what the heck is down there!"

Harold Olgeby continued yelling, "Get me out Conti, now!"

Mr. Conti rebounded with his skill, and a rope was sent down within seconds. The scientist peered over his shoulder while he tied himself onto the rope.

Harold Olgeby then set eyes on the snow creature. A large mass encompassed the opening of the back tunnel. The fallen flashlight emitted enough light to expose the outline of the massive sloth-like beast. Harold Olgeby was awe-stricken. He immediately connected his fossils with the beast. A live Megalonyx! At least, a type of Megalonyx plodded slowly towards the opening of the cave.

Harold Olgeby scrambled up the side of the rocky surface, but it was too steep.

Mr. Conti dropped the rope without a harness. Harold Olgeby impatiently waited for himself to be tugged out and up.

Harold Olgeby exclaimed,"Pull me up, now! Hurry up, it's close, and coming!"

Mr. Conti leveraged himself against a tree, trying to gain support to haul the scientist out. He hung a few feet from the cave floor as Mr, Conti had trouble lifting him. He brought the scientist about 10 feet from the bottom. He tied the rope off as he ran back to the sled for another pulley. He needed to alleviate the stress on the rope, and add more leverage to lift Harold Olgeby out. He worked diligently to produce a working system so the scientist could escape.

"Hurry up, it is coming! A creature, like the fossils, alive!" Harold Olgeby yelled. A bleating rabbit stuck in a snare, was the best way to express his predicament. He was helpless, and hanging in the hands of his drunken friend.

The snow creature slowly approached the dangling man. A digesting meal busted the lines of its huge gut. There existed no rush to eat again, but decided to toy with its food. It would capture its prey, and drag the left overs to the lair. The cold climate, the snow creature craved, preserved the freshness of the kill.

On top, Mr. Conti worked desperately. The whole journey to the excavation site accompanied a bad aura. Earlier, he was afraid to complain again, because Harold Olgeby would get mad, again. He wanted to get paid. He wanted to make sure his hard work received the proper payment. Mr. Conti related his attitudes to his lack of luster approach of this job. But how was he wrong. Whatever thing was brewing down in that hole, provoked his inherited second site.

Harold Olgeby realized his body was not elevating. His life was finished. The hulking beast approached 20 feet away with its beady red eyes watching every move. A strip of tissue hanged from one of the fangs. This carnivore has eaten someone or something. The stature of the beast was menacing enough.

A piercing yell echoed in the cave,"Bahoo, Bahooie! Badda bing!", " The Mighty Caveman" shouted.

A sizable boulder hit and bounced over the back of the snow creature. As it stopped, and peered towards the direction of the projectile, a flare flew down from above. The bright, pink light blinded the sensitive eyes of the subterranean mammal.

The wild boy was aiding his escape, who threw the boulder. Simultaneously, Mr. Conti used a flare to spook off the snow creature. A lucky moment saved Harold Olgeby. The snow creature barreled down the cave tunnel chasing Kyle Meyers, and the last thing heard was a weird caveman-like yell. It sounded more like an Indian warrior. This super hero really needed to work on his signature call. The Megalonyx disappeared.

Mr. Conti assembled a pulley for more rope support, and slowly lifted Harold Olgeby to the surface. The scientist was relieved to be out of that situation. He patted Mr. Conti on the shoulder, and plopped down in the snow, fighting a panic attack.

They both sat next to each other catching their breathe, and their wits. An uneasy feeling still settled inside of Mr. Conti, as he peered down into the cave hole. The second sight, his foreboding skills, which he believed was past down from Granny, "The Witch", overwhelmed continuous, like an endless loop.

A whisper in the breeze warned, " Danger, danger is here, danger is coming. Leave this place, before your dead tumbling."

Fall...Desperate...Unknown. Unknown...Helpless...Violent on Stone. Fall...Gravely...Shatter to Earth. Earthquake...Savage...Sudden Alert.

The proverbial omen repeated inside Mr. Conti. After what just occurred, he thought this tune was ridiculous. He was losing it. It being his mind.

Harold Olgeby regained himself, and said not a word. He sat contemplating his next move. What to do. What to do. A live specimen, a prehistoric mammal breathing the air, thousands of years after hibernation. Scientifically impossible! But it existed. It was real- an alive, carnivorous ground sloth from the Pleistocene era. There was only fossil evidence of plant eating sloth species. No one in humankind knew that a meat eating Megalonyx existed.

Immediately his strategic, analytical mind processed several computations. Harold Olgeby must capture the snow creature alive, and this fame would reward him his fortunes. He also possessed the only fossils, worth possible millions. A missing link now exposed for all to wonder at. Even this founded cave site could be a money producer. People will come from all over to see the lair of the snow creature.

Now the alert pulsated, producing pressure on Mr. Conti's brain. The voices said," Get up! Run as fast as possible!"

Before he could turn his head in the direction of his companion, Mr. Conti fell with involuntary force into the darkness below. The life of a man, he just saved, shoved him into the lair of Megalonyx.

His ankle pulsed from pain. He fell hard on his shoulder. The seriousness of his physical wounds were unknown, but panic-stricken wounds radiated in his mental capacity.

He looked upwards, perplexed. The scientist, now looked more like a mad scientist, staring down with a sinister, clownish smile.

"I am sorry I had to do that. But the prehistoric mammal is going to be hungry. I believe it awoke from a long, very long slumber. You trusted my whole college, scientific persona, but actually, I am not what I appear to be."

Mr. Conti laid aggravated in pain, hoping nothing was broken. He laid irritated about the crazy scientist. He now realized he played the fool.

"Yes, I am a scientist, but a simple average student, who holds great ambition." He commented, twirling once to release some inner energy, and next mopped back his hair with his hand.

The imposter continued," I did win awards, but in conjunction with a five student research team. I mostly cleaned the glassware. Two years later, I stole the prestigious, diamond synthesis work from the real Harold Olgeby who became, well, accidentally killed in a fire. Yes, beer drinking Mr. Conti, I am killer, and I love it. I may even be one of those infamous, psychotic serial killers."

He shuffled and shimmied to make-believe music, and sang some old, fifties tune.

Mr. Conti heavily perplexed, did not follow the conversation with all his aching extremities. He connected his uneasy premonitions with this madman. This guy was a certifiable kook. He realized he drank too much, and it distorts your reality.

The fake Harold Olgeby continued, "It turns out that forgery and play acting are my academic strengths. There should be a graduate program for this stuff. I would be A +, top of the heap. However, fossils and meteorology are my great love. Unfortunately, the last year visit here, with the meteorology team, did not end well. Back at the lab, I realized the importance of the fossil find. I do not share."

Mr. Conti moved his bodily position to relieve some of the pain. He could wiggle his toe, and he believed his ankle was not broken. The partial impacts into the cave sides lessened the pressure of the fall. His shoulder ached terribly though.

"Your a nut job! It all makes sense now," hoarsely Mr. Conti replied up to whoever the man was.

"There are a few dead bodies back at the research lab. I hope I did a good cover up. I never knew killing was so therapeutic. A real tension releaser!" He spoke more of his deadly deeds.

Again, he danced a weird foot step, and mocked his assistant laying helpless in the hole.

He twirled Mr. Conti's backpack in the air, and said, " Look what I found!" The mad scientist had it all the time. He then took out the keys, and jingled them during another weird dance move. This time, losing his balance in the snow, the backpack dropped into the cave. Luckily, for him, fake Harold Olgeby held onto the truck keys, but unlucky for the misinformed Mr. Conti.

Mr. Conti grabbed the backpack as a good sign from his dead granny. Hopefully, items packed were useful towards his predicament. He remembered, ah yes, there was a flask of whiskey in there.

The mad scientist said,"Well, that was stupid of me. Oh well, I just had to dance, you know, bust a move. I hope there is something you can use in there, my loyal assistant. You can never claim I was not helpful to your predicament."

He continued speaking his last words, "As they say, be good, and don't do anything I would not do. I leave you with your new found friend, Mr. Megalonyx. That is its proper name."

Then, the gypsy in Mr. Conti overtook his words, "I cast on you the Conti Curse of the Hills". A bitter end for well wishers, a coin drops in, to commit a sin. Eat your meat to commit a feat. It helps the body to stay fit, then its meat for the devil where you sit."

"Whatever." Fake Harold Olgeby commented, and turned to his sled. He started to prepare to leave. His mindset entered his conniving plan to capture the snow creature.

Mr. Conti thought to himself. What the hell did he just say? He realized fatigue was setting in. In the backpack was a whiskey flask. Quickly, he swallowed half of it, and then stopped. Some of the liquor should be saved for later. Clanking and noise above was heard, and Mr. Conti tried not to think about that double crosser.

About a 100 yards from where he threw in Mr. Conti, was the original cavern with the fossils. After experiencing a real Megalonyx, fake Harold Olgeby realized the importance of the fossils. He pulled the sled with equipment, and stopped by his original site. He decided to take a last look. The fossils collected were enough, but yesterday, with leaving so quickly, there might be something needed of interest at the dig site.

As his aching body headed down the rocky trail, which involved half climbing down, he noticed the damage. The main lighting fixture was falling over, and the light's glass were shattered. As his weary legs stepped downward, closer to his excavation site, the hanging lights were all pulled down.

The damage did not reflect the actions from the earthquake. The generator was smashed. The unit was smashed as if someone or something physically banged the crap out of it. The site was demolished by the Megalonyx. The snow creature stopped by for a visit. Even the metal part of a shovel had a nice bent.

Fake Harold Olgeby browsed around, and was disappointed with all the mess. A folding chair, which he originally left, was not damaged. He sat down surrounded by broken glass, and there was a lot of broken glass. The glistening of glass shards from the sun above, sparked memory cells- past memories which he longed to bury. The sitting welcomed feelings of relaxation, only to dig open those closed coffins in his brain. He moved his foot only to hear the crunch of more glass. His thoughts tornadoed to his "Horror Land of Oz".

Here he sat with the cold wind blowing above him. Suddenly, he was sitting on the beach in Florida, with a warm wind blowing above him. He forgot about Florida, two years ago, when the incident occurred. The broken glass, the hundreds of glass pieces, sparked a return visit to his devious past.

In Miami, working from a college grant, he took a lab assistant job with the real, Dr. Harold Olgeby. The man who really was an expert on production of synthetic diamonds.

His pager beeped on the sunny, windy beach of Miami. The message read- "Needed in lab room 109. Come immediately. Importance of the utmost." The text was sent from Dr. Harold Olgeby.

The laboratory assistant replied,"Oh crap! There goes a nice afternoon. Oh well, the boss calls."

Sand was brushed off his shorts, and he snapped his beach towel to do the same. The wind sent flying sand towards a family who looked displeased.

An old lady, now brushing off her own clothes, with an aura of importance exclaimed," Do you belong here?"

"Excuse me?" the laboratory assistant said.

"This is a private beach."The old lady affirmatively spoke.

Folding his beach towel, the man said,"Okay, and your point is?"

"This is private, secluded private," again, affirmatively, the old lady spoke.

"Do not worry Maam, I am leaving your super, private beach. By the way, all the ocean beaches look the same to me. To answer your question, yes, I had proper approval to access this gated beach community." The laboratory assistant barked at the snobby woman.

He walked away, and the old lady gleamed a smile of content. She was not happy about him leaving, but more that she told him off, and got her way.

He walked into the general laboratory area. Dr. Harold Olgeby waited by a bench, looking displeased, just like the old, rich hag with the sand.

"What happened again? This chemical synthesis is ruined. You set the timer wrong on the oven," Dr. Harold Olgeby spoke irritated.

"I set it right." The young man said, and examined the oven. "See, the timer gets stuck. Maybe, you should spend some money on equipment."

The whole lab was empty. The good doctor brought his failure of an assistant to his office. The scientific floor was partitioned by glass panels. Through the Doctor's office, one could see other parts of the lab. It had its good points. A scientist could observe what was participating in other parts of the labs.

A small label was found on the glass panels- Ginelli & Sons Inc. In a past conversation with the janitor, it turned out that Biochemical Unlimited, supplied kick back money to this manufacturing company. This was the sole reason for having glass walls, than private, real walls. The dirty world of money revolved its corruption even in scientific inquiry.

They sat down in the visible office. " It is not working out," The good doctor exclaimed. " Your work is sloppy, the lateness, and the constant disagreements, inclines me to let you go."

So, what are you saying?" The young man replied.

Dr. Harold Olgeby stared at him perplexed, and said," Is it not obvious? You are fired."

"Fine, I just happened to be the one who pointed out that your metallic stripping process was less stable. By adding chromium flakes, the mass alloy stayed whole with a profound molecular rigidity. Also,do not make me remind you of the added protocol which stumped you for years. One could even say, this is my project." The laboratory assistant exclaimed

"Yes, the chromium ions were noteworthy. In the beginning you possessed a certain scientific ambiance, but always there was a peculiarity which bothered me. Your true, negative colors shined the last year. C'mon, you screwed up, and you received a position in beautiful Miami Beach. How many analytical laboratories exist in such a bikini clad setting?"

"The irritable college worker said, "You screwed up. I am the best. I do not need this child play. I am taking my work somewhere else, or maybe I will branch out on my own."

Dr. Harold Olgeby spoke sarcastically," Now you are delusional. First of all, you are not that good or intelligent in molecular structure synthesis. Do you not remember how your average grades lacked the minimum standard of our meteorology program? I still accepted you. And by the way, it takes money to branch out, and also, you do not know anyone."

Now the young assistant became angry. He stood up, and started digging in his carry satchel.

The real Dr, Harold Olgeby was not finished with this loser. There existed another piece of information which really bugged him.

"Listen, by the way, what is the meaning of this." Dr. Harold Olgeby commented, and pulled out a I.D. Card. He showed it to the disgruntled man. "Well, I found this in your satchel."

"That is a breach of my privacy at my employment!" The young man yelled.

"Whatever, I mean a picture of you, with my name, and credentials? I had enough of the joking around. Were you planning a hoax with the fake I.D.? Is it because of April Fool's Day this Friday? Harold Olgeby said.

Then the good doctor continued with a bragging tone," I understand that people wished they were me. My reputation is admirable and fame worthy. But really, it is not a funny joke playing the role of a joker. Nobody likes a comedian."

The deranged man, the no good lab assistant, spoke with control, "You are an idiot. I have your I.D. Credentials with my picture because I am taking your place. He continued digging in his satchel.

"Oh, really." The real Harold Olgeby answered amused.

"Yes really." The lab assistant replied pulling out a knife from the satchel.

Now, Dr. Harold Olgeby became agitated, lowering his high social standards.

"Oh, you want to play gangster?" The Doctor pulled a revolver from underneath his desk.

The young man stated,"You do not have the guts to use that gun. I bet you never shot it."

The real Harold Olgeby flinched, and a nervousness shown in his face.

The fake laboratory assistant grinned with determination as he lashed out with his knife, He slashed Dr,Harold Olgeby on the cheek. The good doctor sat shocked. Without paying attention, the young man ripped the gun from the his hand.

"I hate you! I hate you! I hate you!" the young man shouted. These words were penned up inside him, and were exploded into the Dr. Harold Olgeby's face.

Both of them looked at the blood dripping onto the desk. It was a lot of blood from the slashed cheek. Fear concerning his worker showed up too late. Doctor Harold Olgeby realized his life was in danger.

The man, who was hired, who might of used a pseudo name to apply for this job from the beginning, grabbed Dr. Harold Olgeby with insane glee.

"Let us go for a stroll through your inept laboratory." He exclaimed, and held the good doctor's hands behind his back.

He pushed from behind with all his force. They both went sailing through the glass partitions. He kept pushing Doctor Harold Olgeby into another glass wall, and then another, and still one more. The good doctor was dead. His body was pierced severely. One deadly glass shard cut his carotid artery on his neck. Blood flowed all over the polished tile floor.

The young man, the killer, joyously replied,"Oh, did that feel good! I needed a release. Oh, how that felt good. It has been about three years ago since I had this much fun."

He remembered when he cut up a stinking hobo, who asked for money every day when he passed him on the street corner.

He always was forced to hear the pleading, lazy bum," Can you spare some money. I have not eaten in two days. Please, can you at least spare a quarter for a coffee?

His mind would become bonkers just thinking about that guy. What could you buy for a quarter? Stupid. The bum did not buy food. Maybe the loser should not of spent his begging money on cheap whiskey. A quarter for a cup of coffee? Keep up with the times asshole, a cup of coffee went for a dollar-fifty and up.

"Here is a fifty cent box cutter you bum!" The lab assistant, then fake accountant, exclaimed as he teared open his throat.

The fake Harold Olgeby zapped back to present, as he stared down at his I.D. Card. At first, he remembered the satisfaction. Then, he glanced up of the cave hole. Nervousness overwhelmed him, and suddenly he did not feel so tough down in a damp, cold hole. His whole life felt like it existed in a hole, now closing in on him.

He mumbled gibberish, and scrambled up the rocky, cave trail. He spoke frantically, to himself," Get me out! Get me out of here!"

The rock walls seemed to move in on him. He could not breathe. The cave would not allow him to escape. The jagged edges ripped at his jacket. Just a few more feet to the snowy surface. The fake Harold Olgeby squirmed like a worm, and wiggled out of the opening of the cave.

Fake Harold Olgeby laid in the snow with relief. After a few minutes he was better. Everything started to become normal- his normal. He suffered a few scratches on his arm. He got up, checked the sled, and started his trek back to the observation building. He had it with holes and caves.

His fear and lonesome paranoia, simply disappeared. His thoughts returned to his prize fossils, and Megalonyx. All those millions of dollars to be generated. Greed and happiness filled the brain of this deranged man.

How was he going to capture the Megalonyx? Fake Harold Olgeby was thrilled with the idea of the capture. His ecstatic thoughts designed complex solutions for his snow creature project.

All those profits to be made. Profits to be earned for him, him, yes for him. Harold Olgeby hummed another old, fifties tune, as he comfortably hiked back to Helix Point.

During the morning walk in the snowy woods, he returned to his successful plot against the real Dr. Harold Olgeby. Out here, in the open air, he savored on his success to replace the good Doctor with himself.

The laboratory at Biochemical Unlimited was a mess, and bloody. Evidence was piled high against him. He did realize this.

Many weeks earlier, he befriended a middle age lady, Heidi Ump. For short he nicknamed her "Hump". She was working a Fire Toxicology Experiment. She by far was no beauty, and a thirty-something old maid. He easily romanced "Miss Hump", and broke her virginity at 35 years old.

Miss Hump was experimenting with risky flammable conditions. Although the parameters were all maintained and within safety protocol, the open chance of an accident could occur. This was a maniac, serial killer's dream come true. Create an accidental fire to burn down the building, and destroy all the diabolical evidence.

He slipped her a sedative in her coffee earlier, so she would be knocked out. Her body would be found with the fire debris, making the accident seem more realistic. "Miss Hump" would be blamed for the catastrophe. Even if, for insurance purposes, a drug test was performed, and found the tranquilizer in her barbecued cadaver, it could have been self-administered. Maybe she would be profiled as a closet addict. Alot of scientists developed addictions from working on extensive research.

The real Dr. Harold Olgeby had one big flaw. He was not much of a socializer. Hardly anyone saw him, here, in Miami Beach. He had a flight to Baltimore today, and would of left town during the fire. The fake Harold Olgeby, took the flight, and communicated to his peers over the phone concerning the Miami fire, and all the scientific stuff which was lost. In the end, the insurance company paid in full.

He could not leave the body of Doctor Harold Olgeby behind. The autopsy, even of a burnt corpse, would identify the real scientist. The fire masked all the other deliberate damage and spilled blood. This killer did what a lot of killers did in Miami. Take a boat, go out on the ocean, start a shark frenzy, and dump the body.

The deranged scientist was free to carry on as usual. He was free to carry on under a new pseudo name.

Bill, Bogey, Meet the Mad Scientist

Fake Harold Olgeby returned to the Helix Point Center. He packed the truck with all his stuff, including his prized fossils. In two hours, he was completed for his escape back to town. He was too excited to rest, but could of used a small break. He started up Mr. Conti's truck, and headed down to Cliff Drop Road.

Every now and then, he needed to veer around obstacles left from the earthquake. All in all, the road was passable. In a short time, Harold

Olgeby caught up with Bogey Wilson, and Bill Meyers at the station wagon. Everybody looked at each other with surprise, but yet felt comforted meeting other people.

The fake doctor said, "I thought I was alone. I am Dr. Harold Olgeby, a scientist from up at Helix Point.

"Earthquake? You did not yet encounter the snow creature?" Bill Meyers blurted.

So these two knew of the living fossil, thought himself.

"Creature? What creature. I was just getting the heck out of here because of that quake." Fake Harold Olgeby stated, realizing these two met up with the living fossil.

Bogey spoke up," There is a thing, a monster creature, which killed and ate people! I think my son is dead too. I feel it in my bones."

"Well, I do not know what you guys are hallucinating on, but that is a pretty wild tale. I think you two need to return to civilization, whatever is going on." he replied.

The scientist, slash serial killer, stayed in the truck while Bogey Wilson buzzed with the chainsaw, and Bill Meyers cleared the cut wood to escape from Cliff Drop Road. At first, Bill Meyers did not recognize the old truck, but felt something familiar about it. Then, he recognized the Italian flag sticker on the bumper,and seen this vehicle around town for years. Shit! The truck belonged to Susan Conti's father! It was Conti's old pick up truck.

Bill Meyers almost quickly gave away the facts. He became tight lipped, recognizing something odd about this stranger. This guy was lying. He continued working while Bogey Wilson cut an opening so a vehicle could pass.

Bogey Wilson picked up some brush while he peered at the newcomer. He wished the fellow would help them because at this point, he was exhausted. Bogey Wilson picked up their chainsaws and stuff, and placed it back on their tractor.

"C'mon, and jump in guys. I will get you out of here." he said.

Before Bogey Wilson could reply, Bill Meyers stated," That is okay. We are not going to leave the tractor here. It is not far to where we have to go. Anyway, We need to speak with Sheriff Gibbs."

"What is wrong with you," Bogey Wilson quickly commented," The tractor has a flat?"

"That is ridiculous. Get in, and I will drive you to the Police station." The stranger remarked.

Bogey Wilson, who looked like he was about to pass out, headed automatically to the truck. Bill Meyers hoped his expressions did not reveal that he knew this man was not telling the truth.

"I headed the seismology study last year, here, at the Helix Point Observation Center. Get in, and let us get all warmed up. I predicted this earthquake was coming, and was studying data this winter. However, It came sooner than I hoped for." The fake Harold Olgeby exclaimed, explaining facts about the current situation.

If Bill Meyers continued to refuse conversation, the awkwardness might reveal he knew about this guy was keeping a secret. This definitely was Mr. Conti's old, pick up truck. The two, stepped in the truck, and drove off, not knowing the exploits of the mad scientist. More introductions were made, and the threesome drove to the intersection at Route 3 .

"Oh yeah, this feels good. We on a real road, and seeing other cars, people. Yahoo!" Old Bogey Wilson shouted.

Bill Meyers sat in the middle between the two. Harold Olgeby casually drove, listening to Bogey Wilson rhetoric.

He then said, "What were you two guys doing on in the woods?"

Quickly, Bill Meyers nudged Bogey Wilson in his side, and explained," I was visiting my friend here who lives at the end of Cliff Drop Road. He sells the real good stuff, you know, pot. I wanted to purchase some prime weed for my girlfriend."

Bill Meyers suddenly became all choked up. Although his story was fake, he could not help pouting for his Suzy.

"She's dead. Ripped apart by that snow creature," Bill Meyers cried.

Bogey Wilson caught on that something was not right with Billy Boy, and acted along with the story. After comforting Bill Meyers, they regained his composure.

"The snow creature, interesting name. Kinda simple, but effective based on your story of this beast. You sure it was just not a deformed bear?" Fake Harold Olgeby spoke, trying to rationalize the creature.

"No, No, No,! This is an evil monster! Smart too! I plan to hang those creature claws over my fireplace. Well, my house burned down, but over my fireplace in my new house." Bogey Wilson spoke annoyed.

Then, out of nowhere, Bogey Wilson blurted out, "This is Phil Conti's truck, is it not?"

All went quiet. Fake Harold Olgeby turned to both of them, glanced seriously for a few seconds, and replied," Oh, you know him. My van broke down, and hey look there it is along the road."

They turned their heads towards the snow covered van as they continued on Route 3.

The imposter continued,"I offered him a nice arrangement to rent his truck for a few days. He stopped along the road, and tried to help me. He called a friend to pick him up, so I could continue my trip to Helix Point. I believe the person who brought him home was a women, his daughter, I believe her name was Susan."

The alert siren in both these country guys sounded off in their heads. Susan Conti was with them the whole time. Bogey Wilson and Bill Meyers made sudden eye contact, and both recognized the concern at hand. How they wished they were already at the Sheriff's Office in Tannersville. Something stranger than the snow creature arrived with this stranger. What was this Harold Olgeby's angle?

Bill Meyers knew to be quiet for the rest of the ride, and waited for an explanation when they reached the sheriff's office.

Bill Meyers started bodily twitching again as his nerves entered overdrive. Fake Harold Olgeby noticed the shaking, but related it to the shocking encounter.

"Are you okay? You are shaking crazy like my seismograph equipment." The mad scientist said, and observed.

Bill Meyers answered," What, are you cold-hearted. I just lost people to a savage beast attack. My brother, my kid brother gone. Dead at thirteen!"

Fake Harold Olgeby realized it was a stupid question on his part. They witnessed a carnivorous prehistoric sloth. A type of Megalonyx which probably awoke from the Pleistocene era. What crazy odds existed for this event. A missing link, which nobody knew even existed.

The mad scientist had concerns, and now, played his card game. He played a new hand to see which cards these fellows held. Could he trust these guys? No killing for now.

The Mighty Caveman or Boy

Mr. Conti peered up from his falling predicament, and realized there was no way to escape through the above opening. Even if he could climb out, his body moved with difficulty, and could not walk very far. His ankle did not seem broken, but no weighted pressure could be placed on it. He constantly badgered himself for being such a fool.

He pulled himself with his good arm towards the back end of the cavern. His dislocated shoulder ached immensely as he crawled over the cold, cave bottom. Once a person has a dislocated shoulder, like Mr. Conti's history did, the bone will pop out of the socket easier on the next physical accident.

He grabbed the flashlight which fake Harold Olgeby dropped earlier. He propped himself against the cave wall, and drank some whiskey. The flask was one third full. The backpack was not very essential to assist him in his dilemma. An extra T-shirt was packed, a whiskey flask, a old pair of back up gloves with holes, a small water bottle, three candy bars, and a small knife. He cut up the shirt with the knife, and tied pieces of fabric around his ankle for support.

"Caving can be dangerous". He murmured, remembering this line from Professor Bates, during his senior year of High School. Mr. Conti signed up for an extra-curriculum club- Caving. This area owned many cave sites, and this hobby was quite popular.

The general safety tips came to his mind as he sat in the rubble of the cave floor :

1) Never cave alone.

2) 4 cavers minimum in team.

3) One injured, one stays as other two go for help.

4) Always pack three flashlights, or light sources.

5) Quiet vocals- vibrations set loose rock/debris.

6) Space blanket for hypothermia

7) Cave Accidents were "Killers of the Unprepared".

This last thought, he remembered well. Not only was he unprepared, he did not expect to be thrown into a unknown cave. Mr, Conti kept checking his body for fresh blood. He feared that he would bleed out and die. Then, no one would know his whereabouts.

Mr. Conti wondered about the wild boy, which fake Harold Olgeby mentioned. He glanced around, down the cave tunnel, to see if the kid stuck around.

"I know you are still here! Come out! I need help. I need a doctor. Let us go back to town before that thing kills and eats us." Mr. Conti loudly remarked.

There existed no sound, and Mr. Conti hoped the wild boy was lingering, observing him from the dark tunnel. No evidence presented itself that any living thing was present, not even the snow creature. His hunting/tracking skills were excellent, and he felt confident nothing shared the cave with him. He wished though his notions were incorrect. Again, he listened in to the silence as he called out for the wild boy. Nothing.

He felt alone, and swallowed more of the alcohol. Suddenly faint footsteps, ever so lightly, broke the drowning silence. There stood a teenager, wearing a beat up blue parka, holding a pointed wooden stick.

Mr. Conti said,"You are pretty quiet. I really thought I was here alone. It takes patience and skill to hide in perfection. You are a hunter ? Have you R.O.T.C training?"

"No, I am The Mighty Caveman." Kyle Meyers replied.

"Okay. That makes sense." Mr. Conti answered back, and worried that this kid shared mentally instability just like fake Harold Olgeby.

Maybe the boy had altercations with the snow creature, and lost somebody he was with. He could be suffering from shock. He hoped the pointed stick was for show.

"What are you doing here?" Mr. Conti asked.

Kyle Meyers said,"That is a long tale. I am going to kill that beast. I saved my brother's life by distracting it away into the woods. I simply climbed up a rocky ledge, and the snow creature lost interest in me. I secretly followed it to this cave. I believe this is its home, its hideout. Down this tunnel is a opening to the forest. I recognize you from town. You are Suzy's father, but I do not know your name?"

"My name is Phil."

Kyle tried to lift Mr. Conti up, but he yelled in pain. Mr. Conti acted cautious, not aware of the true intentions of this kid. He contemplated of the many possibilities to escape out of the cave. He needed this wild boy, and was forced to trust him.

Mr. Conti's sensed a good aura from the boy, but was not familiar with him from the neighborhood. It did not seem so hopeless, and he could be his ticket out to safety. His premonition of inner sight, gave no signal about his "Mighty Caveman" routine. The exhausted Mr. Conti felt relaxed, and calmed with this superhero meeting.

Kyle Meyers asked, "What happened to your friend?"

Mr. Conti replied, "Well that is a long tale as well. He turned out not to be a friend. His name is, I thought, Harold Olgeby. Why did you attack him earlier, Caveman?"

"It was dark, and I was unaware of who or what lurked there. I attacked before it attacked me. That is 'The Mighty Caveman" way." The teenager replied with assurance.

"Well, that turned out to be a pretty smart move. That man is a deranged killer." Mr. Conti spoke more comfortably now with the kid.

Kyle Meyers said, "You are not going anywhere. I can go for help Phil, but that may take awhile, maybe a whole extra day. The snow creature may return at any time. Come, let me help you. I have a place you can hide yourself against the creature, while I go back to town."

"The Mighty Caveman" pulled him down the cave-like corridor. When they stopped, he pointed upwards with the flashlight. A small opening was seen above the outcrops. Mr. Conti trusted him, however, still questioned his well being.

Kyle Meyers said, "This is my cave. You will be safe in there. Try to pull yourself up, and at the same time, I will aid you. The ledge at first is steep, but becomes a more gradual rise at the top."

The hole was no more than 3 feet wide, and narrow. Mr Conti overcame with claustrophobia.

"I cannot fit through there. I will die in there." Mr. Conti replied.

"No. It is quite comfortable. C'mon, let us go in before it is too late. That beast is very unpredictable. I have not figured out its routine yet." The teeneger positively commented.

Mr. Conti pushed and followed behind Kyle Meyers. The inside was a lot larger than it appeared from the other side.

As they settled down, Mr. Conti said," Why "The Mighty Caveman"? Should it not be the "Mighty Cave Boy"?"

Kyle Meyers frowned when he heard this remark. Once again, another flaw was discovered in his super hero character.

"I am a man, not a boy! Anyway, I want to be a man." He stammered.

Mr. Conti stopped questioning this young man's motives. He was stuck in this confined cave, and did not want him going berserk. He grabbed one of his candy bars, and gave one to Kyle. This small cave offered protection against the beast. However, if it broke in- game over. There was no escape route.

For now, Mr. Conti had no other choices. Hopefully, he would bring back help, and maybe then, the kid would know what his title name should be. As far as Mr. Conti was concerned, the kid was "The Mighty Cave Whoever."

Kyle Meyers said, "I need to rest a bit. Let me shut my eyes, and then I will go. It is already past lunch time. I have no idea when I can return. It may be already dark, and that would be dangerous. I might have to wait for the morning. We may need a hunting party for assistance.

"By the way, your snow creature is formally named Megalonyx. At least that kook, pseudo scientist claimed it to be officially called. Some prehistoric species awakening from its slumber." Mr. Conti replied to straighten out the surreal facts of the whacky events.

With these final words both became sleepy, and dozed off. Mr. Conti heard words turn into mumblings, and blacked out. Kyle decided to hike back to town after a short nap. Wasting more time was not an option.

When Mr. Conti awoke, he laid in the dark, and felt the flashlight in his hand. He turned it on, and realized he was alone. He hoped the kid was sane enough to pull off his escape, and not forget him. Maybe some screwball teenager, who believed in super heroes, was the solution to the problem.

Mr. Conti was experienced with his dislocated shoulder. It happened many times. He needed to stand, grasp onto a rocky outcrop, push, turn, and pull. With luck, the shoulder joint would pop back properly into its socket. This would alleviate much of the pain.

Mr. Conti attempted this move twice, and only hurt himself more. It was difficult to stand on one leg, and stabilize his body to adjust the dislocated shoulder. He could of had the kid assist him with his shoulder. He tried one last time. Instead, his body slipped, and fell onto jutting rocks. The pain reached a ten plus level, and he screamed at the top of his lungs.

The ill calculated fall, however, actually popped the ball and socket joint together. Sudden relief followed the acute pain. He felt some relief. Stiff pains still shot in his shoulder, but much less than before. He had one remaining candy bar, and decided to eat it. That boy better return or he was finished. The chances of anyone from town coming out here, especially after an earthquake would be next to nothing. Even if his daughter heard the message that he stayed at Helix Point, this cavern was distant from the observation building.

Mr. Phil Conti then passed out again.

CHAPTER 6

Thee Sheriff Gibbs

THE POLICE STATION FILLED with loud comments, and confusion.

"Hunt it down!"

"It must be destroyed!"

"Capture it, put into a cage, to be gawked at!"

"Blow it up!"

"It killed my girlfriend, and ate her!"

"Death to the snow creature!"

Thee Sheriff Gibbs yelled at everyone to shut up. His police station was in disarray. Everyone just hollered back at him. The disrespect to the sheriff was bringing on friction, and turmoil to his fashionable ways. The commotion was becoming louder. Thee Sheriff Gibbs whipped out his revolver, and sent a bullet into the ceiling. He always wanted to do that.

Thee Sheriff Gibbs exclaimed, "Well, now that I have all of your attention. Shut up! Shut up, and shut up! What is all this crazy talk of monsters, and people becoming eaten. This is a bad joke, and I am not laughing today. Today, is the opening of Winterfest at the Ridgewood ski resort."

"It has large claws, and fangs, it will slice you in half!" Bogey Wilson rattled on and on.

"And I have a large stick to stick up your ass. You, you be quiet before I throw cuffs on you!" Thee Sheriff Gibbs remarked who despised Bogey.

He jailed him for his illegal moonshine many times. Mayor Jackson loved his brew which kept the old timer out of lock up.

"It is true. You all know me from the diner, and family in town. I, Bill Meyers, witnessed a creature never seen before. And a mean, nasty giant it appears to be."

"It is a bear, right?" Thee Sheriff Gibbs obviously stated.

Bogey Wilson answered "No, not at all. The scientist here claims it is called Megalonyx."

"A Megaloo...what? The sheriff replied with a confused face.

"Megalonyx," Fake Harold Olgeby jumped in. " Based on their description,and fossils found in this area. A type of prehistoric mammal." He played neutral, but helpful, like the Professor on Gilligan's Island.

"Right, okay, we are going down this road? It is story telling time? It is a bear. Probably one of those deformed black bears that show up time to time. There exists deranged people, so once in awhile you will have a black bear gone mental."

Bill Meyers stated," It is all white in fur."

The sheriff stated,"Right, a deformed bear. This bruin most likely has discoloration, exceptional long nails, and you guys are exaggerating. You all got scared like a bunch of girls, making up spooky tales. Maybe on purpose!"

Everyone continued to spin their tales, and debate. The volume remained loud in the police station. The secretary, Melanie Cuttles, listened with Frank Porter, the local newsman, who both were about to take lunch. Frank Porter recently took up an interest in Melanie Cuttles, and this was there second lunch date. He definitely listened as a story developed in his little town.

Frank Porter interjected, "Sheriff, let us go to Cliff Drop Road, and find Todd Bloomfield's truck, body, or whatever. Let us see if Suzy Conti is around town." Frank Porter entered the heated discussion.

Thee Sheriff Gibbs said,"Bodies? Listen Franky, you do not write stories of craziness, and half-eaten bodies in Tannersville. If there are dead ones out by Cliff Drop Road, it probably is related to Bogey Wilson's illegal contraband business."

"I never killed anyone," Bogey Wilson replied, and took a swig out of a bottle he found in the bottom drawer of the sheriff's desk.

"Give me that back you boozer!" Thee Sheriff Gibbs yelled. He snatched his hooch bottle, and slapped Bogey Wilson across the back of his head.

Bogey Wilson grabbed his stomach quickly, as the alcohol, including the all night drinking, triggered hunger pains. He was starving. In a corner, a bunch of burritos, left over nachos, and cheesy bean soup, were found on a table. He immediately unwrapped a burrito, and shoved it in his mouth. He sloppily grabbed a second burrito, followed by a hand full of nachos.

Thee Sheriff Gibbs exclaimed,"Do not eat that! That Mexican take-out has been sitting there since lunch time yesterday," exclaimed the sheriff. "Those left overs are from Deputy Wilcox's birthday party."

Bogey Wilson with a mouthful, muffled," Good, it is good." The others were hungry as well, but refused to chance it. A cockroach peeked out from the nachos and scampered over the chips.

The phone rang, and the sheriff answered it with disgust. Thee Sheriff Gibbs was a tall, skinny man, whose reddish cheeks reflected someone who enjoyed a drink at the end of the day. He always looked like a man suffering from an ulcer, and maybe did in real life. He owned notable wavy, salt and pepper hair. A sheriff's hat never was to seen on his head for reasons unknown. Sheriff Gibbs hung up the phone with continued disgust, and scribbled onto a note pad.

His town reflected a law abiding society. He enforced ways which were founded on a simple, narrow minded process. There was a "Thee" in front of his name for a reason- a pompous reputation of peace keeping and domestic harmony. A peaceful harmony demanded by his price. Thee Sheriff Gibbs was from a long line of Gibbs, dating back to the plantation south. Nothing changed around here on his watch.

"Alright, alright, I need your attention." The sheriff spoke still with disgust. "Well, That was Miss Queenie on the phone, that old hag out on Millens street. She claims something killed her cow."

Miss Queenie made complaints twice a month about everything. The sheriff decided to take out the police van, and bring this bunch with him. Maybe her dead cow connected with this alleged snow creature, probably deformed bear, or "Megaloowhat".

On the walk out Bill Meyers spoke, changing the topic," Sheriff, there is something odd with Harold Olgeby's story. My Suzy is dead and eaten by the snow creature. I refused to believe this guy's tale that he met her with her father. This Olgeby scientist is lying, using a cover up story. Suzy Conti was searching for her dad all afternoon, and..."

Thee Sheriff Gibbs stood on the sidewalk, as Deputy Collins drove up the police van. The sheriff pulled away from the lackluster conversation with Bill Meyers, and gathered the group.

To everyone, he exclaimed, "Listen, once again, I will say for the last time, shut up about monsters, and people used for supper. And you, save it kid! Bill, you always were peculiar. What, do people have to spell it out for you! Stop trying to get attention for yourself! I doubt Suzy Conti would be seen with you anyway. Also, you address me as Thee Sheriff Gibbs. Got it?"

That hurt. Bill Meyers became silent, and sneered over his back at the scientist with a look of contentment. Fake Harold Olgeby shrugged his shoulders innocent-like, and stared pitiful at Bill Meyers. He needed to eliminate this kid soon.

"I want to go too," Melanie Cuttles shouted from the doorway with excitement in her voice.

"Who is going to man the station, or err, people person the police office" The sheriff said. In the past, some chauvinistic statements landed him in controversy.

"Nothing ever happens in little ol' Tannersville," Melanie Cuttles cutely responded.

Melanie Cuttles, was one of the more attractive thirty something women in town. The sheriff tried to date her in the past with no avail. He still longed for her, and did not like Frank Porter coming into his headquarters and court her. In his continuing disgust, he agreed for everyone to come, even the newsman, Frank Porter. The sheriff signed out the van. The anxious group got ready to head out to Miss Queenie's farm.

Thee Sheriff Gibbs said, "Deputy Collins, hold down the fort. Our hard working clerk wants to do some field work."

The deputy threw the keys to the sheriff who immediately flung them at Frank Porter. The newsman was not ready, as the keys hit his stomach, and fell to the pavement.

"You gotta work on faster reflexes with a projectile flying at ya. Pick up the keys, you drive Frank, I got to think," the sheriff blurted.

Frank Porter drove the police van with the sheriff riding shotgun. In the second seat, sat Bill Meyers with Melanie Cuttles. In the rear, third seat of the van, sat Bogey Wilson, and fake Harold Olgeby.

Melanie Cuttles disliked the smell of Bogey Wilson, and made sure she did not sit next to him. Frank Porter could not help noticing how pretty Melanie Cuttles looked in the rear view mirror. Melanie added the spark he needed to reignite life. He spent his life, quiet, and conservative. That probably were some of the reasons his wife divorced him. She literally took off with the postman. He was not going to screw this up. He decided to act more adventurous and spontaneous with Melanie Cuttles.

Luscious blond hair illuminated her already appealing face. Her clear, smooth skin, perfect size nose, and cute dimples every time she smiled, allured all in her social circles- both men and women. She spent two to fours hours every other day at the gym. Joe Mepp's business increased with male membership because the patrons exercised to leer at her. She was not a brainiac, but knew the men in the room were always checking her out. It improved her physical stamina while squatting, bending over, and attempting leg lifts.

Melanie Cuttles was pretty, and most admired her sex appeal. When she was a seventeen year old girl, she gained a baby boy, and lost the father. Her good looks were just that, as men desired her, but did not want the child baggage. Her beauty was a curse, because the men only fantasized about physical love, and not to share her family.

Now in her mid thirties, she was definitely not getting any younger. Frank Porter could be her ticket to a stable life. She admitted to herself, she just liked him, but had no real loving affection for the mild-acting reporter.

As the police van pulled into Miss Queenie's farm, one quickly noticed the red blotch out on the field where her dead cow laid- poor, sweet Anabelle. Miss Queenie stood at the edge of her barn holding a shotgun. She, like many, experienced tough times, and a dead, milking cow added to her financial problems.

As the van stopped, Bogey Wilson complained about his stomach. The sheriff yelled at him. He explicitly told him that the Mexican food was outdated. All Thee Sheriff gibbs needed now was a sick passenger.

Miss Queenie waited for the sheriff to walk over to her.

She immediately said,"My Anabelle is sliced open like a butcher busy during the holidays. Something took her brains like a crazed zombie."

Miss Queenie spit out some chewing tobacco.

"Okay, I will take a look and see what is going on," the sheriff spoke politely, even though he hated every inch of her.

Thee Sheriff Gibbs, Bill Meyers, Frank Porter, and fake Harold Olgeby, headed out onto the field to examine the cow. Bogey Wilson stayed back with the ladies because he felt sick, light headed, and well, extremely terrified of the beast.

Frank Porter snapped away with his camera. A bloody mess was left, but it did not seem possible by a person. It looked like a wild animal teared up Anabelle.

"It is a bear," confidently the sheriff remarked.

The mad scientist picked up tufts of white hair, and remarked," Is this from a black bear?"

"Yeah, like I already said, an unusual black bear with white fur." The sheriff replied.

"How about those strange tracks. What bear leaves shoveled tracks. I do not see one bear track in the snow," Bill Meyers added to their investigation.

Thee Sheriff Gibbs remarked,"An aggressive bear shuffling off with some of its kill. Oh, you think it was a prehistoric dinosaur, a Godzilla, here in our Appalachian hills. There is no "Megaloowhat."

The sheriff spoke confidently and sarcastically.

"This was done by the snow creature," Bill Meyers said positively.

"It is a type of Megalonyx, a large ground sloth with great claws,"- Fake Harold Olgeby corrected the annoying young man, who topped his death list.

"That is enough. This is a black bear kill. " the sheriff said, and headed back to the police van, with the others following.

Frank Porter checked the skull with the missing brain, and took a few more pictures. His investigation skills were stuck in neutral. He favored the sheriff's conclusion. A bear made sense. Monsters, and unknown creatures lacked common sense. The scientist even stated that these ground sloths were plant-eating in prehistoric times. This one killed indiscriminately. One could easily be sucked into believing fascinating tales, because people desire to believe in such monstrosities.

"You lucky the snow creature did not slice you up out there," Bogey Wilson nervously replied.

"What you talking about, you old coot," Miss Queenie asked.

"The creature which attacked your Anabelle. It has sharp fangs and long claws to cut you in two." Bogey Wilson continued saying.

Miss Queenie retaliated, "Oh shut up you moran! Anabelle death is the work of a rogue bear."

"Thanks Queenie, that is the smartest thing you said all year," replied the sheriff. He finally was thankful someone agreed with him. He headed to the van to call in for a hunting squad. For such a special crisis, he relied on his buddies from the Boone and Crockett Hunting Club.

Thee Sheriff Gibbs pulled Frank Porter over to the side, and said, "Listen, you are a level headed man. I do not need crazy stories in the paper upsetting the town. Work with me, till we have more information. A tale like a snow creature, a "Megaloowhat", will simply make a mockery of our baptist community."

"Some of us are religious protestants", remarked Frank Porter.

"You know what I mean. I still think those kids are alive. This will all be, by tomorrow, one big joke. I bet those kids are sitting right now at the Tannersville Bar and Grille. This is one, big joke!" The sheriff replied.

Upon finishing the words, big joke, a large crash echoed across the open field. A small pine tree came crashing down. The whole group standing near the van noticed a snow mound speeding over the snow in the direction of the dead cow. The newcomers attention was drawn in awe at the site. The others knew the snow creature came back for seconds. The sheriff looked on with puzzlement.

They also noticed that Miss Queenie headed out to her dead Anabelle with a small sled of butcher items. While the bunch argued, she carried her utensils to cut up some steaks. The poor, old women could not waste all that meat. She savored on many roadkill meals. She sliced around the bite marks, and threw the tainted pieces to the side. Grabbing her small ax, she hacked away at the open ribcage. She whistled while she worked without a care in the world.

Everyone screamed for her to turn around, that the beast was coming.

Bill Meyers yelled," Stay still! Do not move! The "Megaloowhat", uh the snow creature is coming for you!"

She heard the bunch hollering but could not make sense of the words. Miss Queenie noticed them pointing behind her.

She saw nothing. The air was crisp, and the sky was blue. No sound could be heard, and no wind at all. Actually, it turned out to be a nice wintry day with the bright sun shining away. Miss Queenie wondered what was all the commotion about. She always cooked road kill well done in case of germs, or disease. And this was not road kill, but some animal who attacked her cow a few hours ago in freezing temperatures. This meat was extra safe.

Then she noticed the displaced snow leading to her dead Anabelle. Miss Queenie peered down while she heard a faint scraping noise. The snow shook near the ripped open ribcage. She concentrated on the movement below her, but the others aggravated her with all that yelling. Again, that scraping noise continued, and then cracking, like something biting on bone. Somebody or something joined her to share Anabelle.

Before another thought entered her mind, snow splashed with a brown shadow in front of her face. Her instinct swung her hand ax. Miss Queenie let out a half laugh/yell as she stood proudly, stumbling only so lightly.

Miss Queenie shouted,"Look a here you all! I nabbed a red fox smack in the head with my ax. One shot, one kill. The whole town will talk of the time Miss Queenie took out a fox with her handy ax with one whack!"

She quickly noticed that nobody cared about her fox, and the sheriff was heading towards her with his handgun drawn. She wondered what the heck was going on. Again everyone pointed in the direction behind her.

Then, she smelled a crappy animal odor different than her cow. She caught the whiff before when she first investigated Anabelle, but assumed it came from the dead cow. She lived on a farm her whole life, and became tolerant of animal stink. But this was smelly different.

A low, yet deep tone rumbled at her feet. Miss Queenie spun quickly around, but again saw nothing but the displace snow at her feet. A putrid odor mingled and grew in her nose smells. Next the mammoth beast rose up in front of her, towering over her frail, old body.

In an accurate motion, the snow creature scooped out her brains with one claw. The delicate usage of the huge pincers, ripped out Miss Queenie's brain, and kept most of her bloody head intact to her body. The organ morsel was chucked into its mouth with one satisfying gulp. No tearing or chewing was required. Lately, the snow creature hankered the taste of fresh brain. Wasting no meat, it clutched Miss Queenie's body and disappeared under the snow.

Everyone scrambled for the van. Pandemonium set in. The sheriff clipped off a few shots at the "Megaloowhat". Then he too, rushed for the van. Helplessness and fear filled the group, pushing and shoving into the vehicle.

Melanie Cuttles stopped at the middle van door, and exclaimed," This is not the right seating arrangement. This is not the right seating arrangement! I am not sitting next to old Bogey Wilson! This is not the right seating arrangement!"

The sheriff hearing her ridiculous remark, shouted, "Get in stupid ! Who cares where the hell you sit!"

Nothing could of pissed off the sheriff more than a stuck up remark by some high maintenance woman, and a snow creature eating people. He grabbed her shapely rear end, and shoved her back into the third seat. The others pushed behind the sheriff trying to enter the safety of the van. He stumbled into the back, the third seat, and laid awkwardly on top of Melanie Cuttles.

Thee Sheriff Gibbs could not position himself to sit up. The van abruptly started which made the matter worse. The bumping back and forth irritated Melanie Cuttles while the body of the sheriff clumsily laid on top of her.

Frank Porter drove the vehicle in panic with Bill Meyers yelling,"Your are gonna crash, you are gonna crash!"

Melanie Cuttles was yelling," You did this on purpose, you did this on purpose! You pervert, you pervert!"

The sheriff squirmed as he moved his head back and forth. Her breast laid beneath his chin, and with all his rubbing, unclasped her bra. Melanie's beauties flopped right into his face. He needed a plan, and he needed a plan fast. Her cushions helped relieve his uncomfortably position, but increased hers. Melanie Cuttles kept cursing him of foul play, and how he planned this for years. Her one free hand whacked him on his back. Old Bogey Wilson peered behind from the second seat, and thought this was not the time for roughhousing.

The sheriff quickly thought of a bright yet risky move to help him sit upright. His next action would definitely violate an amiable relationship he had or would not have with Melanie Cuttles. He pulled his arm underneath him, and placed his hand on her private mound area. The sheriff pushed himself up, off the screaming Melanie Cuttles. His clumsy fingers ripped her sheer panties, and designer skirt. Melanie Cuttles's eyes popped from their sockets as she felt his fingers invade her private area.

Standing in a half position on the third seat, she swung her fists rapidly all over the sheriff's body. He sat next to her, attempting to block all her shots as he peered out the window for the snow creature. The van swerved back and forth as they headed out Miss Queenie's driveway.

Megalonyx abruptly appeared, smack in front of the van's windshield. The two massive claws rammed into the front grill. The van abruptly stopped with Melanie Cuttles flying into the second seat. During her airborne journey, her damaged top, panties and whole disrupted ensemble, ripped off. Melanie Cuttles fell into the laps of Bogey Wilson, and fake Harold Olgeby, stark naked.

The men, suffering from fear and dread of the approaching beast, could not help to take a moment and appreciate the beauty of a naked women.

A sudden thump with Miss Queenie's teared up body, plopped on the front windshield. The snow creature flung the corpse at the van with contempt and intimidation. Her face smashed and disfigured, smeared against the window.

Bogey Wilson was confused and felt sick. Below, he peered at a gorgeous female body, and in front, a bloody torso missing one leg. Everyone screamed at Miss Queenie's half-exposed skull and one dangling eyeball.

"Stop staring at me!" Melanie Cuttles embarrassed, and yelled. "Stop it, look away you louse!"

"I cannot. I cannot look up, up at dead Miss Queenie. I sick, I am going to be sick. I need to look down at you." Bogey Wilson whimpered like a dog.

She nastily remarked, " How dare you, you pig! You louse, close your eyes, close your eyes!".

He answered, " I cannot do that either. If I close my eyes, I get dizzy, and things start spinning. Please, do not make me look up!"

Bogey Wilson had a complex problem. Melanie Cuttles pushed his face away with her hand. He stared forward, and zeroed in on the mouth of Miss Queenie, with the red ooze creeping down the windshield. He could not look away, as if his mind was in a sick hypnosis. The Mexican food knotted up his stomach like a tight ball. He predicted the following events.

Melanie Cuttles noticed his skin color became lighter. She also could predict the next events. She yelled "Do not dare. Open the window!"

With a melancholy tone, Bogey Wilson casually said," These van windows do not open. I am sorry."

With that, he puked over her nakedness. Her beautiful body was now chunked up with pieces of semi-eaten Mexican food. He definitely ate too fast. The vomit stink filled the inside the van quickly.

Fake Harold Olgeby sat in crisis. He held the female leg parts. He tolerated the vomit, the smell, and her exposed areas below. Melanie Cuttles wiggled, and spread her legs open. Usually, a women's vulva would be a turn on, but the descriptive area of this body part, simulated the descriptive look of the half-eaten burritos.

He grabbed a hand cloth from his pocket, and put it over his nose and mouth. Fake Harold Olgeby closed his eyes, and this worked for him awhile. The sick feelings were better controlled, but he could not help thinking about vomit and oral sex, simultaneously. He, at least, puked to the side.

Frank Porter kept shifting the gears to forward, and reverse. The frantic group were stuck in the van as the snow creature remained anchored on the front bumper. He then only geared in reverse and continued to floor the pedal. The tug of war matched at a stand still. The creature grumbled and grunted, because the weight of the reversing van slowly outmatched its brutal strength.

The bumper became dislodged as the van spun in a semi-circle down Miss Queenie's driveway. The snow creature tumbled backwards still clawing the broken bumper in a goofy head over feet, feet over head roll. The van kicked backwards suddenly, and Frank Porter stomped on the brakes.

Bill Meyers yelled," Go! Move now!" He planted his foot over Frank Porter's foot on the gas pedal. They rushed passed the shaken up creature onto Millen's road.

Megalonyx expressed a ghastly, pissed off grin with its flesh ridden teeth. Even with fangs and all, intelligence surfaced from its demeanor. It stared at the fleeing van as Bill Meyers stared back. It looked annoyed, but not like an animal seeking food. It lusted for revenge. Its aggression ranked high as well as loathing for victory. Bill Meyers peered at a beast which never excepted loss of battle.

The snow creature flung the wrecked bumper at them. It landed with a bang on top of the van, denting the roof. From the windshield. Miss Queenie's body fell off, and laid alongside like roadkill. No one will probably go back to find her. Somehow there existed irony in the natural cycle where she now contributed to the crows and coyotes.

The drive on Millens road seemed longer. The van raced with a greater speed than before. It took forever to reach Rte 3. They all looked ahead at the intersection which never was reached. Witnessing actual cars driving on Rte 3, relieved their fright. Anxious to drive on the highway, Frank Porter pushed the speed limit. This probably was not such a good idea, since the reporter was not a great driver. The van kept sliding, swerving into plowed snow banks along the roadside.

Bogey Wilson stared out the window searching for the snow creature. The beast hustled parallel with its head turned at them. It's whole body was above ground, moving swiftly. With the claws faced inward, the thick front arms lunged forward, and then under it's body. The muscular, clawed arms pulled the snow creature forward, producing an efficient stride. The smaller back legs coincided with the motion of the front, and the beast sped next to the van. The versatile abilities of Megalonyx were inspiring. These actions were quite the opposite of the slow moving, South American sloth.

It still turned it's head to them following with an incredible chase. Before Bogey Wilson could let out a warning, one huge pincer claw sliced into the side of the van, ripping it open like a metal can. Everyone watched helplessly as the tip of the claw sliced cleanly down inside the van. It barely missed Bill Meyers up front, but as it streamlined to the second seat, it cut cleanly through Melanie Cuttles upper arm. This was definitely not her day.

Melanie Cuttles was not aware of the bloody slash, but screamed in pain. Blood gushed over her naked body, now mixing with the pasty vomit. The penetrating claw zinged past the sheriff in the third seat with stuffing from the seat exploding all over him. The back wheel became dislodged from the van sending into a small tumble. The van smacked into a snow pile, which a bulldozer previously shoveled together at the intersection of Rte. 3.

That snow pile blocked them from skidding onto the moving cars. Everyone crawled out of the destroyed van, All were glad to be alive.

A worker on top of the bulldozer yelled," Hey, you okay!? What are you blind, you did not see the huge pile of snow?" No one responded to the highway man, but checked each other for injuries.

The gentleman, volunteer medic, the all around good guy who turned mental, Bill Meyers quickly ripped a piece of his shirt off . He wrapped Melanie's cut arm. The sheriff cloaked his police jacket over her shoulders. Realizing it was the sheriff's jacket, Melanie Cuttles whipped it off into his face.

Frank Porter swiftly put his long coat over her naked, gastric/ bloody body to regain her self- respect. Bill Meyers contemplated to offer his new leather jacket, but it was saved for his love, "Slutty Suzy".

Bill Meyers shouted," The highway, the paved road! It will protect us from the snow creature."

At different speeds, they all hustled out onto Rte, 3. The passerby cars looked upon them strangely, but no one actually stopped. They all stood helpless with mixed emotions, still searching for an attack by the dreaded beast.

The highway worker stepped off his bulldozer and walked near Rte. 3. He stared in awe as the beaten up group huddled out at the double yellow line. He just could not comprehend what was happening.

The highway guy exclaimed,"You all are going to get run over! Step off the road before you get killed."

Before a another word could be spoken, he became absorbed into the snow creature's moving snowball. Behind the killing mound, trailed pinkish snow. Bill Meyers realized that he forgot to warn the highway guy about the snow creature. Then again, he doubted he would fool-ishly walk into moving traffic anyway.

The sheriff pulled out his badge and hailed down an upcoming car.

He exclaimed, "I need to commandeer your vehicle. We have a state of emergency,"

Everyone cramped into the automobile. The driver sat spellbound. Frank Porter realized Bill Meyers was unaccounted for. Everyone could care less, and were just happy they were alive.

In front of them, the exit for Winterfest was all jammed up. They all thought the same scenario. The snow creature has a buffet at the festival awaiting it. The sheriff yapped on his walkie talkie. Harold Olgeby contemplated his next move. Bogey Wilson sat whimpering to himself. In his thoughts, Frank Porter concluded that this Megalonyx does exist. Bill Meyers was absent who never entered the car. Melanie Cuttles, the unfortunate Melanie Cuttles, was really having a bad day.

Thee Sheriff Gibbs said, "Let's head to the Winterfest, Mr. uh, what is your name?"

"Ed Mousy". He replied.

He was a local contractor meeting some friends at the festival heading in that direction.

Sheriff Gibbs commanded Ed Mousy to drive along the shoulder to the main entrance, circumventing the traffic. At the gate, the sheriff flashed his badge, and quickly explained the emergency. They headed to the front door of the lodge taking a service road not permitted for the public

"Let us get Melanie to First Aid. She needs medical attention." Frank Porter replied the obvious with deep concern.

He immediately assisted Melanie Cuttles to the front door as a man with a wheelchair came rushing out. The crew at the main gate radioed ahead to First Aid.

Thee Sheriff Gibbs noticed the surprised looks people showed at the bloody women. This concern demanded a remedial plan quickly. A monstrous beast creating havoc in Tannersville was unacceptable. The sheriff called experienced hunters he trusted, and planned to meet them at Winterfest in the next hour. The Boone and Crockett Hunting Club were the best of the best.

As Melanie Cuttles passed the sheriff, she spoke in a half cry/disgust," You' re terrible! Your a filthy animal. I hope everyone hears what you did to me back in town."

He felt bad for her, but also could care less. This snow creature created this nightmare. Thee Sheriff Gibbs only wished he could of erotically ripped off her clothes as consenting adults.

Frank Porter accompanied her, and the sheriff yelled out," Hey you, Franky! Let us keep a lid on this until a sound plan is hashed out. We need to stop this thing. I mean it. We need to be as hush hush as possible."

Frank Porter glanced over his shoulder with feelings of you know what that means. The truth will be altered for the public knowledge. No headlines will be printed without the sheriff's control. Frank Porter already mentally outlined this incredible, as well as unbelievable event, with or without official approval.

The fake Harold Olgeby nonchalantly meandered over to the sheriff. Time prevailed for him to present his pitch to protect his interests. Thee Sheriff Gibbs was the man to side with, and he knew it. He offered the him a hot cup of coffee, and both sat at the snack bar.

No one spoke for minutes. Thoughts were collected, and emotions searched for realities. Both men glanced casually at the busy cafeteria to keep their minds off the bloodshed.

The mad scientist started with," We need to capture it."

"What? We need to eliminate it. We need to secretly make this abomination magically disappear."The sheriff spoke matter of frankly.

Fake Harold Olgeby said,"Well, keeping this matter hush hush, as you said earlier, won't help pay the bills. Money, real money, could be profited by caging this phenomenal species. Curious onlookers will pay plenty to witness this creature. Again, we need to capture it."

The sheriff thought for a second, but returned in mind and body to his initial attitude. He refused to allow these tragic events to become public. Nothing would turn his nice peaceful town into a cheap, circus sideshow.

"I already called the best trackers in my county. They received orders to kill it, chop it up, and bury it. Maybe set it on fire." The sheriff remarked.

"Sheriff, Thee Sheriff Gibbs, you are making an unfortunate mistake. This will be the find of the century. A living missing link, will help answer questions about our evolution, and unaccountable scientific inquiries. You and I could become very rich." Fake Harold Olgeby replied.

The sheriff remarked,"You and I will be parting ways in a few days, and everything will be back to normal, my normal."

"But how will you explain all the killings, and missing bodies. Accuse me for my boldness, but some of the victims have been eaten,or at least partially devoured." Fake Harold Olgeby commented.

Thee Sheriff Gibbs commanded, "I can take care of the bloody business at hand. You need not to bother yourself with the details. Go back to your University."

The sheriff's seriousness changed with understanding to help this Harold Olgeby comply.

"Listen, I relate to the scientific community's concern with such a find. But, in the long haul, nothing good will come out for us in Tannersville. We have fine, local culture, and I plan to keep it this way. Freaky monster stories adds to making our a town the butt end of a trashy joke."

"You need to reconsider. Maybe, if we can feasibly catch it alive, we secretly could examine it. The Feds probably follow your line of thinking, and would want to keep this story out of the press. The government love to cover up stuff like this, when it happens. We still could make a handsome dollar with the Feds." The mad scientist hashed out his plan.

"Well, maybe I will consider it. But bringing in the Feds welcomes unwanted trouble. They are always messing around in everyone's business. By the way, how the heck did this thing survive all these hundreds of years?" The sheriff asked.

Fake Harold Olgeby said, "A good question, and that is thousands. All the more reason to capture and examine it. I believe this Megalonyx adapted to ice age conditions. The cold environment was its home. It may possess antifreeze type blood, and enter a deep sleep. Under some harsh or critical conditions, the snow creature undergoes a slumber like coma, almost similar to our North American bears."

The mad scientist continued, "As a matter of fact, I believe the snow creature perfected its existence for cold climate, such as winter, and it hibernated during the summer. The biochemical design was optimum for wintry life. For example, imagine how it would feel walking around in the summer wearing a heavy woolly overcoat."

Thee Sheriff Gibbs replied,"So it was a winter predator. I understand. So how come we never heard of it."

Fake Harold Olgeby said,"More reasons for us to study it and not eliminate it. There are possible many reasons for its almost extinction. It may have preyed on a specific food source. The physiology may have been so specific, that it lacked changeability. Its aggressive nature could be its downfall. And who knows, maybe there are more hibernating snow creatures awaiting to awake. These creatures could possess an unusual time clock. The questions about the snow creature are endless. We need to examinine it, and observe its behavior in a controlled environment."

Just when fake Harold Olgeby thought he was convincing the stubborn sheriff, a mood shift overcame the ignorant demeanor of Thee Sheriff Gibbs.

The sheriff stammered,"Poppy Cock! I say poppy cock. This creature is evil all throughout. It came from hell! That is what I believe. We are being tested by the Devil, and Almighty God both."

The sheriff downed the coffee from his insulated paper cup, and patted him on the shoulder.

The sheriff said,"C'mon we have work to do. I am not letting you out of my site. Let us see what my boys and their hunting toys come up with."

The scientist, the mad scientist, the plotting pseudo Harold Olgeby, knew his chat was a failure. Right now, he needed to mix in with the others. The sheriff just made his death list. Those redneck hunters will have to go as well. These dimwits were unaware of the beast's hunting abilities. The snow creature would eliminate them for him. For him, its business as usual. He needed to capture the snow creature to begin his dreams of splendor.

Bogey Wilson did not feel much better. He decided to eat at the cafeteria. He stomached a nice cheeseburger and fries. This time,the food was staying down. His ill feelings disappeared, and contentment filled his insides. Seeing crowds of people was the greatest. Strength in numbers, helped rid the fear of an attack of the beast.

He wondered about his son, Gilroy Wilson. Something inside spoke to him that his son was dead. Even with the high performance vehicle, the chances were slim. His dimwitted son could not use such a vehicle to his advantage. Gilroy Wilson was a flake, a drunk, but a true homosexual, nobody knew.

Bogey Wilson thought about keeping that hot Jesse girl for himself. He should of. Bogey Wilson should of enjoyed her beauty as she prance around his bedroom. He could of. Bogey Wilson could of made love to her sweet body. He would of. Bogey Wilson would of treated her like a queen, and he would have been the king who she would of cherished and been loyal to.

No more sacrificing for others. His son was a failure his whole life. The crime, the drugs, the controversy solicitation with homosexuals, all were irreversible damage. Gilroy Wilson's type never learned the secrets to life. Bogey Wilson just sold the drugs, but did not use it. It was about hard work, and saving the money profits. Only lazy, selfish antics attracted these types, and the parents paid for it in blood and disappointments.

Bogey Wilson bought two draft beers, and sat outside, watching skiers head down the bunny slope.

Happy Birthday Deputy Wilcox

While the others headed to Winterfest for relief, Deputy Wilcox received an assistance call from a concerned citizen on Rte 3. A van was seen having an accident at the intersection of Millens Road. He was on highway patrol, and the report mentioned a van was totaled, and the word " Police" was seen written on the side of it. When Deputy Wilcox arrived, he recognized there official vehicle.

He radioed in, but no one answered at the station. His family was to meet him at Winterfest for his birthday celebration this week. He decided to investigate, and his family fun would have to wait. The scene seemed odd, with no passengers around- alive, injured or dead. He tried calling Thee Sheriff Gibbs but received no answer.

"Boy, what a mess. That van took quite a tumble." The police officer commented.

He noticed the missing wheel, and the side ripped open like a sardine can. Were there survivors? Did someone call an ambulance? The deputy was about to call the general hospital, when the pinkish trail of snow, caught his eye.

Deputy Wilcox guessed a hurt passenger crawled away, possibly seeking help. He followed the trail, but was not sure of what to make of it. Between the trees, there laid a head on the snow. The person looked buried in the snow. The officer scrambled over, and the to his surprise, the person was alive.

The head faintly spoke,"Help, I cannot move. Please help me. I am cold."

Deputy Wilcox quickly assessed the situation, and bent over to try to pull out an arm.

"Are you okay? Can you feel me touching your hand?" The officer asked.

The head replied," I cannot feel my feet. I cannot move. Help me, please."

Deputy Wilcox said,"Okay just relax. I am going to grab you under your armpits, and pull you up."

The head acknowledged what the officer was going to do. The deputy took hold, and in one motion pulled him out from the snowy ground. He realized the man was not too heavy. As he peered down, still holding him, he realized the man had no legs below the knees.

Shocked, the officer dropped him. The man fell onto the ground, past out, and then his heart stopped from the trauma. Deputy Wilcox tumbled backwards as he let the man go due to the sloping ground. He could not regain his balance to stop, and continued to motion backwards with a small momentum. His back smacked into a snow bank, and plopped down into a sitting position, It was not snow leaning against him.

He smelled awful, animal odor, like that of an unclean zoo. Suddenly, he became startled. An angry roar pierced the silence behind him. He stumbled up against the camouflaged beast. New tips surfaced about the snow creature- never awake a sleeping Megalonyx.

The beast roared in a high pitch, and as it turned its mammoth body, it sent the officer tumbling further down the sloping forest ground.

Officer Wilcox reacted instantly. His pistol was flipped out from his utility belt, and it was pointing at the beast, The beast searched irritably for the adversary who awoken his comfortable snooze. Megalonyx leaped at the officer with claws swinging in motion. Before a bullet could be fired, Deputy Wilcox was cut in half, straight across the stomach.

Megalonyx threw a tantrum of swinging claws, slicing the two bodily torsos into shreds. Its general demeanor was uncomfortable and awoke with a headache. The food was not agreeing with it. The broken sleep made it irritable. The tantrum did not help relieve Megalonyx either.

What the snow creature did not realize, was simple. It absorbed the alcohol from Gilroy Wilson and Jessebelle Quentin, who before eaten, were stinking drunk. The virgin beast carried no tolerance to the intoxicants. being a first timer to alcohol. The alcohol infested tissue helped Megalonyx sleep soundly. Then the after effect with a headache, brought on the vicious mutilation of the police officer.

Deputy Wilcox's wife and kids would be waiting in vain at the Winterfest. He was not showing up to continue his birthday celebration.

CHAPTER 7

More Winter Fun

KYLE MEYERS STOOD ON Ski Run Road perplexed. His caveman/ wilderness skills sucked. His internal compass directed him in the opposite direction. He thought his position was near the police station off Rte 3, but instead, appeared towards Ridgewood, near the ski resort. Once again, Kyle Meyers felt remorse about his super hero statis. He longed to be acknowledged as "The Mighty Caveman". His torn, weather beaten, blue parka did not help support the part either.

When Kyle Meyers heard traffic from the woods, he assumed he was near Tannersville. The noise actually reflected the crowds heading for Winterfest. The yearly festival bustled with its full activities. In disgust, he walked towards the entrance of the Ridgewood Ski Resort.

A pointed stick was held for protection, and in his pockets, some roundish rocks. In little league, Kyle was a substitute pitcher, and had a good arm. His aim matched that of a baseball starter. He threw with natural instinct, and not from practice. His accuracy reflected a natural ability.

While he walked in his cave-like strut, he thought that "The Mighty Caveboy", did have a better title for his super hero character. Mr. Conti, back injured at the cave, did present a good point. He was a still a boy, so he will be the caveboy, and not a caveman. In his back story, terrible tragedy affected his life as an abused child. Because of his loss of normal living, "The Mighty Caveboy" dedicated his life to correcting wrong, and fighting the bad guys.

He watched the skiers on the bunny slope. A fearful thought awoke him. The wilderness born, action hero must continue the deeds of goodness for humankind. The snow creature could attack the festival. He must stop his enemy now, and end its bloody rampage.

A new look was needed fast for the super hero. He required a costume, err no, he meant clothing and apparel to support the relentless bashing forth coming to his evil foe.

He entered the gift shop, and saw exactly what he desired. A raccoon coat with matching hat was displayed for him to take. Stealing would not be appropriate, but considering the lives to be saved, it was justified.

The girl attending the gift store was in the back room. Who would miss such an oddball item? When Kyle took it from the display, dust powered the air. This coat awaited in timeless anticipation, for its destiny, the rightful owner, "The Mighty Caveboy". He quickly scrambled outside, and ducked into the rest room with his prize.

It was a bit long, but the large size fit his plump body fine. The 13 year old boy took his knife, and sliced off some of the coat on the bottom, so it would not drag. He saved the raccoon strip to tie onto his wooden spear. "The Mighty Caveboy" was taken shape. He shoved the raccoon hat on his head, and oh, he looked good.

He bellowed a tune, " Looking good, good, good looking. Good, good looking, looking good!" He just stamped the wow factor on his superhero character.

A bunch of kids sat on a bench noticing Kyle Meyers strut towards the snack bar. His weary body needed some sustenance. He glanced at the menu board to see what he could eat for three dollars and fifty cents. His body physically hurt, but not too bad, considering he lacked daily excercise. The other kids recognized Kyle Meyers from school, and laughed at his costume. Was it Halloween in December?

Two men swiftly left the snack bar area, almost knocking him over in his new raccoon coat. The sheriff, Thee Sheriff Gibbs, did not recognize the savior of all, "The Mighty Caveboy?" Kyle contemplated that it was time to save unfortunates in distress, and build his popularity. One day, he may need the assistance of the law.

Thee Sheriff Gibbs turned his head briefly at Kyle Meyers while walking away, and murmured, "These festivals bring out all the whackos."

He took off and adjusted his raccoon hat. The other school mates could not hold back their laughter. They had to mock him in that get up.

Donald exclaimed," Look at that dope, it's Kyle Meyers. What the heck is he wearing. Hey Donna, promise me you will stay away from that weirdo."

Donna shook her head in agreement as the kids laughed at him in his ridiculous coat. Then, Kyle let out a caveboy yell. The kids laughed harder until there stomachs hurt. They could not believe, that Kyle Meyers actually sounded a dog barking noise.

"Hey raccoon man, go feed in the garbage! Did you find some road kill to make that coat? I will keep Donna warm near the fire." Donald exclaimed.

Kyle Meyers immediately recognized his classmate foe, Donald McRonald. Kyle, and his geeky friends branded him as the class clown. Kyle Meyers never forgave the incident with the pancake syrup all over his school locker. "The Mighty Caveboy" tackled the snow creature, witnessed people dying, and saw his share of spilled blood, real blood. He had no more time for small, childish jokes. He ignored the ignoramus, and bought a bag of cheese doodles, and a can of coke.

Donald came up behind him, and pushed him in the elbow. The cheese doodles flopped onto the floor. Kyle bent down and picked up his snack. His stomach ached from hunger. He went with the five second rule that his mom always used. He picked them off the floor, and into his mouth.

Donald exclaimed," Look at the filthy animal! He eats off the floor Donna, Jimmy, Dan, and Lizzie!"

"The Mighty Caveboy" took no heed, and gobbled up his cheese doodles. He gulped down his soda fast, and created a huge belch. Everyone ridiculed Kyle Meyers non stop. There existed more serious business at hand, and he ignored the child mischief. His pride was still intact, and he ignored them.

As he strutted away, a proud emotion overwhelmed himself. The lessons from school, and things his mom lectured to him, he now understood. One should overlook other's spite and ridicule. One should treat others as one would want to be treated. This maturity molded him to be a true hero, to be responsible in society, and now, become a protector of the down trodden.

Donald nastily remarked,"Hey dopey Kyle, your like your weirdo brother, creepy Billy. He is the biggest asshole in town!"

Oh no, Donald did not! No one messed with his great brother. Screw maturity! He took out a rock and flung it around 30 yards, targeting the clown boy. Maturity and righteous behavior lasted a historical 30 seconds. It smacked into Donald's shoulder with a sting. This kid would never forget the sharp pain resonating through his left side of his body. "The Mighty Caveboy" left his mark, a mark stating- Do not threaten the Caveboy and family.

"You are crazy! That hurt, you moran! I am telling Vice Principal Stevens. You are suppose to be on the field trip with us. You are not sick." Donald replied.

The arrogant kid ran with fear searching for the vice principal inside the ski lodge. Kyle Meyers treated his classmate the way Donald treated others. His mother would not be proud of the reverse logic.

Kyle Meyers did forget about Mr. Conti back in the cave.The sheriff at the snack bar, if he could of remembered, would of assisted in an official rescue for the hurt man. He promised to help Mr. Conti, and be responsible. The fight with his class mates made him forget about him, and his physical injuries. What did Mr. Conti truly expect? He really was just a some stupid kid.

He turned a corner by a large patio. Many booths and tables were set up for the crowds to shop and be entertained. As he focused on the forest ahead of him, a hand briskly grabbed him by his raccoon collar.

"Son, where are you going? Playing hooky I see," responded Vice Principal Stevens.

"What do you mean? It is Saturday?" Kyle answered slyly.

Vice Principal Stevens replied,"You are on the roster, and agreed to join the class on our field trip. Now, join the others. By the way, I love your costume. It is nice to see someone getting into the spirit of Winterfest!"

Kyle Meyers started to say"I have important business..."

"Now be quiet! What is your phone number. I bet your parents do not know your sneaking around here alone." Vice Principal Stevens said.

Kyle Meyers said, "Well, you cannot reach them. There visiting family in Richmond."

"I will leave a message. Who is watching you?" The teacher asked.

"Err, um, oh my brother Billy of course!" he said.

"Fine. I will leave a message at your house, and you join the other classmates." Vice Principal Stevens spoke firmly, and officially.

Kyle saw the rest of the crew sitting in the cafeteria munching on their lunches. He noticed the giggling, but the kids kept to themselves-,worried about getting in trouble. He sat at a bench with the kid from India, who stayed to himself, a loner. He immediately plotted his escape to continue his hunt for the snow creature. More bloodshed was coming, and he must save the day.

To his surprise, Donna Curio joined him. He put her in the top five girls he liked. She used to be sixth, but Rhonda Biggs, number five,called him "spasmo" one day, when he tripped on a crack in the sidewalk. Kyle Meyers bumped into her, and spilled a red slushy drink all over her bright blue dress, one summer.

Donna Curio exclaimed," I like your coat. You are entertaining. Donald was an idiot."

"Thanks. Listen, there exists a snow creature in the forest, and I need to getaway from the class trip, to hunt it down, and kill it with my spear." Kyle Meyers replied.

She laughed," Yes, you really are entertaining! Your a bit too much, but your fun. I want that fur cap!"

Donna Curio grabbed the raccoon cap, but to her dismay. It was all sweaty inside the rim, and it stank. She politely handed back to him.

She then remarked, "You smell. I mean really, you smell like crap, Kyle."

"The smell came from fighting the beast." Kyle Meyers diligently told his story. He descriptively explained how he jumped on its back with a pitchfork to save the others on a tractor wagon in the middle of the night. How proud he spoke of his adventure, while Donna Curio attentively listened. He described his super hero character- "The Mighty Caveboy".

"I will help you escape. But I want to join you in the woods." She replied, and tried to bargain.

He was not sure if she truly believed, but "The Mighty Caveboy" needed to get back on his snow creature hunt.

He said,"Okay, I think I can trust you, Donna. Do you have any ideas. The Vice Principal is pacing back and forth over there, constantly taking a head count."

"Well, maybe Donald can help."Donna commented.

"He will not help me, Donna." Kyle Meyers insisted.

She positively said,"Maybe that is true, but Donald would do anything for me."

Donna Curio jumped up from the table without Kyle's approval. She bent over, and whispered into Donald McRonald's ear. He squirmed from the tickling feeling her lips made against his ear. He liked it, and she knew it. She walked slowly back to Kyle Meyers, as Donald and Lizzie stood up and walked to the fixings station at the cafeteria.

Suddenly, a quarrel broke out between the two classmates, and Donald threw ketchup, mustard packets, and napkins at Lizzie, who returned the fire with the same condiments.

"Quickly, Let us go!" Donna Curio whispered to Kyle, grabbing his arm.

They scrambled across the patio out onto the snow, and headed for the tree line.

"Boy, that was easy," exclaimed Kyle Meyers. "The Vice Principal has no idea we disappeared with all that commotion.

"I do not think it was smart, that Donald hit Mr.Stevens with an open packet of mustard," Donna Curio replied.

At first, she felt excited, and adventurous. Entering the woods, it appeared eerie and intimidating to her. It seemed different here, in the real forest, than walking among the trees in her neighborhood.

Before much of any conversation or interaction between the kids happened, a crack of breaking branches sounded in the woods. Donna Curio brushed up against Kyle Meyers frightened. A good size, six pointer buck, leaped and dashed within 30 feet of them. The deer kept a steady pace, not paying any attention to the two. The buck seemed frightened, more than the girl, for some odd reason.

"It is just a deer. He is harmless. We probably spooked him when we entered his territory, Donna." He stated to calm her.

"Oh, well I was not sure," She replied, and let go of his arm. She stepped away not realiizng her body wrapped around his in her frightened moment.

"I will protect you," The Mighty Caveboy exclaimed.

The sound of the forest was quiet and serene. Faint noises of the crowd and the band's music could be heard. As the seconds past, uncomfortable feelings between the two surfaced, as they had nothing to say or have in common out here away from the festival. Donna Curio was thinking of heading back.

Before Kyle Meyers could produce another word, he then heard it. A howl resonated from the woods. It was a coyote howl. Then, to his left he noticed a gray, brownish shadow trot among the pine trees. Before he could react to his left, behind him branches broke, and turned to see. There sat a coyote licking its paws. The inexperienced, outdoors girl witnessed a sitting coyote, and of course screamed.

Her first instinct was to run. Donna Curio ran frantically towards the festival area, down the hill. "The Mighty Caveboy" became activated. He had no time to follow her, and waste his energy. Another two coyotes sneaked up his back when he turned to stare at the sitting one. Quickly, naturally, "The Mighty Caveboy" grabbed his rocks, and flung them at the two as fast as they were drawn from his pocket.

The airborne projectiles were direct hits. Both landed right in their snouts. He grabbed another, and flung it at the one of the two which hesitated. The coyote looked about not expecting an attack. The third one, which was licking its paws scrambled back to the other trees. Its job was a decoy as the other two coyotes investigated.

"The Mighty Cave Boy" sensed that the small pack of coyotes left. They probably were tracking the buck, which they saw gallop past them. Within seconds of realizing all was safe, he took off after Donna. She ran almost half the distance already to the ski lodge.

"Stop Donna! It was just harmless coyotes. They do not attack, unless provoked." The Mighty Cave Boy spoke loudly, attempting to bring her back.

"Keep away, you are a nut for bringing me out there! I could of been killed! Donna exclaimed.

"Trust me, come back. The coyotes were attracted to the festival, and all the food smells, that is all," Kyle Meyers pleaded to her.

She was not coming back. He plopped down in the snow. That was not much fun. Does she not know coyotes do not attack humans?

He thought about a phrase that was said a lot by his Dad- "Women, cannot live with them, cannot live without them."

Fun times could not be had anyway with the snow creature prowling freely. "The Mighty Caveboy" needed to return his focus on the important issues at hand. His mission was not completed as long as the beast roamed around Winterfest. Guard duty was implemented. He was to be a watchman along the trees, the dense pine, awaiting for the snow creature to begin its havoc.

His ears became attentive. A few black-capped chickadees flew around him. These woodland birds were curious by nature. He realized a few cheese doodles were in his pocket. On his open hand the snacks were placed, and within a minute, the friendly, little birds landed to eat. Kyle Meyers broke up the few doodles in smaller pieces so the fun would last. After the snacks were all eaten, one black-capped chickadee stayed on his hand, and began to clean its feathers.

The curious bird jumped on his shoulder, enjoying the raccoon fur coat. The fur was fluffy, and warm. This little guy closed its eyes satisfied. Kyle enjoyed his new friend. Bringing aid to his little bird, made him feel important, and good. This was far more fun than hanging out with scared Donna Curio.

The wilderness would be his new home. "The Mighty Caveboy" acted similiar to "Tarzan of the Jungle". The animals of the forest were his companions. The animals would assist him in his fight against evil. These woodland creatures were mistreated as well. Hunted and killed, their innocent lives ending sometimes just for human pleasure.

The thirteen year old grabbed his spear. Roundish rocks were searched for, and must be of a special quality for him to throw with accuracy. He felt tired though. "The Mighty Caveboy" gathered a bunch of pine branches, and laid on top of them, quite cozy. Thinking to himself, his last thought, before he fell asleep, stated, "This is the life".

He Who Casts The First Stone

Melvin Washington jumped off the ski lift only to take a fall in front of the family. He grabbed his son's arm to gain balance, and took his kid down with him. Everyone laughed, as earlier during lunch. Melvin Washington was the brunt of jokes. He has not been on skis for over fifteen years.

You did not experience Winterfest without doing a ski run. His so-called family and friends from the Black Baptist Church, took the ski lift to the top for some skiing fun. They claimed Big Mel was going to make a fool of himself, especially with the extra 50 pounds he now carried. This bunch of black christens were not the polite, holy rollers up here on the slopes.

Poor Little Mel felt embarrassed while the group continued ridiculing his father. Little Mel was an excellent skier, and wished he had time to shape up his Poppy.

A very fit lady, their Aunty Sheila exclaimed," Lordy, lordy, Melvin do not take the laughs so serious. It is all fun in God's presence. It's just, that belly, the protruding belly around your tight sweater, was special for sitting, not skiing."

"Us people were not made to ski," an undertone remark blurted by Mr. Melvin Washington.

"Oh no, oh no. You did not say that, did you? You are a racist, black man. We beat the whitey folk at all the sports. It is only time we own skiing as well." Aunty Sheila remarked, and held her own. She constantly spoke about the strife, and how they will overcome with believing in Jesus.

One after another, a shot was fired of uninvited criticism towards Melvin Washington, and then they headed down the slopes. What started out as innocent fun, became hurtful, and sarcastic.

The last to go, Aunty Sheila laughed with a remark," See you lost among the pines, belly boy!"

Little Mel stated,"Forget them Poppy. I will be with you skiing the hill, and help if you have trouble."

Little Mel led his father on, as they stood on the top slope. Big Mel Washington knew he could do this, but admitted to himself, that maybe he rushed to the more difficult slopes to soon. He recognized his body's lack of physical stamina. A little training and exercise would have been a plus. Melvin Washington stared down the hill intensely, and felt intimidated.

Little Mel broke the silence and said," Okay, I will go first, and you follow my trail. I will keep you in my sight. If I lose you, I will stop and wait for you. Just take it slow. If it is too much, take off your skis, and walk towards me."

"What! Take off my skis? Son, how much sarcasm can a man take. You are too good my boy. I hope all your christen learning does not distort you. There exists harsh realities among people." Big Mel said.

"Believe in Christ, Poppy. That is all you need." Little Mel took off, zipping downward, this way and that. His son skied a good distance in front of a major turn, stopped, and awaited for his father.

Melvin Washington was very proud of his son. Now sixteen, he lived for others. Responsible, caring, and helpful were all part of his son's middle name. This remained worrisome. Soon, his son would be a man, and all religion could be misleading. Others could commit trouble which Little Mel might misinterpret.

The boy dealt with critical issues like brushing lint off a woolen coat. This was fine, but first, one must be able to buy that coat. Religion and earning money do not always meet eye to eye. Little Mel represented a good christen boy. Big Mel, well, was sort of good.

His father's back pulled tensely, and off he pushed. His skis were not kept aligned, and his body fumbled as if he was already going to take a plunge. He gained his composure, and snow plowed a little. He saw his son below waiting, and decided to go for it. Big Mel molded a good tuck as he ripped down the slope. His ability became reinstated. It felt like he never forgot, like how to ride a bike. He flew passed his son.

Melvin Washington jokingly yelled,"See you later slow poke!"

Little Mel let off a huge smile, and had faith in his father. He knew his Poppy remembered. They swooshed down the snow filled path. Big Mel began to enjoy himself. It all slowly came back to him. He kept his speed down because he admitted to himself about his lack of practice. The father and son enjoyed a family moment together. The others were forgotten with their nasty comments.

Little Mel took on a small mogul on the inside of a sharp turn. His body was airborne, and came down hard, but accurately on the steep left. His Poppy traveled the right, the more casual route. With the slower speed, Big Mel was able to enjoy watching his son on the left. How elegant and professional Little Mel skied. His son flew through the crisp air, and landed with an explosion of snow, dusting the surroundings.

As the snow cloud disappeared, suddenly, Melvin Washington became fright struck.

Little Mel sped on down, not witnessing what occupied to his far left. Around the curve, hung Uncle Bobo from a huge craning arm, attached to a gruesome looking beast. He hollered upside down. The uncle caught sight of Big Mel who stopped and stared from the other side of the ski trail.

"What in living hell". Big Mel murmured.

In milliseconds, Big Mel's brain attempted to register what was real or not real. He drank no whiskey like Uncle Bobo did, before riding the ski lift. That creature was real. In milliseconds, he wondered if Uncle Bobo was thinking the same, that the alcohol was producing this unholy beast. He bet Uncle Bobo wished it was concocted from the whiskey.

Melvin Washington stood horrified. Still in shock, he stared frozen, watching this beast toy with his brother-in-law. He should of attempted to help, but for some dumb-stricken reason, remained awe-stricken. Instead, his mind turned backwards to earlier that day, earlier when he, and Uncle Bobo, engaged in a frictional encounter.

Big Mel sat munching on his egg/bacon muffin at the breakfast pavilion. Sneaking up behind him, Uncle BoBo grabbed his hanging stomach gruffly. Big Mel realized he could not breathe and fell to the floor. Uncle BoBo stood laughing, but Little Mel knew immediately his father was seriously choking. His son headed over to his father to administer the Heimlick Maneuver, which he learned at school. Luckily, Big Mel forcefully discharged food debris from his mouth without any assistance.

As Big Mel slowly stood up, he automatically shoved Uncle BoBo aggressively, even though faint.

"Take it easy ol' boy! It was just a joke." The Uncle turned and replied.

"You almost killed me! That is a sin, scaring a man enjoying his food." Big Mel exclaimed, Noticing the chunks of bacon on the floor, Big Mel actually thought how it was a waste of good food. He definitely had a eating problem. Should not he had been more concerned about his life, than thinking of the uneaten food on the ground within those seconds?

"Okay, I am sorry Bacon and egg man." A big hug smothered him by Uncle BoBo. Big Mel noticed little compassion, and more of a " I gotcha sucker" attitude. The bacon incident was not forgotten.

No helpful strategy came to mind on the slope. Big Mel initiated a skiing move, or side step, horizontal to rescue Uncle BoBo. Madness must have entered his brain to think he could take on this beastly creature. The snow creature caught site of another meal coming its way. Big Mel locked eyes with it at roughly 50 yards.

The woolly head turned with a growl back at the hanging UncleBoBo. Two skiers flew past, not noticing the huge beast. They concentrated their sights down the mountain.

In sudden swift slices, the snow creature cut up Uncle BoBo into strips- just like bacon. Somewhere, Big Mel thought there was some irony occurring. The beast ravaged on the strips of flesh, and flung half of Uncle BoBo's parts all of the slope. Big Mel received a booted leg in the head. He took it has a sign to get the hell out of there.

He skied as fast as he could, becoming more clumsy in his moves. His balance teetered. Sometimes he only had one ski down, or his body was air lifted awkwardly, heading for a crash. Somehow, Big Mel kept enough balance on his skis while plunging down the hill.

At one point he turned his head to chance a look. Big Mel felt confident about his distance from the beast. With fearful dismay, the snow creature rumbled a few yards right behind him. He witnessed a snow ball of fury with the huge clippers rotating in speed. The backward glance was perfect timing because the snow creature was about to pounce and finish him.

The fearful apprehension, that the end of his life represented a meal ticket for the snow creature, produced a spasmodic loss of body control. Big Mel crashed down in the snow as the beast swiped the air above him with its huge claw. His body sleighed backwards moving at high speed, with his head tilted up toward the slope.

With the snow creature still tracking at his heels, Big Mel helplessly slid headfirst. He imagined the back of his head crashing into a rock, making it easy to eat him. Instead of Uncle BoBo bacon strips, Big Mel would be menued more as an egg/cheese, bloody sandwich.

Like a sled, he continued downwards.

Big Mel not knowing, that on a slope below, Cousin Joseph, Cousin Robert, and Little Mel stood waiting for him.

Earlier, the two cousins played catch with Big Mel's woolen cap. Of course the burly man could not keep up with the younger men, as they easily flung his cap over his head. It landed twice into the wet snow. After humiliating Big Mel in this game of tag, Cousin Joseph shuffled behind him and tugged the wet cap onto his head. Again the family group had a good laugh at the expense of Big Mel's feelings.

Even their Aunty Sheila, with her constant religious rhetoric, chuckled, not realizing that Big Mel took this personal. Little Mel also was ridiculed as the boy chased his older cousins trying to assist his Poppy.

Big Mel exclaimed, "What am I going to do now you idiot! I cannot wander up in the cold hills with my head wet from my cap. I am already chilled to the bone."

"Oh here. Wrap this scarf around your head." Cousin Joeseph replied.

"That was my lucky cap," Big Mel sternly stated. Cousin Joseph helped bandage Big Mel's head with the scarf.

"Wow, Melvin, you look like a terrorist with a turban." Aunty Sheila remarked as all, yes again, laughed.

"That was my lucky cap," Big Mel seriously replied.

"Oh in that case, I will keep it." Cousin Joseph said, and slapped the woolen cap over his own hat.

"Okay men, that is enough. Let us take our tummy man for some fun skiing, Okay tummy man?" Aunty Sheila replied as she always spoke, automatically putting herself in charge.

"Just do not crash on your big tush!" Big Mel answered in sarcasm.

"Oh no, you did'nt. Oh no you did'nt! No gentleman are you. Stop looking at my tush! You foul creature of habits. This is because you skip church."

"Uncle BoBo, your beloved skips church too. He does not want to look at that tush too ." Big Mel ripped out a zinger.

Aunty Sheila and the rest of family scolded Mr. Melvin Washington. No manners, trouble making, and disrespectful, were some of the verbiage branding Big Mel's behavior. He thought, it was okay to poke at him, but he cannot poke back? She joked with the name tummy man, but he cannot reply with big tush?

Little Mel forgave his Poppy for the uncalled for remarks. Deep, sacred in his christen heart, he could not forgive his relatives for their antics. This developed a conundrum for Little Mel's soul. His family, who he loved, shared in catholic activities, now were acting opposite.

The group was releasing energies which Christ's teaching were supposed to eliminate. The hidden urges seemed to build up, and now released here in the hills. Tomorrow was the church day of obligation. Little Mel wondered how each then will interact. Could his bossy, over zealous, Aunty Sheila feel guilt?

Down the slope, the cousins waited with Little Mel due to the boy's concern of his father skiing. The hill above them took a deep turn downward at them. In other words, they could not see far up the ski run. The trail above them met with the sky instead.

Still, the cousins joked about Big Mel, that he was so slow, and nowhere in site. Little Mel continued to fight his irritation against his family, and tried to forgive them in his soul.

Big Mel suddenly flew off the deep part, and sailed over the cousins and his son. Before they realized what occurred, the two ton beast plopped heavily in front of them. The snow creature raised its pincer claws, and let out a terrifying roar.

Little Mel peeled out of there as fast as he could in terror. Cousin Joseph and Cousin Robert stood frozen in terror. The large pincer claw swung across decapitating Cousin Joseph, and Cousin Robert in one swoop. The snow creature sank his fangs into the headless bodies for a delicious, warm, drink of blood.

The two heads rolled and bounced down the ski trail along with Big Mel. Little Mel skied in total fear not knowing which direction he headed.

Big Mel's momentum remained constant, and still slid backwards. His back still exposed to a deadly crash. He noticed the heads rolling along his sides. His first order of business was simple, besides the life threatening crisis. His hand, still wrapped with a ski pole, reached out at Cousin Joseph's head, and in one miraculous move, snatched back his lucky woolen cap. His heart filled with satisfaction, and thanked God. He needed his lucky cap. Melvin Washington looked upon his action as a good omen.

Cousin Joseph had a sad, miserable expression stamped on his dead face. Big Mel felt Cousin Joseph's spirit present. It conveyed- I am sorry I snatched your lucky cap. Bloody, rolling heads, was the price they paid for their actions. For Big Mel, it was a moment of tribulations.

Out of nowhere, a force was felt slowing him down. Little Mel grabbed at his Poppy. Finally the crazy ride ended.

"C'mon Poppy, get up!" Littel Mel yelled.

Achy, and bruised, Big Mel was able to right himself, and stood with only one ski still attached.

Little Mel said, "We need to go! We got to get to the bottom, Poppy. That evil beast, it will come after us, I know, I just know."

"I cannot. I have only one ski. I am exhausted. I hurt, I feel numb, I, I want to faint." Big Mel spoke trembling.

"You can do this! Or we will die! Believe in Christ. We are in a test by God. Do not give in now. One ski is all you need." Less fear but confidence, was preached from Little Mel.

Big Mel glanced at his woolen cap. He felt the energy, a supportive energy. He was not sure if it radiated from Christ, Little Mel, or his lucky cap. Maybe It was all of the above.

"I will survive. We will beat this beast my son!" He said with a roar of ear shattering victory, Big Mel took off skiing and yelling.

His stern roar echoed everywhere. It challenged Megalonyx. On one ski, Big Mel headed down the ski trail, making weird monkey-like moves to keep his balance. His son followed along. The snow creature took pursuit after hearing Big Mel's territorial howl.

"No one can stop us now, Poppy!" Little Mel said excited.

The beast caught an ear full of the bellows. Big Mel's loud statements mocked its strength, but exhaustion slowly was setting in. All the gorging, and gulping of food started to slow him down as well. It's gut irritated the beast. The present food tasted different. Where was the prey, the good stuff it loved and savored. But those roars were a challenge, and it continued the chase of Big Mel.

After it's long sleep, the snow creature ate too fast, and too much. The hunger blinded its normal habits from its past existence. The brain cells started to reconnect, and register different environment conditions. But those offensive hollers, challenged it to battle. Instinct possessed him to kill and eliminate this adversary.

Aunty Sheila continued her ski patterns, alone, down the mountain. She knew she was the best skier. Her family were somewhere far behind her. She expected not to bump into any of them. Out of the corner of her eye, she caught a dark moving mass. Surprise, and more surprise filled her eyes, as she recognized that clownish skiing anywhere.

"Big Mel, next to me?" she spoke low to herself. Little Mel made sense, but him out of all the family, speeding next to her?

"Out of the way! I cannot stop! Move that Big Ass fast!" Big Mel yelled uncontrollably.

His skiing was all over the place. Uncoordinated, Big Mel would bend to the left, and be righted up with a sudden poke in the snow with his pole. At any moment, it looked liked he would fall, but then corrected himself. His body contorted into unnatural figurations, still balanced on that one ski. This motion clip easily would have made the cut on "Funniest Weird Skiers of All Time".

However, Aunty Shelia, was intimidated by Big Mel's antics and impressive moves. She overflowed with jealousy.

To herself, she mumbled,"Look at that tubby showing off, and on one ski. He wants to play, I will play. He is deliberately poking fun at my skiing."

She darted left, and quickly to the right, with a swoosh passing in his front. Big Mel, out of control, yelled, calling her a crazy bitch. Little Mel moved just behind them trying to get his Aunt's attention She once more cut across his front by inches almost knocking him down, laughing all the time.

Big Mel headed straight into the woods, blindly without choice.

"That knuckle brain is going to go between the pines? Asshole. Shit!" Aunty Sheila said.

She realized she cursed, and began a prayer while trailing Big Mel through the forest. Even for experienced skiers, racing among the pines could be deadly. Behind her, darted Little Mel, who, with no avail, could not get her attention. The 2,000 pound, people eating monster, who digested her husband, Uncle BoBo, followed not far behind.

In her mind, the race was on. No one was about to embarrass her, and that was not to be tummy man. Again Aunty Sheila skidded close by Big Mel who desperately tried not to crash among the trees. His method so far worked. He would stab his poles into the ground, pushing himself bodily away from the wooded obstacles.

Big Mel's dexterity was that of an artful amateur, and yet, somehow, he circumvented the forest without a collision. At this speed though, death was eminent, even for the experienced Aunty Sheila. Little Mel handled himself well because of his youthful, physical skill.

Both men feared that the fanged creature would appear around a tree trunk, and slice them to death. Aunty Sheila feared she would lose to the tummy man, and be ridiculed at church.

Big Mel noticed a clearing ahead, and the ski lodge in the distance. He made it. Well, Big Mel would of escaped if it was not for a thick granddaddy of a tree. He leaned to his left, using any skill he possessed to veer away, and miss it. Well, he mostly missed it. He flew, and brushed onto the bark, tearing at his ski jacket. The contact was enough to throw him off from all pressure of being on only one ski. Little Mel watched as his Poppy tumbled, and rolled into the small clearing.

Aunty Sheila increased in momentum beyond her expertise. She could not veer away as well, and collided into her brother. The impact sent her over her head. One of her ski poles snagged onto Big Mel's jacket, and dragged him a few more yards.

Little Mel came to a stop off to the side of the clearing. To all their dismay, branches smashing and cracking, were heard approaching closer by the second. The snow creature tunneled through the snow with its trademark style. Small rocks were kicked up, and thrown all over. Sapling pines were uprooted, and flung all over. Dirt, mixed with soil, tainted the trail the snow creature made. It destroyed everything in its path. Some trees were partially pushed sideways with squeaks and cracks. The energy exerted by it was tremendous.

The big, bad, snow creature popped into the clearing next to Little Mel. The young man exhausted just stood in awe. The beast stood on its strong, short legs with pincer claws waving above its woolly head. Again, showing the sign of dominance, it let out an incredible roar. Little Mel, for the first time felt doubt. He could not even muster a prayer.

Now entered our super hero- "The Mighty Caveboy". His entrance was grand, leaping out from a thicket bush. His plan to stalk the festival perimeter payed off. His arch enemy, the snow creature, arrived as expected. He did his trademark half Tarzan, half apelike howl, challenging his foe.

The snow creature turned its beady glare at Kyle Meyers. It recognized the little annoyance like an irritating fly, buzzing around your face. How dare this pathetic looking being challenge the "Master of the Winter World". It let loose another dreaded howl to invoke timidness. It toyed no longer, and pulled his pincer claw back ready to rip "The Mighty Caveboy" in shreds.

Back at the snack bar, Kyle Meyers pocketed small bags of hot sauce. Luckily, the ski resort's selection at the fixing station, stocked different, potent hot sauces. They had "Cha Cha Cha 's El Spicy", a connoisseur choice for the extreme burn. After leaving Donna Curio, he soaked the roundish rocks of choice in the used cheese doodle bag with the spicy sauce.

Utilizing the old doodle bag, was now part of his signature moves. "The Mighty Caveboy" reconstructed garbage to use and fight against his arch enemies. At the same time, he supported recycling, keeping the wilderness clean, and preserved.

He flung all five rocks directly into the gaping mouth of the bellowing creature. One after the other, his loaded projectiles hit its target, before the snow creature released its fury. The spicy loaded weapons hit the back of its throat with exceptional accuracy.

The snow creature swung at the air with misdirection, while "The Mighty Caveboy" quickly grabbed Little Mel out of the battle zone.

At this point, a few factors were weighted against Megalonyx:

1) The overeating caused sluggish action effecting its precision hunting.

2) All the physical activity worked negatively on his full gut, developing nasty indigestion.

3) Twigs, dirt, fowl water, and clothing, added to its discomfort, and all ingested into his belly. This in turn brought on a striking headache and nausea.

4) The spicy, hot rocks pushed all the buttons for it to physical implode.

The small, red eyes suddenly dilated three times larger. This followed with a disgusting, short belch, then a longer belch. It settled back on all fours, sat silent for 4 seconds, whimpered, and was silent again. It next heaved its stomach contents. Guts, body parts, blood, bile, branches, dirt, and rocks, gushed out all over Big Mel, and Aunty Sheila. The odor alone easily would chase anything alive into the deep hills for miles.

Both sat there covered in the toxic disgust. Big Mel literally could not breathe, and thought he would die from lack of oxygen. So excruciating was the filthy air, everyone forgot about the snow creature attacking.

This day was a victory for the "Mighty Caveboy". The beast's whitish red cheeks turned pale blue. With droopy eyes, the "Master of the Winter World", felt for first time, defeat. It registered in memory that these beings were a worthy adversary. Past times were simpler, and the food tasted better.

Nothing in the past, challenged this beastly warrior. Vain attempts of the prehistoric cave bear, with predictable swipes, and tiny fangs, it clobbered. The saber toothed tiger, who could not pierce its thick woolly skin, laid in a distance like a pet, as the snow creature would fling it morsels from its kill.

It returned to the thick pines, and lumbered away. It would fight another day. Megalonyx was cunning, and intelligent, something these humans may not be counting on. It gulped down some fresh snow to settle its gigantic gut before disappearing. The defeated snow creature tunneled back to its lair to take a nap.

Big Mel and Aunty Sheila looked at each other covered in the expelled mess. Both hugged with desperate forgiveness.

"I am sorry Mel." Aunty Sheila cried.

"No I am sorry Sheila." Big Mel added.

"No, I am sorry" Cried Sheila still.

"No I am sorry." Big Mel spoke forgivingly.

"I am sorry about the insults." Aunty Shiela confessed.

"No, I am sorry for saying big ass." Big Mel confessed.

"It is a big ass." Aunty Sheila laughed even with the animal stink oozing on her.

Her brother laughed as well, as he picked off a partially fingered hand, and threw it over his head. Both sat in the biological muck, glad to be alive.

He knew it! He knew it. The Lord, Jesus Christ, was truly the savior. Little Mel praised joy while watching his family reunion. He knew God worked in strange ways, but this was weird, whacko strange.

He next thanked the strange boy who saved his life.

"Thanks for your help." Little Mel said.

Clearing his throat, and attempting to speak in a deeper, show off voice, Kyle Meyers stated," I am the Mighty Caveboy. This is what I do. That was the diabolical snow creature who I will kill. I got him fleeing now. I know where it hides."

Little Mel really was confused, and did not know how to answer the odd hero. He was glad to be alive and joined his Poppy and Aunty Sheila. They attempted a vain clean up by rolling and rubbing themselves in the clean snow. Little Mel turned only to find the raccoon boy gone. He definitely had stealth.

The three, exhausted and perplexed, had a new surprise showing up.

Suddenly, six men, dressed in hunting gear with guns, materialized from out of the trees. Some were on skiis, and accompanied by an all-terrain vehicle. With them, was the infamous, Thee Sheriff Gibbs.

"Okay people, you okay?" The sheriff politely replied.

They nodded with approval.

Before any of them could voice their mouth off about the attack of the snow creature, Sheriff Gibbs interrupted, and said,"Before you say crazy remarks, think first, before you answer. I know what happened. It is a tragedy about the human life which suffered. Your grievance, and loss of loved ones will be compensated. Come boys, help these unfortunate citizens down the hill to the Ambulances."

Big Mel, Little Mel, and Aunty Sheila felt uneasy, but safe. They carried themselves down the slope with aid of the hunters,and did not say a word. They kept glancing at each other.

Thee Sheriff Gibbs confidently said,"Everybody, after we get you all patched up, I will get you something to eat."

"And then?" Big Mel remarked.

"We are going to have a quiet chat," The sheriff spoke with sly uncomfortable words.

It occurred to Melvin Washington that Aunty Sheila's husband, Uncle Bobo, was ripped apart by the beast. This tragic event seemed to horrifying for him to explain right now. He decided to wait at the warm, comfortable ski lodge to convey her loss. How she would accept his death with all her religion, Big Mel had no idea. As they were escorted down the hill, Aunty Sheila kept asking about the other family members, and hoped they were alright.

Big Mel explained," They are all fine. God is protecting them."

Racoon Boy

"The Mighty Caveboy" walked proudly through the forest. He saved those helpless victims, and now, officially transformed into a super hero. He sat on top of the world, with the best attitude a young man could own. Soon, the tale would be told, the tale how he saved the skiers from a diabolical monster.

Earlier, as he walked away from the rescued skiers, he remembered
what the young boy commented. He used the phrase, "Raccoon boy",
to describe the "The Mighty Caveboy". He wondered if his action hero
name should be changed. Did this name sound foolish- Raccoon Boy?

Kyle Meyers did not like it, As a matter of fact, he hated that name.
His worrying mind concocted a newspaper article using the childish,
stupid name, Raccoon Boy. His dad always baited poison under their
porch, to kill the annoying pests. Pest? Who, What, him?

With the glory, came the problems. He now needed damage control. He strutted through the snowy wilderness conflicted by such
matters. Life of a super hero sure was not easy.

A sound out of the ordinary sparked his hearing. A snow crunch
with a muffled branch cracking. No, it was not the snow creature, or
his animal friends of the forest. Megalonyx would be silent, or bombas-
tically loud in its attack. This was human. Someone was tracking him.

Back at the clearing with Big Mel and Aunty Sheila, the wild boy
with the raccoon coat was mentioned. Thee Sheriff Gibbs needed to
keep control of things. He sent Tommy and Matt Drake, his two best
trackers to find that "Raccoon Boy". With all this bloodshed, it was not
the time for leaving lose ends.

Thee Sheriff Gibbs found the story by the Baptist christens to be
unusual. Some kid fought off the "Megaloowhat"? How was this possible. Either pure luck was drawn, or the boy knew something about the
beast. Thee Sheriff Gibbs decided their was a connection. The wild boy
knew tidbits of the beast's habits, and this would assist in its capture.

"The Mighty Caveboy" knelt down behind a pine tree. He peeked
ever so slightly around the trunk. A tip of a moving brown hat surfaced, on top of the past slope, he just climbed. He hid about 50 yards

from their trailing position. He figured these guys were experienced. Somehow, his super hero mind needed to outwit these hunters. A bad feeling came over him, especially if they nabbed him.

His footprints were clearly marked in the snow. These guys took the direct route, and were hot on his easy trail. They did move cautiously, and this would be one of his advantages. Backtracking was a thought, but the two hunters already reached the top of the slope, and too close. He had to take action quickly before they could visually make contact.

The two scoped out the terrain ahead of them. Again, they were being careful not to give away their position. Their experience showed for itself as Boone and Crockett Members. "The Mighty Caveboy" possibly could backtrack about 20 yards, and veer off to either sides, buying him some time to escape. This plan seemed iffy at best, and perfection was a priority against these hunters.

The decision was made, but not a great one. He would high tail as fast and quietly as possible. Heading towards the left, the hill descended. He would jump down the slope into more thicker pine trees, and hopefully lose them. Evergreens, the pine trees, keep their leaves all year, so positioning oneself in the density of trees, would bring dry spots with no snow. "The Mighty Caveboy" could limit his noticeable tracks. Maybe a hide out could be found.

There existed no right time. He took off. His stealth was good, as he nimbly hopped and jumped over obstacles, trying not to make noise. He never looked back. Zig zagging, and pushing his speed, he headed over the top and down the slope.

"The Mighty Caveboy " stumbled as the slope over here was steeper than he anticipated. He could not gain his balance, and his body rolled uncontrollably. Near the bottom, covered in white from the snow, he was able to stand and regain his stature. Immediately, he entered the tree line. Just as he expected, the forest floor shown through in areas from escaping the falling snow. He hopped, and leaped onto rocks. He stepped as carefully as a superhero should precisely do.

He wondered if the two saw him take off down the slope. He came upon a small clearing, cutting the forest in half. He deliberately made tracks with a brisk walk to the next set of pine trees. Entering the other side of the forest, the ground presented dry, no snow areas as well. His tracks could be masked under the pines. He did leave though, subtle marks to lead the trackers through the woods.

Then, "The Mighty Caveboy" turned back, and returned to the clearing with his boot tracks. He tiptoed on his snowy footprints in the small field, and headed daintily back to the first dense woods. By back-tracking, stepping carefully into his prints already molded, He hoped to outwit the trackers, and direct them deeper into the forest. He hoped for a hiding spot. Then, he simply would move in the opposite direction of the hunters, back up the snowy hill, he originally stumbled down.

He re-entered the first section of pine trees. Quickly, he scanned for a hiding area. Climbing onto a tree, would limit his escape if they located him. He needed to find something on the ground to hide, and not obvious.

Again, "The Mighty Caveboy" hopped about, attempting not to leave evidence of his trail. He heard the slushing, and crumpling of snow. The two hunters entered the tree line as they just stepped down the steep slope. Steadily the cautious tracking continued, and knew this wild boy was at hand.

Nothing could be found for the super hero to hide away. He caught a glimpse of a moving body hugging the tree line. He jumped down, and landed in a small indentation of the forest floor. He snatched a sizable pine branch to cover himself. The two hunters were less than 20 yards away when he dropped to hide. The camouflage had to be acceptable. He could see in the direction of the two hunters, who obviously did not catch on of his wherabouts.

Tommy and Matt Drake were exceptional trackers. There was one flaw. The description of the victims back on the ski trails, spoke of a strange, odd boy, who seemed rather innocent. They accepted the fact that the boy was a school kid from the class trip at Winterfest. Matt Drake remembered a teacher nervously complaining to the sheriff that he lost one of the students.

These Boone and Crockett Hunters did not believe the story about a kid fighting off the beast. They witnessed the body parts, and all the blood. Tommy Drake was a commando in the military. They hardly believed some stupid kid could commit such a feat.

"The Mighty Caveboy" did an exceptional job in covering his tracks, or he was just plain lucky. Both men walk confused. Noticing the clearing through the trees, they immediately headed for the open area. Quickly, they saw the boot prints. Instead of examining the trail like good trackers, they moved forward into the next forest patch naively- a trackers number one mistake.

They meandered through the scattered trees again looking for signs. When they entered the second patch of woods, "The Mighty Caveboy" sped back up the slope he stumbled down. The distance was far enough, that the two would not here much noise from our super hero's movements.

The last few days, brought on physical conditioning. He hustled up the slope, and continued going up on high ground. His breathing was better, as he did not have to bend over from feeling faint. He looked, and marched up the high ground. Within 10 minutes, Kyle Meyers brought himself to a peak overlooking the valley below.

"The Mighty Caveboy" spotted the two hunters walking in a snow clearing. He won, he lost them. Overcome with victory, he let out a yell with deep, voracious sound, like a mix of a lion and a bear roar. The threatening call caught the tracker's ears as they peered up.

There was the super hero waving his hands in a mocking fashion. The two knew they were had. His caveboy call was excellent. At least to Kyle Meyers, it was the trademark call he searched for. His wilderness vocals sounded with the voracity of a lion, and the strength of a bear. He turned back to the woods to continue his hunt for the snow creature.

The beast turned, and stood up with surprising awe. What foe, again, dared to call out in his territory. The Megalonyx snooze was over. Spite built inside of it. There roamed to many territorial opponents. It needed to tear apart this howler. It's adrenalin increased as it flexed it's muscles. A few clashes of its claws knocked together, and sounded through the forest. Who dared to take on- "The Master of the Winter World".

Again, Kyle Meyers, "The Mighty Caveboy", expelled his new, signature call.

CHAPTER 8

Bait, Decoy, and Snare

THE MORNING SUN GLOWED orange as it crept slowly upon the horizon. The snow ridden field gleamed like orange popsicle, ice cream. A raw chill with twenty-five degrees Fahrenheit stung on the hunters' cheeks. All already manned their positions. No wind, no sound, but just a few caws from some passing crows. It was perfect fair weather conditions for hunting. This Sunday morning the bells rang for Megalonyx, and not the church goers out here in the remote woods. The trap was set.

Fresh killed, deer carcasses laid in the opening. Out in the center of the field, the bait hopefully would entice the beast. The seasoned hunters, tactfully and patiently awaited in their stations. Some drank hooch, which fake Harold Olgeby took no deep interest in. These fools were too confident, and this would become sloppy. Fake Harold Olgeby giggled like a boy when he listened to their "macho" tales and talent. Any loss of life would be the sheriff's problem. These idiots had no conception of the cunningness this beast possessed.

Last night, fake Harold Olgeby busied himself in a barn while the Boone and Crockett Club Members bragged about their skills at Charlie's Diner. The sheriff had Charlie close up early for a secret meeting. For a Saturday night, this was a loss of money for the owner. Everyone conformed to Thee Sheriff Gibb's command. No leaks about monsters terrorizing the countryside would ever be. In other words- don't ask, don't tell.

The mad scientist dissected on deer carcasses. He removed the brain matter, the stuff this creature was partial to. In the forest, trails of brain chunks would be scattered to direct the predator to the trap. Fake Harold Olgeby also sprinkled a strong aftershave along with these delectable morsels. He remembered the story of Bill Meyers, and how he believed the beast connected food with Suzy's perfume. The curiosity of the snow creature's nose could be its downfall.

The seismograph equipment was utilized as well. Tremors could be detected from the motion by the snow creature. The mad scientist randomly placed sensors throughout the forest. He could pin point locations of the beast with his equipment, coupled with his computer notebook. The signals relayed to a central data base. All parameters were hashed out to every detail. Thee Sheriff Gibbs appreciated the intelligence, and scientific planning by Harold Olgeby.

Everything, however, relied on the fact that the snow creature showed up in the designed trap. A decoy made be needed to further entice it. Some of the redneck hunters would act as the rabbit to catch the fox. So positive they bragged. A claim was stated, suggesting they would capture this predator before the trap would ever be released.

Fake Harold Olgeby wanted the snow creature alive, but Thee Sheriff Gibbs wanted it eliminated by any means possible. The hunters were given orders to shoot to kill, if possible. Again, the mad scientist silently chuckled about these Boone and Crockett Hunters bagging this prize trophy. The elaborate scheme to snatch it alive was a cover by the sheriff. He wished to convey a professional side, and show he cared for its life.

Thee Sheriff Gibbs offered secret cash bonuses for the shooters to terminate it. His money source was funneled by silent citizens, and/ or financial people of interest. A small town represented "Big Fish in a Small Pond". Tannersville raised the bar concerning local jurisdiction and corruption. The lack of transit business and tourism, isolated the area of living, and certain individuals controlled the business, media, and social structure for their own personal end game.

A central headquarters was camped away from any possible altercations from the trap. Thee Sheriff Gibbs, Frank Porter, and Fake Harold Olgeby worked out of the heated, huge tent. Isolated in a woods, this operation was very hush, hush. A helicopter was utilized for transportation. Secrecy expressed constant diligence from all. Frank Porter, never briefed on the actually trap, had no idea of its operation. All he knew was the code name- Bait, Decoy, and Snare.

Frank Porter scribbled notes, and stuff for his article. He kept the story he planned to expose from his adversary, the sheriff. Drinking hot coffee, viewing the beautiful sunrise, he decided to support the right moral choice. The people bared that right to know the truth. This snow creature may have been unknown up to the present time, but its discovery revealed it to be part of the local culture. The new Megalonyx species belonged to our world, and everyone needed to be re-educated.

Frank Porter recalled the finding of other fossils, which redefined history. Thomas Jefferson. one of our founding fathers, took many interests in his career, and one of his favorite subjects- fossils. In the late 1790's, skeletal remains were discovered in the western part of Virginia. This animal called Megalonyx, " great claw", existed during the Pleistocene era, 12,000 to 6 million years ago. It was named in honor of Thoma Jefferson's discovery.

Megalonyx Jeffersonia, was a large ground sloth. At first, Thomas Jefferson assumed it was a large carnivore, like a lion. However, examining of the bone structures, revealed an animal of a plant-eating nature. The ground sloth ate roots and tubers as well as other plant fauna. Sometimes it grew at such a huge size, scholars believed that the animal trapped itself underground in caverns. Megalonyx fossils were not abundant, and like other extinct species of this era, no one truly knew the social behaviors and why they became extinct in the first place.

This live Megalonyx could be a cousin to the plant-eating one. If fossils were not plenty for the plant-eating sloth, was it so unusual that no one identified this prehistoric carnivore? The meat, human-eating, sloth/like, bear thing, with crustacean-like claws, terrorized the Virginia countryside now in 1985. Thoma Jefferson's love of investigative science, would probably be ecstatic in his grave.

Fake Harold Olgeby sat keenly, observing his equipment. No signs of the snow creature were registered. He drank out of a water bottle, and nibbled on some crackers.

Not much of a breakfast, Frank Porter thought. He remembered how Bill Meyers showed concern about this man's integrity. The scientist fitted his analytical role perfectly, so his character seemed credible. What did young Bill Meyers know which Frank Porter did not?

He also thought about this troubled young man, who disappeared. He took off into the woods after the van accident on Millens Road. Bill Meyers yelling for revenge of his dead girlfriend, Susan Conti. Living his life in a small town like Tannersville, Frank Porter knew everyone well, and he had to agree with the sheriff. It seemed highly unlikely that Suzy Conti, with her outgoing reputation, would date the type like Bill Meyers. Frank Porter doubted that they were an item. He believed Bill Meyers suffered a mental breakdown, and now, he was loose and unstable, out there, somewhere with the snow creature.

One of the hunters radioed in as his voice spilled over the speaker.

Matt Drake said, "We got nothing. It is 7:30 A.M., and still not a noise or a grumble. Any suggestions."

Thee Sheriff Gibbs replied," Just sit tight. Your men are better off in your fortified positions, than if you start stalking about."

"No problem, over and out." Matt Drake said.

The sheriff had some serious concerns. He posted five deputies around town, including the Winterfest. Being Sunday, the festival would attract crowds again. Thee Sheriff Gibbs cleaned up yesterday's bloody incidents very covertly. Most visitors never witnessed the beast, and a story was concocted of a tragic family skiing accident. Those slopes were closed off, and no one became the wiser.

The sheriff could think like a science guy too. He realized there was quite a bit of body parts left at the scenes of attack. He believed the snow creature lacked the taste for human, and preferred its usual prey from its past. Deer existed during that era, so the bait should attract the hungry predator to their trap. All seemed to be thumbs up for the capture.

At 10:00 A.M., still no sightings. No beeps or signals motioned on the equipment. The plan looked glim, at least for the morning. The hunters near lunch time needed to stretch their legs, and exposed their positions. Later, they continued with the plan, but still, not even a small tremor showed up on the seismograph. Nothing was reported at the ski lodge or anywhere around town. The guys discussed the situation in their tent, and decided to follow up tomorrow morning.

Maybe the snow creature was physically decimated. Maybe, it took off to another territory. It could be ill, or even hurt from some of the return gun fire it already received. Could this species be more intelligent than this group gave it credit for? Just because modern professionals named past species, pre-historic or extinct, it does not mean it had no actual intelligence. Was this "Master of the Winter World", scheming against the stupid looking humans?

Fake Harold Olgeby knew about the beast's lair, which Thee Sheriff Gibbs, and Frank Porter remained ignorant of. Maybe it feasted on beer drinking Mr. Conti back at the cave, the mad scientist thought. Mr. Phil Conti could develop into a problem. Harold Olgeby knew he was sloppy on this point. If your trademark branded you a serial killer, make sure your witness the death of your victims. Tomorrow was another day, and Bait, Decoy, and Snare would be given one more chance.

Another Go For Megalonyx

Hunter Davis already took to his tree stand a half hour before the 6:30 A.M. sunrise. It was day 2 of their project. This man utilized with what considered him a well seasoned hunter. He positioned himself up in the tree canopy with a stand. Here, his expertise for shooting hundreds of deer, a dozen bear, several coyotes, two bobcats, and varmints, excelled.

Based on the information, the snow creature's predatory skills were ground, and cavernous oriented. Hunter Davis was nobody's fool. He witnessed the bloody gore on the ski slopes, and his mind was set at ease up here in a tree. His target range consisted of three good sites to take down this nasty predator. The brain matter was scattered properly as well as a few other tidbits on the snow covered floor. He wanted the extra bonus to personally eliminate the snow creature.

Most wildlife species were territorial, and returned to their hunting area. Underground animals usually possessed a keen sense of smell. Hunter Davis brought a garbage can full of the bloody snow from the skiing incident. This would attract the beast to the kill, it already knew. Confidence dominated high up here, where it could not sneak up and slice him.

He waited patiently in the dim morning light. Behind him, the forest was thicker, and his shooting view limited. He secured his platform so his back faced this section. There existed the risk the snow creature could come behind, and he would miss it. It also would smell him because his position was upwind to his back. Cavernous animals possessed poor eyesight. It would be unaccessible to his tree position, and be confused of his human whereabouts.

Faint scratching was heard below, but he visualized nothing. A squirrel scurried around most likely. His experienced identified this consistent, intermittent scratching to be that of a squirrel. A twig snapped every now and then as well. No real alarm raised in Hunter Davis, but concern. The sun was yet to break the morning gray as he glanced around for a squirrel to ease his thoughts.

A piece of something struck his cheek. Hunter Davis peered around. Was it a piece of pine cone falling from the tree? He could not tell of its direction. While he looked upwards, another piece of something, now pricked his forehead. It seemed to come from below. Again nothing to be seen. While looking downwards, Hunter Davis got pricked with another piece of something, which stuck to his face. He pulled it off and examined the piece- it was a piece of brain.

Anxiety accelerated inside him. He wished the morning sun shed more light onto the forest. Suddenly, a rush of rumbles vibrated his platform. He looked down as the large tree shook with snow clumps falling to the ground. The snow creature shimmied up the back of the pine, and plopped on a huge branch behind Hunter Davis.

Shit, was the only word in his mind. Hunter Davis was upwind, and still did not smell the predator. Where did it come from? Did the beast stalk him from the backwoods? Megalonyx, this beast of a bastard, adapted to tree heights. Who would of guessed.

One pincer claw swung and rapped around the tree stand with Hunter Davis. Luckily, a cross bar stopped the blade from cutting him in two. The strength of the creature's upper arms, squeezed tightly, bending the metal frame. The hunter was trapped in his stand. He felt the pressure on his mid-section, and could not escape. He let go of his rifle which stayed slung on his side. He frantically attempted to free himself.

Hunter Davis was locked solid. He grabbed a revolver from his utility belt, and randomly fired behind him. Safety was the essence for him, as he originally picked a huge, stable section of the pine tree for his makeshift platform. The bullets flew aimlessly around the large trunk, missing his target. He now smelled the vile odor of the beast. Events quickly became reversed against him as the hunter was now the hunted.

The durable straps which held his weight and stabilized his stand, was not so durable to the sharp claws of the snow creature. The snow creature remained comfortable on a broad branch, and secured itself with one of its claws from a hanging stem above. The other pincer claw hacked away at Hunter Davis around the trunk, and finally ripped the straps. The whole apparatus fell with him smack to the ground. Although the snow piled around two feet, it did not soften his fall. Part of the metal frame came down on his leg underneath, and broke it.

Screaming in pain, he watched the huge beast gracefully climb down the tree like a monkey. No sooner could he yell for help, Hunter Davis was dragged through the forest by the beast. The broken leg was unbearable. His choices were none. Terror-strickened, he slid along the snow behind the snow creature.

The pincer claw clung onto the metal frame with him trapped in it. Hunter Davis noticed the claw was half broken. He figured at least someone did some damage to the beast. He realized that was the reason he survived the attack in the tree. The full claw would of easily crushed him in half. But now, he also realized his time left for survival was going to end. Somehow the painful trauma lessened his fear of death.

They approached the top of a high cliff. The snow creature placed him in a position that he could look at the view. The beast shook his head with surprise, then down with awe at the height. It stared with its small, beady red eyes at him. Then, the eyes became wider as if to convey a message. Megalonyx peered over the edge, making himself seem frightened, but like it was acting.

"You are a son of a bitch", Hunter Davis scowled." You going to throw me over, right? You are mocking me for sitting in the tree. You threw the brain stuff at me. You are not some stupid animal at all!"

The snow creature released small grunts, and kicked its stocky hind legs. It attempted to relay a message. The human hid high in a tree, thinking it could not climb. The snow creature possessed evolutionary, climbing traits similiar to the present day tree sloth.

Megalonyx conveyed a message, staring at his beating foe- Oh, you thought there was a fear of heights. This was what happens when you fool with - "The Master of the Winter World."

The snow creature flung Hunter Davis in his contraption out over the cliff. The hunter sailed downward, enjoying a last fresh breathe of air. He smashed hard on the broken rocks below. His bodily flesh was riddled with rips, and gouges from the sharp, rock bed. The Megalonyx exploded with one of its vengeful howls.

Hunter Davis let off a shot from his high performance rifle. He practiced trophy hunting as a member of the Boone and Crockett Club. He never ate the meat of his kill. This weapon was saved for a special prize, for that one of a kind trophy. The high priced gun now laid lost in the snow at top of the cliff. The name "Terminator" with a skull and crossbones were etched into the gun's stock. No joy from hunting came from it, yet.

Tommy and his brother Matt Drake heard the gunshots. They quickly headed to Hunter Davis's position. Nothing came back on the walkie talkies, and the central tent had no idea what happened. Fake Harold Olgeby ordered them to hold their area, but they refused. Matt Drake shut off his talkie.

Loud howls were heard in the distance. That was their buddy out there. If Hunter Davis sited the beast, they decided to assist. The trap was failing thanks to the sheriff. The bonus money invited the hunters to take matters in their own hand, and shoot it dead.

The Drake brothers surveyed the baited spot, and noticed the shoveled snow where the tree stand came down. They patiently tracked the trail noticing blood along the way. No sooner than walking a few minutes, a snow mound shuffled across in front of them, left to right. Immediately the two hunters shot rounds of ammunition with their semi-automatic rifles.

Nothing moved as the snow mound laid still. Quickly, they became thrilled by the kill. All of a sudden, more shuffling noise came from behind them. They turned to see a snow mound speeding right to left, and again they fired. The mound laid still as the two puzzled hunters quickly reloaded. To their far left, a snow mound began to shuffle, increasing distance away from them.

Confused uncertainty replaced their thrill for the kill. Calm, cool, collect, the hunter's trademarks, disappeared. How fast was this beast? Stalk mode was utilized, as they sight patrolled their surroundings. The hunters did not want to be flanked, and be victims of a sneak attack. Patiently, they paced, following the disrupted snow trails. The trails lacked conformity, and criss crossed all over. Plus, the snow creature left snow mounds as bluffs, confusing the hunters of its position.

No more visual motion was detected. Not a sound was heard in the forest. All was quiet as they stood, contemplating their next move. Tommy Drake developed a nervousness about the whole scenario. The beast plotted against them, and they were not doing the stalking. His brother Matt glanced at him with a look of unknown.

Fear called inside of Tommy Drake, and his hunting skills felt inadequate. He decided to call back to central camp. As soon as he turned on the walkie talkie, a loud buzz with the sheriff loudly yelling, pierced the quiet of the forest serenity. Breaking silence, gave away their position.

A snow mound rushed at 20 yards away towards them. Arming the rifles swiftly, shots were fired at the rolling snow ball. It smacked into their standing bodies. Both fell over like bowling pins. Little did they understand that the creature laid low as the muscular pincer claws rotated, digging the snow above. The bullets fired, flew over the body of the snow creature while it tunneled.

Two bullets made contact, but afflicted minor damage. The snow creature felt the bullet sting, which just slightly burned. Burrowing up, through the snowy ground, a claw sliced into Tommy Drake's chest. He sounded a few gurgles from his gaping mouth. The pissed off beast surfaced above the snow. It took vengeance upon its foe, and stomped on his body, over and over again. Tommy Drake was mushed like cherry fixin's topped on vanilla ice cream.

Matt Drake bounced to his feet in complete horror. He witnessed the death of his brother as if in an unbelievable nightmare. One of his boots slipped off while frantically running through the deep snow to escape. Mat Drake haphazardly, and unknowingly, headed straight towards the trap. He acted as the decoy to ensnare the snow creature.

The central camp was in disarray. Harold Olgeby argued with the sheriff. The plan seemed foiled. The mad scientist blamed the infamous sheriff that his men were amateurs, and screwed up the trap. Anxiety set in on the hunters stationed around the open field. Contact was lost with a few men, who actually were dead. The confused team challenged the possible success of the capture.

One hunter, Bobby Friedman, caught site of Matt Drake hysterically plodding through the snow near the clearing. There were three hunters positioned around the baited field, all secured in rocky outcrops. The facts dictated that the tunneling snow creature could not attack you on rock. Matt Drake headed straight for Bobby Friedman's spot. He climbed the rocky terrain, and stumbled next to the hunter, sweating profusely.

"The beast killed my brother, it killed him dead!" Matt Drake cried with hysterics. "This thing is a monster. The claws are longer than a person! Poor Tommy, oh my poor mother."

Bobby Friedman tried to calm him down as the antics were giving up his hidden position. Bobby Friedman noticed a medium size rock zip by his side, smashing into the rock bed. Then a rock the size of his head collided center into his face. He fell down unconscious and lost grip of his rifle. Matt Drake freaked, looking upon his friend's bloody face.

Then, he peered directly at the snow creature climbing casually onto the rocky outcrop. It grabbed another rock, and flung it with its claw. He thought the beast was unable to do these things. Climbing and throwing rocks? It kept coming and growling at him, meandering casually on top of the jagged ledge.

True, Megalonyx did not favor the rocky floor, and enjoyed the soft earth and snow to dig in. Although it felt exposed on hard surfaces, it did not mean it could not travel on it. How foolish its prey to believe it lacked cunningness, Stereotyping the cave dweller was a big mistake. It truly was-"Master of the Winter World".

Matt Drake hurriedly moved the other way scared out of his wits. His foot, the one without the boot, went down, and took a good twist. The pain was masked by his fear. He scrambled with a fractured ankle over rocks to the snow covered ground. He limped quickly to the center of the field. Maybe out in the open, someone could take it down with a rifle shot.

Megalonyx heard Bobby Friedman moan back on the ledge. The semi-conscious hunter glanced up, and witnessed the humongous beast. The snow creature chopped down on his head, and sucked out warm blood for a refreshing drink. It flung another rock, out at Matt Drake, almost hitting him as well. It threw the rocks just to show that it could, and with fair accuracy. This whole time the snow creature was toying with the stupid, human creatures. Matt Drake saw the rock tumble by his feet, and more hysteria overtook him.

Fake Harold Olgeby set a remote camera by the field. The staff at the central camp visioned the beast lumber out to the open. Quickly, he ordered the last hunters to stand down, and not to fire on their walkie talkies. They still had a chance at this. The hunters watched and were intimidated at the site of threatening beast.

Matt Drake stumbled as his sprain foot got stuck. His foot was tangled in something unknown. He sat reaching down his leg to loosen his entanglement. At the same time, the snow creature moved in his direction at thirty yards. He panted and cursed at his stuck foot. It was netting. It was high tech netting with steel enforcement. In the background, a helicopter hovered, zeroing in near the field. The air noise caught the curiosity of the snow creature, which stopped in its tracks.

On top of a tall pine, adjacent to the clearing, pointed a reversed giant hook. This hook was attached to steel cables looped to a tremendous net, buried in the snow. This netting encompassed a third of the field's center, along with the carcasses of deer. The helicopter accurately snapped its gear with the giant hook, and locked securely. The aircraft flew up and over the field slowly tugging the net together.

This noisy, flying thing was peculiar for the prehistoric creature. It upset the beast's demeanor enough, as it turned to retreat. The broken claw and one back leg, snagged into the netting, just like Matt Drake did.

The huge net slowly withdrawn on the snow creature, the helpless hunter, and deer bait.

The tech-advanced netting closed smaller and smaller as the cable was withdrawn up into the helicopter. This was not your everyday aircraft. This helicopter with powerful thrust, pulled up, wavered forward, pulled back, and strategically hovered different formations to enclose and secure the capture. Snow dusted and whirled everywhere, confusing the snow creature more.

The trapped hunter pressed against the woolly back of the beast, and slowly smothered. He desperately pleaded for God to help, praying in short breathes. His body cramped in the enclosed space of the net as Matt Drake watched a antlered deer squeezing toward him. He wished quickly to die and end his misery. But this would not occur. Still with shallow breathes, he watched as the deer antlers pushed, inch by inch below his chin. The antlers pierced into his chest, cracking his rib cage. His last breathe was one big, bloody discharge as the sharp antler cut through his lungs.

Matt Drake joined his brother Tommy. They left their poor mother with a concocted story from Thee Sheriff Gibbs. Their deaths were admirable in the man hunt for the maniacal killer of the townspeople. This would be the cover story of the going ons of Megalonyx. Mother Drake for years after would proudly speak how her sons protected Tannersville. The real irony of Matt Drake, remained in the facts that the seasoned hunter, who killed and poached hundreds of deer, was pierced to death by a deer antler.

Megalonyx, truly pissed off, battled with no success to free itself. Being immobile and confined, aggravated the beast immensely. These feelings, plus being airborne, brought on uncomfortable sensations. Weaknesses surfaced to defeat the beast.

The helicopter returned with its prize back to camp central. Fake Harold Olgeby, aiming with an elephant tranquilizer gun, shot a few darts into the snow creature as it hovered 10 yards above ground in the net. They needed to knock it out. It wriggled in the captured net with a few short hollers. The growls were more passive than usual, sounding off as small grunts instead. Then, with no movement, their 2 ton prisoner became incapacitated.

While it remained unconscious, the cage diligently was constructed. A portable steel frame interlocked with the webbed net to transform intro a non escapable habitat. The poles slid through prepared slots within the netting fiber. The team worked efficiently. The webbing expanded into a structural housing for the beast, which it already laid inside comatose. The interlocking joints were reinforced with titanium creating a sturdy, unbreakable zoo cage.

The net originally landed down on a concrete floor, from which the housing was compatible with to secure the beast. In the middle, the snow creature remained unconscious, laying on top of the dead hunter's legs. There was no way to remove dead Matt Drake. Lunch awaited to be served when it hungrily awoke.

Frank Porter grabbed the sheriff, and yelled," That hunter died as the bait! There was no chance for us to save him!"

"Casualties of war, Franky. A couple guys took to the grave for this freaking monster! Blame your Harold Olgeby." The sheriff exclaimed and pushed Frank Porter to the side.

Frank Porter noticed the broken pincer claw. The snow creature took some damage at least. He kept thinking- how will the camp's personnel deal with Matt Drake's body eaten in front of them?

The rest of Monday involved securing the beast in captivity. Around mid afternoon, the snow creature rolled its body over. More tranquilizers were injected to keep it in a coma. Due to the rush of their portable set up, the dosages were not well managed. Hopefully, the creature was not physically affected by adverse symptoms. A twenty-four hour.watch was mandated. They decided to keep it in snooze mode.

Frank Porter was amazed at the financial support the sheriff collected. This project generated major bucks, from the simple supplies to the high tech helicopter. The Federal Government could barely pull something like this off, given the amount of time, and they access the military forces.

"It is amazing how you got your hands on such a sophisticated system in such a short notice." Frank Porter politely said.

Thee Sheriff Gibbs replied," The extra day helped. I know some people at Norfolk, the military hub."

"You are a man of many talents Mr. Gibbs", replied Frank Porter.

As the sheriff walked away he snapped," It's Thee Sheriff Gibbs to you, and do not forget it. I am not your friend."

"Yes Sheriff Gibbs, or wait, Thee Sheriff Gibbs." He mockingly replied.

Fake Harold Olgeby joined the two arguing, and said, "I flew in an item, which I wish to share with you. I am going to grab two of your idiot huntsmen to give me a hand. Is this okay, I mean, does it meet with your approval."

The sheriff answered, "If it has to do with the large crate you flown in with your equipment, absolutely-tively."

"I figured you were a 'hankering' what its contents was." Fake Harold Olgeby exaggerated the word hankering with a country twang, making a local joke. He left the conversation like that, and exited the tent.

Near the cage, Frank Porter astutely stared at the huge, beaten animal. His feelings shifted, and realized it represented a predator like a wildcat, or a bear. A predator was a carnivore, and played its role in the scheme of the life cycle. The snow creature was not really a monster at all, but a mammal like all other warm-blooded mammals of earth.

The sun has been the source of all nourishment of our world. The energy emitted from the sun, becomes trapped by plants in photosynthesis. Herbivores always ate plants. Carnivores always ate herbivores. Omnivores have been eaten both. Predators, like the snow creature, developed techniques to insure food. Food has always been essential for existence, and has created life-death situations.

One would hope, the carnivorous Megalonyx weeded out the old, and diseased. However, its intrusive nature probably captured young ones, and the healthy animal population as well. This presented an imbalance in nature's cycle. Animal species insured survival by remaining healthy, and not to be eliminated or extinct. Did the snow creature upset the balance of nature?

Can one connect severe aggression with evil intent. Or was the snow creature's brutal, predation skills, a random gift to insure specie's survival. If so, where was all the fossils, and scientific facts of its grand existence?

Frank Porter felt a sorrow for the lost creature of the past. It just needed to answer the basic need for survival- hunger. What was so wrong with this deduction. Maybe this animal species could be assimilated back into the environment. Frank Porter doubted this idea. The chance of adaptation could be impossible, and its destructive nature could change the world against us- humans.

Frank Porter returned to the central tent, Thee Sheriff Gibbs stood waving a bunch of papers with a pissed off expression.

"No, this will never be printed. No! I told you to comply or else." The sheriff exclaimed.

Frank Porter replied," Poking through my stuff? What does that mean. You are going to kill me."

The sheriff waved papers and loudly said, "It has crossed my mind. This monster tale will not be read by the good, god-fearing people in town."

"That file report was locked in my luggage. You had no right. Well, what is your decision? What are you going to tell the world?" Frank Porter replied.

Thee Sheriff Gibbs explained,"You will see. Deputy Collins, keep this man in custody. A special quest will be visiting us tomorrow."

"Locking me up will not stop me one day from writing the truth." The newsman stated.

"Tomorrow the faith of the snow creature will be discussed." Thee Sheriff Gibbs exclaimed, and tossed the news reporter notes into the wood stove.

Upon that, men with the crate entered the command tent. Fake Harold Olgeby showed quite an enthusiastic smile, while a crowbar cracked open the hidden contents. He ordered the two hillmen to step aside. The crate's dimensions ran in length of roughly ten feet by five feet. All accounted for, shared an interest of the mysterious carton, including Frank Porter.

Deputy Collins grabbed his arm to hold Frank Porter in custody. He gave the officer a dirty look and said, " I am out here in the sticks. Where the hell do you think I am going to go?"

The deputy holding a pair of handcuffs, was about to answer him, but the sheriff exclaimed," Leave him alone. Our newsman may still be of great use to us."

Fake Harold Olgeby lifted the large item covered in a tarp, and placed it carefully on a table. It seemed light in weight, as it presented no problem for him to carry it. He uncovered the tarp to display the magnificent fossil of a giant scissor-like claw. Probably, a huge pincer from a past, dead Megalonyx.

"Here is the evidence of our snow creature from the past. I found more bones. The exposure of this missing link will bring us a fortune. We now need to conspire on how to deal with our newly found prehistoric pot of gold." The conniving scientist stated.

One of the hillmen, a large, 250 lbs. Wilbur Juggs, pushed Fake Harold Olgeby aside to take a closer look at the old fossil. The Boone and Crockett Club member admitted that he never killed anything with that bone structure. He showed signs of intoxication as he bumped into the table, and grabbed at the it clumsily. Fake Harold Olgeby became irritated, and warned him to step aside.

Wilbur Juggs ignored the asshole, which the hunter's all called him. The scientist was irritating with his sarcastic orders the last two days. Fake Harold Olgeby grabbed his shoulder to lead him away from the table. The old timer gave him an elbow check in the chest, which sent him flying backwards. Wilbur Juggs lifted the 8 ft. claw in his hands, and shakily stood, admiring the piece of fossil.

He commented with slurs," I lost good friends out here. I wanna look at the bone, I will looky here. My buddies are dead and eaten! Buzz off city slicker!"

Fake Harold Olgeby was no city slicker, but a maniacal killer. He approached Wilbur Juggs with offensive intent. Both wrestled with the fossil in hand, each tugging to possess it bodily. The sheriff became frantic, and he joined the mix to retrieve the fragile fossil. All were unbalanced and tumbled into the table with the huge claw. The old bone hit the floor into several pieces. They all laid there looking annoyed and guilty.

Fake Harold Olgeby softly stated, "That should not have happened. Fossils are not that delicate. This is highly unusual. Actual pieces disintegrated into dust."

"Well that ain't worth anything at all. Your bone is a fake," Wilbur Juggs remarked like he was educated in these matters.

Fake Harold Olgeby stood up in disgust. The bones were kind a lightweight. He would need to analyze the bone structure for strength, and density. Could Megalonyx suffered from a disease? When they fell, the fossil took most of the brunt on his chest. It cushioned the impact, and merely rolled off him onto the floor. Disintegrating into pieces should not of happened.

Was the downfall of the snow creature in its anatomical frame? New questions arose. Thee Sheriff Gibbs yelled at the Boone and Crockett Man, and hauled him out of the command tent.

The burly, Wilbur Juggs, winged a beer can at the snow creature's cage. A metallic ting resonated in the air. One eye popped open from the beast. It comprehended the predicament, realizing it was caught. It laid still while the huntsman verbally attacked it with profanity.

The snow creature wished to rip open the gut of Wilbur Juggs, but not to eat, but to satisfy its anger. It smelled Matt Drake's lifeless body surprisingly right next to it instead. The good claw poked at the human head, and casually chomped on the skull. Megalonyx then deliberately, savagely tore at Matt Drake, so the fat human, Wilbur Juggs, would be disgusted, and mad.

"You bastard! I will kill you someday!" Wilbur Juggs yelled. He shook his fists as he bolstered back to his tent. Exactly the strategy, Megalonyx, somehow desired.

Deputy Collins, escorting Frank Porter, looked on in horror as Matt Drake was ripped apart. They then continued to the chopper with a helpless attitude. Wilbur Juggs lied on his bunk yelling obscenities, which only gratified the beast more. The snow creature initiated its control, even in capture.

Back at the police office, Frank Porter was locked up. One night in jail was decided until the next morning. Frank Porter, against his will, still was included in the snow creature meeting tomorrow. Well, at least he will see Melanie Cuttles at the police station. He wondered how she fared after her intimate, shocking moment at Miss Queenie's farm.

A Day Earlier at Secret Cave

Mr. Phil Conti ached continuous. The drab lighting of his flashlight, the claustrophobic surroundings, and a chill escaping from some rocks, brought paranoia and extreme nervousness. Hunger overwhelmed him with abdomen pains. Drinking his last whiskey on a empty stomach, drove his comfortability rate to zero. He rolled restlessly, expecting that monster to sneak up and finish him.

He spoke aloud," Where is that stupid kid. I will not last. I cannot make it like this. I am going to die."

Mr. Conti, every bunch of seconds, kept conforming to different positions in his secret cave. This was definite high anxiety. Every move reminded him of his shoulder pain. He stood up, and stumbled on his hurt ankle, back and forth. He guessed this was good news. Limping on his ankle proved it was only fractured, and not severely broken.

Mr. Conti still had half a bottle of water. He downed it. What would be next? He had no idea. Getting out was the solution. It was ludicrous to trust that crazy kid. The boy thought he was a caveman? The kid out here alone, was playing games, thinking he was a crime fighter like Batman? Yeh, Kyle Meyers was batty alright. Was it day? Was it night? Mr. Conti had to do something to make things right.

Hell, it was time to go. Mr. Conti shimmied through his small cave entrance. His hand shone the flashlight around the cave tunnel from his cavern hole. Good so far, being there was no sight of that snow creature. He plopped forward, or really downward. It just felt safer going head first. Half way, near the bottom, he fell off the rocks. Again, his aching body radiated with striking bolts of pain.

A relief did overcome him. It felt better being out of the small enclosed cavern. The flashlight was dim, and Mr. Conti hoped it would last. He desired to see the light of the forest. That was, unless it was night time.

The wild caveboy mentioned there existed a back exit at the tunnel. No way he could climb up the open crevasse he fell from. He steadied himself against the rock wall, and stood listening. All was very quiet. Like piercing silent quiet, not a creature was stirring, not even a mouse.

Mr. Conti, with no walking stick to aid his injuries, stumbled along the back tunnel. He limped no more than ten yards when he heard breathing. Breathing. This meant a living thing lied ahead of him.

He quickly thought. He lived as a country boy, an experienced outdoorsmen. How many different animals could be breathing down in a dark wintry cave? He wanted to believe it was not the snow creature.

Panic-stricken feelings replaced the aching pain.The breathing came from something sleeping. No problem. Mr. Conti would reverse his steps, and head back to his lovely hole in the wall. Confident thinking was essential, and so he forcefully attempted to suppress his fear. He would simply hop, climb, and jump back into his cozy man cave.

Then, a small growl resonated in the tunnel. His dim light shone against the wall. Slowly, inch by inch, he adjusted the beam of light towards the center of the cave hallway. To his surprise, a black bear raised its head back and forth, sniffing the air around him. Its eyes flashed from his light. It then lowered its head and sniffed the rocky floor.

Oh, this was not so bad. Thinking, this guy was better than that abominable snow creature. Mr. Conti stepped backwards only to collapse to the floor, kicking rocks noisily. His brain was delusional, and his body still had major physical injuries.

The fall excited the black bear who expelled a louder growl. It was not just simply a black bear, it was a giant black bear. It was about to lunge at the injured Mr. Conti. After another giant bear growl, Mr. Conti's reasoning returned, and knew it was game over for him. What, was he freaking stupid! That was a mean, man-eating mother ff...ng bear!

A massive explosion blasted down in the cavern. Another nasty roar bellowed from a different mother ff...ing giant. Megalonyx slammed its pincers claws into the cave rocks with missile force. The beast was infuriated at the furry newcomer, trespassing on its territory. Not only that, but the audacity of this bear to enter into its personal lair. Mr. Conti stared helplessly as he laid amongst the rocks. He had front row seats to the fight of savage beasts.

Quickly, the black bear clamped his huge paws onto one of the massive pincer claws of the snow creature. It held tightly while the two struggled. The snow creature was twice the bear's size, and had difficulty biting or hitting the bear within the confined space. Both wrestled as Mr. Conti inched backwards, heading to the bottom of the entrance of his small cavern. He shone his flashlight on sinister faces, threatening expressions of exposed teeth, and flying fur among the dusted air.

The black bear bit down hard on the pincer claw, still grasping tightly with its own claws. The huge pincer broke in half! The black bear's power grip cracked the snow creature's claw. Mr. Conti was shocked. How could that be of such low durability. It dug through all that snow, and pushed huge boulders. Black bears were strong, and with one swipe could take off a man's head. But something like this did not add up right.

Mr. Conti had time to escape. The two cave titans grappled each other, not paying attention to him. He scrambled up the ledge to his secret cave entrance, just before becoming stomped to death. The snow creature howled ferociously with ultimate aggression. It smacked the bear center in the chest with the other good pincer claw. The bear was sent rolling over upon itself down the tunnel. Mr. Conti hung by his entrance as the repulsive, smelling snow creature lumbered underneath. It's woolly head moved inches below his dangling legs.

Megalonyx moved in for the final blow to its invader. Mr. Conti laid in his cave hole, flashing light on the two giants. He now had good balcony view of the match. The bear unpredictably charged and aimed for its neck. The stout neck gave little room, and so the bear chomped down onto the snow creature's face. The bear's head was smaller, and its bite lacked potential for damage.

Megalonyx ripped the bear from it's cheek, leaving a flesh wound. One clean samurai-like slice flashed down on the bear neck. It cut the head, hanging half off the body. It quickly followed a second blow to the neck with the good claw. All was quiet within seconds from the decapitated black bear. The snow creature picked up the bloody head and sucked out its winnings.

Unexpectantly, Megalonyx quickly turned and reached out the good pincer claw at Mr. Conti sitting above. The flashlight knocked out of his hand, and fell to the tunnel floor. The snow creature was not finished yet, and constantly aware of Mr. Conti. The exhausted man did not expect this fast motion. He crawled backwards into his small cavern. He moved to the rear in pure darkness. The large claw jammed into the opening, barely missing him. Mr. Conti could feel the air displacement from the claw's motion as it shoved into every nook and cranny of the small enclosure.

He huddled in a fetal position, and thought of viscious thoughts to kill the beast. The snow creature relentlessly smashed at the entrance, hoping to create more space for it to get in. Mr. Conti peered about, but could not see. He was scared.

Mr. Conti shut his eyes with helplessness. His thoughts escaped to the flub facts from his caving school course. A large smash occurred in front of him. Okay, what was a cave? He remembered some tidbits. A cave was a natural formed void located beneath the earth's surface. Passages must be large enough to admit humans for caving exploration. The huge claw scratched against the rocky wall. Sounds of falling debris could be heard. This cave was not big enough for Megalonyx. It signed up for the wrong course.

Deeps vibrations and rumbles were felt from the rocky walls. Okay, unstable ceiling rocks could be set loose by vibrations. Caving can be fun, but be safe first. So always remember to be voiceless, slow and quiet. Another loud smash was heard. Mr. Conti refused to open his eyes, even though there was only darkness. He prayed that this hole would not cave in, and be his funeral plot.

The air became musty as the dust content increased from the snow creature's digging. His claustrophobia started to kick in again. He did, however, felt the cool draft, which previously annoyed him. The cavern breeze blew from a hole which was sizable for his body to fit. He remembered when he checked it with the flashlight. It did not present a rewarding escape.

Mr. Conti had no choice. More rumble became displaced around the cave entrance. The snow creature was gaining ground into his trapped spot. His beaten up body crawled into the tight opening, hoping it to be a valid escape. He now had some rock separating him from the beast. The crashing of the claw sounded muffled. The enclosed crawling wreaked havoc on his claustrophobia.

Before he continued, the rocky ground underneath his arms collapsed, and his body fell aimlessly. He became soaking wet, and rode along a slippery surface in darkness. An underground river carried him downwards. Darkness, little space, and now water, pumped the stuff nightmares are made of into his head.

Time for more speculation on caving. Cave beginnings developed from slow moving water by millions of years without sound. Majority of caves occurred in limestone. Limestone beds were built from layers of shellfish, debris, and sedimentary rock. These beds were deposited unevenly of different rock, sand, silt, which intermixed with the limestone. Over the ages, beds shifted, uplifted, forming horizontal and vertical cracks by volcanoes, and earthquakes. The rain, floods, and ice ages, added to the development of caves over geological ages.

Suddenly Mr. Conti stopped moving on the underwater river. He was caught on a low ceiling hindering his body. Mr. Conti started choking, and frantically turned his head for air. He was stuck in a tight spot. Pushing forward, was thought to be his only true escape. The enclosed river could lead to a dead end, seeping into smaller cracks.

Everything occurred too fast. He just went with the events as they happened. He heard a mighty muffled roar, and sounds like explosions. He then became unstuck as chunks of rocks intermixed with the water flow. He now rode faster with the underwater current. Air was gasped anytime he managed, but also took some water. The underground river was to small.

Could Megalonyx be right behind him? Where and how? Again, Mr. Conti could hear muffled roars, during his choking fits for air and unwanted water.

A jagged edge added obstacles to his journey. Of course his bad shoulder bumped into it. Luckily, the underground cavern had breathing space. He swallowed more water which presented utter distress. His cavern swim consisted of choking, swimming, aching, and praying.

Anything alive which existed in the cavern, would of constantly heard, "Oh my God, Oh my God, Oh my God ..." Mr. Conti next felt himself airborne, His body became weightless for a few seconds. He splashed down into a large pool of collecting water.

Immediately, instinctively, he waded in the cavern lake searching for land, a hard surface.

The collision with jagged outcrop earlier, displaced his shoulder again, making the action of swimming difficult. Joy overcame him when he actually felt his feet touch bottom. He walked/floated to the bank. Light protruded from several holes in the rocks, and the water seeped outside from the several openings.

His pain was not too unbearable because he basically was numb from the water chill. He maneuvered himself as best as he could. His fear and paranoia became less as he witnessed light shining through rock crevaces. He dragged himself on the wet rocks, attempting to bodily escape the soaking cave water.

It was time for more useless, safety facts. Hypothermia consists when body loses heat faster than it can be replaced. This was caused by prolonged activity in the cold, exhaustion, wetness, and loss of will power. His cave knowledge dictated the wise caver rule again- caves can be the killers of the unprepared! Where was the space blanket every caver equips in his supplies?

Mr. Conti realized he laid in a dome pit. A dome pit with a lake. He breathed the fresh air seeping through the cracks in the wall. The clean, less musty air felt good. The outside was within feet. He felt positive that he would find an opening, and escape. He also needed to adjust his displaced shoulder again.

Light seeped and scattered into the large cavern. These natural holes to the outside were useful for yet another type of animal. Mr. Conti noticed movement on the ceiling above. Hundreds of bats were hanging in their daytime dormancy. As he lifted his hand, which gave him support from the floor, it was caked with guano, bat droppings. The floor around him was loaded with bat crap.

Like switching a television channel, a bat fact was realized from his caving days. The disease, rabies, can be contracted from breathing the air with dense bat populations, as well as other serious sicknesses. His fall into the lake, fortunately, did not start a panic. The excited bats would of flown in disorder and possibly, scratch him, bite him, piercing his skin. Physical, direct contact could bring on rabies easier.

A shocking explosion sounded throughout the dome pit. The snow creature fell from roof. Megalonyx broke through the ceiling due to its weight, and landed with a hardy splash into the lake.

It was bat time. The air above teemed with the flying little critters. But this concern was small against the snow creature now paddling with the huge claws, pushing its way towards Mr. Conti.

He was useless and exhausted. His dislodged shoulder aided his negative handicap for escape. Mr. Conti watched the beast, straight line right to him. He could not move. It was all over.

Suddenly nowhere, his witchy senses kicked in. A voice spoke to him with words," You are a smoker, there is a water resistant lighter in your pocket. Hey stupid, your are a cancer-stick smoker!"

Finally, a useful flub fact popped in thought at this crucial moment. Bat guano was flammable! Quickly Mr. Conti grabbed in his pocket for the cigarette lighter. Hundreds of bats swarmed inside the cave dome. As they circled, several would take exit out the cave openings to the forest. Megalonyx cared less about the little things. He hunted Mr. Conti and tugged along in the water for its just desserts.

Ten yards and closing, the lighter flipped on for a flame, and fire, fire everywhere! Mr. Conti rolled just as a huge claw came slamming down. The flames quickly spooked the beast as Mr. Conti with extreme pain pushed himself over some rock formation. He hid behind a huge stalagmite – stalagmites were formed from splashing action of water dripping down from hanging down stalactites. (No more time for Caving Course 101).

The fire burned fast, and covered a large portion of the dry inside of the cavern. Megalonyx despised fire. It took its heated dose of Mr. Conti's surprise attack, and headed toward the light from outside. It moved quickly to the wall of cave openings, smashed an opening, and then disappeared to the outside. A distant roar could be heard as it tunneled away.

Mr. Conti used every effort in his body to crawl to the new access out. Thanks to Megalonyx, he miraculously crawled out of the cavern. Jubilation was the best word to describe his feelings right now. The sun brightly beamed on the crystal snow. He escaped.

He glanced about, squinting from the sunlight, and only saw a way out upwards. This would be difficult.

He mumbled and said, "The hell with it. I am going for it."

Mr. Conti's glee helped mask the cold sensation, and he was not going to sit around here. He grabbed a stable stick to support his weight, and limped up the sloping terrain. He constantly peered over his shoulder awaiting the beast to crash out from somewhere, and finish him off.

The air was cold, but Mr. Conti seemed to be tolerable of his environment. The climb was welcomed over sitting in that nightmarish cavern.

It seemed endless in time, finally reaching the top. The physical moving generated heat, but now, as he stood at the top of a cliff, the cold sharply penetrated his body. He propped himself against a tree as a urge to sleep overwhelmed him.

No! He exclaimed to himself. He quickly surveyed the area. His body shook a bit as the thought of hypothermia came back. The cliff top was full of deep pine trees. Underneath the tree canopy, there existed dry spots with old, fallen pine branches. Quickly, as shaking increased all over him, he grabbed bunches of branches, sloppily in a bunch, and immediately torched the pile with his life saving lighter.

Crackling, the flames presented pure joy for Mr. Conti. The warmth of the fire penetrated his body right away. He laid next to his lovely, little campsite. He closed his eyes, and longed to sleep. But no, he forcefully interrupted his feelings with a fast survey of his area. Look around, keep busy, he reminded himself. If the fire goes out now, he could be dead.

To his unbelievable surprise, over his shoulder within 30 yards, a shiny, metallic object attracted his view. Mr. Conti could not wait. Any useful supply would be a plus right now. He crawled over to the object. An impressive rifle laid in the snow on the cliff top, like a gift from a Forest God.

He picked it up, and felt an icy sting to the metal touch. Mr. Conti dropped it, put his hand inside of his jacket, and then grabbed it. It was a fancy gun. A high quality material, performance rifle, which appeared to be a collector's item, which laid there in the snow. Only a hunter with money to waste, would take this baby outdoors. On the rifle buttocks, an inscription read- The Terminator. Mr. Conti did not ponder on questions, but simply took it.

And then he welcomed another surprise. He found two energy bars. Quickly, he unwrapped them, and ate like he did not eat for five days. Well, it actually was two. He crawled and rolled back to his fire. More dry branches were fed to the warm fire. Mr. Conti snuggled with "The Terminator". The rifle was fully loaded.

This item looked like a leftover from the snow creature. Somehow his witchy sense called out that a hunter lost his life. This rifle, with the skull and bone insignia, was left from an unfortunate encounter with the beast. Mr. Conti tracked the trail of the snow creature. "The Terminator" obviously did not do the dead hunter any good. The energy food bars were a plus.

Mr. Conti, as he dozed off, could visualize this gun owner, home by his cozy fireplace, dreaming one day to use his prized gun. The hunter probably would have been off better with his older 30.06 Remington, Although it needed constant maintenance, the gun probably never missed the bullseye. Mr. Conti knew a name in his dream vision, Davis, and visioned him shooting his 30.06 without a miss. The hunter lacked experienced with the fancy rifle.

Mr. Conti awoke in the twilight of evening. He had no idea where he was in the vast forest. He would follow the trail of broken snow which lead away from the cliff. Now, he would rest more. Somewhere distant, Mr. Conti heard rifle fire. His witchy sense signaled trouble to the sounds of distant yells. He blacked out.

CHAPTER 9

Blast From the Past

THE CAR RENTAL PULLED in at Monticello, Virginia. Tourism was low this time of year, but a special weekend before Christmas, attracted a good crowd. Monticello was the estate where Thomas Jefferson, our third President of the U.S.A., lived out his days. The grounds were awe inspiring, even without the green landscapes and warm temperatures. The architecture captured your presence with simple and yet complex structure. Thomas Jefferson's Monticello represented a home, which breathed life, and welcomeness.

The renaissance building itself was beautiful. The manor was designed uniquely from early American style. The front foyer, and impressive balcony, held your attention upon viewing the front facade. The octagonal roof, imitating the dome of Halle aux Bleds in France, shaped the Jeffersonian home with uniqueness. This signature roof installed a gem like quality to Monticello. Thomas Jefferson believed in his ideals and philosophy, which he incorporated in his home.

The third president once said,"I shelter myself in the fine arts to escape the vulgarities of our society."

The winter time visit denied the guest a full experience of Monticello's potential. It was known for its elaborate gardens, orchards, and outdoor connections. Monticello reflected rural life, which Thomas Jefferson incorporated into his philosophy. It was called the agrarian way.

Thomas Jefferson had also commented,"My home was a continuation of my own body".

There existed structural secrets, only known to Thomas Jefferson to enjoy. He believed a house should be partly hidden, just like a man's body.

Where did the snow creature's role played in this Jeffersonian way of life?

The love of the outdoors, possessed him towards an intrigue of earth's past. His discovery of the prehistoric clawed sloth, Megalonyx Jeffersonia, might shed new information concerning their situation. The prehistoric sloth, though, was not exactly like, but similar to the carnivorous snow creature. Knowledge discovered over 200 years ago, could have been misunderstood, and now extremely helpful.

He accompanied Melanie Cuttles who was in dire need for a getaway. The trip to Monticello helped relieve her stress from the beastly confrontation. She remained quiet most of the car trip. Every now and then, she rubbed his shoulder. This action seemed to relax her, as well as Frank Porter. Her calmness needed the presence of a man. It felt good escaping the motherly responsibilities of her son, and added challenges in raising a teenager.

Few Days Earlier

Frank Porter met her at the police station, the morning of his incarceration. Her presence was not to work, but to pick up a few things she left in her desk. The day of the Miss Queenie's horror show, left Melanie Cuttles very withdrawn, She muddled through her stuff, and became surprised to see Frank Porter sitting in a jail cell. He stared directly at her.

"Hey hot stuff," he called out .

"Really now. You enjoying a free peep show? What are you doing in there." She replied.

Frank Porter said in jest,"Doing what all us real news reporters do. Charged with criminal activity for writing the truth."

Melanie Cuttles said,"So, did you also enjoy my nakedness, my public ridicule because of that jerk of a sheriff?"

"At Miss Queenie's farm, I was busy trying to drive and escape. I never took a good look." He replied trying to make the incident like it was no big deal.

Melanie Cuttles replied with light humor,"Well you missed the best. So, do I have to bake a cake with a file for my new boyfriend?"

Boyfriend? She actually said boyfriend? This was a first. So the feelings were mutual after all.

Frank Porter thought of Bill Meyers, with his infatuation of Susan Conti. He wondered if he followed the same incorrect interpretation of his romantic emotions for Melanie Cuttles. The boy's longing for a girl, blocked his rational ideas for both a physical and platonic relation-ship. True Love was always a two way street. One way, would lead to a dead end.

Melanie Cuttles looked very attractive with her plain appeal. She used little cosmetics today, and her hair laid casual over her shoulders. She looked more appealing than when the hair was all done up. He remembered how his fingers would stick in her hair style, full of spray products to shape it. Her interest in him, bolted his confidence, and his attraction steered on the right track.

He said,"How are you dealing with all the tragedy, Melanie. I bet it is not easy for you to witness all this dreaded shock."

She replied."Well, I guess. Thee Sheriff Gibbs spoke lengthy to me after I settled down. He apologized about his van groping. Not only did he strip me of my clothings, but stripped my will to live. He threatened me with all kinds of angles about this monster. I promised to shut up about everything, but he had to promise not to brag about seeing me naked."

Frank Porter heard shallowness in her comments. She cared less about the danger of there lives, and more of her social stasis.

"Our lives changed, that was for sure, Melanie."He replied.

She walked up to the bars, and through them, she grabbed his shirt by his shoulders. Frank Porter was pulled towards her, and received a nice kiss. It was good for each of them. Melanie Cuttles needed some compassion, and wished to drag him home with her. Frank Porter felt emotions stir, and wished to do the deed right here through the jail bars.

Frank Porter stated,"When I am released. We will get together - I Want You to Want Me."

Melanie Cuttles giggled with a stupid impression. She wondered, what was this- a Cheap Trick song? What was he thinking. Was he sixteen years old and she impressed with his teenager incite.

Frank Porter realized the connection after he blurted the statement, and yes it was kind of dumb. He lacked the flowing connection to lead romance. Melanie Cuttles was the leader in this department, and controlled the love show.

Frank Porter could not bring the stability, the union. Their passionate interactions lacked mutual ground. He went along with her suggestions, like a pet dog following its owner. He was falling in love with her. Or was he? Without realizing it, he could be mimicking Bill Meyers. Was he madly bound to misinterpreted emotions?

All the years with his wife, amounted to nothing. How stupid could he really be? His ex-wife, Mary, was ravaged by the postman for a year, in his bed, and wearing his robe. Something which movies were made of- sex with the postman? Why did she despised him so much? He would never learn. Some would say, the answer stood right in front of his face.

Maybe, Mary's glasses of wine in the afternoon filled a void, a void Frank Porter unknowingly invited. Adventurous ideas, diverting her internal frustrations, materialized into reality. He failed to realize that having few physical relations over a year, might have sparked the divorce.

Frank Porter lived a teenager, inverted kind of life. For him, his child years were fulfilling. He enjoyed reading science-fiction books. He contently sat on the summer beach with shorts, socks, and sneakers. He hated sand. So, he never caught a baseball during his little league years. He and his friends enjoyed board games, and spent Saturday afternoons inside playing video games. Frank Porter realized his life mimicked that of Bill Meyers.

His creative nature matured into investigative professionalism, and now, was greatly respected as a good writer- an underpaid, unknown newspaper writer.

"I am suppose to meet with our asshole sheriff in a hour. He wants me to attend some meeting about this bloody mess in Tannersville,"Melanie Cuttles continued.

He answered,"You too? I guess our Sheriff Gibbs once everyone who witnessed the snow creature to attend. Some surprise guest will be part of the solution. I am guessing a "Big Shot", government type official. Probably, very covert. We need to trust each other. These events could have serious altering issues in our lives. Maybe even, ending our lives."

She exclaimed,"You are scaring me, Franky. You are smart. I trust you . We stick together. Thee Sheriff Gibbs, well there is something about him. I sometimes feel in a uncomfortable way."

"It is a deal. We will be a secret team. Let us leave this nightmare safely behind." Frank Porter finalized.

After saying that, Deputy Collins returned with breakfast,and gave Frank Porter something to eat. An hour later, they gathered there belongings, and drove to a farmer's field to catch a helicopter. They flew to arrive for the 10:00 A.M. secret meeting.

Back at Monticello

Never in a million years, would Frank Porter of thought, that this institution would be associated with the freak business of the snow creature. One of the many talents of Thomas Jefferson consisted of his personal inquiry of fossils. One of his manuscripts, caught the eye of Frank Porter. The Jeffersonian article explained how many fossils discovered were in poor condition, and developed unstable storage conditions.

There was a lack of technology for detailed investigations back in colonial times. The incomplete bones left puzzles and questions unanswered . Thomas Jefferson did, however, have them recorded, categorized, and stored at Monticello. Frank Porter hoped these records would shed some answers to their alive Megalonyx.

In one of these old manuscripts, A unique group of fossils were mentioned. These bones became frail and decayed over a short time in storage. Some would crumble into pieces by a simple touch. Thomas Jefferson's examination concluded that their existed different bone composition of this species.

Originally, these delicate fossils shared similar traits with his Megalonyx Jeffersonia. He never established any solid facts or correlations. Who or what these bones belonged to, was left as a mystery. The fragile bones were equipped with large sword-like claws. The sturdier fossils of the herbivore, Megalonyx Jeffersonia, utilized burrowing, fingered claws like an armadillo.

Thomas Jefferson gave up on his inquiries, and pampered his failing health in his old age.

This information supported the same findings of Harold Olgeby's fossils. His too, with much disappointment, disintegrated over a short time. The scientist only had a few intact fossils left, thankful to cold storage. Frank Porter felt positive, that the fragile fossils of Thomas Jefferson were that of the snow creature. Maybe Megalonyx, the carnivore, owned bone structure effecting its demise. This trip also meant, they were not the first to discover this new species. Of course, Thomas Jefferson now again stole the glory, adding to his list of accomplishments.

Melanie Cuttles accompanied him into the main hallway of the astute mansion. She could not hide her excitement, and first, freshened up in the ladies room to start the tour. Frank Porter immediately noticed his contact, who openly greeted him. A medium sized, black man, with a serene smile, and quiet composure, waved politely from the middle of the busy hallway. The other knew as well this was the man he expected. The two shook hands and spoke complimentary salutations.

"I am Rupert Jones, welcome to Monticello." This gentleman was family related to the original slaves who worked for Thomas Jefferson.

Rupert Jones held information about Megalonyx, and related fossils. Frank Porter hoped this man knew information to help understand the snow creature. Frank Porter decided to keep the live capture a secret, via his agreement with Thee Sheriff Gibbs.

"So, this is your first visit here". Rupert Jones said politely.

"Yes, I never expected to find my reporting leading me to Thomas Jefferson's home. Fossil hunting of prehistoric animals does nor seem to correlate with the revolutionary war." Frank Porter replied.

Rupert Jones replied," Yes, our forefather was truly a man of many talents."

The passive black man looked admirably at Frank Porter every now and then. He searched for the newsreporter's true purpose. This archaeologist was a master in his field for a reason. He studied fossils for a purpose, like it established his destiny.

Rupert Jones said,"Although the giant ground sloth attracts interest, especially with children, there really is not much to share. These personal letters you seek do not release much scientific data. Instead, reflect a man, Thomas Jefferson playing a detective, and attempting to understand the universe. The place of God, and the history of the earth always challenged the mental acuity of many intelligent thinkers. For goodness sake, they did not even have electricity yet. Just think of their world, over 200 years ago, without the advances made from oil discovery."

Frank Porter replied, "Yes, God answered the unexplained, and things happened for a reason. God's will was the solution. That is, until science filled in the puzzle pieces, confusing the supreme position of God."

"You are a bright fellow. Look, here comes your beautiful lady. Let us not bore her. Go take the wonderful tour, and I will meet you back here in one hour. Our Christmas festivities feature many fruit jams from the trees, here, at Monticello. Go visit the heated tents outside, and purchase some of the homemade products." The historian concluded.

The two enjoyed the pleasantries of Monticello. Strolling among the fine rooms, and different decor, helped masked the problems at home. Frank Porter walked hand in hand with Melanie Cuttles with passion. She rubbed up to him closer every now and again. A small kiss was given here and there down the historic hallways.

At the end, they met up with Rupert Jones, and together, ate a wonderful lunch. Both men eyed each other as they slowly entered conversation of the subject matter at hand. Frank Porter gave Melanie Cuttles 40 dollars, and mentioned that she should shop in town. The men were going to talk business.

"I noticed a scar on her neck, leading underneath her coat." Rupert Jones mentioned. "Did she have a recent accident."

"Yes, I told her to stop scratching it, and try to forget the pain." Frank Porter mentioned.

"So you are interested in some letters. I have access to personnel rooms here at Monticello, I am allowed to use. As you know my kin were servants here." The historian said.

They headed to a private wing of the mansion, and took stairs down into the basement. It was clean but muddled. File cabinets placed everywhere, and some tables had bone fossils.

Frank Porter glanced around the basement room, and Rupert Jones gathered some papers.

"You can look through these documents. As I said, it is mostly general, and not very conclusive." he replied.

Frank Porter said, "I am interested in the findings of unstable fossils. The team, which I represent, discovered bones which disingrated too easily, when removed from their natural setting. Their structure slightly differentiated from the typical plant eating, Megalonyx Jeffersonia. The exposure to air, after they were dug out, turned brittle within weeks."

Rupert Jones raised an eyebrow, and guessed the direction of the conversation.

He stated, "Yes, Thomas Jefferson, or I should say the slaves, first discovered these fossils. They were different than the prehistoric ground sloth, Megalonyx, yet similar. The first bones reflected teeth, molars of a plant eating species. The brittle ones, were had a type of scissor claws, and a fanged skull."

"And then the artifacts probably disintegrated." The newsman added.

"That is correct Mr. Frank Porter. The other bones were stable, and could be fully examined. The first set of bones were considered an accident, and thought to be the same as the Ground Clawed Sloth. Which as you know was a plant eater."

Frank Porter concluded, "They were not the same, but considering the time, the technology, the results brought confusion. Their were two sets of fossils belonging to different creatures, but both Megalonyx cousins. Thomas Jefferson did not access of information to distinguish the unique facts."

"That is correct." Rupert Jones continued with the same trend of inquisitive thought.

"This creature had defected bone composition, leading to its instability. But as you said, the letters written are not very detailed." The newsman continued.

The historian added, "These letters are not, but there are other documents. My past great uncle, Paddy Jones, was a learned slave turned free man, back in 1810. He wrote of his experiences with Thomas Jefferson, concerning the fossil hunting. A private diary, but not publicized of course."

This caught Frank Porter's interest quickly. His black scholar in arms, brought out a vintage whiskey from a desk draw.

Rupert Jones said, "Try some of this liquor. Homemade recipe dating back to the origins of Monticello. A special blend of corn and grain grown here on these private grounds."

They shared two shots of whiskey. This was the stuff you sipped on a cold wintry night, with its production of overwhelming body warmth.

Frank Porter continued, "Excellent brand. So, your great uncle, Paddy Jones, wrote fossil documents as well."

"Yes, of course. He was the actual expert, Thomas Jefferson relied on. A lot of Uncle Paddy's work was rewritten under Thomas Jefferson's name. As you know, due to slavery, my uncle's skills could not be exposed. Thomas Jefferson struggled with the concept of black freedom his whole life. But in the end, still conformed to the norm of political incorrectness. Some slaves were freed at his death, such as Paddy Jones." He stated.

Rupert Jones handed copies from the originals for the reporter to examine. "These letters report that the unstable bones belong to an animal species- a ferocious, vile giant."

"How do you know it was vile?" The newsman answered with curiousness.

Rupert Jones conflicted with his emotions, and was concerned how to play the next move. He did not know this man. However, all these years of secrecy, did not produce anything significant. He decided to go for it. He poured two more whiskey shots, and remained silent.

Frank Porter said,"Boy, this stuff is golden, Rupert. I am surprised Thomas Jefferson did not sell his original whiskey, in considering all his other endeavors."

Rupert Jones stated,"The liquor was kept private, personal to him. Thomas Jefferson believed certain truths to be kept secret, secret to a man's self worth. Also, personal was the giant monster. Many nights were sleepless because of this vile pestilence."

"I do not follow. You speak like it was more than just a fossil." Frank Porter remarked.

The historian slyly said,"You know exactly what I mean, Mr. Frank Porter. You have one, alive too, right?"

Frank Porter looked on with shock, and blurted, " How do you know? We call it the snow creature."

"The Jefferson team called it the savage giant. This whiskey was produced about the same time of the awakening of the evil thing. Both were kept a secret. His special brew always reminded him of this savage giant." he remarked.

This conversation seemed unbelievable. A connection, present to the past of fantastical, terrible truths. Thomas Jefferson did battle with the snow creature? Both men sat in the dim basement getting high on alcohol. Both men told of dreaded stories, actual realities, and not scary fiction spoken like two teenage movie fans.

Rupert Jones said,"I present to you confidential letters written by Thomas Jefferson. You are now part of a few who set eyes on these documents. Paddy Jones was entrusted with these letters to hold, and the complimentary ghost writer. Thomas Jefferson upheld him to a sacred oath, until he needed to share it with others. That day never happened. Upon Jefferson's death, Paddy Jones passed it down with his ancestors, not really sure what to do."

"That was some secret to bare, especially for a black man in colonial times." The newsman claimed.

"Most people were spiritual in those days, or let us say more mystical religious. This creature was marked as a demon, the devil itself. There was a righteous honor to keep this secret, and to destroy the demon in order to save humankind." The historian said.

"So they actually battled the snow creature?" Frank porter concluded.

Rupert Jones searched through journals and papers, which he placed on the desk. He always handled the material with extra care because its fragile nature. The letters were sleeved in transparent, plastic folders to preserve them.

"This letter marks the original overview of your snow creature." He said.

Frank Porter quickly took an interest, and examined it. The letter was as follows:

Confidential Record October 1795   The Savage Giant

The unfortunate process to remove an unsightly rocky growth, brought a sinister presence into our world as we know it. The savage giant immediately sprung from the hole which was produced by Charles McCormick's explosives. The property purchased by my in-laws needed some sprucing up with the removal of a annoying rock bed, blocking a scenic overview from the Master Home.

The vile, smelling animal attacked two working men. This included Charles McCormick, and digested parts of his human flesh. All fled in fear, as for myself, the wagon which I sat, took off with two spooked horses. My life almost ended with the chaotic ride through the woods. Luckily, I grabbed the reigns to able to control the frightened animals.

One could never forget the withdrawn red eyes of the savage giant. They peered with evil intent, absorbing the surroundings to maraud all that is good. The movements and presence, installed fear itself into a man's soul. The red eyes, fangs, the large damaging claws, the putrid odor, and the sinister growls it reverberated, were all signs of the demonic being.

Quickly, we assembled, to draw plans against this savage giant. I believe some of my fossils are that of this missing link. I hope salvation his reached, and *elimination brought onto this pestilence, which I blame myself for entering our christen world.*

Concerned And Fearful,
Thomas Jefferson

The thought of men with muskets fighting the snow creature, was too surreal. The concept did not sink in. The mind refused to accept this as possible, and that of the impossible. How would the present day officials tackle the Megalonyx.

Rupert Jones said, "I think it is time for some coffee. I wish the solution to the problem was simple. Simple it is not. The colonials attempted to contain the savage giant at the cavern opening. They fed cattle, goats, sheep, and anything they could muster up to satisfy its hunger. By keeping it in one area, they hoped to finalize a plan to destroy the beast."

Frank Porter glanced at some additional letters, and said, "It claims they lost over a dozen men in dealing with it. They attempted some traps and tactics which ultimately failed. The only positive note was the savage giant prowled near this cave.

"Yes, this gave them time to hash out a more decisive plan. However, pure luck was the answer. Here is a another document, where Thomas Jefferson reports the final days of the savage giant. I will go upstairs to the kitchen. I will bring us some hot coffee and snacks. The women who works here, at the mansion, bakes a delicious apple pie. You read, and I will be back." Rupert Jones replied.

He left as Frank Porter stood up for awhile to stretch his body. So much information revealed, in such a short time to deal. He rubbed his eyes wishing for the coffee, but could not wait. He sat down again on a classic, wooden swivel chair. Frank Porter needed to know how this ended, and shook off the sluggish feeling from the whiskey.

Delicately, the 200 year old document laid on the desk, Carefully, he removed it from a folder, and again the letter was preserved in a transparent cover. These papers were well kept, and hardly were torn or unreadable from age.

CONFIDENTIAL REPORT MARCH 1795

Our will to overcome became suddenly rewarded. Just when all seemed to be a failure, a heavenly miracle. The savage giant was seen snoozing at the cavern opening on a bright, sunny day. For early spring, the March temperatures were a balmy 55 degrees, with the birds chirping, and the evil beast sleeping. It seemed too simple, just to walk right up to the demon animal, and kill it. Rocks were thrown at it only for it to roll onto its other side. Some felt the devil itself was trying to deceive them. Too much blood was already seen, and loved ones killed to be partially devoured.

A month earlier, in the freezing cold, the savage giant remained active. It roamed actively, attempting to break our perimeter. Three, well positioned cannons kept the beast from escaping. No shots were well aimed enough to end the life of the savage beast. But many of our lives were taken by the demon, who seemed to relish every encounter with us.

I realized over these few months, that this demon monster was actually behaving like other animals. From the dark continent, Africa, exotic creatures are discovered, and the news of them brought back on ships returning to port after every journey. This new world is still new to us, and with it, new living species. The savage giant possessed no mystical powers, but relied on its unique biology, and reacted to the environmental surroundings, like all wildlife.

The loss of slaves who were killed became an issue. The religion and tall tales assisted myself to keep my staff in line with this crisis. A demon it looked like, and so a demon of an other world it was. The savage giant was a sacrilege against human kind. A few held ceremonies from their African homeland, accompanied by chanting and rituals, which normally were considered taboo or witchcraft.

The lethargic behavior of the savage giant even astounded myself. I contemplated over leaving to Paddy Jones, my trusted servant, the documents of the savage giant situation. Was the animal sick? Maybe, it grew accustomed to our presence. The behavior changed to a tameness from the feeding sessions, like having a pet dog. It could be just old in age. Whatever reason existed, it was time to act.

The three cannons were well placed directly at the savage giant as it laid in slumber. At the moment of attack, an emotion of sorrow overcame me. It reminded me of a trapped bear, who needlessly has to suffer death because of its own call to natural instinct. The Savage Giant did not mean harm like an evil demon, taking vengeance against the righteous us. But then again, could an animal of lower intelligence exhibit hate?

The attack was sounded and two out of three cannon balls were direct hits. Upon impact, the savage giant stood up high as could be, eyes jolted wide open, and expelled a ferocious yet defeating howl. It fell and *quickly dead. So simple the deed was done after all the fear it spread during the winter. All cheered great hoorahs except I. An unexplained sadness filled my soul. The final solution was not really a solution at all. Why does our God Almighty, test us, in such complications in our mere simple lives.*

It seemed the warm temperature affected the savage giant. We will never know as my energy has become low due to my ailing health. The third cannonball exploded into the rocks, destroying the opening of the cliff. Any answers may have existed inside those rocks, but I decided to leave it be. All in all, with my understanding of people and politics, my greatest secret of the savage giant was to remain a secret. No one wished to speak of such matters in fear of being ostracized. The slaves, who consumed in religion, were proud of this secret, and how they defeated the devil, itself.

I have recorded the events to possibly take future action. Right now nothing will be done. I leave Paddy Jones, my truly trusted servant, my documents of the savage giant situation.

Finished and Tired,
Thomas Jefferson

Frank Porter questioned himself about the events concerning the death of the savage giant. Anything was possible. It may have just been diseased. He hoped he could figure a solution to control their captured snow creature. Did the Jefferson's beast just give up in the end?

Frank Porter recalled the meeting of the morning of a lot of unanswered questions back at the command tent in the woods. After he spent the night in jail, he, as well as Melanie Cuttles, were demanded to attend the 10:00 A.M. meeting with all associated with the horrid events. Little did he know such colonial information would be exposed at this point when he sat in a jail cell, restless and aggravated.

He thought back to the Megalonyx meeting while he awaited Rupert Jones return. Frank Porter felt hungry, and so distracted his thoughts back to the command tent when he met two odd, official individuals. New players entered the game. Frank Porter received the information about his contact, Rupert Jones, from these government guys.

The 10:00 A.M. Meeting

Everyone who needed to be here, was here. At exactly 10:00 A.M. the sheriff walked into the command tent with two government officials. They were dressed plain, with everyday parkas, and wore nothing to reflect they were C.I.A., military or something special. As far as Frank Porter was concerned, they could be fakes, designed by the sheriff. The stage curtains were drawn, and the show about to start.

"Good morning, and hello! I am Agent Finks. Yes, I work for the government, and I am a fink." One official said.

No laughter in the tent. Nothing could break the seriousness from the recent tragic events.

The same official, Agent Finks, said, "Okay, well let us move on. This is my science half, Dr. Hippotalumous, and yes, you can see he is very fat, and the word hippo is portrayed in his legal name." Again, no laughter.

This official then said, "We need your cooperation concerning this unbelievable matter in our believable world. These are high stake times in a world of low stakes."

The rhetoric continued by Agent Finks. The direction of the meeting headed towards a solution which had no solution. Whatever the plans were by these guys, they were not revealing it.

Next up, was Dr, Hippotalumous, with a soothing, French accented voice. He spoke little of the science value of the snow creature, but more concerned about the confidentiality. He explained how the world would not understand. Such matters needed research first, before media coverage.

Dr, Hippotalumous stood in front of the small crowd, and spoke comfortably. He toyed with a medical bag, and grabbed one of the contents, from time to time.

While he held a syringe, Dr. Hippotalumous replied in a funny way," In other words, if you speak of this snow creature, we will have to kill you."

Again, there was no laughter. Everyone got the point [get it, the point of the syringe]. Even before the meeting took place, everyone decided to conform, but only because what could one really do. These guys were official, the so called professionals. So let them figure out this maze of monsters and dead bodies.

During the useless speeches, Frank Porter noticed something different about the snow creature. The broken claw was mended. It grew back. Never in evolutionary history, has he heard of a mammal regenerating a limb, or grow nails within such a short time frame. He decided to keep this observation to himself. He was not on their good side, and why assist them with their devious plans.

Only Frank Porter remained a rebel at heart. He conspired with himself, to reveal the truth about the snow creature. When the time was right, his story was to be printed. Once the information leaked out to the press, what could the sheriff do. The people sworn to secrecy will blabber faster about the facts, than any other gossip around a small town.

Coffee and cake was served in the command tent. Thee Sheriff Gibbs still had plans for Frank Porter. Agent Finks introduced himself to the news reporter, along with Dr. Hippotalumous.

While the doctor shoved his face full of cake, keeping up his reputation as a fat person, Agent Fink spoke, "So, the rough treatment does not have to be. The sheriff here, speaks highly of you. We could use a sensible man like yourself."

Frank Porter replied," What makes you believe that none of these people will spill the beans about the snow creature?"

Agent Finks casually stated," That is easy. I, myself, came from a small town. This bunch do not want the hassle to be called names, like "nutso". Trust me, there will be no evidence of Megalonyx- period. And the ones who gossip about monsters, will learn fast how others will scorn them, and not associate with them in the town."

"Well that happened to "Rudolph the Red Nose Reindeer", and he became famous."

"You mean a child's tale?" The rebuttle from Agent Finks.

"Touche'", added Frank Porter.

The annoyed reporter continued, "Wipe the icing off the cake. Although it looks like Dr. Hippo licked that up already. What do you need from me. I will decide should I agree to your terms, Finky."

"We need you to do this one thing. The chopper awaits for your freedom." The official said.

Frank porter asked,"Where are you sending me?"

Doctor Hippatolumous, in his french accent replied, " My home country, France, greatest ally, Thomas Jefferson. We are sending you to his estate- Monticello."

They walked with Frank Porter towards the helicopter. Melanie Cuttles already was on board. Frank Porter stepped onto the chopper with an inquisitive look and said," Monticello, Virginia?"

"I will ride with you, and explain your task. I know you will go because your reporter instincts possess you to." Dr. Hippatolumous replied, and stepped clumsily into the helicopter, giving the impression that his weight actually shook the structure.

Frank Porter gave his inquisitive look inside at Dr. Hippo taking up two seats.

The fat doctor remarked,"C'mon, get in. I flew in, and the helicopter did not crash, so we should make it back to town. The pilot removed the emergency equipment for flight failure to compensate my weight. (No laughter). Let us move on this. I need to return and continue my examination of the beast."

These guys did play Frank Porter well. The news reporter's curiosity was hooked in easily. He sat across from Dr. Hippatolumous, and wondered what these guys were dragging him into.

The helicopter left the command post.

Agent Fink remarked as the helicopter head back to town," Are you sure he will comply?"

Thee Sheriff Gibbs replied," He better, or it will not turn out healthy for him."

Back at Monticello

Rupert Jones returned with a tray of coffee and slices of apple pie. They both indulged themselves.

Frank Porter finished his coffee, and he said," So, how did you meet Agent Finks?"

Rupert Jones replied, "They found me. Actually, the government knew about the documents held in confidence, even when Paddy Jones was alive."

The man poured a second cup of coffee, and offered some to Frank Porter who refused.

The historian replied,"There are organizations, who 110 % of their time, are devoted to espionage. Someone as popular, significant like Thomas Jefferson, could never really own secrets. We are not truly free, but freer from living in other countries."

The two men spoke more about government conspiracy, and their dislike of the political interplay with scientific venture.

"Back in the 1920's," Rupert Jones continued," A team of researchers excavated the cliff where the savage giant was discovered. To their dismay, the archeology team, alias government covert team, found no evidence- no bones, no living creature. Basically found nothing. The whole " Under the Table" inquiry was dropped. Whether they expected a hoax or not, no one ever came looking for these documents again."

Frank Porter lost interest in past events of espionage, but returned to his problem at hand. He thought about the raw facts surrounding the snow creature. Back at Tannersville, they captured a live, carnivorous Megalonyx, and needed to move forward with the issue.

Frank Porter veered the conversation away from government games to pertinent issues about the captured snow creature.

"Why was the beast lethargic in March? Maybe the Jefferson team poisoned the snow creature." The newsman inquired.

"Well, Mr. Frank Porter, they actually attempted to poison it. They distributed arsenic into the goat meat. They tried three times. Some how the beast disliked his free meal. It knew, smelled or tasted, the arsenic tainting the meat. The savage giant only ate fresh kill." Rupert Jones commented.

He then said," I can sort through more papers, and hopefully some of it may aid you, Mr. Frank Porter. As for what to do with your snow creature, I first, would like to join you, and see for myself."

Frank Porter said the obvious,"Rupert Jones, you were already included in the gang. Agent Finks ordered me to return with you. Like you said, the government already knows all about the living Megalonyx. You have no choice in the matter."

They reviewed some more documents, and gathered what they felt was needed back at Tannersville. Rupert Jones was to meet them here at Monticello in the morning, and drive back to Agent Finks and the snow creature.

Melanie Cuttles sat in the lobby awaiting her Frank Porter. She waved bags in the air, exclaiming she had presents for a special some-one. A nice, big kiss met his cheek as he approached her. Her cheery presence helped Frank Porter forget about all the complexities. He felt such pleasantries as he looked upon Melanie Cuttles's satisfied smile.

Rupert Jones gave his good byes. The two headed back to their motel. In the car, He again felt relaxed being with a women. Maybe the terrible creature should simple be destroyed. A simple ending to all the complicated disaster. The real issue lied in the facts that should this story be told. Frank Porter longed to expose the tale of the snow creature, He planned to publish the story in tomorrow's Tannersville Gazette.

They both stood in the hotel lobby with luggage. Frank Porter pulled from his pocket two pass keys.

"I reserved two rooms. They are opposite of each other. I did not get them adjacent with the interlocking door. In case you thought I designed certain intentions."

Melanie Cuttles looked complexed. " You are kidding, right?"

"What do you mean, Melanie? I did exactly what you requested yesterday?"

"Yesterday, I was pulling your chain. I planned, today, to tear off your clothes," Melanie gestured seductively.

Frank Porter took a miss on this one. It did cross his mind to invite her in his room after a few cocktails, and see which way the wind blew. Melanie Cuttles already planned to sleep by his side tonight.

Frank Porter answered,"Okay, well this sounds fine to me. By the way, we are being followed."

Frank Porter noticed the same man from the Monticello tour, now sitting in the lobby, reading a magazine. It could be coincidence, but his reporter instinct alarmed differently. Those government guys were not really going to let him take this trip solo. There was too much at stake.

He pointed him out to Melanie Cuttles, and she replied," That is Hans Rheinhart! I went to high school with him. You remember Hans right?"

Frank Porter said, "Oh yeh, Hans. He was quiet, and very good-natured. I remember how he would take lashings from the other kids being German decent. In history, class with the lectures about the Nazis, they ridiculed him that his family were evil Nazis, and cooked Jews. Hans Rheinhart took the encounters sadly, and was embarrassed."

She said,"Well, I know something about his relationship with the sheriff. Hans Rheinhart had some trouble with neighboring hillbillies. The sheriff did him a solid, and those rednecks never bothered him again. What Thee Sheriff Gibbs actually did, I have not the faintest. But it seems, Hans owed him back, and was used as a errand boy, and what not."

"So you think he is stalking us for the sheriff? Hans does not seem the type for that kind of work." He replied.

She said,"That may be true, but I seen him around the station, meeting with the sheriff. His inconspicuous nature might be a plus for him."

"What should we do?" Frank Porter questioned.

"I will go over and bump into him with surprise. As I keep him busy, take my spare card key, and wait in my room. Hans will not know, and believe you just took your own room. It is believable, based on your gentleman like qualities." Melainie Cuttles remarked.

"I not always a goody two shoes," Frank Porter responded in defense.

She simply said, "Well, yes you are."

Frank Porter was not sure how to take Melanie Cuttles attitude towards him. She casually, with surprise, started banter attracting Hans Rheinhart's attention to her. Frank Porter slipped in the elevator, and immediately entered her hotel room. Hans enjoyed the flattery by Melanie Cuttles, and thought nothing out of the ordinary.

Nobody was seen on their hallway floor, so a second stalker was doubtful. He realized his stuff was in the other room across the hall, but feared taking a chance to grab items and other clothes. He knew Melanie Cuttles would not agree to his griminess from the day, and jumped into the shower. In fifteen minutes, Frank Porter sat in a hotel robe on her bed.

Melanie Cuttles finally showed up. Before Frank Porter could express a word, she shushed him, and peered through the door peephole. Slowly, Hans Rheinhart walked passed listening to the walls, and observed anything which would discriminate the two.

After a few silent minutes, she said," Hans claimed he has business in town. He would love to have breakfast. At first, I mentioned, I really needed to move, that I am visiting relatives. But Hans insisted on breakfast."

Frank Porter remarked, "What about me? Did you tell him, I was accompanying you?"

"No." She replied.

"No? I do not understand. Would not that raise flags, because Hans obviously is aware I am here for the Megalonyx papers." He said.

She remarked,"Actually the cunningness, would reflect that we both are abiding to the secrecy. To us, Hans Rheinhart represents a innocent bystander."

"You are sneakier than I gave you credit for. You seem experienced in secret hotel meetings, Oh Melanie." The newsman commented.

Melanie Cuttles replied cutely, "Oh Frank. There are certain women abilities which men are completely blind to "

Frank Porter was not sure how to compute that statement. Somehow he needed to slip his article on the snow creature to Melanie Cuttles without any one catching on. But right now, right at this moment, a beautiful women undressed in front of him.

Melanie Cuttles romantically headed over to him. The robe was removed as she massaged and kissed him. Frank Porter made a hand gesture, and was about to speak when she stopped him.

Melanie Cuttles whispered," Hush, be absolutely quiet. Do not move. I am in control here, and so- lay down."

She grabbed him, and pulled him into the bed touching him in different ways.

Everything she did was intimately perfect. How she also enjoyed herself, pleasing him. Frank Porter could smell the day's odor on her, and her perspirations, perfume, added an erotic flare to the love making.

Melanie Cuttles enjoyed her visit, and felt her duty to pleasure him. After his ecstasy, it was time for him to pleasure her. He felt her here, and then grabbed there, but all in all, the stimulation of Melanie Cuttles was fair. She began fake humping on him, even though his erection already had been finished earlier. She grinded on his inner thigh, screaming with erotic satisfaction. His mere body and presence was enough to bring on her orgasm. Or at least, she claimed.

It did not matter for her. She was glad Frank Porter had a good time, and again, this trip was something she needed. The travel relaxed her. There would be more times to repeat their love connection. Both laid comfortable in each other's arms, but were not sleepy. Frank Porter needed to concoct his plan for Melanie Cuttles to covertly send his article to the Tannersville Gazette.

He expressed clearly to her. She should give the manuscript, he secretly wrote, to Stan the Editor. He would comprehend what was going down. They both had history, and Stan trusted Frank Porter's judgment. Melanie Cuttles could slip the story about the snow creature off at the Tannersville Gazette easily, and inconspicuous. The newspaper office was in the same building as her beauty salon.

For now, they shared a comfortable, enjoyable moment together. Frank Porter and Melanie Cuttles had not slept liked this in days. A small lamp was left on across the room. It gave enough light for him to take a peak once in awhile lifting the covers. Boy, she had a great body.

CHAPTER 10

It Began, and Shall Will It End

THE MEGALONYX REMAINED INACTIVE. It scarcely ate, and it physically showed signs of weight loss. If someone spoke or yelled at it, the snow creature returned little response. When the huntsman, Wilbur Juggs, banged onto the cage, the snow creature did not even flinch. Zero aggression presented itself. Once in awhile, it strolled in circles inside the cage, and again, showed no emotion. No one knew if it was angry, afraid, sad, planning an escape, or what.

Frank Porter shared his tent with Rupert Jones. His new companion was fascinated by the live beast. After reading all the documents from his ancestor, Paddy Jones, with the witnessing of the real, savage giant brought him completeness.

Thee Sheriff Gibbs entered their tent with a tray of coffee and breakfast. Although their existed mutual animosity among themselves, casual conversation was initiated. Outside, a droll machine noise faintly was heard as the morning camp became alive.

The sheriff addressed the gentlemen. "So fellows, we still need a few days to draw a conclusion concerning the faith of our horrid guest. My feeling supports Harold Olgeby's thoughts. These government guys are going to haul the beast's smelly ass out of here, and experiment on it."

Frank Porter replied," Where are they going to take it."

"I would figure somewhere secluded, and unknown?" The sheriff answered with sarcasm like that was a stupid question.

Thee Sheriff Gibbs continued," As for all us involved, we need to come up with a confidential agreement. Agent Finks is attempting to generate financial funds. In other words, everybody would be nicely paid off!"

Frank Porter replied as a typical news reporter," Money, the solution to the world's problems. Even with government involvement, nobody here sees the importance of the find. Money buys us luxuries, and buys the snow creature our happiness at its expense."

"La dee da da," joked the sheriff.

In a hurried step, fake Harold Olgeby entered the tent. "So they plan to take it away, and research our Megalonyx." He spoke straight to the point with a moody seriousness.

The sheriff turned to him, and exclaimed," Well, that was what you always wanted, right?"

The mad scientist now looked mad, and said," No. This is not what I wanted. I want the snow creature for myself, and make a whole lot of money from it."

Everyone looked confused with fake Harold Olgeby's changed mood. Then Frank Porter replied," How were you planning to profit off the snow creature, and were you including us?"

To the surprise of the group, the mad scientist pulled out a handgun and pointed it towards the men in the tent. His ear to ear, psycho smile said it all.

"Where did you get that pistol", said the sheriff with surprise.

"In a hour or two, one of your men will find the night watchmen dead behind a tree. That is where I got the pistol. It was interesting how the snow creature stared attentively as I slit the soldier's throat. Why the shocked faces? I do not fit the profile of a killer? A killer I am, and a proud, cold-blooded one."

"You are proud, dumb ass!" The sheriff spoke with contempt. " You are a double crosser and a loony!"

"Yeah, those probably are fitting names, sheriff. Oh, I mean Thee Sheriff Gibbs. It is not loony introducing your name with Thee? I hated that title you pompous ass! I cannot wait to feed you to the beast. Oh yeah, hand over the firearm." Fake Harold Olgeby spoke with control.

The sheriff reluctantly passed his handgun over to Harold Olgeby. Frank Porter did not foresee these turn of events. Rupert Jones looked on with shock. Thee Sheriff Gibbs turned redder in his face.

Fake Harold Olgeby was not done with his anger towards these men. He tossed a newspaper onto the table, and said,. "I see you were busy during your trip to Monticello, Mr. Frank Porter. Look what the helicopter just delivered. You ruined my morning coffee, and my well thought out plan. I guess that goes the same for the "dumbass" sheriff's plan as well."

The sheriff grabbed it quickly and read the title," The Snow Creature, a Missing Link Monster, Terrorizes Tannersville." The sheriff read on, and yelled obscenities which became drowned out from the increasing machinery noise outside.

"You idiot, writing this article will escalate matters! I knew I could not trust you. You were under surveillance all the time." The sheriff yelled.

"I knew that." Frank porter replied.

The sheriff continued," I had an operative stalk you on your trip to Monticello. How did you deliver the article?"

Frank Porter slyly replied," What about Melanie Cuttles?"

"She is to stupid! Melanie could not, impossible, what the... damn!" He replied.

Melanie Cuttles was left back in town. Agent Finks, and the sheriff felt she could do no harm, and would keep quiet. Never trust a women.

"I slipped her my story for the paper at night in the hotel." The newsman proudly said.

Thee Sheriff Gibbs annoyed, said, " Hotel, at night? My man saw her go into her own room alone. You two did, no, you know, she was not that desperate to, well, participate in some- horizontal mambo?"

The sheriff looked at the silent, Frank Porter. Silent, Frank Porter grinned, even with a loaded gun pointed at him. Thee Sheriff Gibbs disgusted, realized he got the double screw while they got really screwed.

"Enough of this! All that noise your workmen are making, will help my cover. You guys are finished. Sorry that we just met, Mr. Rupert Jones. Your arrival to witness the snow creature was a life threatening mistake." The mad scientist announced.

The rumbling noise became louder. The sheriff noticed a bulldozer pass by, outside the tent opening. He realized there was no work detail today, and, they had no bulldozer. What the sheriff also noticed was Bill Meyers riding on the bulldozer. It was the bulldozer from Millens

Road where the police van had its accident. Bill Meyers borrowed the machine from the highway clean up crew.

Harold Olgeby peered at the bulldozer heading for the cage, while he held the others at gunpoint. The bulldozer smashed into the metal captivity. It immediately dented, but did not crack an opening. The snow creature watched eagerly, awaiting the next move. Bill Meyers went in reverse, and forward, as the hydraulic forklift and bucket continued to tear at the framed network.

Loud metal screeches resonated throughout the camp, while the bulldozer worked on its demolition. One metallic bang cracked loudly, piercing everyone's eardrum. The noise threw fake Harold Olgeby's attention off, as Frank Porter jumped him within a second. The two others assisted, and took the guns.

The sheriff exclaimed," Good work, Franky. I did not think you could make such a gutsy move! Olgeby could have shot you dead."

Frank Porter did not answer, and acted on natural instinct. Actually, he surprised himself. He quickly looked over at the snow creature's holding cage. The frame was kinked and severely damaged. Suddenly, an opening formed out of the bent metal in the dilapidated cage.

The bulldozer busted through. Quickly the snow creature hustled along the side of the moving machine. Megalonyx recognized Bill Meyers, its old foe, sitting on top, but desired freedom right now. The beast zoomed in on Bill Meyers eyes.

The delusional, young man heard the beast speak to him in growling words, "I will be back for you. Suzy was delicious. Loved her succulent breasts!" The beast, monster, pushed all his physical buttons, producing ultimate rage. He smacked and grabbed the controls with disarray, and the bulldozer conked out.

The snow creature squeezed out the opening, and felt its old self again. It was time for more mayhem.

The camp personnel moved haphazardly, not really thinking of what just occurred. Once the personnel sited Megalonyx prowling freely, chaos set in, and recapture, or destroying it was not immediately considered. The snow creature let out a few more roars, and an alarm finally was sounded.

Megalonyx took a defensive stance on the camp grounds. A young man, new to the military, ran at full speed around a tent directly into the body of the snow creature. He fell, and laid on his back looking shocked at the beast. The smell alone penetrated dread inside his soul. The camp team could of at least hosed it down once.

The snow creature turned its head, peered down at the young man, and bellowed another frightening roar. The soldier fumbled quickly to stand up as the snow creature's saliva sprayed in his face. He peeled away as fast as he could, scared out of his wits. The snow creature's energy returned, and relished the moment of spooking the soldier.

Dr. Hippatolumous headed for the chopper, moving slowly due to his weight. Before he was near it, the snow creature lumbered in front of him. His rolls of neck skin shook, as he stood frigthened with his open mouth. The snow creature swung his forearm, and knocked him in the head with its elbow. It rendered Dr. Hippatolumous unconscious. The beast recognized his blimp size, and connected it with a tasty, delectable meal, a mixture of tender, fatty meat. The snow creature was going to keep Dr. Hippatolumous for a later snack back in its lair.

The chopper pilot began to lift off after visualizing the beast grop-ing Dr. Hippatolumous. Instinct overtook Megalonyx, and attacked the moving flying machine. Its incisors hooked onto the landing bars of the helicopter. It tugged forcefully as the helicopter became unbalanced in the air. The snow creature let go, just when the pilot lost control, and the helicopter spun above the tents in the camp.

It came crashing down, and exploded near the guys, who were detaining the fake Harold Olgeby. They became dispersed, falling to the ground. One of the guns came lose, and was thrown at the feet of the mad scientist. He picked it up, and ran swiftly away. The sheriff suffered a nice gash on his forehead. Frank Porter, and Rupert Jones were roughed up a bit, but okay.

Fake Harold Olgeby headed to the snowmobiles. Agent Finks bumped into the mad scientist, who headed in the same direction.

Agent Finks remarked, "Where are the others, Olgeby? What a disaster. How are we going to detain the beast?"

Fake Harold Olgeby simply stated, "We are not doing anything. You are going to die."

He pointed the handgun at Agent Finks, who was totally not prepared. He never guessed that the scientist was a fraud. Agent Finks was a veteran government agent, and never thought he would be put at gunpoint anymore.

Agent Finks took a few shots in the chest, and hit the ground. He laid in extreme pain, though his bulletproof vest worked successfully. He barely could move his good shooting hand, and decided to play dead. How glad he thought, because he debated to wear his vest this morning.

Fake Harold Olgeby jumped on a snowmobile, and tried to start it. He lost all his medical pills back at the scuffle with the other guys. He moved with panic, and nervousness. Finally, the snowmobile started as Bill Meyers showed up. The mad scientist stared with anger while he stood, blocking his escape route.

Bill Meyers said,"I knew your story was not true. You are a crazy lunatic! I bet you killed Suzy's father!"

Bill Meyers took a stance with a shovel. This man killed his girlfriend's beloved dad. Bill Meyers was going to take him down, in honor of his lost love, Susan Conti.

Fake Harold Olgeby decided to drive the other way. He needed both hands on the snowmobile, so it was impossible to take a gunshot. The snow creature was heard in close proximity, and he only wished to escape as soon as possible. The mad scientist turned around, and had to take his ride through camp. Bill Meyers chased behind, operating another snowmobile.

Agent Finks propped himself against a tree for support, so he could try to stand up.

Frank Porter, Rupert Jones, and the sheriff, took a utility vehicle, and also decided to high tail out of camp. Without the chopper, a safe means of escape was limited. Putting distance between themselves, and the snow creature, was the best laid plan. Thee Sheriff Gibbs held his revolver, and that was going to have to do for defense. Rupert Jones sat in the back seat holding tightly onto a crossbar. He imagined how Thomas Jefferson,and his Great Uncle, Paddy Jones, defended themselves against the attack of the snow creature.

Wilbur Juggs, the Boone and Crockett Hunter, was busy defending himself. The beast had him trapped by the supply tent, as the desperate hunter hid amongst a bunch of barrels. He held his rifle, but had no shot. The snow creature was hauling boxes, metal rods, plastic containers,or anything it got its pincer claws on, at the cornered man. Wilbur Juggs decided to throw the crap back. The two had a throwing contest.

The fat man became exhausted, and knelt to the ground. The snow creature raised a barrel over its woolly head, and brought the barrel crashing down on Wilbur Juggs head.It smashed him like a pumpkin. Megalonyx possessed memory like an elephant, an elephant which never forgets. The Boone and Crockett Hunter threw empty beer cans at the cage, every time the he passed during the last week. It was a can for a can.

Before the snow creature finished him off, Wilbur Juggs, the hot-shot hunter, had no plan for defeat. Before he threw the garbage and stuff back at the beast, he spilled a barrel of gasoline where his last stand was soon to be. Wilbur Juggs knew he was a goner, and hoped to take this monster along with him. As he knelt exhausted, his hand held a lit lighter. When the snow creature's barrel came down and took his life, the lighter fell and ignited the gasoline. Balls of fire exploded, bringing a surprise attack against Megalonyx. Unfortunately, little harm was afflicted, and singed only its white, woolly fur.

Agent Finks stumbled along the perimeter of the camp. Fire spread on the tents from the helicopter crash, and from other explosions. He moved away from the camp disasters. He, watched for the beast, which somewhere continued its havoc on the command center. Agent Finks thought about his next choices as an outdoor utility vehicle headed in his direction.

The guys in the terrain vehicle noticed a man stumbling towards him. Frank Porter recognized Agent Finks. They stopped about twenty yards away because of physical obstacles. The Agent moved slowly, walking in front of a snow filled slope. The pain in his chest was un-bearable from the gunshots. In training, they were shot wearing bullet proof vests, and it did not hurt like this.

"Hurry up, and get in!" The sheriff yelled.

Agent Finks stood a few feet from them. " Everything happened to fast. What a disaster. Thank God you guys showed up. I really thought I was a goner. Your Harold Olgeby is insane."

Before anyone could answer, Frank Porter noticed unusual spots on the protruding slope behind Agent Finks. It looked like two red beads. Then, the two red dots blinked. As Agent Finks attempted to step into the vehicle, a sudden explosion of snow sprayed over them all. The snow creature blended itself with the slope of snow. It busted out, clutched Agent Finks, who became creature food before he could blink his eyes. His struggle was useless as he bodily disappeared under the forest's blanket of snow. Maybe, the the gunshots without the vest, would have been a less painful death.

Harold Olgeby drove randomly into the unknown forest. He lacked experience on snowmobiles, so he covered distance sparingly. Bill Meyers followed behind, also not talented riding one of these recreational machines. Both took their time circling around trees, slowing down on purpose in fear of crashing, and stopping short because of hitting the brake incorrectly. If someone had a bird's eye view of them, the whole race would of looked clownish.

The mad scientist had enough. He stopped, and turned with the gun, pointed at Bill Meyers. He had six shots left, and had to make it count. One shot was fired as Bill Meyers heard the twang of the bullet ricochet off the snowmobile. He veered towards his left and took cover. He hunkered down behind the snowmobile as another bullet whizzed by.

Bill Meyers realized how stupid his plan panned out. Without a weapon, defeat and death presented itself. Soon he would join his beloved love, Susan Conti, his "Slutty Suzy".

Without medication, erratic behavior worked fake Harold Olgeby's psyche. He now joined the deranged mindset of Bill Meyers. He concentrated to shoot dead this annoying, young man. He slowly stalked forward to get a closer shot. Attentively, he aimed the gun ahead, awaiting for Bill Meyers to flee from his hidden spot.

His physical shaking effected his aim, so closing the distance was a smart move. Harold Olgeby now realized he overused his medication again. Barely, he could hold the gun as his extremities vibrated, and a chill shook him to the bone. He needed a fix, but had no pills.

Soundless, Kyle Meyers, the superhero, stalked in the woods. Fake Harold Olgeby never realized "The Mighty Caveboy" approached his position. Upon hearing the snow mobiles, the super hero headed in that direction. So skillful he sneaked up behind fake Harold Olgeby, Kyle Meyers could not help give himself a successful rating concerning his tracking abilities. His superhero skills finally had become fine tuned. He mentally approved his actions while he surveyed the situation. He recognized his brother, Bill Meyers immediately. "The Mighty Caveboy" was off to the rescue.

The mad stalker was now stalked. Harold Olgeby heard a twig snap behind him. As he turned his gun in that direction, a large stick whacked him across the chest. The super hero leaped on him with his trademark yell, knocking away the gun. Although the assault took the mad scientist off guard, he easily overpowered the thirteen year old boy, and sat on top of him.

Bill Meyers noticed the scuffle, and immediately rushed over to overcome fake Harold Olgeby. As he attacked, fake Harold Olgeby quickly grabbed his gun and let off a roughly, aimed shot. The bullet shattered Bill Meyer's elbow. His younger brother below, clumped up snow and mushed it in his face. This distracted the mad scientist enough, to allow the brothers to tackle him.

Bill Meyers did not yet recognize his brother Kyle Meyers, who he thought was already dead. Bill Meyers assumed it was another person who was aware of the true identity of this madman.

Kyle Meyers said with glee, "Billy Boy, it is me, Kyle!"

Emotions flooded the brothers with unexpected joy. Feelings forgotten since all this hell appeared. Bill Meyers awoke from the torrid events of his mind, and accepted that he was standing in front of him. Whether it was dream or not, he embraced his living brother.

"Hey, did you forget about me?" There stood fake Harold Olgeby pointing his gun, brushing snow off his pants. The mad scientist watched as the two brothers continued hugging, and smiling at each other. He wondered what craziness was this. He cared less, and needed to move on with his demented plan.

The madman pointed his gun at the two warmly embracing each other. He wished them a crappy trip to hell. Before he uttered some more farewell obscenities, an ear shattering, rifle shot exploded. A blood splat formed on fake Harold Olgeby's abdomen. All his bodily feelings became numb, as he helplessly dropped the gun.

He slowly looked down at his blood dripping on the white snow. Stepping away from a tree, there stood Mr. Phil Conti holding "The Terminator", the special edition rifle. The gun he found earlier, the gun from the dead, Boone and Crockett Hunter Davis, finally shot a true trophy.

The mad, serial killer scientist whimpered, "I left you for creature fiddles, but I should have stayed for the feast. I guess the dinner bell never rang for you. I knew leaving you still alive was stupid."

"Should of, could of, would of. The downfall of most famed luna-tics. In your case, insane maniacs." Phil Conti spoke with a smile of all smiles.

Mr. Conti survived, and served his vengeance with extreme grati-fication. Grandma the witch would be proud of him.

"What is your real name anyway. If you do not mind me asking." Mr. Conti said. With last mumbled,"who the hell cares" words, the serial killer replied,"Irving Ninapoot."

That made alot of sense to all there, why this guy stole other peo-ple's identities.

Suddenly, a snow mound rushed past, and snatched the bloody corpse of Irving Ninapoot. The three felt for a split moment that Megalonyx joined the capture and death of the madman.

For a moment, peace relaxed them. They needed a few seconds, be-fore getting all pumped up with adrenaline again. As Mr. Conti checked the "Terminator" rifle for bullets, the ground vibrated. The ground vibrated and rumbled as the pine trees dropped snow from its branches, once again. Bill and Kyle Meyers were experts now on earthquakes, and this was another one of those tremors.

All was silent. Quickly, Mr. Conti spoke," Helix Point! Helix Point! We are near the observation center. We can share the snowmobiles, and hide out there for safety."

Without much conversation, they mobilized themselves to con-tinue their escape from the earthquake and of the snow creature. Quickly the ground shook again, and quickly the unpleasant rumbling lessened and stopped. Then, all silence occurred.

The beast zipped by just five minutes ago, and no one wanted more deadly encounters. Mr. Conti suffered from his physical injuries, and needed help from Kyle Meyers to drive the snowmobile. Bill Meyers stayed alone on the other one, and coped with his shattered elbow. They prepared themselves on the snowmobiles, and were ready to head for the Observation Complex at Helix Point.

They plowed through the snow-filled wilderness. Mr. Conti seemed to know the way with his natural gift of the senses. Although his "witch senses" did not predict the sudden tremors, he knew the route to Helix Point. Mr. Conti lacked the skill on how to turn his gift, on and off. Maybe, a clairvoyant could not control it, but it controlled you. They drove in the right direction up to Helix Point.

Bill Meyers kept peering over his shoulders, awaiting to be grasped by the snow creature. Nothing developed. No chase came about. The constant fear of being ripped apart, made the drive difficult. Once in awhile, they lost control, but got back on track, and continued buzzing through the pines. They tackled up a last hill to the observation center.

Upon reaching the parking lot, a parked utility vehicle was seen, as well as a police jeep. In the doorway, Thee Sheriff Gibbs stood with his hands on his hips, awaiting the new comers. Out by the back of the jeep, a police deputy aim a high powered rifle, guarding for any trouble. As fast as the snowmobiles pulled up to the front door, the parking lot wall exploded with the snow creature rumbling swiftly behind. There would be no party without Megalonyx.

The deputy aim and fired, but all in vain. The beast railroaded him with such speed, he barely got the shot off. The snow creature turned and rolled over the deputy's body several times. The police officer laid dead, full of broken bones.

The others rushed inside, and slammed the door on the incoming pincer claw. It sliced in, and jammed the doorway ajar. All of them pressed hard against the metal door. The locking system was state of the art, and if they could just get the door closed securely, all would be safe. The snow creature's weight and strength overpowered them, as the door bolted open. They retreated down the hall to a second door. The second door had a lock, but not as durable as the front.

Quickly they sprinted passed the next door, and slammed it shut. Initially, the bulk of the snow creature pushed into the hallway, but it was a bit of a squeeze. It felt uncomfortable in the closed space, and literally stuck in the entrance hallway. The beast could not grasp the fleeing men. Megalonyx easily could of smashed through the second doorway, but decided to retreat back to the outside. Even for a cave dwelling animal, this tight enclosure overwhelmed it.

Inside, to Frank Porter's surprise, sat Old Bogey Wilson with Deputy Collins. Bill and Kyle Meyers looked on with recognition at their battling buddy, Bogey Wilson. He expressed insecurity and fear in his facial expression.

Thee Sheriff Gibbs had an ax to grind with this old coot for years. Tannersville represented idyllic moral values. The sheriff valued these American institutions- a way of life in these parts of Virginia. Illegal drugs of Abuse, mind altering substances, worked against his wholesome township. Bogey Wilson was routinely involved with illegal drug sales and moonshine. This old man was the patsy the sheriff needed to cover up all the bloodshed of the snow creature. Bogey Wilson was the accused madman, murderer of the Tannersville Killings.

All stood in the center room with exhaustion. Thee Sheriff Gibbs kept the cover story a secret about sticking the blame on Bogey Wilson. The past held many secrets, and reasons why the sheriff hated this man so much. Deputy Collins had his pistol drawn, attentive to defend himself and the sheriff. The sheriff needed to convince these men to kill Megalonyx, and to join him. He was to explain that Bogey Wilson was handcuffed for drug charges which ranked to important, even during the conflict with the snow creature.

Thee Sheriff Gibbs announced,"Everybody now, calm down! I had enough of the confusion, the destruction, and the lack of cohesion. We need to rethink, and come to our senses. What I said days ago, will now be accomplished. The beast is to be eliminated. Simple. We are personally going to kill this Megaloowat. Everybody man up! Man up now! No one will never know this dreaded snow creature ever existed!"

The sheriff, while Deputy Collins stopped pointing his gun, pulled out weapons from behind the couch. He handed the men rifles,even young Kyle Meyers received a gun. The sheriff sported a slick looking machine type one. Only Bogey Wilson did not receive a weapon, who sat on the couch with his hands cuffed.

Thee Sheriff Gibbs preached,"Let us go out the front and have our final showdown! This ends now, even if it ends us. Too much death piled up. I refused to follow my better instinct. We destroy this evil menace with our firepower, and blow this beast into bitty pieces. Out on the pavement, the snow creature cannot dig and escape!"

So profound, did the sheriff loudly procure his battling speech, that Frank Porter convinced himself to shoot dead Megalonyx.

The men stood in a circle. Thee Sheriff Gibbs, Frank Porter, Rupert Jones, Mr. Phil Conti, Bill Meyers, and "The Mighty Cave Boy"- Kyle Meyers,shouted positive remarks to boost each other up. It was time to do or die. Deputy Collins had strict orders to guard Bogey Wilson. Without their patsy, the charade would not work.

The sheriff yelled," Let's get it boys..." The ground shook. Another earthquake started, and this one was to be a big one. The vibrations were not just left to right, but up and down. They all fell to the floor. No one had control, and nothing could be held onto. Everything was busting apart. A split opened in the floor of the main room. Cement chunks flew upward, as high as the ceiling. Windows shattered.

Rupert Jones was hit in the head with cement debris. He felt weary, but attempted to stay conscious, he laid helpless on the disintegrating floor.

A huge gap increased below their feet. The earthquake was splitting the Observation Complex in two. Frank Porter peered down into the developing crevasse, and it looked bottomless. A side wall gave away, and Bogey Wilson took his chance, and stumbled to escape out the opening. Deputy Collins tried to stand without falling, aiming his gun towards the fleeing Bogey Wilson.

Megalonyx rose above out of the growing opening, Its massiveness filled the main room, making the space look a lot smaller. Fiercely, the beast scanned the room as the building became dismantled. It arrived to finish them off. First business- Deputy Collins head was sliced off. The vengeance of the beast fueled its fury.

No one could take a shot because they all were trying to secure themselves from delving helplessly into the giant pit. Even Megalonyx held on to an exposed floor beam with concern. The severe quake disoriented the snow creature, and slowed down its vicious attack.

The concrete slab, below Frank Porter and Bill Meyers, buckled, They slid towards the snow creature, hanging onto to their very lives. The beast swiped with its claw within feet of the two as their fingers clawed into the cracks of cement. The snow creature also showed signs of alarm due to the surrounding damage. Frank Porter could not make a move, and prayed for the earthquake to stop.

The beast's instinct marched its hatred on with a committed oath to kill. This carnivore possessed an intelligence, a more intelligent value than killing just for food. Its brain registered these beings to be more than food. Megalonyx owned potential ability. The snow creature understood that offense was essential to defend its life, an important understanding for an animal's survival. An evolutionary enhancement, conscience, deems a quality most living species never possess, except humans. Megalonyx must destroy these human beings for its own existence.

Bogey Wilson's escape was in vain. He was knocked backward by a collapsing ceiling fan, before he could step to the outside. He tumbled on the slanting floor unable to stop, heading back inside towards the snow creature. Desperately, the sheriff reached out to grab Bogey Wilson, the important chess piece that he wished not to lose. Thee Sheriff Gibbs tumbled with Bogey Wilson to their tragic faith.

The two slipped down closer to the snow creature. The beast awkwardly took a swipe with one of its claws. Due to the severe shaking, it could not stablilize its body. The middle part of the claw smacked into the sheriff, sending him flying to the front hallway. Bogey Wilson plopped onto the huge stomach of the Megalonyx. He held on with his dear life. The sheriff landed bruised, by the main entrance hallway. Hurt and disorientated, the sheriff fired aimlessly away, attempting to hit the dreaded beast.

Frank Porter, and Bill Meyers both knew their fingers could not clutch onto the disintegrating floor much longer. Frank Porter witnessed Bogey Wilson hollering, who looked up in terror at the fanged head. His grip was strong, grasping the long tufts of woolly hair. This irritated the snow creature. It attempted to relieve its position, and the floor beam cracked in half. The snow creature fell, down into the open pit. Megalonyx disappeared along with Bogey Wilson.

The shaking, and quaking ceased. The Observation Complex was in ruins. The men slowly regained their wits. Carefully they moved among the building debris. The cold air penetrated the inside, because the building was no longer intact. Bill Meyers nursed his injured elbow, and Kyle approached from behind, patting him on the shoulder. Rupert Jones chatted with Frank Porter, verifying they both were not serious hurt. Thee Sheriff Gibbs, sulked with his wounds.

Suddenly, snow showered into the wrecked building, and was brought to their attention from the intensity of the whipping flakes. Before these survivors could even catch a break from the earthquake and attack of the snow creature, more commotion came their way.

Two helicopters hovered downwards with overwhelming noise. The copters landed just outside on the parking lot. Although the lot suffered with major cracks, it still was intact. Men jumped off the two choppers, before they even landed. More snow and lose debris flew aimlessly, making the survivors more uncomfortable.

Armed men in black scurried into the ruins. The soldiers pointed their weapons at the survivors. The leader exclaimed," Who is Harold Olgeby! We want Harold Olgeby!"

Kyle Meyers took a few steps forward to greet the soldiers. They ordered him to halt or they would shoot to kill. The boy in a raccoon coat was odd enough for the soldiers to shoot first, and ask questions later. The emotions in the room were panic and more confusion. No one wanted bullets flying, and no one wanted to be dead, especially now, after surviving the battling snow creature.

Mr. Conti replied," He is dead. I shot him. The imposter Harold Olgeby tried to kill me."

One of the soldiers said,"Everyone out to the copters!"

At gunpoint, the group was led along the parking lot. The helicopters in large letters, printed- F.B.I. Inside, the compartments were warm and comfortable. Thee Sheriff Gibbs took the lead, after showing his credentials. The sheriff demanded his bunch to be tight lipped, and he would describe the details to these special forces. The snow creature was totally left out, and a concocted story about fake Harold Olgeby,and Bogey Wilson was told. No one dared at this point, to challenge the sheriff, and explain about the beast.

"So, Harold Olgeby met with this Bogey Wilson. You think they joined forces to make a profit over these fossils, and scoring illegal drugs as well? The official in charge said, who actually believed the tall tale.

It seemed the evidence, back in Baltimore, matched this story, and that fake Harold Olgeby was a maniacal killer who acted as real scientist. The F.B.I. Agents found five dead bodies connected to the fake Harold Olgeby doings. The where abouts of the real scientist was unknown to the F.B.I., but figured he was dead or shark meat back in Miami.

The flight in the helicopters seemed to last forever. Medics dressed their wounds as Thee Sheriff Gibbs spun his tale of the false facts now given. Frank Porter, though defeated, favored the relief attitude that it was over. But he wondered, was it really over for Megalonyx?

It was too much, too fast, to absorb after the deadly mayhem of the snow creature. Frank Porter cared less of the truth. He wished he was in the arms of Melanie Cuttles. He wished he was at home, in front of a fireplace, enjoying a hot coffee and a piece of cake. The others also were exhausted and kept quiet. They all had enough. Let the sheriff handle the mess.

Bill Meyers sat, looking absent minded. He played back his thoughts concerning the facts of the night, the night the snow creature appeared. Todd Bloomfield was dead. Suzy Conti, his beloved Suzy was dead. She never went out on a date with him. Slutty Suzy mocked him at the diner, in front of everyone. There was no love, only blood, and death.

"Are you okay? Billy, are you in there?" Kyle Meyers spoke to a none respondent brother. He touched his older brother, who was stiff, cold, and unresponsive.

"He is catatonic," replied one of the medic soldiers. "He will need medical help immediately."

Bill Meyers heard, saw, reacted to nothing around him. The young man gone mental, only responded to abnormal dream sequences. First, he shared a romantic moment with Susan Conti. Next, she is all bloody, laughing at him, calling him an asshole . Then, he imagined screaming out loud as he bodily was caught in the snow creature's claw. One scene blurred into another as suddenly he was smacking his younger brother across the face, back in the old station wagon. Over and over, with different events, some based real, some fantasy, and some both. Dreaming of different people with painful memories, Bill Meyers entered a brave new world- his convoluted mind.

The F.B.I. Helicopters landed in Norfolk, Virginia, at a military hospital. The medical staff attended to the injuries. Everyone was diagnosed stable, at least stable enough, except Bill Meyers. A week past for recovery, and again, all committed themselves to erasing all events of the snow creature. The attitude shared was mostly relief, and glad to be alive.

Frank Porter was flooded with reporters, concerning his peculiar article of a creature creating havoc in Tannersville. He decided at this moment to deny the story, and claimed he wrote the article to draw off the truth of the maniacal killings to support Thee Sheriff Gibbs investigation. He despised himself for this flaky stance of lies. Frank Porter told the other reporters he needed the money.

The craziness continued for weeks. By the month of February, all were discharged, and returned back to whatever lives they sanely still owned. Thee Sheriff Gibbs escalated the propaganda, and denounced Frank Porter who mocked their town with a tale of a silly monster, only to line his pockets with profit.

Bill Meyers was not so lucky. Officials admitted him to Ridgewood Psychiatric Ward. He blurted nonsense and incoherence. A beast called Megalonyx was spoken of, as well as his love, "Slutty Suzy". The medical staff did not believe a word of it. The deaths were accomplished by the hillman, Bogey Wilson.

Kyle Meyers spent two weeks, in house, for psychological evaluation. The thirteen year old, boy finally admitted that The Mighty Cave Boy was an illusion, and did not believe he actually transformed into a super hero. Kyle Myers visited a psychiatrist once a week for his past delusions. Any mention of monsters, fighting devilish creatures, was related to his over zealous reading of comic books. No snow creature really existed. The teenager upon returning home to distraught parents, secretly slept outside in the wood shed, not in his cozy bed.

Thee Sheriff Gibbs acted like nothing out of the ordinary happened. Filing paperwork, discussing police matters about criminals, and keeping peace in Tannersville, became back in the normal routine. No sheriff report ever referenced about the snow creature. He played a crucial role in the mock manhunt for Bogey Wilson, still criminal at large.

Bogey Wilson currently has not been found. He is listed on the top ten wanted F.B.I. Criminal List.

Mr. Phil Conti readdressed his whole lifestyle. He mourned deeply the loss of his beloved daughter, Susan. A sober living replaced the alcohol drinking. He also denied any existence of a creature called Megalonyx.

Rupert Jones gathered his information on the snow creature, and added the new evidence to his documents. The government continued to keep tabs on his life, covertly. He simply kept close-mouthed, and continued his research of the Thomas Jefferson's fabled- The Savage Giant, alias The Snow Creature, or the personally named- Megalonyx.

Frank Porter became miserable. He never forgave himself for quitting his morals. The cover up about the snow creature slowly brought on alcohol drinking. His relationship failed with Melanie Cuttles, who sparked a serious intimate relationship with the sheriff. The mild manner reporter, disappeared into seclusion. The blooming love affair between Thee Sheriff Gibbs and Melanie Cuttles was a whole other story.

The snow creature, Megalonyx, only became a tall tale. The actual existence was never proven. The days of the December/January earthquakes were the unofficial last sightings of the beast. Dead or still alive, it was not seen again in the area of Tannersville.

Buford's Circus of the Bizarre

Frank Porter drove back on the I-95 South. A day has past, since the Georgia State Police Department released him from prison. The two weeks in jail were needed for him to recuperate from his opiate addiction and leg fracture. He even received free medical care. More time would have been better, but he needed to get back on track. His hunt for Bill Meyers, Bogey Wilson, and Megalonyx continued.

He traveled in Florida on a dirt road. The dirt was compact and wet, but not soaked. The earlier rain now has stopped with a gray sky. The scene was similar to the day of the car chase on the road back in Georgia. His body and soul were clean of toxicants, and common logic dictated his conscience. His dead mother did not appear since the car chase- at least not yet.

A makeshift parking area was roped off with orange contractor tape. A teenager sat on a folding chair by a wooden table. On the table consisted of a metal money box, and a roll of tickets. The lot looked half full with plenty of parking. The teenage wore a pair of headphones, and began to remove the music as the damaged Ford Taurus pulled up.

With a lack of enthusiasm, the young man stated, " Welcome to Buford's Circus of the...(pause)... Bizaaare." He lengthened the vocals of "Bizarre" for dramatic effect.

It did not work. Frank Porter paid the kid five dollars for parking, and fifteen dollars to enter the pavilions.

"When does "The Tale of the Snow Creature" start?"

The teenager replied," It begins in a half hour, two shows in the afternoon. That exhibition was almost closed down yesterday. The animal, the deformed bear, I think was sick. It looked unusually worse than normal."

"The deformed bear?" Frank Porter asked inquisitively.

"Well, I mean the snow creature, if you believe that crap. I personally, would put that sorrowful looking animal out of its misery." The teeneger replied.

"Smart Kid," Frank Porter said and drove off to find a parking space.

Frank Porter guessed that the circus was not too popular. Considering it was Saturday, there should of been more cars. He sat and pondered as the ignition was turned off. How lucky it was that he survived the whole horrific ordeal. Standing next to his wreckage of transportation, he took a piss. His mind recalled the surreal encounter with the old milk truck off the I-95 highway.

Frank Porter remembered how he laid on the roadside after having words with Bill Meyers. A command was given to the snow creature,and before he knew it, he was hauled on the back of the beast. How did Bill Meyers train the beast so fast in little over a month? How did he tame the vicious animal at all. He hoped these questions would be answered at this freak show.

Surprisingly, back in Georgia, Bill Meyers left him in his car at a Hospital Emergency Room. Frank Porter figured he was a goner like Officer Bongo. He spoke honestly to the police at the Georgia jail, who assumed him quite insane. He was locked up in connection with the disappearance of the state trooper. After his wounds healed, the detectives released him without any evidence of foul play or breaking the law.

Although not official, the incident was connected with the wanted murderer, Bogey Wilson. This statement was concluded from the reports of Officer Bongo encounter with the old milk truck, and the accounts of Frank Porter.

Frank Porter walked with a cane, slow at first. The doctors prescribed mild sedatives, for the pain, and promised to take his prescription properly. The overdosing of the morphine was a one time thing, and done out of desperation. It still hurt every time he put pressure on the leg. Constantly, the pain brought on the horrid memories of the beast, and now he approached the final showdown.

In his pocket, was a handgun. A trashy, old revolver. He lacked knowledge of the model. He figured it was accurate within close proximity. Approaching in point blank range, was his plan. Frank Porter purchased it, outside of a cheap massage parlor, back in Georgia. He decided to use the gun to get in the last word.

If only his dead mother could have seen him yesterday. Her son, the honor student, getting jerked off by a nickel and dime, out of shape hooker. The slurred speaking woman was named "Luscious Lucy". A more fitting name would have been "Luscious Lush". A real career name could have been "The Girl with the Flabby Belly but has a Vagina". It did not matter. He needed, it. Luckily his dead mother did not appear. His expectations that she might ghostly pop up, almost hindered his physical pleasure.

Yes, Frank Porter lost Melanie Cuttles.

He thanked, in a weird way, that he met up with the snow creature. Megalonyx helped him to see the true self of people, and the selfish values they really lived by. Also, he finally saw his true self. Only through experiencing real, horrible evil, does other evil become unmasked from the normal.

He knew the night at the hotel, back at Monticello, lacked the magic one wished for. The awkward love making, in the end, was for him at least, satisfying. She faked. Melanie Cuttles must have faked, and was not honest with him. They enjoyed a great day of friendly companionship. But somehow, in bed, something lacked, at least in his mind, for Melanie Cuttles. Emotions were miss felt for the exciting chemistry, needed for their relationship to last.

A spontaneous beginning of Thee Sheriff Gibbs and Melanie Cuttles blind sided Frank Porter. Yes, those two formed an intimate alliance which has been tight for now a two months. When his thoughts strayed to their romantic union, he erased the events from his mind, never to be spoken. Maybe it had nothing to do with him anyway. Those two possibly were meant to be, and had nothing to do with Frank Porter's personality.

The local relationship became the talk of the town. The story, as Melanie Cuttles explained it to him a week ago, was simply that it was one of those things. It just happened. What could she say to Frank Porter without hurting his feelings. It turned out, the sheriff was a terrific lover. Who would of guessed? Melanie Cuttles claimed the sheriff vitalized her into a new person, and he became a different person, which she could relate to.

She longed to forget and all connection with the snow creature. Initially, Melanie Cuttles stayed with Frank Porter, but the constant resurfacing of the beastly stories, conflicted with her life. She liked her daily routine simple, and Frank Porter's obsession with the truth, brought unwanted glances, and negative gossip in the community. She needed her society conformity. Even with her sexy skirts and past wild evenings with men, she modeled a soccer mom to perfection. Being the sheriff's girlfriend, hammered the final nail on her coffin for the permanently acceptance into the "Village Green".

Frank Porter paced himself as he past the various carnival tents. He glanced at the typical side shows- the bearded lady, a man holding a 15 foot. python coiled over himself, a sword swallower, and a midget poking fun at a very, obese man in bikini briefs. Most of the acts held no unique fascination.

Then, the tent he sought, was pitched with mountainous, snow wilderness, canvas murals.

The snow creature pavilion requested another three dollar entry, It ranked as one of the star attractions of Buford's circus.

A huge banner hung over the entranceway, "The Tale of the Snow Creature".

A small crowd sat dispersed. Frank Porter took a seat near the back. He quickly noticed an old man sweeping around the stage. It was Bogey Wilson. The man on the run, who Frank Porter thought was dead back at Helix Point. The lights grew dim, and a spotlight shone on a ringleader dressed in a raccoon coat. It was Bill Meyers.

Music played a country, rockabilly sound with sinister undertones. Artificial snow fell onto the stage, while Bogey Wilson faked chopping wood with an ax. He sported a beard, a white-grey one, fitting him an old woodsman look. It matched with his short frizzle hair, now all bleached. He carried extra weight, and now had a small gut as they called it.

Old, Bogey Wilson moved with a limp. He barely could lift his right leg, and it was dragged with every step. It reflected an injury brought on from the attacks with the snow creature.

Bill Meyers continued with more profound rhetoric. He grabbed the top of the raccoon cap, and announced the introduction of the snow creature. A dark curtain on the corner of the stage rose as a spotlight popped on, onto Megalonyx.

Frank Porter could not believe his eyes, as the saying goes. First off, the mammoth animal lost much weight. Its fur draped the snow creature like an over sized coat. Rolls of skin existed where past muscles stoutly erected. A general sunken look encompassed the beast as a whole. The huge claws were cut off, only leaving stumps, which were cuffed with large, strong looking chains. The red beady eyes, modeled a pale rose color. Megalonyx carried a morbid look.

The news reporter's brain began to function again, The general appearance of Megalonyx reeked of opiate addiction. A rash distribution of illegal heroine had recently flooded the American states. The sales were cheap as the stuff somehow entered the country easily. The hunger, the addiction, sedated the snow creature, and replaced its savage appetite for live meat.

The show continued with lack luster. Frank Porter felt pity towards Megalonyx. When Bill Meyers cracked a whip at the defeated beast, it flinched as eyes widened from a fear of past hurtful lashings. At one time, Megalonyx would of retaliated with bloody revenge, slashing away with its great claws. It seemed to lack a healthy physical appearance, and simply sat and accepted its new life in the stage lights.

Bill Meyers enjoyed every second of the theatrics. He specially added emotion to the part with "Slutty Suzy", and used some trashy blond for the role in the show. It turned out to be Bill Meyers new women, who cheated a lot behind his back. This information was later shared from a short conversation with Bogey Wilson. Susan Conti and the loving relationship would remain in this young man's mirage. Even the show girl changed her name from Ethel to "Slutty Suzy" for real.

The finale ended with an alteration with the capture of the snow creature. The final outcome was the existence of Megalonyx, here in front of the audience. The show received fair applause, considering the lack of believability. Sitting in the darkened benches, Frank Porter glanced down at the rusty revolver. It was over. His revenge fizzled into useless feelings. The animal suffered enough. He was not going to put it out of its misery. Instead, he decided to shoot Bill Meyers, and free Megalonyx.

Frank Porter approached Bill Meyers and Bogey Wilson after the show. They all stared at each other with this expected yet unexpected meeting. Hopefully, by gones would be by gones, and the past would remain in the past. Ideally, no hard feelings would surface between them. What good would come of it at this point anyway. Everyone related to the true tale of the snow creature. All were exhausted, and preferred to forget.

Bill Meyers spoke first," What is the gun for. I find it funny. A man like yourself would never had raised a firearm. I thought the police would of locked you up for good. I never would of let you live, if I truly thought you would be standing here."

"Wrong once again poor, deluted boy," Frank Porter answered.

Bill Meyers continued, "Megalonyx brought change, and a challenge to the potential of what is expected of the human spirit. I believe this horror was for the better."

The newsman stated,"Of course you do, you are deranged. You know, you never had sex with Slutty Suzy."

"Don't call her that! You came here to insult me? This creature will forever be punished for taking my girlfriend! I, I, can only call her by the name – Slutty Suzy." He droaned on.

Bill Meyers began to explain the events reaching here, to the circus. When he was discharged from the psychiatric ward, he headed straight to the snow creature's lair. He packed some stolen morphine, and an ax. The same morphine which Frank Porter stole during his last visit at the psychiatric ward. His doctor refused to prescribe more potent pain killers.

Upon reaching the secret cavern, he found Bogey Wilson hiding out. The snow creature was motionless, and entered a type of hibernation. The carnivore was a wintry predator, and the warm spring months triggered its dormancy.

Bogey Wilson lived in a rough camp with a fire, and hunted off the land. That meant he scavenged for food at night, mostly hitting garbage retainers on the outskirts of town. How unusual the scene, when Bill Meyers entered the lair, and saw Bogey Wilson sitting in front of a fire, fifty yards down the cave from the sleeping giant.

Bogey Wilson explained that he thought he was a goner after the battle at Helix Point. The snow creature carried him back to the lair. Light from the major opening of the cavern shone down the tunnel where Megalonyx dropped him. He immediately saw a huge, bloody body laying in front of him. It was Dr. Hippatolumous.

The obese doctor was still alive, and muttered for help. Bogey Wilson laid listless, and played dead. The snow creature tugged Doctor Hippatolumous to the lighted entrance down the tunnel, and enjoyed its lunch. It needed to shine some light on the meal. Bogey Wilson kept his eyes closed, and refused to look. He listened to the eating noises of Megalonyx, and the corrupt doctor's last yelps of life.

Bogey Wilson continued the tale. He continued to play dead, maybe for a day or two, and dared not venture to look about. He was starving, and had to make a move. He heard the huge woolly beast snoring. As Bogey Wilson moved, and grabbed onto the cavern wall, some rock crumbled off loudly. The beast did not move. He threw a small rock at it, and again, the beast continued to snore.

Bogey Wilson explained that the secret lair was a good hideout. He was not going to jail, and not back to jail for something he did not do. Killing? That was not his style. He gathered stuff from his destroyed home, and built a makeshift camp next to the sleeping giant. He also contemplated what to make of this snow creature. Would he, Bogey Wilson destroy it?

Frank Porter listened as they all stood behind the huge tent in the muddy dirt. Bill Meyers broke into the discussion as threatening rain clouds approached.

Bill Meyers needed to seal the deal with a simple act of revenge. He injected the morphine into Megalonyx. He whacked and whacked with the ax, and chopped off its deadly claws. He devised a schedule with Bogey Wilson, and spent the next two weeks working on physically removing the snow creature from the hills. Insanity invoked a perfect plan.

The beast remained sedated, and the two tamed Megalonyx. The snow creature was an intelligent species, and being hooked on opiates, willingly worked with Bill Meyers on a mutual basis. Bill Meyers did switch to street heroin, which became readily available. This longing for the drug, the syrup concoction his new master supplied him, was new and extremely satisfying.

The new food was satisfying just like the delicious metallic aftertaste of fresh blood. The snow creature blindly followed Bill Meyers, forgetting its enemy's past. No desire existed for it to hunt for food. Megalonyx was hooked on cheap packaged bologna. When the snow creature heard the sound of plastic crunching from the wrapper, it rushed to Bill Meyers like a puppy dog.

Megalonyx was easy to control. The spring season started its hibernation. It remained lethargic, and stayed awake, desiring its opiate fix. The mighty "Master of the Winter World" was useless now, outside his zone. The stumps showed signs of growing back into its intense size. Bill Meyers would simply saw them down, inhibiting any sudden aggression.

And that was that. Frank Porter disrespected the whole side show cheapness, but it worked. It also kept their secrecy because no one took the animal seriously. The defeated snow creature fit in totally as a bizarre circus freak. Megalonyx has now been captured and defeated.

Bill Meyers spoke, switching topics," I was surprised, bumping into you in Georgia. You were quite insane. I found your state of mind actually intriquing. How did you follow us."

Frank Porter answered," Come on, a newspaper with an add of a circus, and displaying a showcase of- The Tale of the Snow Creature? You are not to smart, are you."

"Well, my obsession with the beast could be my flaw So far, my plan has moved like clockwork." Bill Meyers insisted.

Frank Porter continued,"After your release from the mental ward, I followed you into the forest. However, my damaged leg hindered me to stalk you to your true whereabouts. I stayed on Cliff Drop Road, well hidden I might add."

"Hmm, not bad. I did not catch on you were there. Touche!" Bill Meyers added.

"The day you moved Megalonyx into the old truck, I followed very secretely, but all the traveling for two weeks on a unpaved road, brought on a flat for my Ford Taurus. You escaped my grasp, only to catch up with you in Georgia." The news reporter explained.

"And the insane part?" The young man asked.

Frank Porter softly and sadly, said," Melanie broke up with me, and joined the sheriff in bed."

Laughter came from Bill Meyers.

Frank Porter stood between Bill Meyers and Bogey Wilson. The rain began to patter down on everything. The washed up news reporter could not do it. He desired to shoot Bill Meyers, but instead lowered the gun.

Bill Meyers stepped towards him, and took the rusty revolver from his now shaking hand.

Bill Meyers quickly raised the weapon and hit him hard on the back of his neck.

"Stupid Idiot", Bill Meyers sharply replied.

Frank Porter went down, and laid in the mud. In a blur, his dead mom appeared standing down a bit by the end of the tent. She smiled at him.

She gestured with her hands, and said,"Your a good boy."

He heard in his mind her voice, "You took a long time, but finally are choosing the right path. You found your prize, your meaning. Keep it up. This monstrous game is not over. Keep it up. More challenges await. I am proud of you, and always will be."

Before her presence dissappeared, she commented,"By the way, stop fucking fat whores!"

The motherly imagery vanished as Frank Porter was about to pass out. What was this connection, or would there be none? Maybe he truly became insane from the terrible ordeal.

Frank Porter awoke with an aching neck. The sun shone bright with the ground damp and muddy. The warmth of the sun felt good.

The circus grounds were cleared out. Some garbage laid about with a general stink in the air.

If Megalonyx escaped, what new mayhem could occur? The fickle newsreporter finally switched again in thought. He remembered his dead mom quote- The monstrous show was not over.

Frank Porter filled with fresh confidence. The creature, the monster Mr. Megalonyx, must be destroyed- no more Flaky Franky. He sat in the trashy field among a few standing structures. In front of a him, was a green meadow all dug up. Frank Porter noticed long runs of top dirt, protruding up from the green field. It reminded him of the snow tracks left by the snow creature.

What might happen when Autumn approached. The air engulfed with coolness of the change of seasons. Could the monster, yes monster, overcome the opioid addiction with the oncoming winter, and return back to its carnivorous self. Will there be a sequel to "The Tale of the Snow Creature".

Will there exist a:

"RETURN OF MEGALONYX — MASTER OF THE WINTER WORLD"

ABOUT THE AUTHOR

Al Zach moved from New York City in 2010 and now enjoys country living in Central New York State. Here he wrote "Megalonyx", a classic creature horror. His writing style expresses twisted, fun escapism for the reader's enjoyment.

His other interest is a hobby farm. Al refers to his animals as friends not pets.

As a retired Medical Technologist, analyzing drugs of abuse, Al Zach has only one statement to share: "Read a book, do not do illegal drugs!"

Printed in the United States
By Bookmasters